PERFECT
WEAPON

PERFECT WEAPON

AMY J. FETZER

BRAVA

KENSINGTON PUBLISHING CORP.

http://www.kensingtonbooks.com

BRAVA BOOKS are published by

Kensington Publishing Corp.
850 Third Avenue
New York, NY 10022

All Kensington titles, imprints and distributed lines are available at special quantity discounts for bulk purchases for sales promotion, premiums, fund-raising, educational or institutional use.

Special book excerpts or customized printings can also be created to fit specific needs. For details, write or phone the office of the Kensington Special Sales Manager: Kensington Publishing Corp., 850 Third Avenue, New York, NY 10022. Attn. Special Sales Department, Phone: 1-800-221-2647.

Brava and the B logo Reg. U.S. Pat. & TM Off.

ISBN 0-7582-1105-8

First Kensington Trade Paperback Printing: March 2006
10 9 8 7 6 5 4 3 2 1

Printed in the United States of America

*To my editor and friend
Kate Duffy,
for believing I could do this and
giving me the writer's ultimate dream:
creative freedom.
And that world domination plan?
I'm right there with you, girl.
Thanks,
Amy*

One

Southern girls could charm the pants off a scarecrow.

Dr. Sydney Hale was only trying for one U.S. Marine guard. She didn't want him sans his camouflage uniform, of course. She drew the line at robbing the cradle. She just wanted to soften him up enough to let her go above ground for some fresh air. But when he saw her coming down the long corridor, Corporal Tanner snapped to attention and gave her that *no one gets past on my watch* look.

Not a good sign.

"Come on good lookin'," Sydney said with a smile. "Let me through."

"I can't, ma'am." His gaze remained straight ahead. "Wait for the end of the shift like the rest of the staff."

"That's a long time off, Corporal. We've been cooped up since before midnight. Besides"—she cocked her hip—"I've been going up topside for two years, Corporal. You'd think a body'd get used to the routine."

Only his gaze shifted. "My entire life is routine, ma'am. I like *routine*."

He was trying hard to be stern, bless him. "I thought Marines craved adventure, danger?"

"Working down here with all those chemicals is danger enough. I want an enemy I can see and shoot . . . ma'am."

She understood that. Surrounded by chemicals was tough work. Surrounded by the elements of Sarin gas was quite another. Wanting to see the sky more than chat about dangers and the ethics of warfare, she moved past him and stood near the stainless steel elevator disguised behind artificial cinder block. She tapped her foot. When he didn't key her in, she folded her arms and gave him her best boss-to-underling look.

He held tight to his resolve for about three seconds, then folded like a retriever under a petting hand. Growling under his breath, he punched the codes and inserted the key, then glanced behind him to check if the corridor was clear. Fake cinder blocks slid back to show the steel lift.

"Do I have to search you?"

She held up the penlight and water bottle. The granola bar he could see sticking out of her pocket.

Syd leaned close. "Was it my smile this time, Tanner, or my hard-ass look?"

He snickered. "Hard-ass? You?" The door hissed open. "To be honest . . . it's your tight ass in that short skirt." Shaking his head, his gaze locked on her behind as she stepped inside. "Sweet . . . ma'am."

She grinned, facing him.

"I'm gonna be dragged before my C.O. if you get caught," he warned softly.

"I'll say I forced you. Pulled rank. Pitched a hissy fit."

He made a face, folding his arms and just staring. Nothing could get past this guy, she thought. Armed to the teeth, he towered over average people, and her by about nine inches.

"Stay out of sight." He glanced back again when he heard something. "I swear I don't know why I give in to you."

"Because you want to get into my panties."

He flashed her a grin that brightened his features. Oh, to be ten years younger, she thought.

"Is it working?"

The doors started to close. "No." She winked. "But then, Marines never give up, do they?"

She heard a soft *ooh-rahh* before the door sighed closed and she leaned back against the steel hull. Nothing like being locked inside your lab like a rat, she thought and couldn't even feel the elevator shoot to the surface. When the door opened, she hurried down the short corridor of rock, then pushed on the outer escape hatch. She couldn't count the times she'd missed it coming back down because it was disguised to look like a pile of dead logs and vines.

Cloak and dagger spy stuff. She hitched up her jacket to pull her notes from the waist of her skirt, then twisted off the top of her water bottle. For a moment, she stood still and inhaled the unfiltered, un-reconstituted air, then she moved between the trees, her steps high. Shoulda worn jeans, she thought; instead she wore her best black skirt and a new Dior blouse. Because *she* was being inspected today, as well as the facility. She hated that once a year people who knew next to nothing about her work would be prying into her files, looking into the way she ran things six hundred feet below the surface. And pull her funding if they didn't like what they found. The inspectors weren't due to arrive for another three hours. Let Handerson take care of it, she thought. It'll make her assistant feel official.

Sitting on a rock and leaning back against a mossy tree, she propped her feet on a rotting log. The hint of the rising sun coated the world in a hazy purple glow. Clouds bumped and threatened rain. Time strolled by out here. Closing her eyes, she snacked on a granola bar. Low carbs are a waste for good calories, she thought and wondered if Tish would join her for a decent breakfast. She awarded herself five minutes of empty thoughts, listening to the breeze push against the dry leaves. Then she snapped on her mini flashlight and studied the latest test results, excited enough to know she was a couple tests away from a perfect formula. Mentally calculating the process, the degree changes she'd take next, her palms went clammy. Gulping water, she blinked at the printout, reading it twice.

Oh my God, I did it.

6:45 A.M. EST

A forty-forty rifle cradled in his arms, Jack sat in the tree stand, needing coffee and contemplating his life as he usually did when he was stuck in a tree waiting for deer to conveniently cross his path. Since returning to the States, his life had gone from dull to boring so he skipped dissecting it and watched the terrain below. Thinning the deer population for Fish and Game was never a challenge. Hunting one deer, that was sport, and some good eating.

A whisper of conversation came over the radio. Jack put it to his ear. "Radio silence mean anything to you shit heads?"

"Sure, in combat. Where it counts." Lyons. Jack could tell by his Georgia accent.

"What I want to know is where are all the deer that are getting in the way of tourism?"

Jack whispered into the radio. "Flapping your jibs is scaring them off, Decker."

"Silent but deadly you ain't, Deck," Lyons said, chuckling.

"I crawled out of bed for this?" Decker ragged back.

"We all did." Mateo, Jack recognized.

"Unlike your bed, Martinez, mine wasn't empty." Despite the nose that had been broken more than once, Decker's "wore braces till he was seventeen" smile drew women. Jack wondered if his mama knew her investment was paying off for her boy.

"The question is, did she care if you left?"

"Can't say. I'm a gentleman," Decker said and the other three snorted. If Decker's bedpost wasn't notched, Jack'd be surprised.

"It's more than quiet out here, sir."

That's what he liked about it. Silence, the chance for meandering thoughts, life-altering decisions. But with too much company, he wasn't getting any of that today. "Keep your yaps shut for the next hour and we'll move down the mountain two clicks."

"Is that an order . . . sir?"

Jack leaned his head back and smiled through camouflage netting covering his face. "Does it have to be, Gunny Lyons?"

The radio went silent. Jack stuffed it into his leg pocket and practically ached for coffee. The breeze chilled the air around him, and when he heard movement from below, he sat up higher for a look, quietly shifting the rifle to his shoulder. Bingo. He sighted down the scope and put the doe between the crosshairs. He pulled the trigger. The crack echoed and the deer dropped like a stone. Jack radioed his buddies before climbing down and heading toward the carcass.

7:14 A.M.

People should be warned when their luck was about to change. When she dragged her butt out of bed to work six hundred feet below the surface of Luray Caverns, Sydney should have listened to that inner voice telling her to stay put, call in sick, and languish the day away with books, a pint of Häagen-Dazs, and her trusty vibrator.

When the elevator doors shot open on her floor, her first thought was *an explosion*. Smoke engulfed her, stinging her eyes, cloaking everything. For a second, it was deadly quiet. Then Corporal Tanner smacked into her, his dead weight dragging her to the ground.

"Chris! Oh, Jesus."

Blood flowed from a hole in his chest and onto her. She ripped open the man's utility uniform and frowned harder at the Kevlar vest. A neat hole pierced right through it. She yanked the vest open, Velcro tearing loudly. She covered the wound with her hand and blood bubbled up between her fingers.

It's in his lungs. She could hear it rattle inside him.

She cupped his face, checked his eyes. "Don't die, Corporal, that's an order." Her gaze flicked wildly around the corridor; a body dressed in black lay on the floor beneath the haze of smoke. She got to her feet, trying to drag him into the elevator. But she couldn't move him across the threshold. Smoke and frustration made her eyes tear.

Blood trickled out of his mouth. The sound of gunshots with silencers echoed back to her like a dozen soft pops. Bad guys. Coming this way. The Marine struggled to talk, but only gurgled, sluggishly lifting his weapon and pressing it into her body, into her hand.

She knew what he was trying to do. "I'm not leaving you!"

He closed his fingers over her hand. "Ammo, right . . . leg pocket." He coughed. Blood splattered.

She found it, cocking the weapon and stashing the ammo in her waistband. "You gotta help me help you, Chris."

His eyes were bleak with his coming death. "*Run.*"

She couldn't. He was young and alive. She refused to leave him, gripped him under the arms, and pulled. Footsteps pounded on the stone floor and she didn't know if it was a rescue or his killers. She rolled him inside and smacked the panel. The doors didn't close.

"Codes, Chris. Gimme the codes!"

Weakly, he held up fingers and she pushed reset, then jabbed numbers. From the door at the end of the long cement hall, a man in head-to-toe black appeared, stepping over a body, and moving toward the elevator. When he saw her, he sprinted.

Closer. Closer.

"Come on! Come *on!*" She hit the panel hard. The man stopped, widening his stance to sight down the long pistol. *I'm not gonna make it.* Sydney swallowed hard, lifted the gun and fired first. The pistol's kick threw her back against the steel wall. The elevator door shut and this time, she felt the unit shoot to the surface. She took a deep breath, shoved the pistol into the waistband of her skirt, then crouched. "Chris. Chris?"

His eyes fluttered for a second. "A danger . . . I could see."

Her heart broke right there, but she forced a smile. "You did good, Corporal." She stroked his cheek. He was already growing cold. "Who were they, Chris?"

His eyes glazed and she checked his pulse, then choked when she didn't find one. Oh God. Dead, dead, *dead*, pulsed through her brain. She tried CPR but his lungs were filled with blood.

She couldn't imagine what might be going on down below. Her friends. Handerson, Piccolo, Dysart? Harmless chemrats like herself. She swiped at her tears, her hands covered with his blood and for the last few seconds of the ride topside, she lovingly held the dead marine in her arms.

When the elevator stopped and the door hushed open, Syd kissed Chris's forehead, laid him gently down, then stepped out. Instantly she spun back and tried to stop the doors from closing so she could lock the unit on this level. The thick metal nearly took off her arm and she jerked back, cursing.

It would go back down and they'd know of the escape route. She gripped the gun, turned and hit the ground running. She needed a phone, cops, NSA and anyone else she could gather. She busted out of the hatch and into the forest, running toward lower ground, for the main road over a mile away. Branches yanked at her clothing, holding her back. She tripped and fell, tore her jacket sleeve and scratched her arm. The gun flew from her hand, and she scrambled to find it.

Distant thrashing from the woods snapped out a warning. Frantically, she dug under the leaves for the gun. Her fingers closed around the metal grip and she pushed to her feet. She chanced a look back.

Men in black were heading directly toward her.

And they were armed way better than she was.

She booked, the Marine's nine-millimeter heavy in her hand. Her legs throbbed with strain, her lungs near bursting. *They killed Chris.* Innocent, flirting twenty-year-old Chris. Rage pushed over fear and she ran harder.

Jack walked down the mountainside with the dead deer across his shoulders. One already lay in his truck, a half mile down the mountain. He stopped to radio his buddies, and when he didn't get anything but static, he moved to higher ground. A sound drew him around and the weight of the doe nearly toppled him backwards. His gaze scanned the area, first low, then higher up the hill.

"Now there's a picture you don't see every day." A woman in a suit jacket and skirt running down the hillside. He got a look at her face, her hands. Scared and armed. Dangerous combination in a female. She was bleeding. He tossed off the deer, and radioed Decker. "Fan out, guys, we have an intruder and she's armed, hurt, and heading toward you."

Then he saw the armed men following her.

Jack took off toward the woman, running to intercept her. Her assailants ducked under trees and one man took aim. Jack lunged for the woman, knocking her to the ground and covering her with his body as bullets zipped overhead.

Whoa. Silencers.

Beneath him, she struggled and howled. He tore the weapon from her hand and covered her mouth, his weight pressing on her. "U.S. Marine!" he said close to her ear. "U.S. Marine!"

She made a pitiful, relieved sound and went slack beneath him.

Jack scanned the area, released her, then motioned her toward the nearest tree.

Sydney rolled to it, crouching, and trying to keep her granola bar down. "Give me the gun."

"Are you hurt?"

She glanced at the bloodstains. "No. Give me the gun."

"What the hell is going on?"

"Give me the weapon!"

Without taking his gaze off the terrain, the man covered in ferns, leaves, and branches kicked it toward her. Sydney grabbed it, checked the load, wondering what the hell he was doing here in deep cover camouflage. Another shot fired. Quiet. Deadly. Like the whoosh and click of a sliding door. It pierced the tree above her head.

"Go!" Lying on the ground, Jack radioed his pals. No answer. His gaze remained on the attacker's location. Where'd the hell the bastard get to? He inched closer to her. "Down the mountain, there's a black truck."

"Don't stay here! Jesus! They're not going to let you walk away!"

He scowled. "I say again, lady, what the fuck is going on?"

"I don't know!"

Someone shouted, but it wasn't English. Shots pierced the ground near his arm, and he returned fire. The sound of a bullet impacting the body was muffled under the backfire of his weapon.

Sydney heard the cry of pain and seconds later, the peppered spit of bullets chipped and thunked into the ground and trees. The Marine's attention snapped to her, but she couldn't see behind the camo netting.

"Who are these people?" he demanded.

"Who cares! They're trying to kill us! Come on!" Syd took off toward the truck.

Jack slid backwards on the ground, then stood behind a tree before racing a few yards behind her. Silencer-enhanced gunfire cut around them. Hell of a morning, he thought. The woman lost her balance, slid to the ground and he grabbed her up, and together, they ran. Why were they after her? Who were "they" and where the hell did she come from? He'd been on this mountain since before dawn and hadn't seen anything but deer and a few chipmunks. The armed men had just appeared.

When they reached the truck, Jack surveyed their path, then pulled off the Gilly hood, reached inside the truck bed, and flipped back the tarp.

Sydney nearly lost that fight with her granola bar when she saw the dead deer in the back.

"Get in."

"You can't be serious." She winced at her own voice. Like saving her life wasn't worth lying with a dead deer? She climbed onto the flatbed. The scent of blood filled her nostrils and sank into her heart.

Her savior was inside the cab, rummaging. "What are you doing?" she shouted and tried to inch away from the glassy stare of the deer lying beside her. "Let's get out of here!" Syd held onto the pistol so hard her knuckles whitened.

"I have three buddies out there and I haven't heard from them since you came on the scene. Stay put."

"Stay? They're coming this way!"

"If you keep yelling they will be," he snapped, then tossed her a small, green plastic medical kit. She frowned. "Your arm," he said, then whipped the tarp over her and the carcass.

Pulling the camouflage Gilly suit back on, Jack left his rifle behind and kept his 9mm. If he hadn't been working with the Fish and Game, he would have left it at home. Now he was glad he hadn't. The woman's attackers were still near. He could smell them. Their last meal and new fabric. To them he'd smell like stag piss, so he wasn't too worried. The Gilly suit did its job.

He moved toward Decker's location first, low and quiet,

his time spent covering his own back. When he approached, the man was sitting, his shoulder braced against a tree, his rifle across his lap. He was too still. A sick feeling washed over Jack as he scanned the area, then knelt beside his friend. The blood splatter and the scent of scorched flesh were hard to miss.

He pulled off the hood. Jesus. Jack turned his face away and choked. Decker was dead, half his face blown off. He breathed hard, struggling for focus, to not lose this battle in himself and go nuts. Forcing himself to look around, he checked the body of his friend. A single shot to the back of the head. Jack's gaze ripped over the ground. No footprints, no struggle. Nothing to follow. *Snipers.* Jack looked to the trees, the high ground. The entire forest offered cover.

The shooter could've been anywhere.

Rage rocketed though Jack's blood as he thought of the woman. The bitch. She'd set them up for this. Anger and adrenaline pumped through him. Leaving the area untouched for the police, he moved fast and low, covering the next hundred yards. They'd planned it that way, face north and stay close so they didn't accidentally shoot each other. *Ah, jeez,* Jack thought and wanted to stop and howl and mourn his friends.

When Jack found Martinez dead, he knew Lyons would be, too. But he had to find him. When he did, his heart broke. All three of his friends, each with one shot to the head. They still held their weapons and there were no footprints that weren't theirs, no struggle. That meant the bullet had come from long range with a laser sight. Jack hadn't heard a thing. No backfire meant a custom silencer, he thought, blinking back his emotions and running toward his truck. To the source of his grief.

He aimed his pistol on the lump in his truck bed. Those guys in the woods had done the shooting, but the woman would know *why.* Jack jabbed the body. "Gun first, toss it out." No movement and Jack yanked back the 9mm slide.

"Weapon first. Slow, hands up!" When the woman refused to move, Jack thought for a second whoever killed his pals, had come back and killed her.

He yanked on the tarp.

The little bitch was gone.

Jack wanted to hit something, shoot someone. He grappled with his temper, his outrage, carefully laying his hands on the tailgate, his finger still on the trigger. He realized now his shot at the deer had alerted the shooters to their presence. He'd been point, farther north than the others. And now his friends, three men he'd trusted with his life were dead, executed like dogs. He'd no idea why, and his only clue to the truth lay with that woman.

His eyes burned and Jack thought of the wives he was going to have to face, the mother he'd have to tell that her son had been murdered. It was his duty. He'd survived. By sheer luck, he was still standing. But inside, he was dying.

Someone's going to pay.

He'd save his revenge for just that moment.

He surveyed the territory, weapon out. Shooters were still out there. He took a step and beneath his feet, the ground trembled.

7:18 A.M.

Agent Gabe Cisco glanced at the ringing cell phone attached to his dash. "Too damn early for a mess," he muttered and hit the call button. "This had better be good; I haven't had coffee yet."

"Mother is down. The Cradle has fallen."

"Christ."

"Good enough, sir?"

"Details." Cisco listened to the sketchy facts as Agent Wickum spelled them out. It was bad. Internal alarms unresponsive. No contact from the sentries. Air supply couldn't be monitored. At least there weren't any civilians at the park yet. It didn't open till nine. He hoped the tour buses hadn't made it near yet. But first things first: the people inside the laboratory.

"Priority one. Close off all entries to the park. Shut it down two miles down the mountain." Strays, Cisco thought. He was going to get strays off Skyline Drive in the area. "No one gets in or out. No one. Plainclothes, no military. We don't want to scare the locals. Call it a gas leak. I want a man at every store, gas station, and outhouse in the area. Canvas the mountain in a two-mile radius. Infrared and visual. I'll authorize helicopters. Bring in the bomb squad, but we search for survivors outside the Cradle and isolate them. Do not allow anyone to get inside, understood?"

"Even the bomb detection?"

"Even them. We don't know yet what we're dealing with." Bomb squads expected explosions, not what was down in that lab. He checked the time and knew it would take him at least an hour to get there. "I want you on a chopper to meet me at helo pad two. You drive my car to the site."

"What about the FBI, sir?"

"They aren't aware. It'll be forest rangers and local cops first if anyone's hurt. Keep them back. Say nothing. This is my ball game." He hated being questioned. It was *his* job to question, to secure secrets, to hide them if necessary. And if the Cradle really had fallen, this mistake was going to take some fast moving. "Wickum?"

"Still here, sir."

Cisco could hear the man breathing hard. "Get a CBC team on standby."

"Good God."

Gabe cut the line and steered the car toward the Cradle.

7:31 AM

A truck rolling past shook the asphalt under her feet. Above her, gray clouds billowed. Rain would be just so fitting, she thought and kept walking. She pulled her jacket closed to cover the blood smeared across her shirt, but she smelled it. It was in her hair, seeping into her skin. Hurrying into a convenience store, she glanced at the clerk, then slipped into the restroom. She locked the door and sighed back against it, feeling ridiculously safe. Pushing off, she walked the three steps to the sink and gripped the edge. She couldn't look at herself in the cracked mirror. She'd see more evidence of Tanner's death if she did.

Chris's face flashed in her mind, like a snapshot, clear, quick. Then the man in the hall, the ice blue eyes in a black hood, pointing a gun at her. She'd never forget the way his eyes had almost glowed as he aimed at her heart. She hoped her shot got him between the baby blues. But she doubted it. It was the first time she'd ever held a gun.

The Marine covered in foliage like a Yeti was almost stranger than the rest of her morning. Why was he wearing a Gilly suit? Snipers wore stuff like that. If he was part of the attack, then why save her life. She pulled the weapon from her skirt, wondering why no one had noticed it—since her jacket wasn't big enough to conceal it well. Her hand trembled as she laid it on the edge of the sink. Her fingers were crusted with drying blood. Suddenly, she turned to the toilet and lost the fight with her granola bar. She choked and coughed, then rinsed her mouth and her face. She washed the blood from her hands. The water turned bright pink and she forced herself to look in the mirror. Her blouse was stained with blood but most of it was low, and she buttoned up her jacket. Smoothing her hair back, she picked out leaves and twigs, then brushed at her skirt and jacket, wincing as she hit the cut on her arm. Stripping out of her torn panty hose, she pitched them in the trash.

She replaced the gun in her waistband, frowning when something crackled. She reached behind herself and expecting leaves, she got her notes. Oh God. This information was never supposed to leave the Cradle. Stuffing it back into place, she matched it with the gun and left the rest room. Follow procedure, she told herself as she walked immediately to the phone at the back. A TV blared from somewhere in the front of the store. A bell jingled when someone came in. A couple of people shopped up and down the narrow aisles. Early tourists. She heard a child fussing, then glanced at a little boy trying to reach the slush machine. She was tempted to lean out and help him. Instead, she turned her back and dialed.

The line didn't even ring. "9854-Kilo," she blurted.

"Dr. Hale?"

"The Cradle is down."

"Are you injured?"

"No. Get me out of here."

"Where are you?"

People were staring. She cupped the phone. "Where the hell do you think I am, dammit!"

"Please state your position, Miss Hale."

She was barely holding it together and his "calm the womenfolk" tone shredded her last nerve. "It's *Doctor* Hale. I'm at the convenience store past the third mark. Now get me out of here. There are killers on that mountain!"

"Rendezvous at mark eight."

Sydney frowned. "There's nothing there."

"We'll come for you."

The line went dead. Sydney hung up, daring a glance around. No one noticed her. Trying to look like she belonged when she didn't, she pushed her hair back and walked toward the front as if she had a car waiting. Outside, she forced herself not to run, kept her pace even, and lowered her arms to keep from clutching her churning stomach and looking more obvious than she was.

"Fine. It'll be fine." *Like hell.*

What the attackers might have taken from the facility really terrified her. The cold room was supposed to be impenetrable. But then, so was the Cradle. Her mind shifted to the man in the Gilly suit. She hoped he'd gotten the hell out of there.

He'd been stupid to go back. But then, he was a Marine. Which meant courage most often won out over personal safety.

Considering what had happened, it was a little too convenient to think that an armed Marine, complete with buddies, was in the area. A four-man team. Snipers maybe? It was a U.S. government project.

Her mind sifted, plucked at information. It's what she did for a living. Gather data, theorize. Experiment, test, try a new route. If this had been a chemical reaction she could have figured that out easy. But she had a result without the cause. Why hit the Cradle? Why kill a bunch of tech nerds?

Okay here's your stupid card, Syd. It was top *top* secret. That alone attracted bad guys. But the Cradle was more covert than the NSA, and aside from an elite group of military and finance council officials, only a couple of handpicked agents knew about its existence.

Now everyone would.

Sydney stopped at the appointed mark, glanced up and down the road, then did as ordered. She stepped into the forest to wait.

She knew what those people were after. The elements in the cold room. Maybe the bomb. No one was supposed to know about that, either. She touched the notes wedged into her panties. If they were after her research, then they had an incomplete formula.

She had the rest.

And now, she had the only copy.

Two

Like an ancient Apache, Jack put his hand on the ground, feeling the vibrations.

The trembling stopped as quickly as it had started. Frightened deer loped deeper into the valley, away from the scent of blood. Smaller animals dug frantically into hollows and underbrush. Earthquake? Cave-in? Crouching, he sniffed the air, scenting only mist and morning.

Slipping his binoculars from his leg pocket, he sighted on the mountaintop. His fingers flexed, and he wished they were around the killer's throat. Tucked against the truck fender, Jack examined the area three-sixty. He was far enough from Skyline Drive not to feel the rumble of trucks or buses. No personal vehicles could have made such a rumble anyway. So what caused the shaking? There was nothing, no one. And, there was no easy line of sight for shots accurate enough to kill three men a hundred yards apart. That meant more than one shooter.

He was hoping for a head to scalp. Instead, he was alone with three dead friends and no one to blame.

And possibly with a shooter still sighting on him.

He threw a fistful of rocks, keeping low and expecting the

soft pop of silenced gunfire. None came, but he still wasn't taking chances and using the trees for cover, he moved slowly back to the point where he'd first seen the woman. He found large footprints, blood smeared on the underbrush. The man Jack had shot was hit badly. To die and left for the animals, he thought. The woman's prints were there too. The toe of her shoe made more of a mark than the heels. That meant running at top speed, he thought, then hotfooted it to his deer stand and climbed past the jump seat. He sighted again through the binoculars, his gaze clawing the hillside from the cavern entrance. Nothing. Impatient rage rushed inside him, but he moved slowly, finally swinging right and higher.

The air was dusted, and from this distance, he couldn't tell if it was smoke, or lingering morning fog; the smudge in the sky was too faint. He climbed down, dropping the last dozen feet into a pile of leaves, then heading toward the top. He hadn't gone a hundred feet when he heard the whine of motorcycles and knew he was too late to catch them.

He didn't stop.

7:58 A.M.

The dark sedan pulled up to the contact point, the door popping open without help. Sydney climbed in and shut it. The locks clamped down automatically. Her gaze snapped to the driver, but he was hidden behind black glass. Probably wearing dark glasses, black suit, and no recognizable jewelry, either, she thought, feeling creeped out even as she was relieved to be on her way to safety. She wanted to ask the driver about the others, her colleagues, the sentries. But she knew no one she encountered would talk. It was their job not to.

She stared out the window, her stomach churning miserably, then she looked around, saw the small leather hatch and opened it. It was filled with water bottles, and she took one, cracked the seal and drained a third of it. Her hand shook as she swiped it across her mouth, and she held it out to steady it.

Blood was knitted deep into the cracks of her nails and knuckles. The urge to rub it was overpowering. The young Marine's death played in her mind again and again.

I've never seen anyone die.

She didn't want to again.

She gulped more water, then tossed the empty aside and grabbed another bottle. She drank.

Her composure wavered and she clamped her hand over her mouth, her eyes stinging. Don't. *Crying won't help. You're stronger than this. You have to be.*

In the back of her mind, she heard her dead father's voice, cold and imperialistic, telling her *logic defeats emotion, fear is the easiest to conquer.* She'd bet a grand her father never had anyone shoot at him, either. But he was right, her fear was drowning under the flood of anger flowing through her like overripe wine. Thick and slow. Bitter rage churned in her, spilling over any remaining terror until there was nothing left but the urgent need to find out what happened—and see that someone paid.

She leaned back and waited. Let her thoughts brew. The ride toward Washington would be long. She ought to be flaming mad by then.

How nice.

8:22 A.M.

Cisco grabbed the oh-shit strap and held on as the chopper took a dive over Annandale. "This isn't an F-18, hot dog. Go silent, we're alerting the entire county," Cisco said into the mike, and when the noise inside the chopper died down, he pulled off the headset and tossed it aside. The roadblocks were up, but he had to lock down the mountain before suspicions got out of hand and the local cops pushed their noses

into his business. The park opened in—he checked his watch—
less than an hour. He'd been forty minutes from Langley
when he'd gotten the call, and the gridlock traffic had chis-
eled into his time. He didn't have any left to make it clean
and accepted it. The fictitious "gas leak" was going to be
deadly.

Turning his attention from the view out the chopper window, he stared at the bank of monitors. The sensors were off,
way off. He sent the computer an arched look, his gaze hopping across the data spitting across on the small screen.
"Copy?"

"Yes, sir," an agent said, pulling at his headset. "It's the
latest relay."

The data pour stopped, the screen blanking to a gray
haze. He didn't look at anyone else. He didn't need to. They
understood. The surveillance feed from the Cradle to Mother
was gone. Something had taken it—or the power source—
out. Cisco turned his attention to the mountain below.

"Sir?"

He could almost feel the other agents in the chopper ex-
changing confused looks. "Do nothing," he said. "I can't
judge what I can't see."

An agent turned back to the screen in a desperate effort to
pull up the images. It was useless. The security cameras and
sensors were able to survive a blast that would wipe out a
city block. If they weren't receiving, then Mother, the elec-
tronic caretaker, wasn't just down. She was dead. That meant
the air supply was enough to last maybe ten hours if it wasn't
contaminated. If it was, then he couldn't vent the facility.

Whoever had hit the Cradle knew its most tender spot.
That didn't leave Cisco many suspects. "I want infrared before we set down," he said.

An agent looked at him, doubtful.

"You want to walk in there blind? Make it happen."

Jack saw a black combat boot, then a dark pant leg, and
found a body nestled like a sleeping child in the underbrush.

Circling for unfriendlies before approaching, he knelt, the business end of his gun pressed to the man's temple, just in case, though the hole in the man's back that had blown flesh and fabric four inches wide was a real clue. So, his aim was dead on. Good, Jack thought. But was this guy number one, or number two? He'd no idea how many there were up here.

He searched for identification, knowing there wouldn't be any. Not if they were good—and they were. They'd infiltrated into this area without a sound, right under his nose, then slaughtered his friends and did God knew what else in the hills. He pulled off the dead man's hood and pushed the body over.

It was cocky not to wear Kevlar, he thought, frowning at the dead man's face, hair. He yanked off the black gloves, peeling the fingers back. What the hell is this shit? Quickly, he hunted through the front pockets and found C-4 fuses, and a detonator. This ain't Radio Shack crap, he thought, leaving it where he found it. Moving against the ground in slow increments, Jack found the machine pistol a couple yards away. It was cold. Since he'd no intention of anyone slipping past using it on him, he removed the ammo and disabled it, left the weapon for the Feds, then headed up the mountain. Toward the area where he'd heard motorcycles.

One killer down. Satisfaction still didn't taste nearly good enough.

On the hill, he tracked the woman's footprints into the dense woods till they just stopped. He covered the area like a madman, trying to find more and put his foot on something soft. He dug and found a parachute pack. No chute, no release buckles, just the pack. He gave it the once-over, knowing he'd have heard a plane, and although a silent fall was possible with a HALO drop from thirty-five thousand feet, no one had free-fallen while he was here. That meant the attackers had staked their territory before he and his friends arrived. Before five A.M. Or they simply hadn't seen them until he and his buddies had advanced up the mountain. That would explain why the shooters hadn't shot him out of his deer stand. Jack had been the only who hadn't moved. He'd been point man and the others moved forward in a straight line toward him, pushing deer his way.

Under the canopy of trees, he threw down the chute pack and looked around. Find the reason and you'll find them. The woman could have free-fallen dressed like that. Not wise, but doable. Where had she come from and what were they after? Big questions, he thought. There was something hidden in the Shenandoah Mountains, something worth killing for. He let his gaze move over the forest and felt as if he was hunting down a grain of salt in a sea of snow. There was just too much ground to cover alone.

Wind blew across his face, leaves rustled and he saw a reflection that appeared and vanished with the breeze. The ground was scraped near the flicker of light and moving slowly, he parted the brush and hit pay dirt. A laminated I.D. tag. The back bore a magnetic strip like a credit card, the front, a thumbprint and the woman's picture. Dr. Sydney A. Hale. Doctor of what? And what the hell was a doctor doing out here in the cold with a man in black ops gear shooting at her?

It didn't add up, but it didn't matter either. He'd never let this rest. Not until he had the satisfaction of a life for a life. He canvassed the area again before heading toward the cavern entrance below, each step magnifying the grief he wouldn't allow himself to feel right now. If he did, he'd go postal on the wrong target. So he banked it.

Right now, rage was his only comfort.

8:45 A.M.

The rank smell of blood and her own fear filled the back of the sedan. People were dead, killers were on the mountain and it was a stroke of luck she hadn't been caught in the crossfire. The cold eyes of the hooded man flooded her mind.

He saw me. And he really wanted to kill me. It wasn't easy to accept that another human being wanted you six feet under. She didn't have to ask why again. The gas. It was like candy to hungry terrorists. That meant someone directly involved had talked. The list was short, but someone had slipped up.

Chilled, she reached to turn up the heat and realized the driver was breaking the speed limit about the same time the car rocked hard over uneven ground. She looked out the tinted windows at the terrain shadowed with trees. They were climbing higher. Oh, hell. It's not D.C. Behind them, another car and an SUV pulled up and flanked them as the car skidded to a halt outside a cabin surrounded by trees. A man in a dark suit and heavy coat hurried to open the door. He offered his hand, but Syd ignored it, stepping out on her own power. He didn't even glance at the blood covering her clothes and took her arm, two more men rushing close and walking backwards as he led her inside.

She felt almost presidential.

No one spoke, no one informed her where she was, or what was happening. Inside, she stood still as they moved around her in a choreographed dance of secure and lock. The interior had a great room, kitchen/dining, a hall leading off to the right. Lots of wood, and rustic. A nice retreat, but she could see that the windows had steel shields that would slide into place, the locks computerized. And there were, of course, five men with guns.

A safe house. She let out a long slow breath, then heard the vehicles outside move off.

"Someone tell me what happened." Sydney waited for an answer.

No one stopped doing their check of the house, going about their business with a silent determination. Creepy. Syd shivered just as lights blinked on, and warm air pushed up through the vents.

Worry nibbled at her insides. "Gentlemen, it's going to get rough if one of you doesn't start talking."

Still nothing.

"I'm working up to some major hysterics, people." Only fair to warn them.

They paused, glanced at each other, then one blond-haired man stepped near and stared down at her. He was gigantic, a Mac truck with arms. "We have orders to secure you and nothing more, ma'am."

Okay, they were keeping her safe. That was good. But she needed to know more and *somebody* had better start talking. "Then get on your nifty radios and find out what happened! Why didn't the alarms and sensors go off? How did those people get inside my lab? Where is the rest of my team?"

"Ma'am, you need to calm down."

Sydney removed the gun from her waistband. It was muddied with Tanner's blood. "Calm is *not* an option. You be calm when a man dies in your arms, pal."

The others reached for weapons hidden inside their coats until the big guy waved them off. The agent's features tightened, even though he tried not to show a thing. "Yes, ma'am. I do understand. And I'm sorry for your loss."

Sydney wrapped her fingers around the weapon as she stared ahead, seeing Corporal Tanner with a hole in his chest and breathing his last. She looked at the 9mm pistol, blood prints over metal black. And for the first time in her life, she wanted to watch someone die for that.

Deliciously slow. Yeah, that worked for her.

"You want to give me that, ma'am?"

She met his gaze. "No, I don't."

"You're safe here, Dr. Hale."

"I was supposed to be safe in the Cradle too, Agent . . .?"

"Combs, ma'am."

She didn't think that was his real name, but it would do. "But now my team is probably dead, a Marine guard is dead and I'm here, under house arrest."

"Protection, Dr. Hale. For your own safety."

Sydney wanted to hit him just for the emotionless chill in

his words. But she accepted that she wasn't getting a thing out of him and he likely didn't know any more than she did. NSA agents had taken her away within minutes of her phone call and left the disaster of the Cradle behind them.

"There are bedrooms that way." Combs nodded to the hall. "With clothes in the closets and drawers." He sized her up and looked doubtful. "You might find something to fit."

Sydney flipped the safety on the gun, but kept it. "I'll be in the shower." She took a few steps to the hall, then stopped and turned. He hadn't moved, but now the others were staring at her. "You aren't asking any questions, Agent Combs. Why is that?"

"Following my orders, ma'am."

And not letting one hand see what the other's doing, she thought. NSA field agents, a necessary evil. "Let me know when they change."

Luray Caverns 8:58 A.M.

The pilot started his descent. Pebbles and dry leaves spun upward like a twister, then were beaten back down by the slowing pound of the blades. Infrared painted the area clean, which wasn't a plus on their side. Cisco didn't doubt that if there was a "they" out there, they were long gone. He had to assume they'd made off with the gas vials. It was the only thing of value down there aside from the research. But until he received the satellite shots in increments, he wouldn't know a thing. Infrared was wading in official channels.

The building came into sight below. *Mother*, a cheezy acronym for Mechanized Operation Tether/Habitat Environmental Regulator was a fireproof building that housed the air filtration, sewage, computer, surveillance and electricity systems—and just about anything else the Cradle needed to operate. Cisco didn't know who had come up with the cute names, but at least they were easy to remember. Mother was self-contained, designed to not need a keeper. There were only eleven people in the underground facility, including armed sentries and there was no way now of telling if anyone was alive.

Without a list handy, Cisco knew the name of only one person—Dr. Sydney Hale—on shift. Average height, better than average-looking. Reddish brown hair, brown eyes, with a smart mouth and a brain like a vault. She was the reason this facility was in operation and as much as he'd trained himself not to feel a thing, the thought of her dead pissed him off.

Cisco shoved open the helicopter door, hopped down. Field agents were combing the ground in a line up the mountain like black bears scouring for honey. He headed toward the flat-roofed building surrounded by an electric fence. Fishing in his pocket, he tossed his keys at the fence. Nothing. Damn. He punched a code and still nothing.

Lock-out. Cisco popped open the keypad and jimmied a wire. If it were that easy, he thought, anyone could get in. It took another ten minutes for the explosive experts to set the charges and blow the gate. It took prima cord, and a considerable C-4 to get through the eight-inch-thick doors.

A flood of men and women followed him inside the yard. He hadn't had time to brief them, and wouldn't now. The closer he played this to the vest, the better. He opened the steel door and stepped inside Mother. He motioned to Marcuso.

"Get in there."

The technologist opened the back of a tall box that looked like a freezer. "It's probably fried."

"Of course it is. Find out how. This pumps air below and as far as we know there are a dozen people down there."

People scrambled.

"Don't turn on the generators till I give the word."

They frowned collectively. He didn't give them a reason. Aside from the scientists and technicians working in the Cradle and NSC, less than five people knew what was really six hundred feet below the surface. He was one of them. If the cold room had been breached, and the vials damaged, he didn't want Sarin gas sucked up the air vents and into this building. He almost hoped that the attackers had left with the vials. Better it killed them than Cisco's team.

"Wickum's here, sir."

Cisco glanced at the door as Pete Wickum rushed inside with a silver case. He reached for it. "You get a speeding ticket?"

Wickum smirked and shook his head. "Stellar evasive maneuvers."

"Cocky little bastard." Cisco kept an ear tuned to the radios, sliding the silver case on top of a steel gray utility box. Opening it, he slipped on a set of thin headphones and flipped a switch. A pulse beat across the screen without sound. Around him, agents tried to get the sensors up and running. Cisco listened to the sonar pulse.

If confirmed the Cradle's tunnels were under rubble, yet as far as he could tell, the main body of the facility was intact—which wasn't much. Nor was he certain if anyone was still alive down there. Thermal imaging wouldn't pass through that much stone. "Wickum, get excavation equipment up here." He closed the case, taking it with him as he moved to the door.

"That'll scare the tourists."

"It's a gas leak," he reminded them, then swept out like a black wind.

An agent watched him. "When I grow up, I wanna be just like him."

A few chuckled, and Wickum glanced back from the door. "Trust me. You don't," he said and followed his boss.

Jack was about two seconds away from killing a park ranger. Which would damage the hell out of his military career, but what the hell. He was pretty much on the edge right now.

"What do you mean you can't go get them? They're up

there on the mountain and they'll be raccoon fodder if you don't."

"There's a gas leak. We've been restricted until it's contained."

"Where? They're caverns, for crisssake!"

The ranger, patient, huge and Jack counted, dumb as a bag of hammers, said, "The area has lodges, the tower, gift shops."

Not that close, Jack thought, frowning. "Who reported it?"

"We have official word."

Jack gestured to the walls of the dinky office. "Who's official here except you guys?"

Then he knew. Government. He leaned over the desk to put his face in the pansy-assed ranger's. Smeared black and tan camo paint sharpened his features. The effect was scary and he wanted to see this man piss his pants. "You listen, pal. I have three buddies who are dead, murdered, and you'd better hotfoot your ass up to where they died."

"Murder has to be investigated by the police."

He slammed both fists on the desk. "Then get them in here!"

Ranger Pearl reached for the tottering water bottle. "Sir, calm down and please take your seat. I'll record your statement and the Luray police are here."

"Hey, Pearl?"

Jack's gaze snapped to the door. A blond man stood half in, half out. He wore jeans, a sports jacket, and Jack recognized the bulge of a shoulder holster. "Who the hell are you?"

The blond man's features tightened, then he motioned to the ranger.

"I'll be back to take your statement in a moment," the ranger said as he left with the big blond guy.

Jack dropped into the chair, and leaned forward, his head in his hands. *Gas leak, my dyin' ass.* Bristling, he scraped his hand over his head, then shot out of the chair, walking the room, flipping at files. A lot of litterbug citations, he smirked, then got a drink from the water cooler.

They were still out there. His friends. His men. Decaying, attracting creatures and insects when they should be draped in their country's flag, paid the respect due for men sworn to protect their country. He crushed the thin paper cup, staring out the office window, then pushed the blinds down.

Cooling his heels just got old.

Cisco approached the escape route, stopping to study the footprints.

There was enough moisture and dead leaves to give them a hand full of casts, but he saw three sets, one was very small. Female.

The escape entrance in the underbrush was intact. Gravel crunched beneath his shoes as Cisco moved behind the partition and walked the corridor. Power had been routed to a generator and lit the stone interior. The sensors were already registering the area free of toxins. At the end was a single steel elevator, bullet and impact proof to ten thousand PSI. It was unmarred but for the bloody handprints smeared all over. He leaned near.

"Small. Frantic. Female. Look how many times they touched. Get a sample."

"There's another blood trail here," Wickum said and Cisco turned.

His assistant squatted near the entrance and gestured with a pen at the bloody stones.

"Type match it to the blood on the doors. Let's see if we have more than one runner."

"You think this was one of the attackers?"

"I hope so. There were two females working the graveyard shift." And alive, he hoped. Neither were the killer type.

Cisco's pager went off. He leaned toward the light to read it. The bosses, he thought bitterly. They could wait. He had to collect something other than theory before he could give an initial report. *He who makes the gold makes the rules*, he thought as he moved out of the stone corridor and into the morning light.

He slipped his cell free and punched numbers, securing the line, then moving to his car.

"We have Dr. Sydney Hale," the agent said on the other end of the line.

Instead of being relieved, Cisco was instantly suspicious. "Anyone else?"

"No, sir."

Cisco cursed. "No discussions, Combs, and double check your security. Remove all outside traces. Dr. Hale is a witness and a suspect."

"Sir?"

"So far, she's the only one alive."

Cisco cut the line, then dialed again. His boss went off on him the minute Cisco spoke. "No, sir, I don't know exactly what happened."

"Your best scenario, Agent Cisco?"

"I'd rather not speculate just yet."

His boss growled into the phone. "Give it a shot." It was an order.

"The attack occurred at zero seven hundred hours. Mother was down seconds before that. We're locked out of the system, still. The escape lift is covered with blood, three, possibly four sets of footprints on the mountains. For unknown reasons, Dr. Sydney Hale escaped and is now secured." There was a small stretch of silence while Cisco waited for that to sink in. "We have reports of ground tremors and considering nothing is opening the doors, my first analysis is the Cradle suffered an explosion. We have to assume they took the gas and anything else of value, killed the inhabitants and escaped out the emergency lift."

"Good God. How?

"That I can't speculate, sir. Until I have something, I'd ask that you not inform the council yet."

"And just why should I do that?"

"This assault team got into one of the most secure facilities in this country, sir."

There was a grunt, and then the line went dead.

Cisco cut the line and tucked the satellite phone inside his coat. He scrubbed a hand over his face, then walked down the mountainside.

Wickum was right behind him.

Cisco stopped, gauging footprints. He touched something, rubbing his fingers together. "Someone definitely got hit." He showed the other man the blood on his fingertips. Cisco snapped out a handkerchief, bright white against the dark clothes. As an agent took pictures and a sample, he stared toward the cavern's tourist side. He'd bet a hundred that the carefully disguised door at Tatiana's Veil hadn't been destroyed. Inside the cavern formation Tatiana's Veil hid the interior doorway into the facility. The only other route in or out was the escape lift. Likewise disguised from the untrained eye, the escape hatch was locked from inside the Cradle and a Marine guard had the only codes and turnkey. The inhabitants of the lab didn't know it existed. Except, apparently, Dr. Hale. Wickum met up with him, pressing on the earpiece that wasn't hidden all that well. Cisco wondered if that made him feel important. He hated the things. Communication aside, it was like someone in your head just to annoy you.

Wickum spoke softly while Cisco lit a slender Cuban cigar. He dragged on the smoke, his gaze narrow and moving over the mountain, the caverns. He tried to visualize how it went down.

"We've found a body."

He glanced at Wick. "Excellent. Now we have something."

"Victim's wearing black ops gear and has a semiautomatic machine pistol."

Cisco clenched the cigar between his teeth. "Crap."

Three

This was bullshit, Jack thought, opening the office door. The ranger station looked like a command post at Threat Con Delta. There were more cops, rangers, and firefighters in here than necessary. Three murders didn't call for this. Okay, sure, a gas leak was plausible, and maybe there *was* an explosion somewhere—he'd certainly felt the earth move—but then, where was the equipment used to dig out after such a blast? Air tanks, compressors, bulldozers, backhoes? The crew?

Too many doing too little, he thought, easing out of the room and down the hall. People ignored him despite his uniform. His Marine utilities had been stripped of insignia, too frayed for service, but perfect for hunting. He'd bet five bucks everyone here figured him for a local boy hunting, since anyone could get old camouflage uniforms from Army surplus. It made things easier. He moved to the end of the corridor, listening. Ranger Pearl, a bulky man who needed to do a few sit-ups, was talking with another guy, short, Asian. Between them, Pearl held a videotape. The little Asian man was gesturing wildly, but no one could understand him.

Jack could. Two tours in Iwakuni and Okinawa gave him a small handle on the language. But the man was chattering so fast, Jack only caught words. Woman. Long head hair, he translated loosely and would have been amused if he wasn't listening so hard. *Ding wah*. Phone. Stain? No. Blood. Well, the little guy had Jack's attention. The ranger motioned to a man in jeans with a police shield on his belt, and when he approached, the Asian man started all over again before the cop led him into another office, taking the tape.

When Pearl turned toward him, Jack said, "What's that about?"

Pearl hesitated. "Just a local convenience store owner. Words out to a few locals about your buddies." At Jack's look, he added, "We capped the rumors, I swear, but this guy's got a video from his store. We think it's got a suspect on it."

Jack would bet it didn't. "I want to see it."

The ranger stared back, and Jack felt him waver. "Come on man, these are my pals. Marines. They've been to Afghanistan, Iraq; Lyons and Decker had Purple Hearts, for crying out loud. They've seen hard corps battle and were shot in the head like fish in a barrel. You either have something or not. And I was up there, I could tell you if you have something."

Pearl sighed. "I saw the tape. It's a woman."

Jack reared back, scowling. "Describe her."

"Average height, hair looked dark on the video. She was wearing a black skirt and jacket. The store owner's English is bad, but we think he saw blood on her when she came in. That's why he gave over the tape."

"You're wrong about her."

"Sir, I know you're upset about your friends, understandably—"

Just then, the cop stepped out with the Asian man and Jack pinned the officer with a hard stare. "You're wrong," he said. "That woman didn't kill my pals."

"Remind me never to take you into confidence, Pearl," the cop groused and the ranger reddened.

Jack ignored him. "She was with me and running for her life."

"Maybe she was running from the murders she'd just committed? You said she had a gun."

"Yes, I did. But her nine millimeter military issue didn't make the holes in my Marines' heads. Long-range weapons did." Jack flicked a hand toward the Asian man. "What did he say?"

"We need a translator, his English isn't great."

Jack looked at the little man, bowing a bit, then said, "Tell me the story," in Japanese.

"You speak it?" Pearl asked, impressed.

Jack glanced his way, eyeballing him. "I can swear in five languages, but little beyond that." He looked back at the storekeeper. "Tell me," he said in Japanese.

The man's eyes rounded and he started talking again, fast.

"She went straight to the bathroom, then made a phone call." Jack tapped his watch. "How long was she there?"

"*Ju.*"

"Ten minutes. When she left, she headed south. He said he looked down the road and she was already gone." Jack thanked the man, then looked at the cop. "I want to see that tape."

"I need to review it again, then maybe."

"I'm your only witness."

"Yeah and the only one alive to tell the truth, too. Kind of works against you."

Jack wasn't going to point out that if he had actually killed his friends why would he report it and hang around. "You know, I don't see you doing much about my pals. And when the press gets wind that three decorated U.S. Marines were murdered in cold blood in your county, and left on a mountainside . . ." He let that hang for a second. "Are we communicating here?" Jack gestured between himself and the cop. "I think we are." He glanced at Pearl. "Don't you?"

Pearl smothered a rude sound. Neither man realized Jack was about to blow a gasket.

"Are you threatening me?" the officer said.

Jack shrugged, giving him his best good ole boy look. "I'm about five minutes away from pounding you into the concrete; you be the judge."

The officer glanced over him, unimpressed. "Must be the trauma making you act so stupid," he said. "Did you know this woman?"

"Nope, never saw her until she was running down the hill with men chasing her. And I'd been out there since five A.M., which I already told Pearl here."

The cop ignored that. "And you believed her story."

"You're not listening. I saw them, heard the gunfire. I'm sure there are a few rounds in the ground, the trees—my men," Jack growled back, wanting to wipe the floor with this guy. "What're you gonna do about it?" It was tough keeping all this inside and not having at least his punching bag to pound.

The cop scraped a hand across the back of his neck. "And you say you shot one man."

"I found a man dead with a hole in him. She could have shot him, but I'm guessing I have better aim."

"Where did this woman come from? There is nothing up there but the caverns."

"Maybe she fell asleep after a tour, how the hell should I know? I didn't get her name and number." But he had the ID tag, and survival instincts said don't let the cops in on that just yet. He wanted to find her, question her before the cops stopped every bit of information from flowing his way.

The detective seemed to battle with something and when he reached for the doorknob, his shirtsleeve slid upward. Jack saw the USMC tattoo. "Wait in there." He jerked his head to the room with the files. "I'll see what I can do."

Jack nodded and quietly stepped inside. "Semper Fi."

The cop met his gaze. "That's the only thing keeping me from locking you up right now."

Jack folded his arms, his patience snapped. He was tired

of being shuffled off without answers. And he wasn't leaving without them.

Peter Wickum bagged the weapon and handed it to Cisco. "No prints," he said.

Cisco held it up to the light. "No firing pin either."

"A cleanup crew?"

Cisco shook his head, his ponytail slipping across his back. "They'd have taken the body, or at least hidden it." He handed the gun back, then squatted near the body of the intruder. "Whoever was here, didn't care what they left behind." He pointed to the footprints. "Cocky sucker." A pause and then, "Like you, Wick."

Peter snickered to himself and squatted, too. "This guy didn't pull off his own mask," he said. "With a wound like that he would have been dead before he hit the ground and the impressions in his skin from the knitting says he was talking to Lucifer around then."

"Cute, Wick."

"I try, sir."

Cisco opened the dead man's jumpsuit, peeling back the folds.

Wick swallowed at the sight of torn flesh and blood as his boss pulled something from the lining. "What's that?"

Before Cisco could answer, Agent Hodges rushed up to the scene.

"Jesus, you're pale, Hodge," Wickum said as he rose, and the agent glanced between the two. Cisco stood.

"We have a problem."

"A bigger one than I have now?" Cisco gestured to the body at his feet.

"Oh, yeah."

It was the first time Pete Wickum had seen Agent Gabriel Cisco run. He usually stalked an area like a wolf on the scent, slipped quietly away in a dark sedan, but rarely did he get worked up over much. He didn't take anything personally. At least not in the three years Pete had worked with him. Cisco was ruthless in his pursuits and emotionless while he performed them. Wickum hurried after him.

Cisco stood rock still near a lump on the ground and Pete's first thought was: they've found a body that's been there a long time. Small, too. His stomach tightened and he reached for his Maalox tablets. *Please don't be a kid.*

Cisco lifted his gaze from the body. "A Gilly suit?"

"We have it from the Fish and Game that some men from a hunt club were out here thinning the doe herd," Hodges said, handing Wick what they found on the body. "I guess the deer were getting into traffic, eating garbage. Destroys the ecosystem."

The Gilly suits were used by military in combat to hide their approach in the field. It made them invisible and part of the terrain, and it wasn't something that could be easily bought. Of course there were copies, but this was the real McCoy.

Cisco squatted. "What do you see, Wick?"

Peter took a hard look. Cisco liked testing him. "I don't see any signs of a struggle. Two sets of footprints, this man's and one other." He pointed to the dead man's boot cocked sideways. "This guy has small feet, the other marks were from someone with the same boot, same tread, but larger. Weapon and ammo were left behind. But"—Wick leaned out for a better look—"it's been disabled, like the other guy's."

Cisco reached for the netting.

"It's a head wound, sir." Hodges looked ready to puke.

"Did you look further?"

"Not yet. Pictures are done."

Cisco nodded. "Gonna be ugly," he murmured and lifted the netting hood. He looked, and dropped the cloth.

Wickum handed over a wallet. "He's a Marine."

Cisco stood, and flipped to the ID.

"There are two more," Hodges was reluctant to say.

Cisco didn't speak, his expression unchanged as Hodge led him to the next man. And then the next.

"About a hundred yards apart," Cisco said, his voice tight with disgust. "Regardless of what Fish and Game says, dressed like this, we can't ignore that these men could possibly be part of the attack. Maybe staking out a spot to kill anyone who escaped the Cradle, but someone got to them first." The dead man on the hill? Cisco did a three-sixty, his attention flicking high and low. In this dense forest, anyone could hide well.

"But those are hunting rifles," Wick said.

"With high-powered scopes." Military types liked having state-of-the-art, even for game, but Cisco had to exhaust all possibilities. "I need facts. Hunting licenses, records, associates, family, friends, duty stations, everything."

"The bodies?"

"They're ours for now."

Wickum moved off, radioed for stretchers and a forensic team. Hodge and another man were laying the first victim flat on the ground. "Treat them as you would your mother, Hodge."

Cisco glanced, eyeing him for a second, then walked off. But his anger was just below the surface. Wick had learned that that narrow look and long stride said stand clear or be knocked clear.

Gabe Cisco stopped beside the last man, thumbing open his wallet. Carl T. Lyons. Gunnery Sgt. USMC. He wasn't even thirty yet. Then he found pictures. He hated seeing this. Pictures made it personal. He slid them back into the plastic cases, ignoring the face of a little girl smiling at the father who'd never come home.

"Cisco," Wick called. "CBC is here."

Cisco turned, scowling. Chemical Biological Containment. Army. He tossed the wallet to him. "Bag it."

"The tourist side is secured."

"Air quality?"

Wick spoke again into the lip mike, then looked up. "Contained in Mother and so far in the corridor only."

Cisco nodded. Sarin gas lacked color, odor and taste.

Invisible and deadly. "Do not begin excavation until CBC give you the okay." Excavation would be slow and dangerous.

"What's down there?"

Cisco just stared at him.

"Never mind, forget I asked," Wickum said, knowing better and expecting the worst.

Lifting his gaze to the mountain, Cisco watched the choppers circle, the noise like the beating wings of a hawk. Time to march on the locals.

With the door cracked a bit, Jack listened to the noise, picking out one voice and holding onto it. They couldn't move on the mountain and the cops were getting pissed. Who was messing with their jurisdiction, they kept asking, but Jack could have told them that. Your government dollars at work.

He needed to see that videotape, and when Pearl headed toward him with it, he thought, finally. But someone called the man back. Jack moved to the door, leaned out just enough to hear better. Gut instinct said stay hidden. The gas leak was a warning that it was smelling pretty bad around here and was only going to get worse. The lack of equipment and the wrong people to contain it screamed when it should have whispered. He watched, listened. Reconned.

A tall man with dark hair pulled back in a ponytail swept into the station like a winged creature. Two men followed, each wearing dark clothes, long coats. The first guy looked ready to eat a small child, his eyes cold, blue, and moving over the faces in the room. Nothing in there, Jack thought. Must be hell being that empty inside.

Ponytail took the tape from Pearl, handing it to the man flanking him. The cop stepped forward, arguing over jurisdiction. Ponytail rested his palm on the guy's shoulder like they were old pals. His expression went kind and soft.

What a player.

Jack eased back a bit more, but listened intently. They weren't giving up the bodies and it took everything in Jack to stay put and hear the rest. FBI had the power to override locals, but they were usually clearer about it. Ponytail wasn't making any declarations. In fact, he was talking to the cop and Pearl. No one else.

The noise in the station muffled their words, but when Ponytail handed over a business card, Jack's senses went on alert. It wasn't so much the white card, but that the instant the cop read it, Ponytail took it back.

NSA.

Had to be. NSA agents had to collect back their cards.

This is a bigger shit pile than I thought.

Pearl wasn't included in the conversation and when the young man glanced toward the room Jack was in, he jerked back out of sight, looking around for an escape. Staying here was no longer an option. Not with Ponytail out there quietly flexing muscle and overruling local authority. Getting out between that flood of officials was the only thing on his mind now. Especially when he was covered in blood and smelling like a horny stag. He'd be detained, used, accused. He'd never find the woman, or the son of a bitch who murdered his friends.

Too many cops outside the windows to climb out, Jack thought, then moved behind the door, peering through the crack between the jamb and the wall. Ponytail was doing a lot of asking and no answering. He wondered how much this guy had to do with the woman and if he could lead Jack to her. Ponytail advanced, ignored Pearl, and spoke with the cop. Jack couldn't hear but body language said a lot. The cop was ticked off; NSA was taking over, or restricting them. Ponytail leaned closer and whatever he said, shot the officer's plan out of the water. Pearl, his ham-like fists clenched at his sides, turned on his heels. Beyond him, Jack saw the ponytailed agent slip out as unassumingly as he'd arrived. Smooth.

Pearl stepped inside, looked around for him. Jack cleared his throat.

"They aren't releasing the bodies to us."

"I heard. Who are they?" he said innocently, but he knew.

"I can't say."

Jack nodded, accepting that the young man had screwed up by telling him about the tape and wasn't going to walk that path again. Besides, Jack already knew who he was dealing with. He stared, silent.

Pearl folded in ten seconds. "Dammit, they can't do this!" Pearl said. "I mean, something's terribly wrong here and we're supposed to just shut up and take it? National security, my ass."

"I know."

"Do you?" Pearl bit back. "What'll you tell your friends' families?"

"The truth."

Pearl shook his head. "Hell, man, I don't know what the truth is right now. I've been here for three years and didn't know there were gas pipes up there. Natural steam, sure, it plays the organ in the caves, but, oh, hell . . ." Pearl rubbed his neck and muttered something Jack ignored. "Detective Harding says I've got to hang with you. Material witness. Harding's pissed."

"Did the agent mention me?"

"I don't know. That guy was talking, not listening. I don't see where the murders of your friends have anything to do with a gas leak, though."

It has everything to do with it, Jack thought and saw his chances of learning more going from slim to none real fast. NSA would clamp down and that'd be it. They were already manipulating the ranger's world.

"I understand, Pearl. Take it easy. I lived with this kind of red tape crap."

Pearl nodded and reached for a stack of forms sitting in the in-box. They were yellowed and curled, and Jack knew this place hadn't seen trouble in years. Now they had more than they could handle.

Pearl searched the desk for a pen. Jack just noticed there wasn't even a computer in here.

"Your full name." Pearl frowned, cocking his head. "You know, I don't even know your first name."

Jack moved up beside him, laying his hand on his shoulder. "I'm aware of that." He popped the kid hard on the back of the neck, and Pearl went out like a switch and down like a sack. Jack caught him, leveling him into a chair. Quickly, he knelt, pulling at the park ranger's shoelaces. "Sorry kid. NSA'll cramp my style."

Ten minutes later, wearing Pearl's too loose uniform, Jack walked out the back door and to his truck. The area was peppered with men in uniforms, yet no agents. Jack was good at spotting agents, covert or otherwise. They rarely looked at the usual and searched beyond. Pulling the cap low, he offered Pearl's wallet to the cop standing post at the edge of the lot.

"Where you headed?"

"Out for donuts and food. With the gas leak, they won't let 'em open the diner."

The cop snickered, handed him five bucks, and ordered breakfast. Jack took the order like he meant it, then drove. It took him another half hour to get down the drive and when he passed a police cruiser, he tossed the wallet into the open window and sped on.

He had a new prey to hunt.

It hit her in the shower.

Sydney slid to the tile floor, water streaming over her hair and mixing with her tears. Grief swelled like foam, poured so fast she couldn't catch her breath as she cried, the faces of her colleagues, her friends, filling, then fading through her mind. All those people, that drive and innovation gone. They'd had one goal, stop the deadly chemical threat of Sarin gas. Save lives. And for that, they'd lost theirs.

This assault presented a bigger threat. The attackers had the gas. The amounts were small, too small, in her opinion, to warrant an attack of that magnitude. But they'd done it, slipped inside before anyone had realized it.

How? How did they get into the lab, or into the cold room? Hell, how'd they get into the Cradle at all? Her reasoning that the attackers could have easily killed the guards and taken the keys and codes managed to get past her grief. Hot water slapped at her like tiny needles, prodding her to move. She climbed to her feet, finished her shower, dried and put on the sweatpants and thermal shirt she'd found.

Then she noticed the gun she'd left on the bathroom counter was missing. Bastards.

Grief slid deeply into anger, and she was already wired for sound. Her internal clock was set for night hours and beneath the surface of her skin, she could actually feel her blood rushing through her veins. Prickling with energy. Adrenaline and endorphins, she thought. The hot shower had done no more than remove the stench of death, but sleep was impossible. Hunger and uncapped energy slid so hard through her she wanted to run, fast. Anywhere. Alone.

She stormed into the great room. One agent stood near the window talking into a head mike set. Another was in the kitchen, without his coat and jacket and preparing something to eat. He wore a shoulder holster, the leather grip latch open.

The agent gave her a mild glance, then went back to work. "Feeling better Dr. Hale?" He slid a sandwich and chips across to her, then started cleaning up. If he noticed she'd been crying, he didn't give any indication.

Ignoring the sandwich, Sydney moved past him to the fridge, took out a soda and wished for a beer. She popped the top and drained a third, then looked at Agent Combs.

"You guys get a good show while I was in the shower?"

Combs was silent.

"I want the gun back."

"I'm afraid I can't do that. It's evidence."

She figured that. But the weapon gave her power when her world was crashing. The Cradle was supposed to be safe. Impenetrable. Well, not anymore. So why should she believe that these guys could keep her safe? She wanted a weapon, yet now all she had were her notes, tucked inside too big sweatpants. She hoped the paper didn't crunch when she moved. Opening the freezer, she found a pint of Ben and Jerry's and took that, the sandwich and soda to the living area. She curled up in the corner of the sofa. Her watchdogs whispered amongst themselves. She didn't try to listen. NSA talked in code and never made much sense.

She ate, her mind on trying to figure out how the attackers had made it up the mountain without setting off Mother's sensors, let alone getting inside the facility. The park wasn't open, the day guards weren't there, but the checkpoints she usually had to go through were enough to catch anyone trying to sneak in. The inspectors scheduled to arrive had probably been turned back when Mother went down, so that cut them out of the equation. The day shift? Had those scientists been accounted for? And the data? Her work?

The elusive "they" had known how Mother operated, knew how to get close enough to shut Mother down. So much for state-of-the-art security and technology. She tried to remember if the emergency lights were on when she got off the elevator. She couldn't recall anything except Corporal Tanner dropping like a stone, helpless and bleeding to death, and the gunman who'd killed him, pointing his weapon at her heart.

Shaking off the fear, she mentally plucked at the events since she'd arrived at work just before midnight. Arrived by car—a chauffeur was a perk of the job so cars weren't seen outside the facility when tours weren't operating. Day security parked with the tourists and walked. During park hours, only two guards were outside the facility, dressed like guides for the caverns or mingling with tourists. Sydney suspected they were just downright lucky to be on their way to work at the time. Key locks and codes, hidden steel enforced doors, palm scans; in the cold room was a retinal scanner. All sensors linked to Mother, then from Mother to someone who knew what all that stuff meant, somewhere in Langley. Three Marines were inside the Cradle twenty-four seven, shift changes were at 2200 hours, and they left in civilian clothes. Corporal Tanner favored baggy khakis and big shirts, she recalled, her throat tightening.

All information was filtered and yet, she understood there were at least fourteen possible leaks in military personnel and scientists. Then there was the Defense Department, finance committee members, NSC, their staff. Anyone who could get a look at certain "eyes only" papers if one DOD personnel slipped up. But she doubted that. Data went to the Under Secretary of Defense first, then was filtered down. She frowned, chewing the last bite and dusting off her fingertips.

At least she was *told* that's how it worked. Security wasn't her bag.

She dove into the Ben and Jerry's, which was just the right consistency for her to finish off what was left in the pint in record time. She was glad now she hadn't given her unexpected savior her name. It was a little too convenient that he was in the forest and armed at the time. Deer or no deer. Was he part of it or had he been stationed there to stop a suspected attack? Why, then, hadn't she been warned? She was the project manager; it was her research that garnered millions from the government and enabled the Cradle to exist. Okay, think smart. If he'd been part of it, he'd have killed *her* instead of risking his life to protect her.

Tossing the spoon into the empty pint, she glanced at her watchdogs. Combs looked at her, bland and so very special agent–like.

"Get the chief up here. I have some things to tell him."

"He's got his hands full right now."

And you don't have the clearance to take my statement, she thought snidely. "Really? Well how about you tell him my ID tag, which I had on this morning, is missing."

Combs's features tightened, the first sign of life. He grabbed the radio.

Cisco's people found chute packs, and another body. Two terrorists and three dead Marines, and motorcycle tracks. Worst case, no one was alive up here to have heard anything. Except Dr. Hale. He had to assume that everyone inside the facility had been killed by the attackers—too many dead aboveground to believe otherwise.

He couldn't order the air compressor to the Cradle turned on if the vials were broken. The toxicity would kill everyone aboveground. Below ground, a dozen people were dead, or dying.

Standing under a tree, Cisco tried to comprehend what happened. The intruders had dropped silent and waited to take out Mother. How they did that was a mystery in itself, but somehow they managed to delay the internal alarms, or he would have heard about it before it was too late—and it was painfully late. Stupid place to put a lab, he thought.

"Wick. Contact SETI and see if anyone reported a UFO; assign men to canvas any homes in the valley. If they parachuted in, someone might have seen something." Not that it would do him much good, he thought. "I need satellite photos of this area, from twenty two hundred yesterday till now."

"I can do that. But infrared didn't tell us anything. Not even showing the men running when, with all the footprints, is proof positive they were here."

Cisco braced his back on the tree. It was a beautiful day. "You're getting slow, Wick. You didn't notice the suit, the black fabric, but more specifically, the lining."

Wick frowned, and remembered Cisco pulling out threads through the bullet holes.

"It keeps the body temperature even to avoid infrared.

Those particular thermal liners are classified. They knew we could track them, so they chilled themselves up for it."

"Great. Now what?"

"We need delayed infrared, Six A.M. to sunrise. After the attack. They might have chilled up, but not the motorcycle engines. Cast the tracks and footprints, I want to see if the ones near the Marines match any we find here near the escape hatch."

"I know I'm going to really feel stupid for asking, but why?"

"Dr. Hale got out of here alive, was she the only one? Why?"

"Evasion? Luck?"

Cisco shook his head. "The escape hatch."

Wick frowned down at his notes. "Her checkpoint is logged in at the HQ. Her palm print says she was in there. I don't get it."

"She was. But she wasn't inside the facility at the time of the attack."

Wick looked at him blandly. "I take it back, I wanna be you."

Cisco scoffed, pushed off from the tree and started walking.

"You really think she had something to do with this?"

Cisco didn't answer, and Wickum drew his own conclusions.

Four

Never leave a man behind.

It clawed at Jack, brewed in his chest with the grief he'd suppressed for the last couple of hours. He dealt with it the way he always had. He shoved it to the back of his mind while he addressed the here and now. There'd be time enough later to drink to the dead.

Parked in an alley a couple blocks from his house, he watched his place, smoking a stale cigarette he found in a crushed pack under the seat. He didn't know if the cops and NSA had shared information yet, but he wasn't taking a chance at getting hauled in before he learned more about Hale and what really happened on that mountain.

Time to call in some favors. He dialed his cell phone. The pick-up was instant.

"Hey, Jack."

Caller ID at NCIS. He'd have to remember that. "Hutch, I need a favor."

"Name it."

"You been contacted by NSA?"

"No." A pause and then, "What's wrong?"

"I can't say. Not yet. Run a check for me." He pulled out the ID tag and read off the name.

Jack heard the computer keys tapping.

"Nothing. No record, no address. You sure this woman exists?"

Her image popped into his mind; small, long reddish-brown hair, bloody clothes and leaving bodies in her wake. "I'm sure. Go level five."

"Negative." Dennis Hutchinson's voice was muffled, whispered. "Not authorized."

Jack battled for a second then said, "Decker, Lyons, and Martinez are dead, Hutch. Murdered while we were hunting at Luray. She's the reason."

"I'll get back to you on that." The line went dead.

Hutch would come through. He owed Jack for pulling him out of a little mess in Iraq a few years back.

With NSA swinging the big dick around, trying to sweep the murders under the carpet of national security, he had to back up and regroup. He'd already tossed the dead deer in a Dumpster near the park, and went to a self-serve car wash to rinse out the blood. The ranger's clothes joined the carcass and Jack was wearing jeans and a sweatshirt he'd planned to change into after the hunt and had stashed in a duffel in the truck.

He was freezing his ass off. He scanned the area, his two-bedroom house outside Quantico and was locked as he'd left it. Most of his neighbors were still at work. He couldn't wait till nightfall. People would be coming home, kids would be near and vulnerable. If the intelligence network connected, they'd be looking for him before morning. He was a material witness, and when NSA figured it out, Jack would have to turn himself in. He was hoping his military record spoke loudly enough for him when NSA learned he'd slipped away from the rangers. Breaking the rules wasn't something Jack did easily. Ever. But three dead Marines made the difference.

Leaving his truck and edging down the alley, he slipped in his back door.

Inside, he didn't turn on lights. He pulled the shades, feeling like an escapee from prison. He kept his cell phone near.

After a quick shower, he changed, then took inventory of his Ops gear, and stuffed it into duffels and packs, loading it by the door. He started to dial Lyons's wife, then stopped and dropped into a chair. What would he say? He'd lost men before. When they knew the enemy and saw them coming. But this?

A goddamn massacre. And he couldn't give their families answers yet.

He stared at the phone, then laid it down, and gripped his head, fought the grief, the images of shattered skull and blood. The expressions and tears he knew he'd see when he told his friends' loved ones their husbands and sons were dead. It was his duty to be the one to inform them. But with the sad news, he needed to tell them why, and that the murderers were behind bars. In caskets, would be better.

Pushing out of the chair, Jack went to his liquor stash over the stove, and poured himself two fingers of twenty-year-old scotch. He held it up in salute, murmured, "Semper Fi," then tossed it back in one shot. It burned over the ache swelling his throat. He gripped the glass, his vision burning.

It should have been me. Dammit. The glass popped in his fist. He stared down at the shattered glass, the blood blooming on his thumb. *You're alive for a reason*, he thought. *Get control.* He rinsed his hand, gave it a quick first aid, then sitting in front of his computer in the darkened house, he went online to search for Doctor Sydney Hale.

College photos and newspaper clippings of numerous awards digitized on the screen. Child prodigy, gifted. A masters in microchemistry at Clemson, another in microbiology, then a freaking doctorate from Johns Hopkins in chemical immunology. Jesus, did this woman even have a life beyond school? Then, five years ago, everything stopped. Using his access codes he had only because he was a team leader, Jack bent a few more rules, skewered his ethics, and accessed files few could. Still, nothing came up in the last five years. No water bill, no mortgage, not even a driver's license. She'd been wiped out, and that meant someone didn't want Sydney Hale to exist.

Her image gelled on the screen again, and Jack memorized her face, the curvy body and bright eyes. The man in him recognized her beauty. The Marine in him saw the answers to his friends' death.

Who are you, Dr. Hale? What were you making up there?

The cell phone rang. Jack looked at the number and answered.

Hutch spoke briefly, then cut the line.

Cisco sat alone inside a long, black windowless van, the satellite communications phone to his ear. His skin turned a slightly darker shade as the director raked him over the coals. Mother had failed and it was Cisco's responsibility. "I'm looking at the satellite thermal shots now, sir," Cisco argued. "Three escaped. No sir, the two bodies we have were wearing thermal liners." The director asked how he knew only three escaped. "Aside the bike track, those men were running uphill, and their body temp didn't keep up with the cold liner suits under their clothes. Obviously they'd planned to ride double."

Cisco scanned the photos, the doors of the van closed. Outside, several agents waited in the cold evening. Gabe wished they were in here facing the big guns instead of him. "I'd ask that you not inform anyone of the dead Marines, sir." Cisco didn't want to tip any hands just yet.

"The council and the Under Secretary must be informed," the director said.

"We have a leak, sir, and until I cap it, I insist. I'm sure you'll agree it's best that the country doesn't know that three Marines—on leave—were murdered anywhere near the Cradle."

"Agreed, however, watch yourself. You're inches from accusing a member of the council of a criminal act."

"With the exception of you and the Under Secretary, everyone is a suspect . . . sir."

There was a long silence as the director weighed the options and scenarios. As Cisco had done since dawn this morning. "Agreed."

"I've accounted for the five researchers not on that shift. All have valid alibis, but can't be undisputedly proven. It was dawn. They were sleeping."

"And Dr. Hale?"

"Alive and secured. I'll be questioning her soon."

"She's a valuable resource, Cisco. Her brain child garnered a billion dollar project funding."

"I understand that, sir, but she is the only living witness." Cisco pressed his advantage. "I'm aware the R & D team was working on Sarin countermeasures sir, but what type exactly?"

"You're tasked with finding the terrorists and the vials," was his boss's answer.

"You're tying my hands, sir. How can I hunt if I don't know what to look for?"

The director made a frustrated sound. "It can't be helped."

"Then don't expect miracles."

"I'll see what I can do."

"Yes, sir." Shit. He needed more information to work this.

The director cut the call and Cisco did the same, tapping the heavy satellite phone against his knee before sliding the door open. He inclined his head and agents climbed in. "Wick, get the car."

Wickum looked forlornly at the warm van, then hunched in his coat, and obeyed.

Cisco shut the door and stared at the men crowding the van.

"Get comfortable, no one leaves." No one balked, either. "When CBC gives the go ahead, excavate. We need to get down there." The Chemical Biohazard Control Unit would clear the air for toxins before anyone was close enough to be affected. Cisco silently deliberated, then spoke. "The Cradle was a working lab for Sarin gas countermeasures."

Expressions changed, eyes widened.

"It's a level five, no discussion without secure locations. We have whisper devices; they can, too. I want everyone to be suited up if they go near the entrances. There were vials of gas stored six hundred feet below. We don't know if they got to them or what else they might have seized. We have to work from a clear objective." He held up a finger. "One, they took the gas and will use it to blackmail the U.S. Two, everyone below is dead and possibly the research data destroyed or stolen. These attackers easily killed three hunters; they won't hesitate in killing anyone else. I want to know where those shooters were positioned—today. Dr. Sydney Hale escaped unharmed, yet lost her ID tag. She says it's on the mountain, so I want people searching the kill zones for it. If the wrong people find it, the wrong questions will surface. And worse case . . . we have an internal leak. It could very well be her. We treat her like one."

Cisco's narrowed gaze drilled each man. "At this point we can only speculate. We won't know the truth till we get to the security tape linkage from the Cradle to Mother up and running. I want Hale, the entire R&D team, security forces, and the dead Marines researched thoroughly. Especially Hale. I want to know the last time she had a date, her hair cut, her favorite restaurant, everything. Hodges, you take the lead."

Cisco slid open the door and climbed out, leaving Hodges to close it and address the men remaining inside. Wickum picked Cisco up in the sedan. The heat was blasting and Cisco sank into the leather seat and stuffed his feet right below the vent.

"To the safe house?"

"Yes. Take your time." Cisco rubbed his face, then stared out at the beautiful scenery. Find the leak and it will lead us to the gas. He didn't let himself think about the people who'd died today. Instead, he pulled Dr. Hale's file from his briefcase. She was his only link and during the ride, he considered how he could use her.

When Sydney would normally be dropping face first into bed, she was wired, her nerve endings frayed. She couldn't sleep, couldn't even be still. She was damn tired of being left in the dark, too. If anyone should be kept abreast of what happened, it was her. She was project manager. Or, she had been—until her world went up in gunfire and smoke.

She moved around the cabin, hunting for something to take her mind off the attack. You'd think they'd stock a safe house with books or video games, but there wasn't even a TV that she could find. She tossed out the burnt coffee dregs, started a fresh pot, then rooted in the cabinets.

"Anyone want a sandwich?" she called out. "Play poker?"

"No thank you ma'am," came from around the house.

She found a bag of Bugles. She wasn't hungry at all—a surprise since food was a vice for her—but stuffing her mouth was better than tearing into the agents. They had orders and were following them to the letter. Still, it ticked her off.

Radios crackled, men mumbled. Syd was walking the perimeter again, shoving corn horns into her mouth when a car pulled up. She moved to the window and was pushed back by an agent. She rolled up the bag, wiped her mouth and waited. It didn't take long.

A tall, slender man entered from the side entrance with another, slightly shorter man following behind him. More men in black, she thought as the great room emptied except for the pair. Sydney folded her arms and regarded them.

"Cisco." She'd met him once before when her handprint and retinal scan were registered.

He nodded, eyeing her too large clothes. "Dr. Hale. This is Agent Wickum."

Sydney shook his hand. It was ice cold.

"Are you comfortable, Dr. Hale?" Wickum asked.

"Fine, peachy. What happened?"

Coming into the living area, Cisco removed his coat, turned it inside out and laid it over the back of a chair. Details like that told her he was meticulous and careful.

"That's what we're trying to ascertain, ma'am," Wickum said politely.

Cisco just stared. It was unnerving.

"What about my project staff?"

His eyes went flat and Sydney felt the thread of hope snap. She sank onto the sofa and covered her face.

Over her head, Cisco and Wickum exchanged a glance.

"You were outside the Cradle when it was attacked, weren't you, Dr. Hale?"

"Yes." She looked up.

Cisco ignored her glossy eyes and asked, "Who knew about your absence?"

"Corporal Tanner, he's the only one with the codes."

"And he's dead."

She felt slapped. "Yes. He let me go topside often. I'm a little claustrophobic. I like air that's fresh. Clears the mind."

"What did you see, Dr. Hale?"

"Aboveground, nothing." She shook her head, reliving it all again. The silence in the woods and the horror below the surface. "It was still a little dark. I had a penlight. I was up there maybe fifteen—twenty minutes tops. When I came back down, there was heavy smoke in the corridors, Corporal Tanner had been shot and he fell on me. I dragged him into the elevator and we went to the top. But he was dead before we reached the surface."

"He was shot where?" Cisco asked.

"In the chest. It went right through his Kevlar vest. That means armor piercing, right?"

Cisco nodded. He didn't bother with making notes or a tape recording. But his number two man did.

"When I realized the elevator would go down again, I tried to stop it." A harsh laugh shot from her throat. "Like slapping the eight inch thick steel door would stop that thing? They must have used it to come back up the shaft because they were right behind me."

"Who was behind you?"

"The killers."

Cisco didn't bat a lash.

Her gaze flicked to Wickum. He looked normal—blond hair, brown eyes. Average cute, like someone's big brother. But while Agent Wickum had life in his eyes, Cisco's looked vacant.

"Continue."

"I ran and fell once." She showed him the scrapes on her palms and arm. "I had Tanner's gun. Combs took it. And my clothes. When I fell, I must have lost the ID tag. They shot at me a couple times and that's when the Marine dove at me."

Inside Cisco went still as glass. "Marine?"

"Well that's what he said. He wore a Gilly suit, you know, those netted things with fake leaves and branches all over it."

Cisco nodded.

"He knocked me to the ground, covered me and fired back at the man shooting at me. He had a hunting rifle. The attackers used silencers because I didn't hear anything more than soft popping till the bullets hit something. The Marine's rifle was loud. Then we ran to his truck. I crawled in back with a dead deer and he went looking for his friends."

"This man who helped you, did he say how many were out there with him?"

"He said pals, plural, Agent Cisco. More than one. He left me and that's the last time I saw him. I ran to the store, made a call and got to Mark eight. Followed the rules."

"Except for being outside the facility at dawn."

"I'm alive because of that, so back off." She stared across the room at the agent and if she wasn't so pissed she might have put her girl brain in gear and admired his looks. But she knew better. Cisco would do anything for the cause, and if that meant pointing a finger at her, he would.

"Yes ma'am. You should know, those men don't need a permit or license to hunt there."

"Yes, they do. It's a state park."

His thin look was like saying *very good Dr. Hale, next question*. She wanted to drop-kick him.

Wickum handed him a large envelope. Cisco slipped out the photographs and offered them to her.

She recoiled, dropping them on the coffee table. "You son of a bitch!" It was of the dead men in black. In full Technicolor, one's chest blown open. "You could have warned me." She shoved them at him with a snide look. "The men I saw were dressed like that, but they wore masks. One had bright blue eyes."

He tucked the pictures away. "What did you hear and see after you came down the shaft, Dr. Hale?"

"Smoke so dense I couldn't see far, gunfire, and the terrorist with blue eyes aiming at me and Tanner." She flexed her fingers. "Blue Eyes stepped over a body. I didn't see anyone else except him."

"Did Tanner return fire?"

"Maybe before I got down there, but I did."

There was a slight lift of a brow. "That was very brave."

"Are you always this much of a condescending asshole?"

"Yes."

Wickum cleared his throat.

"The chemicals I worked with could be used as weapons of mass destruction. Shouldn't you be looking for them instead of grilling me?"

"We are."

"They have the gas, don't they?"

"We don't know yet."

"What do you mean? You go down there, open the cold room and take inventory."

"We can't get into the Cradle by Tatiana's Veil. It's been sealed from the inside."

"The escape elevator?" He shook his head and she frowned.

"Mother didn't automatically turn on the emergency compressors and vent?"

"Mother is down and with the Sarin threat inside, no."

Slowly she stood, her voice a cascade of shock and outrage. "Good God, Cisco, they may be alive! If they're trapped on a level, they have ten hours of air down there. Twelve max. But there was smoke and that eats the oxygen."

"And if the vials were broken, they were dead in seconds anyway."

"You know, I suspected you didn't have a heart, now I'm sure you're missing a soul, too."

Cisco stood very still, his hands behind his back, his gaze direct. He'd had to weigh the deaths against the final outcome and the consequences. "If we turn on the compressors everyone above could die, too, Dr. Hale."

"Not unless the dead guys had something like atropine and contamination suits on them. I didn't see suits or lugging them either. No"—she shook her head—"they didn't release the gas. The risk is too high. They attacked to steal it."

"Yes."

"So my entire staff is choking to death down there. Jesus, how do you sleep at night?"

His fists tightened.

"This is your mess, Cisco. The Cradle was supposed to be impenetrable. Mother should have operated on her own."

"Yes, but it didn't. And I'll find out why." Without another word, he moved to the kitchen and poured himself some coffee. Syd watched him dump heaps of sugar into the cup. Wickum followed him and the two spoke softly enough that she couldn't hear. They did it to make her nervous.

It wasn't working. He let her staff die. She wanted to hurt him. Bad.

"I know you worked on nerve gas countermeasures." Cisco had his back to her.

"Goody for you."

Cisco faced her, arching a black brow.

"I'm not breaking security, Agent Cisco, so either you two show me your clearance, or shut up." He obeyed and she could tell it irritated him. "Yes, the Cradle team developed a cold implosion bomb."

"How does it work? And explain it so I can understand."

Syd had to think for a second, several formulas whizzing through her brain. "Since Sarin lacks odor, color and taste, we needed to create a way to see it and stop its spread, to dissipate the gas once it's released. The implosion sets off high volume high pressure phosphorous Freon. Freon attacks and paints the gas first, suspends its drift because it gives it weight. The chemical mix goes airborne and neutralizes the most deadly pathogen components. The real success was that we made it work without heat generating blasting material so it remains highly effective after detonation."

Wickum's mouth hung open. "Wow."

Cisco stepped in front of him. "Could it seal the doors?"

"No. It's not that kind of bomb. It creates a flash burn if you're close or holding it, but it's cold. You'd end up with mild frostbite unless you got the mix in your eyes. That would blind you."

"Was there one of these bombs inside the Cradle?"

"Yes. They were stored one level above the cold room."

"We have to assume the intruders have both the chemical weapons and a means to stop it." Cisco scowled, rocking back on his heels. Only his gaze shifted to her. "Is that the only project?"

Now it was Sydney's turn to be silent.

"Please answer the question, Dr. Hale."

She simply tipped her head to the side. Cisco wanted to push it, but admired her resistance. He was overstepping his authority as it was. He asked her to repeat what she saw and what happened for the third time. Cisco considered that the Marine who saved her life and went back into the fray was one of three lying in a makeshift morgue. But he'd find out for certain.

He reached for his coat, slipping it on. "You're to remain here, Dr. Hale." He headed to the door, his black coat flapping like wings.

"Cisco." He paused to look back. "There were three vials of liquid gas left. Those were used to test the effects of a completed implosion bomb. We used the accelerants for development, in small amounts. They're not easy to get after nine-eleven, but any good chemist with the formula could make a deadly gas like that."

"One strike would be plenty. And right now, we don't have the countermeasure. They do."

"If they have the countermeasure bomb, they have three prototypes. We did development, not manufacture. They can't recreate it quickly. It took biochemists and physicists two years to make that work."

Outside the house, Wickum hunched in his black coat. "She's not what I expected."

"They never are." Cisco had learned that brilliance didn't have to be explained and most people with minds like Dr. Hale had a sheltered shyness. Dr. Hale was the exception. She'd come a long way from the woman he'd fingerprinted five years ago. She could barely look him in the eye then. Now, he suspected she'd like to see his ass kicked all over the mountain.

"Why didn't you tell her about the dead Marines?"

Cisco opened a thin cigar and bit the tip, turning his head to spit it aside. He struck a match, the flare turning his features demonic. "No need right now. She's lost her staff and her life's work. Her house been filtered yet?"

Wick checked his watch. "It should be done by now. I think you have her all wrong."

"What I have is a suspect and a witness. She's smart enough to make a cold implosion bomb, what else could she do?"

"Hell if I know. I flunked chemistry."

"I don't trust her, neither should you. Get your hormones under control."

"Hey, she's pretty, intelligent, and she does have a nice rack."

"Yeah, well. She used those charms to get past the Marine guard in time to escape the killing field. Who else did she con?"

"I'll bet you twenty she's clean."

Cisco eyeballed him. "You're on."

"You're going to release her."

"We can't mark her without her knowing it. She'd expect it. Get her place wired, and put a tail on her. Let's see who comes to Dr. Hale. If she's in this, she's the brilliance behind it."

"And if she's not?"

"We'll know within forty-eight hours."

"Yeah, she could be dead by then."

Cisco squinted thought cigar smoke. "Hence, the tail, Wick."

Jack slipped inside the darkened house, moving quietly into the living room. Suzie Lyons was curled in a chair, a wad of tissue in her fists. She stared blankly at a TV, the sound turned down.

Jack called her name.

She flinched and hopped out of the chair. "Who's there?" She grabbed the nearest object, a heavy alabaster ashtray.

"It's me Suzanne, Jack." He stepped into the light.

"Oh, my God." She dropped the alabaster and launched at him. "I thought you got killed! What happened? Why can't they tell us anything?"

He grabbed her, muffling her mouth with his hand. "Shhh. Sit down." He forced her into the chair. "No, no lights." She stared, her pretty tearstained face aglow from the TV.

"How did you survive?"

Anger and bitterness tinged her voice. He didn't blame

her. She was young with a baby and no husband. He was a bachelor with no one. It didn't make sense to anyone—especially him—that he was here and Lyons would never come home again.

"I'm alive by pure chance, Suzanne. If I could change it, I would gladly have died in his place."

Her expression softened. "I know you would have, Jack. Carl always said you were the first man in, last man out."

Jack's jaw tightened. "He was a good man. He didn't deserve this; none of them did."

Tears burst free. "Make me understand, please."

He told her enough to ease her mind, but not enough to put her in danger. She sat there and whispered the word, *murder* as if saying it would help her understand.

"I don't know why it happened, but I'm going to find out." He gripped her hands. "I swear I'll get the bastard who pulled the trigger and the one who gave the orders."

She inhaled. "You can't. Are you crazy? Think of your career. Oh, Jack, let NCIS handle it. Please."

He frowned. "Who's contacted you?"

"No one except the chaplain and the CO. Both said it was a hunting accident."

Oh, yeah, that washes, Jack thought bitterly. Three expert marksmen shot each other? In the head? The CO didn't know anymore than the cops did. "Stick to that story for now." Jack stood, rubbing the back of his neck. His gaze fell on a picture of his team and he picked it up, memorizing the faces of the men he'd trusted the most.

"Take it."

He looked at her. She pulled it out of the frame and handed it over. "Carl would want you to have this."

He pocketed the picture. "I have to ask you not to tell anyone I was here."

She set the empty frame back on the mantel and nodded.

"I'm really short on time, Suzanne." Although he was

legally on leave, he had seventy-two hours to conduct a Line of Duty investigation. It was his right as their ranking officer and the only thing that might keep his ass out of a court martial for going rogue. "I need some of Carl's gear."

She nodded and went to unlock the hall closet. "It's all in there. Take it."

Jack gathered everything he could. Carl was a southern boy who liked his guns and all the toys that came with them. Gear stowed, he moved it by the door.

"I know what'll happen to me and Lizzie, Jack. I've known this since I married a Marine and I've prepared myself for it, but what's going to happen to you?"

It touched him that in her grief she even considered that. "Nothing I can't handle. Don't you worry." He touched her chin till she looked at him. "If the government comes here and asks about me, don't lie. Tell them I was with them."

"They don't know?"

"They aren't forcing their hand enough to find out or I'd be standing in front of the general right now." Jack laid a gentle hand on her shoulder. "Until they catch up to me, I'll do some looking. I have somewhere to start."

She nodded and he kissed the top of her head, then pulled her into his arms. He held her as she clung to him and cried her heart out. "You have someone coming to stay with you?"

"My mom should be here in an hour or so," she murmured, wiping her nose.

Softly he whispered, "Listen to me, Suze." She looked up. God, she was just a tiny, fragile thing. A widow at twenty-five. "I swear on my oath as a Marine, I will get them."

"I'll pass that to Decker's and Martinez's family." She squeezed him and bravely stepped back. "Now go. Because if you're hunted, they'll look here."

Slinging the gear, Jack motioned her away from the back door, and gripped the knob. Before he opened it, he plucked keys from a rack near the door and left her alone in the dark.

five

If looks could kill, Cisco thought as Dr. Hale stopped at the threshold, *I'd be nailed to the wall.*

"This is your screw up, Agent Cisco. You were part of the design team. You swore the encrypted security measures would keep anyone out and could withstand a nuclear blast."

"Apparently, I was wrong."

Dr. Hale's look was bitter with grief. She wanted someone to pay and he was the perfect target. He didn't blame her. "I will find them, Dr. Hale. Make no mistake."

"That's no comfort when my people are choking to death down there and you're still breathing easy."

His brows shot up. "If I didn't know better, Dr. Hale, I'd say you wanted me dead."

Her features tightened. "Then you don't know me at all."

He stepped back as she barreled past to the black Lincoln Town car and climbed in. She shot him one last damning glance before leaning back into the seat. The agent closed the door.

As innocent as her story sounded, trusting her wasn't a luxury at his disposal. She offered too little and was the only survivor in a holocaust of destruction. She'd broken the cardinal rule of leaving the facility without authorization. However, at this point, she was not aware that the Cradle was under hundreds of feet of rubble. That alone said that if she were in on this plan, then she'd been betrayed. He wanted to know by whom.

Agent Hodges approached. "The tail will pick up about ten miles on the highway," he said, moving close to Cisco as the car sped away. "We have sound surveillance, but no cameras inside her house."

Cisco had debated that. Hale had already been under watch, just not so close. Her daily routine was recorded, yet the council insisted that since she'd passed the background screening, and was the brain child of the project, she'd earned her privacy. Cisco needed to have a look at the records of Dr. Hale's recent surveillance and speak to the agent in charge. As he recalled, she led an incredibly boring life. Pity.

"I want men posted around her twenty-four seven. Four hour shift changes, nothing slips past, and watch their backs. The attackers killed a dozen already, they'll kill again."

Hodges nodded and went to the van.

Wickum trotted near, talking into a hand radio. "We've located snipers' nests."

Cisco looked at him.

"There are two."

Jack drove, moving in and out of traffic toward Hale's house in the suburbs. The sun was dropping in the sky, the air growing colder. He cranked up the heat as his cell rang.

He hit the hands free switch. "Wilson."

"Just what the hell do you think you are doing, Marine?"

Colonel Clay Jones, Operations Commanding officer. He'd been waiting for this. And hoped to God Jones would back him up.

"I'm undergoing a Line of Duty investigation, sir. It's my duty and right as their commander."

"I'm aware of procedure, Captain, but if you want to keep those silver bars, then you need to let NCIS handle it. You're too involved and too close to the matter."

"Begging the Colonel's pardon, but the *matter* is the cold-blooded murder of my men."

"Captain, the authorities insist it was a training accident." He said it as if it left a bitter taste in his mouth.

"Impossible. We were on leave, hunting for Fish and Game, sir. And our positions were a hundred yards apart. All of us are sniper qualified; do you really believe that?"

"Regardless, we have orders to stand down. Orders that supercede the generals."

Jack frowned. The colonel sounded as if he had a gun to his head and was repeating a script. "Sir, it's not like you to go along with that bullshit."

"Like you, I have to take orders, too. Stand down."

He couldn't. It was a matter of honor. And justice. "They didn't release the bodies, did they?"

"Autopsies need to be preformed."

"Ask for photographs, sir. If you saw Lyons, Martinez, and Decker, you'd know that wasn't necessary. It was an execution. Martinez didn't have a face left." The colonel muttered something sharp and ugly. "There's already too much smoke and mirrors. NCIS will be shut out, no bodies, no case. FBI wasn't even involved. NSA is in charge at the site."

The Colonel was quiet for a moment, weighing what he now knew. "Have a good leave, Marine. Semper Fi."

The line went dead.

Colonel Clay Jones was stepping aside. It was all on him.

Sydney couldn't get out of the car fast enough, ignoring the agent who was behaving like a first date, escorting her to the door, and even touching her shoulder and giving her a tender look. It was for anyone who was watching to maintain whatever cover they'd cooked up.

"Take your hand off me, Agent Combs."

He drew back.

"And leave. I'm fine."

"You know the rules, ma'am. You are to remain here until Agent Cisco says otherwise."

Cisco was a geek with a gun as far as she was concerned. "Cisco can kiss my ass."

She stepped inside and shut the door in Combs's face. She didn't bother to watch the agent leave. He wasn't going far; climbing into a car or van, watching her front door and wanting to be home with his girlfriend or wife.

Too bad, she thought, then looked at her house. The small two bedroom cottage sent an instant wash of peace over her and she let out a tired breath. She walked through the living room, flipping lights, and although she couldn't see it, she knew NSA had been here. They'd probably copied her hard drive, and tapped her phone and if there were listening devices, then they'd be bored as hell. But the attack was far too serious to let her go without protection or surveillance. It was an odd comfort. Cisco didn't trust her anymore than she did him. He'd practically accused her of being a part of it, the bastard.

In her kitchen, she made some herb tea, her stomach grumbling at the first sip. She poked in the fridge, but nothing appealed right now. Deciding on a pizza or Chinese delivery a little later, she changed into her own clothes, then settled onto the sofa, and clicked on the news. She surfed several stations and was satisfied that the attack was covered up nicely. The American public didn't need to know they were mixing chemicals under a national park. The deadly components were one reason it was six hundred feet below the surface and not a very big lab near homes and people.

She stared into her cup, reality surfacing and she realized that containing a leak underground was the best they could hope for; just not at the expense of her friends and colleagues. Something else could have been done.

The phone rang and Syd flinched, sloshed her tea, then read the Caller ID and picked up. It was Matt Collier.

"Jesus, Dr. Hale, what happened?"

"This isn't a secure line, Matt, I can't say."

"Well men in black stormed my place at seven A.M. and roused me out of bed, to what? See that I was wearing my new boxers?" He calmed for a moment, then said, "They wouldn't say why."

"There was an incident at the facility. Don't report to work until you're called. You'll be paid, don't worry." Collier always had financial trouble though he was paid better than a general. *People with big brains should take a course in balancing their checkbook.*

"Ransely and Cooper and the rest have been questioned too."

"Good, then you're in the clear."

"For what?"

Obviously, Cisco's flunkies didn't mention a thing about the attack. Ethically, she couldn't either.

When she didn't respond he said, "Okay, okay, fine. But how're Handerson, Pic, and Hanai, the others?"

Dead, she thought, but wasn't allowed to release that information. "I don't know." She rubbed her forehead, a lump thickening in the back of her throat. "I have to go, Matt."

"Yeah, sure." It was a cautious sound, doubting her. The effects of the day left her little room to care. She hung up and it took the last bits of her energy to call her mom and check on her.

"Hello, darling. Shouldn't you be at work?"

"I have the day off." Even her mother didn't know where she worked or what she was doing. No one did except her colleagues. To anyone who asked she was doing research for the government. "So, Mom, what are you up to?" She tried to sound cheery when she just wanted to cry for the rest of the day.

"I'm planting purple pansies. It's a lovely day for planting."

It's also September. They'd die in the frost, but she didn't ruin the small pleasure. In her eighties, Mom had so few, and

Syd wanted nothing more than to be planting flowers with her scatterbrained mom right now. They chatted for a moment until Mom got distracted, which was often lately, then hung up. Putting aside her mug, she drew her grandmother's quilt over her shoulders and sank into the sofa cushions. Sleep came easy, yet in her dreams, the horror lived.

The sky was dark purple when Jack circled the block once, then pulled over two streets west, on the far side of a dog park. He watched Hale's place for the better part of an hour, noting movement, cars, locations. The neighborhood was old, lots of retired people, and hardly any children. Even teenagers. The homes were like gingerbread houses frosted with Victorian scrollwork and small porches. It made him wonder why Hale lived here, then thought, it hid her from the public. Old folks might be curious, but they were too polite to butt in her business.

His attention focused on a dark car parked across the street from Hale's place. A luxury sedan with tinted windows, and the engine was still running. The exhaust was kicking up a lot of fog. The license plate wasn't a standard white government plate, but Jack recognized it. It was a car from the mountain. One that was with Ponytail, idling outside the ranger station. NSA.

This complicates things.

Jack considered how to stall the agent without hurting him. The man was just following orders; Jack grabbed a rag from the behind his seat and left the truck. Walking toward the car, he kept himself in the blind spot, then dropped to a squat, and shoved the rag into the pipe. The car would stall in a few minutes. It would be enough.

Hunched, he moved away, then circumvented Hale's house in a wide birth. His steps faltered when he'd spied a blue van two blocks further up the street. But it was the two men standing yards apart that got his attention. They were cleaning up the grounds, shoveling street debris into a cart.

At this hour? The average person wouldn't have noticed anything except when the man's head was down, his eyes weren't on the job. They were on Hale's house.

More NSA? Jack stayed on the far side of the park and north, and passing the van, he punctured the rear tires with his K-bar knife, then made a sharp left out of the field of vision, and kept walking. One of the men moved somewhere in the trees, out of sight on three sides. Jack walked past to the shoveling man. He was storing his shovel and picking up the handles to the junky looking apple cart.

Jack took it all in and kept going; the dark hair, unshaved jaw, jeans and work boots, a ratty hooded sweatshirt. His steps slowed as his mind reproduced the image, bringing in clarity. The watch, he realized. Citizen. Expensive.

Jack curved his path to watch the guy. The man pushed the cart to the trash cans, then set it down. He didn't empty it or gather more debris, and instead walked to the bulk of trees near where the first man had disappeared. Then he vanished too. Jack couldn't see a thing, it was so dense. Not even their feet.

Jack doubled back to their hiding spot, keeping his distance and using the trees for cover. From his vantage point, the pair scarcely shifted the bushes, but he saw the flick of movement. Hand signals. Moving behind another tree, he went down on one knee a few yards back, his heart pounding. It was dinnertime, the neighborhood quiet, lights blinking on in the windows. Hidden behind a thick line of bushes that edged the park between the clusters of trees, he slid to his stomach, saw their boots, then low crawled toward their position. Urban warfare, he thought as he curled to his knees. He rose slightly, putting his foot down slowly, careful not to make a sound as he moved forward.

I cross the line right here.

Whatever he did now, risked his career. He was outside the Uniform Code of Military Justice. But the death of three outstanding men reminded him that anything he suffered would never compare to their sacrifices.

He moved in, making his breathing low and shallow. Instinct and training took over. Silent and careful, he eased closer. He spied the men, a less than clear view inside the covey of bushes. Jack rose slightly, an arm's length behind the men. They were watching Hale's and the sedan. That brought him up short. Before he could think on it, the man shifted and Jack had no choice. He delivered a brutal blow to one man's temple. He dropped. Instantly, the other spun, drawing his weapon. Before he could fire, Jack grabbed the silencer muzzle, yanked it downward as he jabbed him in the throat. Hard and fast, cutting off his air and crushing his windpipe. A reflex shot went into the dirt as the man dropped and choked. Jack pressed hard on his jugular and watched the guy fade out.

He searched them both. It was typical of covert Ops to erase all telltale signs of identification, no labels, ID, or even dental fillings. But no fingerprints? Burned off, slick with scars. Like the attackers on the mountain. Jack rubbed his mouth, the rage leaping into him, and he wanted to choke the life from these two. Instead, he searched, found weapons, binoculars, and each man's plastic card with a bar code across one edge. No words, numbers, just intermittent black lines.

Pocketing the cards, he pulled the pair farther under the bushes, secured them with their own belts and left them for the NSA before he edged his way back out of the park. Scanning the area for watchers, he rose and walked. His gaze flicked to the van. No movement, though it listed to the rear like a bull on its haunches. No one came out. Empty. Just the same, Jack stayed out of the surveillance arena. He couldn't afford being caught on camera right now.

He climbed into his truck and was driving it around the park toward Hale's place when a compact car bearing a pizza logo zipped up the street, cutting him off. The teenage driver pulled around to the back of Hale's house, climbed out, slapped on a Pedro Pizza ball cap, then turned to get the pizza in the backseat. *He's delivered here before.*

Jack threw his truck into park, then hurried to cut him off before he made it to the door. He came up behind the kid and put his hand on the boy's shoulder. The teen jerked around, but Jack gripped tight, pulling him back against a neighboring house.

"Jesus mister! You scared the shit out of me."

Jack flashed his ID in the boy's face. "You shouldn't be here."

"I-I got an order to deliver."

"You just did." Jack took the pizza.

The teenager looked around as if trying to decide whether to complain, alert Hale, or just get the hell out of Dodge.

"You're in the middle of a stakeout, man, beat it."

"I have to get a signature, and my time is almost up. Thirty minutes from placing the order, or she doesn't have to pay."

Jack glanced at the bill, scribbled something unreadable, and paid the kid. "Go, now, quickly." He pointed in the opposite direction, then snatched the kid's ball cap.

The kid was off in a heartbeat, speeding away. Jack put on the delivery cap, drew his weapon and positioned the pizza over it.

Then he headed for her door.

The area was surrounded by ten thousand candle watts of light as Cisco stared up at the sniper's nest. A pine bough and mud packed stronghold in an oak tree. To his right about forty yards, Wickum was stationed at the other. Two nests, two elevations. They were certain to get any strays.

"They'd been there two days at least. The ground is deeply matted," Wickum said. "No evidence behind. No bullet casings, food wrappers, nothing."

"Get forensics up here, they'll find what we can't."

Cisco kept staring up at the nest, slipped off his coat,

folded it, and wearing latex gloves, he leaped at the tree, grabbing a low branch. He climbed. He had to see the view for himself.

He reached the perch, careful not to disturb anything. Then hit the call button on the walkie-talkie cell. "Nothing up here, either. Looks like he tried to destroy it, but didn't have time. There are scrapes down the tree like he fell." In a hurry, he thought, then lifted his gaze to the horizon. "Cut the lights."

The spot lights blinked off and through mini night vision binoculars, Cisco focused on the kill sights. He could see the flicker of the neon orange flags marking the body location, then the next and the last before his attention moved up the mountain. The sniper had a clear observation of the men and the area leading back up to the caverns.

A view to the kills. He could have picked them off at any time.

Cisco called for lights, climbed down, and dusted himself off. He was slipping on his coat as Wickum strode toward him with the phone to his ear.

Wick cut the line. "You were right, SETI had a couple UFO reports, and valley police said a man claimed to have seen a balloon."

Cisco lifted his gaze to the mountain. "They assault at night, wearing state-of-the-art thermal gear, but leave trails for us to follow."

"That says they didn't care and would kill anyone who got in the way."

Cisco brought his gaze to Wickum. "Since everyone except Hale is dead, that would be us then, wouldn't it?"

He headed toward the Cradle site, the partitions and lights splattering a ghoulish haze over the national park.

The anticipation of her pizza made her antsy. Eating was better than reliving her quick, short, nightmare and she couldn't shake the image of Corporal Tanner's death from her mind.

She needed to be busy since for three years her focus had been her job in the Cradle, but with her data destroyed, all she had to show for a billion dollar project was her notes. She read over the crumpled printout, even more certain of her results, then tossed it on the counter and gathered her supplies to make a scented oil for her bath. The hobby was playtime, and like cooking it always helped her relax. It was just a different kind of chemistry, in its simplest form. And it didn't threaten to kill anything except bad vibes. Popping in a Nora Jones CD, she stirred the double boiler, then added lavender essential oils to the mix. She was getting out the bottles and funnels when the knock at the back door startled her.

She glanced at the clock, shocked to see she'd been at it for a half hour, then wiped her hands, turned off the burner, and hurried to the back door. On the way, she grabbed her jar of house cash, plastering on a smile for Ricky. He's grown some, she thought before she opened the door. Bracing it against her butt, she fished in the cash jar, her head down. The scent of cheese and pepperoni made her mouth water.

"That smells great, Ricky, how much do I owe you?"

"More than you know."

Her head jerked up, shock rounding her eyes. Oh, God. The Marine.

The jar slipped from her hands, shattering on the floor. He pushed his way inside, shoving the pizza box on the counter as she turned to run. Jack clamped a hand over her mouth and yanked her back against his chest.

"Not a word, got it?" He pressed the gun to her side.

She nodded and he kicked the door shut and let her go. Instantly, she reached for a weapon, her electric chopper, and threw it at him.

Jack jerked out of the way, glaring at her. "That was stupid." She tossed a kitchen chair in his path, but he kept coming. "I don't want to hurt you."

"Then why are you here—with a gun? What did you do to

Ricky?" She kept backing up, sweeping figurines and frames off the shelves.

"He's fine, gone." He ducked as a book sailed past his head. "Jesus, lady." He lunged, grabbed her arm, shaking her. In her pretty face, he saw fear, like he had on the mountain and something in him settled. He'd get little cooperation if she was terrified, and dragging her with him, he moved, turned on all the appliances he could, then in the living room, did the same with the TV. He tuned it to MTV and cranked up the volume.

"Why are you doing that?"

"Your place is likely bugged."

Hell, yes, and she hoped NSA was listening and running to her rescue.

"Sit." He pointed to the sofa and reluctantly, she obeyed. Jack moved to the window, looking out without disturbing the curtains.

"What do you want?" *Hurry up, Combs.*

"Answers, and you're going to give them to me."

"Like hell I am."

He gave her a deadly look. "You think you have a choice?"

"How far do you think you'll get? There's surveillance out there."

"Not anymore."

Sydney paled. Did he kill them? He looked furious enough right now.

"You've got a lot of eyes watching you. Who are you to warrant so much protection?"

"Nobody."

"Your degree isn't in lying, is it, *Doctor* Hale?" He faced her. "Why were you on the mountain?"

"Why were *you*?"

"I was thinning the deer herd for DNR, Fish and Game. Your turn." She didn't respond, looking like a mutinous schoolgirl in a Johns Hopkins sweatshirt and blue jeans.

"What went down on that mountain?"

Death, she thought. *Only death.*

"Whose blood was on you? Because it wasn't yours."

Her features slackened and sadness spilled over them. Jack frowned, an uneasy feeling sweeping through him, magnified when her eyes teared up a little. But he didn't have time for sympathy. The noise would bring the agent here. Jack knew they had to get lost, now.

"Put on your shoes, get a coat."

She looked up. "No way." God, she didn't want to go anywhere with this man.

He found one, threw it at her. "I can take you without shoes, Doc, but it's damn cold out there. But I *will* take you."

Sydney jammed her feet into her loafers, shrugged into her jacket. Where was the NSA? Why weren't they in here, slamming this guy to the ground and cuffing him by now?

He gripped her arm, and moved with her to the back door.

She dug her heels in, hoping to stall. "You're not a real Marine. Kidnapping isn't in the Marine code of honor."

"It is today. And I'm not keeping you, Doc. I need answers. Fork over, and you're free."

"If I don't?"

He met her gaze and Syd saw only cold determination. "That wouldn't be wise."

She spied the printout. "It will only get worse for you."

More than his men murdered? "I have a right to the truth."

"How do you figure?" She twisted, backing up against the counter. Her hand closed over the printout, the noise in the house muffling the crinkle of paper.

"I saved your life, Doctor Hale, and that got men killed."

"Terrorists, yeah."

"No, *my* men."

Sydney blinked owlishly. He'd said he had friends in the woods. "W-what do you mean? What happened?"

He didn't answer, pushing her out her back door and huddled like lovers, he ushered her toward his truck.

Syd recognized it from the state park. He opened the cab on the driver's side and forced her in. Sydney kept going, shoving her notes down the front of her jeans, shoving the door open. No one came to help. No NSA, no police and Syd knew, she was on her own.

She was half out when he caught the neck of her jacket, jerking her back. "You won't win, Dr. Hale," he said close to her ear. "And I don't want to hurt you. Give it up."

Damn woman didn't listen and fought like a cat snagged in a net. Her nails clawed his cheek, her knee aiming for his groin. Jack closed his arms around her and she slammed her feet into the dashboard. The truck rocked.

Enough of this. Quickly, he pressed her into a head lock, holding firm till she passed out. She fell limply against him. Jesus. He leveled her into the seat, cushioned her head, then patted her down for weapons. He started the engine, pulled away from the curb and gave the rearview mirror a quick glance in time to see the agent talk into his sleeve cuff as he tried to restart the engine.

By the time the agent got out of the car, Jack and his pretty captive were long gone.

Six

Gravel crunched beneath his boots as Cisco strode toward the Cradle. Generators chugged, powering floodlights turning the area to daylight. Men and women in black jumpsuits swarmed over the area like ants. The CBC team was in white hazmat gear, and converging on the Cradle's escape hatch. Cisco walked into the tourist entrance of the caverns and quickly down to Tatiana's Veil.

He ignored the stalagmite formations, the faint trickle of water and stopped at the entrance only a handful knew existed until today. Experts were spread out with equipment, trying to get into the complex through the designated entrance and according to them, it was still sealed from the inside. The elevator was hidden behind rock within what appeared to be a cove in the cavern formations. People passed it on the tours, never giving the space a second look since it wasn't backlit. The false rock face slid back to show a keypad. Once acknowledged, the scientist would slip sideways into the first level of the Cradle. A short corridor, out of the range of the cavern formations to preserve the site, took the scientist to elevators with a palm print scanner activated by their ID tags.

Hale's tag was still missing, lost during the attack. Or had she given it up long before?

The palm scan and tag operated the steel lift, sending them six hundred feet into the belly of the earth to the labs on four levels, each with its own power system, and all connected to Mother.

It was colder down there, he remembered, and Hale was right; seal a level and containment was possible. If they could reach it. *If* the vials were still in the cold room and unbroken.

"It's fried to a crisp," the tech said, sighing back on his haunches. "There is no reason it shouldn't open. I've bypassed the circuits and it's getting power. It's as if there is nothing in there anymore."

"We should just blow the door," another man added.

"No," Cisco said.

"People could be still alive!"

"And this is a natural landmark, we leave the outside as we found it."

"Christ on a cross, Cisco, you're priorities are fucked up."

"I have orders." Everyone inside was dead. The evidence said as much.

The supervisor stood, meeting his gaze. "My sensors say the elevator isn't on this level."

"If your sensors can tell you there's no reason for these men to be here," he gestured to the Chemical Biological team standing by, "then I'll accept that this is not an option."

"Then why'd you call us in?"

"I thought you looked good in the fucking monkey suit," Cisco snapped. "Install a new system, and get it open. CBC rules you, got that?"

The tech's lips thinned with anger, but Cisco didn't give a damn. Containment was priority one, but the truth was that if Mother was running during the attack, it would automatically sense the explosion or a release of toxins, then start sealing floors and venting the air through a charcoal filtering and wash system. Or dumping water if there was a fire. Hale said there was smoke, but the sprinkler systems weren't operating. Nothing worked in Mother. He had to assume inside the Cradle was the same.

They'd have to excavate first, test the air content, then excavate more. It was a slow process.

The tourist entrance to the cavern faced a flat parking lot, a road leading to the highway. Behind the cavern entrance, the mountain rose high and fresh green. Cisco made his way between people to Mother. It was hidden in the forest at the base, her appearance more that of an electrical power transformer than a computer housing. He passed it and went deeper into the forest, gaining altitude until he reached the heavy equipment; Bobcats with backhoes, men lined up with picks and shovels, waiting. He hoped to hell that they didn't have to dig by hand. Six hundred feet of rock was a lot of ground to cover.

He ducked into the escape hatch. The CBC team halted him just inside the stone corridor.

"Sir, we have no indication there's gas in the corridor at all, nor has been. We can open the door."

"Excellent." He started forward.

The man put his hand out to stop him. "It's an eight inch thick door, and that could very well contain any binary agents." He pointed to the hazmat suit.

Cisco sighed and reached for the rubber suit, then dressed. Staring out a Plexiglas face shield, he followed the colonel. They passed through two vapor locks constructed of high-density polymer plastic, rubber, and coiled steel. Easily set up and discarded. Looks like a kid's play tunnel, he thought, ducking inside and walking to the steel doors still covered in bloody handprints.

Men were positioned with sensors and pry bars. "So far, it's clear, sir."

Cisco nodded, standing far back and behind a protective screen as they applied prima cord to the seam, then blew it. The prima cord instantly exploded. The temporary ventilation system sucked the air out of the containment tunnel and passageway like a vapor lock in space. Dirt and small stones stirred. His eardrums pulled. For the next few moments, the noise was deafening.

When the dust settled, Cisco cursed. The explosion barely made a dent in the door. No detection of binary agents.

"Try the pry bars again," the colonel ordered.

Army soldiers positioned the chisel tip in the seam of the door and hammered it in, then pulled. They strained and nothing moved. Two more men applied pressure and still nothing. Cisco joined them, and for fifteen minutes, they pulled without success.

There were no control panels, all operation was from the inside. Cisco didn't have the codes. New codes were issued from Mother to the Marine Security Forces Guard at each shift, so they were screwed in that direction.

The Soldiers refused to give up and were breathing hard after several more tries. Cisco's gaze moved over the blood-stained steel. The prints belonged to Hale, the others, they hadn't identified yet. Two different blood types, too.

They tried again. The door cracked an inch, then suddenly sprang open.

Men scrambled to test, the colonel forcing the rest out with Cisco. He could hear his own breathing, rapid and shallow as they nervously waited, the soldiers risking their lives to learn the truth.

"No detection. None."

Cisco moved back into the tunnel. "Get forensics in here, suited up."

The young Marine lay in a pool of his own blood, the smears of footprints telling Cisco someone else was in here. The prints were in slightly coagulated blood. The Marine's side arm was missing, now in evidence. The crime scene tech stopped several feet away from the tunnel, looking between the hazmat gear, the men in it and Cisco.

Moving toward him, Cisco reached for the bag. "Get in a suit. I can only do so much."

The man was reluctant, but obeyed.

Hell. Cisco wouldn't be this close to the gas if he didn't have to be. He took samples of blood, capping them, then ordered photos of the elevator before he reached high up into the corner. He disengaged the camera links, then pulled the camera from its brackets. A computer chip inside automatically made a copy of the surveillance. At least he'd have a visual.

"Normally, the lift would automatically go back down."

"Could be a cave-in below it."

Cisco shook his head. "If it's stopped on this level means the computer isn't operating. He," he gestured to the marine, "was the only one with the turnkey and codes."

"Who the hell thought that up?" the colonel barked.

He met the Army officer's gaze. "I did. It was to prevent anyone from gaining access from the outside."

"Then we have to remove the elevator. Without controls on this level we can't do a damn thing," the Colonel said.

"Agreed. The main elevator at the Veil entrance is stopped somewhere between levels. Take a break. I'll get some sensor equipment up here, thermal imaging. At least we can tell if there's rubble beneath it and how far we have to dig."

"Christ," the colonel said. "It will be rock by rock! We'd have to test the air quality every second and with every disturbance!"

"Then I leave it in your hands, sir." As Cisco stepped out of the lift, he looked back at the body. *He's just a kid.* And as far as this was concerned, Hale hadn't lied. Tanner was shot in the chest, through and through. Just before Cisco turned away, he notice the dead Marine's forehead—and the perfect lipstick imprint of a woman's mouth left behind.

"What did you do to me? Sydney felt her world come into focus.

"Sleeper hold, thank WWF. The fuzzy feeling will clear in a few minutes."

She tipped her head back, eyes closed. The musty scent of the ocean filled her senses, then the drugging motion of the room. A boat? She opened her eyes. It wasn't hard to recognize the man who'd worn green paint on his face and a Gilly suit. His eyes were the same whiskey brown. Piercing and direct. He sat across from her. Good-looking and dangerous. The gun lay on the cushion beside him.

Yet he appeared relaxed, tucked in the covey of the cabin bunk, his knee drawn up. He overpowered the small space, leaving little room for her. But his expression shut out any doubt. He meant business.

"What exactly do you think this will accomplish?"

"Information." His gaze moved over her, slow and probing and it felt too intimate. "Everything I need."

Under different circumstances, Sydney might comply. The man dripped with a raw sexuality that had her senses jumping. *Good God, Patty Hearst, stop.* But then, handsome was really a meek description for him. He had a wonderfully unyielding jaw, his cheekbones telling her there was some Indian in his background, and while muscles rolled beneath his long sleeved T-shirt, it was those dark eyes that trapped her. She glanced away and reminded herself she was his prisoner. He could crush her throat without effort, and despite her awareness, she wondered just how dangerous this man could be. It was time to find out.

She met his gaze, trying not to show her fear. "How did you get around the surveillance?"

"I have my talents." Jack thought of the bar code cards in his wallet right now and wondered what the hell they opened.

"Did you . . . kill them?"

"No." He looked offended. "And I see we have to work on your opinion of me."

"Kidnapping, assault, and taking me hostage?" She jerked on the ropes binding her hands behind her back. "Working yourself right up there to Boy Scout, huh?"

He looked her dead in the eye as he said, "I wasn't trying for Boy Scout."

Sydney felt her hopes slipping. "In my house, you said 'men got killed, my men.' I remember you going back to check on them."

"And I found them dead."

Her features went slack with shock. "Dead? All of them? Good Lord, how?"

"All three were shot in the back of the head with a high-powered rifle. Without a sound." He lowered his leg and leaned forward, crowding her in the small space. "They were unrecognizable, Dr. Hale. Half their skulls blown away."

The horror in her expression hit Jack like a slap. The color drained from her pretty face. It made him rethink his position. How could she be that uninformed? She was in the middle of this.

"Oh, my God." The pictures Cisco had shown her flashed in her mind and Sydney looked down at her lap, her eyes burning. Three more dead. Corporal Tanner, and this Marine's friends. Her entire team. Her best pal, Tish. There was no one left except the two of them.

And the killers.

"Dr. Hale?"

She looked up. A tear trickled down her cheek and Jack's anger slid a notch.

"This is my fault. If I hadn't been outside, then you wouldn't have been involved."

"Outside of what?"

Her lips tightened. Why didn't Cisco tell her about the Marines? Surely, he'd discovered them. Or was this man lying to her, too? "I didn't have anything to do with the death of your friends. Not intentionally."

He stared at her for a moment before he said, "I'll tell that to their families." She paled, but he went on, not wanting to give a damn about her feelings. "You and whatever you're working on is the reason they're dead. This attack was quick, efficient, and snipers were positioned to pick off strays."

"Me?" She felt ill.

"*Anyone*. What's up there?"

"It's . . . classified."

"Bullshit."

Her gaze narrowed. "I want the killers, too, Marine. I lost a dozen friends in that attack." Instantly, she realized she'd said too much.

He cursed under his breath. "It's underground, a lab."

Her features went taut. *She makes a terrible liar*, he thought. Probably why they kept her locked up somewhere. "You're a scientist, Dr. Hale, and a very good one from what I've read. You were cooking something extremely lethal. It's been my experience that the worse it is, the more classified it gets."

She said nothing, despite her revealing expression. He opened his wallet, showing his security clearance.

Sydney glanced and recognized the ID. "And this should impress me why?" But it did. Only a select group of people had sparse information on the Cradle project. She'd memorized ID levels so she could recognize who was cleared by the National Security Council and the Department of Defense to discuss the Cradle's existence. It made her ask for Cisco's. This Marine's was the same, although that he wasn't included in the existence of the lab wasn't saying much. It was a short list.

"Any higher and it's the president," he pressed.

Even the president didn't know about this, she thought sourly, keeping quiet.

He put his wallet away. "We can go at this all night."

"Obviously my plans have been cancelled." She jerked on the ropes.

He leaned in her face. "I'm not the enemy, Dr. Hale. But you should be afraid, because two, maybe three men got off that mountain and no arrests were made."

"None?" The man with blue eyes, she thought. *He's out there and he saw my face.*

The quick fear in her eyes was almost pungent. "NSA shut out the local police, didn't inform the FBI, and claimed it was a gas leak."

Cisco was clever, she'd give him that. "How long were you on the mountain?"

"Long enough to know that the death of my men didn't mean squat to NSA. For all I know they're still up there on the hillside rotting." He stared at her for a long moment, and God knew what was going through his mind.

Then she knew.

He wasn't giving up, demanding answers again and again. He denied her water, food, rest, his face inches from hers or speaking from behind. She was proud of herself for resisting, mentally cataloging her closets, her panty drawer; anything to ignore him. It wasn't easy. She owed this man her life. He had a right to know the truth. But she'd sworn an oath.

Syd was near exhaustion at around four in the morning. He stopped abruptly, and she thought, thank God. Ha. She should have known better.

He touched her chin, tipping her face till she met his gaze. "We haven't even started." His voice was low, laced with the steel of his resolve. "This won't be over until I have my hands on the bastard who ordered my friends killed. *And* the triggerman."

She swallowed. *He'll kill them.*

"Talk, Doctor Hale, or get dragged along with me. The choice is yours. But I guarantee it *will* get ugly. Are we clear?"

"Crystal."

He straightened and stepped back, staring for a moment before he climbed the short set of steps to the deck above. The slide of the lock made her flinch. Sydney tipped her head forward. Great.

He was set on revenge—and she was nothing but a means to get it.

Jack lay back on the bunk, watching her. She was asleep. She'd lasted longer than he thought, but she was afraid of him. In war, that was his objective; instill fear in the enemy, confuse and create scenarios in their minds. Break them.

The thought of doing that to this woman didn't sit well.

She looked as confused and out of the loop as he was. But she *did* have information. Hoping for something more, he grabbed his satellite phone and dialed Hutch, this time at his home.

He woke him out of a sound sleep. "Jack, you shouldn't be calling me, buddy."

"What happened?"

"You were dead on, all information on Hale and your men is being filtered or halted completely. I found an echo on the files too, just before my boss reamed me a new asshole for looking for it."

Jack scowled. NSA were covering all the bases. "I'm sorry, pal."

"No sweat, but he just about burst a blood vessel, which means some heavy guns are riding his back."

"Who's in the saddle?"

"Can't help you on that, sorry."

"I understand. Thanks."

Jack cut the call, and gripped the phone like a lifeline. His gaze moved to Hale slumped in the chair. What chemical disaster had she been mixing up there? Had to be under the caverns or somewhere near. In plain sight of the public.

That made it the security coup of the decade.

Till now.

He gave the humming cell phone a passing glance, then continued to push the needle into his skin, draw it tight, then repeated the motion, closing up the hole. The bed and towels around him were saturated with his blood. It was less of a wound than a brand, a mark of a mission unfinished. A failure. He got what he came for, he thought with a quick glance at the Styrofoam cooler.

But he left a witness.

Her death meant money, and eliminating Hale was his primary objective. The hunter who interfered . . . he'd kill him just on principle.

* * *

Sydney stirred and lifted her head. Her neck hurt and her shoulders throbbed like crazy. The cabin interior was dark except for a little glow from a battery-powered lamp on a table nearby. Across from her, the Marine was in the bunk, asleep. Now's your chance, the daring side of her said. She wasn't used to it. She wasn't much of a thrill seeker, chemicals aside.

She wiggled her hands, pulling at the ropes. Her hands were small and she folded her palms inward, working at them and watching him. The knots refused to slip, no surprise there, but the nylon rope gave enough for her to turn her wrist and pluck at the ties. It hurt, strained her wrists and shoulders. An hour passed before she got it to move a fraction. What'd he do, put wax on them? She tried not to grunt, keeping her head low and her gaze on the man.

When one line of rope shifted, she used her nails to grab the edges and pull. Her nails threatened to snap off at the quick. Then it gave, and she felt the smooth rope slide over her palm. She had one hand free, the other secured to the chair. She twisted, then flinched as pain shot through her shoulder. She bit her tongue to keep from moaning. *Jeez, my butt is asleep, too,* she thought, and hurriedly undid the other hand. Her gaze flicked to the sleeping Marine, and she sat still, waiting. Watching. *He's playing possum.*

When he didn't move, she rose and went to the small portal. The boat was old, cramped, and weathered. One only a guy could love, and she didn't know the first thing about driving it. She didn't try the stairs, they creaked, and instead she went to the right, peering out at the back trying to see where they were. Nothing except black water and waves. How far were they from shore. *Where* were they? A river? Or did he make it all the way to the ocean without waking her? She pressed her face to the glass, and glimpsed something floating alongside. He was towing another boat. Was he going to get what he wanted, and leave her here?

She glanced at him, then to the well-used cabin. Her gaze

lighted on a group of pictures, but it was the faces that grabbed her. She barely recognized her captor. He was smiling, his cheeks sunburned like the other three men in the photo. His dead friends, she thought. He looked happ; there was a large fish on a table in front of them. There was another picture, the same men, yet surrounded by women and kids. Grandparents too, it looked like. Smoke from a grill curled around his head, almost separating him from the families. She wondered what they were celebrating, then told herself not to care. He'd kidnapped her, threatened—a far cry from the man who'd saved her life.

She turned back and sat, wondering what to do next. This was so far out of her realm of thinking, she tried for logic, looking around for a weapon. She could get the jump on him and force him to take her to shore. *Girl, you've seen way too many movies.* How could she overpower him? He was huge. She was wishing she'd stuck with those karate classes back in high school.

A noise made her freeze and she realized it was her notes crinkling. Carefully, she pulled them out, leaning to the lamp to read them. But she knew what they said. Her memory was photographic, and she'd created Kingsford. She wished she could have done one last test to confirm results. Now she'd never get the chance. NSC would dump the project because of this, citing that the risk was obviously too high.

The Marine shifted and she saw the gun lying at his thigh. Sydney looked down at her notes, then grabbed a lighter and set them on fire. For a second, she watched the flames eat the paper, then instantly recognized her own stupidity. The smoke would wake him. Before it did, she grabbed for the gun.

His fingers snapped around her wrist like an iron band. "Don't."

Her gaze locked with his. "Shit." He looked pissed.

He yanked her wrist, and she lost her balance, landing smack on top of him. "Unless coming into my bunk, you have something else in mind?" He pried the gun from her hand and tossed it aside.

Sydney snorted. "Do all men have a one-track mind, that is, their crotch?" But God, he smelled good, clean, and sorta woodsy. The piles of honed muscle beneath her made her want to just lay her head on his chest and hide from all this. *Okay, that's just twisted.*

"And that's a problem how?" Then he smelled the fire, saw the flames, and pushed her off so fast she stumbled against the bulkhead.

"Jesus, Hale! A fire on the boat! Are you crazy?" He patted out the flames, then realized it was just a couple sheets of paper.

"I was distraught with fear," she said, deadpan.

He met her gaze. She didn't look the least bit afraid now, sitting there with her legs crossed, looking damn confident—and holding his gun.

Hell. She was slicker than he thought. "What was that?" He'd searched her. Where was she hiding it?

"Just paper."

His brows knit for a second. Something vital, too, he thought, glancing back at the ashes.

"What's your name?"

"Joe Shit-the-rag."

She leveled the gun, and her hands trembled with the weight. "I'm not very good with this. I could blow off something . . . crucial."

Jack blew out a quick breath, damned embarrassed to be staring down the business end of his own gun, and he decided the only way he was going to get information from Hale was to gain her confidence. "Jack Wilson. Captain. United States Marines."

"Impressive. I like that I got the jump on America's finest."

"Helps that I haven't slept in two days, you started a fire, and you *were* tied up." How the hell did she get out of the ropes, anyway?

She arched a brow. "Excuses, Captain? Sit." He stood rock still, hands at his sides. He clenched his fist so tightly his knuckles cracked. A chill scratched down her spine. "Please sit, Captain."

He lowered slowly. "What do you think you're going to do with that?" He nodded to the gun.

"Hello? Me with the gun, tables turned. You talk."

"I'd actually take a bullet for some decent information, Hale, so go ahead." He leaned back in the bunk, hands behind his head. "That'll be four Marines shot to hell because of you."

Sydney felt kicked in the teeth. Wounded when she should just be really pissed off. "Go to hell."

"That rapier wit is astounding."

"I'm just warming up," she snapped. "Ever think that it was your shot at the deer that alerted them?"

The hurt in her voice grabbed him, yet the truth of her words hit their mark. "Correct, but you ran."

His look said he didn't appreciate that. "It couldn't be helped."

"I'll have to remember that in a tight situation."

"I'm not a coward."

"Then what are you? Besides lying through those pearly whites." She held his gaze, rebellious as hell, and Jack knew he'd have to work at this. She wasn't scared, wasn't folding. "Those guys weren't government. At least not ours."

"How do you know?" She flinched when he sat up.

"Who's the military expert here, Dr. Hale?"

Her expression soured. "Point conceded."

"Accents were wrong; their weapons fired Teflon bullets. Cop killers. If you're good enough, you don't need them, and if you do, you're making sure no one survives. One went right though Gunny Lyons's head and into the ground."

Sydney's stomach coiled as she remembered Tanner, the hole in his Kevlar vest.

"Classified communications equipment, a redesigned machine pistol with silencer means financing and stolen to do one job. Quietly."

Syd shivered. Rapid fired, a short pop-click. It was a sound she'd never forget. Then she frowned. "Wait . . . accents? You heard them talk?"

"Before I shot one, yes."

"You didn't get that close."

"And you're a judge in firing distance as well as chemistry?"

"Now you're just being snide."

He wasn't amused. "Let me tell you how it is, Dr. Hale. I immobilized a surveillance team outside your place. They weren't military or NSA. My guess is the rest of a well-selected black Ops team, maybe British. Given the situation, I'd say mercenaries."

The images of bloodthirsty "kill everything first" guys with big guns and bandoliers of ammo popped into her mind. "And you came to this conclusion how?

He shrugged. "I've been around."

She wondered what that meant, exactly, but was afraid to ask. Good looks aside, he was a deadly adversary and seemed oblivious that she held a gun on him.

"The men on the mountain and at your house had the same weapons, no IDs, but the real kicker was their fingerprints. They were burned off."

Her grip on the gun faltered. "But then no one can trace them, right?"

Jack snatched it from her so fast she reared back.

"I took out the ammo." She held up the magazine between two fingers, smug.

"Clever girl, but you should have searched the cabin." He reached behind and dug into the cushions, then pulled out a fresh clip. "And that one is empty."

Sydney looked at the magazine, then gave it back.

"You didn't think I'd sleep with a loaded weapon near you, did you?" He popped in the mag, glancing up. The gun was never his concern; her nervous fear was.

Syd flopped back in the chair. "I thought that was a little

weird, but then Commando 101 wasn't offered in college and this whole day is up for grabs in the strange and bizarre." She pushed her hair back off her face. "You were saying?"

"I'm the kidnapper, you're the kidnapee," he said. "You talk." She folded her arms, looking adorably rebellious. She wouldn't win, but she was trying. "I can get nasty, Dr. Hale."

"Hey, I get PMS, you've got nothing in your arsenal that beats that."

Jack fought a smile. What a mouth. "These guys were well prepared, knew exactly how to get in and out. They escaped up the mountain by motorcycle."

"*Up?*" Sydney frowned. "That won't get them anywhere. The terrain is too dense, not to mention pretty darn vertical, and there're only fire roads that high. They don't lead back to the town unless you go on Skyline Drive and that'll take you into North Carolina." Her words trailed off as that registered. "They could be anywhere by now."

He nodded. "True, and unless the government wants an all out manhunt public knowledge . . ."

"They won't."

He uncocked the weapon and tucked it in the back of his jeans. "So, Dr. Hale, are we sharing now?"

Seven

Cisco gave Marcuso the camera, tasking him with removing the chip and uploading the contents. He hoped whatever stopped Mother from working hadn't fired the chip too. He worked with what he had and headed toward the tent erected for the coroner.

Inside, Cisco started down at the dead. "Fingerprints?"

The coroner stood on the other side of the table. "This one, didn't have any. Burned off with a slow-acting acid." The coroner held up the man's hand. "Smooth as a centerfold's ass. I took them anyway and sent them off. Might be a trace of the ridge but we won't be able to get a perfect point match. Sent DNA to CODUS and I've taken dental impressions." He shrugged. "Not that we can connect without a name, and all their teeth are man-made."

Full dental alterations meant these guys were in big business with black bag operations, though he'd never assumed it was a one-time shot. Cisco moved to the clothing and weapons, reexamining them. Russian machine pistols, modified, he decided as he sighted down one. Barrel was longer, less noise. He unscrewed the silencer. Maybe he could trace it to the gunsmith.

"Extracted the bullets yet?"

"Just about to go digging."

Behind him, the sound of a bone saw grinded down on the man's chest. Cisco blocked it out, and examined the thermal suit, checked it for a manufacturer. He already had his computer expert, Marcuso, looking on the net for a seller of thermal liners for cold weather training, hikers, and cross-country skiers. Luge riders in the Olympics would have something like this. He'd bet the killers were sweating their asses off inside the dense liners.

He stood by the first Marine's body, his gaze moving from the boots upward. Nothing unusual, the uniform was faded and frayed, no name tapes or insignia. The boot soles were thin. It was the man's uniform, but unfit for service. Cisco knew a few Marines and they were obsessive about caring for their equipment and clothing.

The coroner stopped sawing. "That guy is a through and through," he said. "The bullet destroyed everything in its path, taking it out on exit, then imbedded in the tree right beside him. What's left is over there."

Cisco went to a small steel table. The Marines' names were on the plastic bags of bullets. One shot each. Cisco heard the squishy sound of the doctor fishing out the bullet and turned as he dropped it into a metal pan.

"This one isn't intact. My guess is that it's a hunting rifle, forty caliber. Probably belonging to one of them." He inclined his head to the dead Marines as he rinsed the bullet and handed it over. "The three bullets that killed the Marines we pulled out of the trees or the ground. And you'll be interested to know that they were all Teflon coated."

Cisco's brows rose a fraction. Now he was getting somewhere.

She felt trapped.
Sydney couldn't look Jack in the eye without seeing his plea for help. Revealing anything would put them in danger. He didn't know what he was asking. If he had even any inkling, he'd leave and never look back.

"Dr. Hale," he said softly, touching something in his pocket. "I have to find out what happened and who put this in motion. People are dead. Can't you see that they need justice?"

"NSA will find it. I can't break my promise. I swore an oath."

"So did I. To protect and defend this country and its citizens, and that includes my men and you."

What a terribly heavy burden, she thought and knew he must be feeling guilty for surviving. She sure was. "You didn't fail them, Jack."

"The hell I didn't!"

He clamped his lips shut and looked at the floor, but Sydney felt the helpless outrage pour off him in waves. Finally, he looked up, his expression showing only a hint of his torment.

"You're all I've got." He thought of Hutch and the Intel lockdown NSA was pulling right now. He'd bet his CO didn't know dick either. When she made a sound of frustration, Jack played his last trump card. "Did you know there was an underground explosion?"

Her eyes flew wide. Cisco never mentioned that. He let her believe he hadn't vented because of the risk of gas, but he *couldn't* vent. That first class liar.

"The damage?"

"I don't know. You were caught on videotape in a store and were accused of the murders of my men."

"Now you're lying."

"I don't lie." His eyes darkened. "A store owner gave a surveillance tape to the local cops, details of you making a phone call. An NSA agent with a ponytail took the tape and split."

Oh, God, he really was telling the truth. "That's Cisco. He was in charge of the security."

"Well, he sucks at it."

"I mentioned that to him."

"Receptive, was he?"

She didn't see his small smile and toyed with the rope on the table. Jack had given her a cup of coffee. It sat untouched next to her. "He practically accused me of being part of the attack."

A stretch of silence then, "Were you?"

"No. It's ridiculous, why would I destroy my own work? But NSA has a different thought process than the rest of the world." She tried thinking like Cisco. She was the only survivor. She was outside during the attack and knew all the codes. Plus her ID tag was missing. That alone would get anyone into the Tatiana's Veil entrance. To Cisco and the people who listened to him, she was more suspect than victim and—suddenly her gaze flashed to Jack's. "That son of a bitch used me as bait!"

"And here I thought that big brain meant you were quick."

She sent him a sour look. "His plan worked." She gestured offhandedly at him.

"I wasn't the only one. Those men outside your house were there to finish the job. You're the last witness."

Her skin tightened with the chilling reality. "They were all wearing masks on the mountain, and there's sensory equipment everywhere. I can't understand how they got in."

She was talking more to herself than him.

"What do I do? I'll be blamed for it. I was outside, taking a very unauthorized break. And I know politics, they'll make me take the heat." Even Dr. Kress and Dr. Nazier, who were both on the R&D committee and had recommended her for the position might back her, but not at the cost of their careers and the money they were paid for their expertise. Nazier and the Under Secretary were frat brothers, for God's sake. She could just kiss off any help from him.

She had to do something to prove her innocence and there just wasn't anything to work with. Dead littered the mountain. The facility was destroyed. Security would be tighter than it was. "Could it get any worse?"

"Probably."

"Wow," she said dryly. "Your positive attitude just blows me away, Jack."

Hearing her say his name changed something and when she met his gaze, he knew she'd crossed over.

"You're going after them, without authorization orders or whatever it is they give you guys before you attack."

"I'll do what's necessary. Without your information, it will be harder, but I will find the bastards."

"We want the same thing."

"Are you asking for a truce, Dr. Hale, or collaborating with the enemy?"

"I don't believe you're my enemy, Jack."

Finally, he thought.

"However, *if* I tell you more, it will just get worse—for us both."

He frowned slightly. "After kidnapping you, I've pretty much shit-canned my career, and you're accused of murder, conspiracy, and treason. What else is there?"

"Well . . . when you put it like *that*. How about having the government and all its resources after us."

He scowled darkly.

"They hid this project in plain sight. Making us both disappear without a trace would be a snap."

He went still. She was dead serious. "Who are *they*?" he said softly, lowering into a chair.

"The National Security Council."

He cursed and rubbed his forehead. He knew it was big, but NSC?

"Cisco will cover this up. Never doubt it. It's his job, almost a spiritual calling. And he's merciless."

Jack considered the consequences, how much, beyond his own life, could be destroyed if he kept heading where he needed. "Why don't you start with what's up there?"

"A billion dollar research and development project six hundred feet below the surface."

He'd figured it was something like that. You don't drop a woman with her kind of smarts out in the middle of nowhere without a damn good reason. "What are you developing?"

"Countermeasures for Sarin gas."

He frowned. "There isn't any, except MOP for hazmat gear and atropine."

"There is now."

Cisco was leaving the coroner's tent when his cell rang.

"We have delayed infrared, and satellite," Wickum said.

"About time."

"Sorry sir, but no one wanted to give them up. And *you* have to sign for them."

Bureaucrats. "Speak to me, Wick."

"It confirms they escaped on the fire roads. Then to Skyline Drive most of the way like a pack. I can't tell one tire tread from another. At a high altitude, it stops. That's when the sightings reported to SETI and locals pick up." Cisco heard the rustle of paper before Wick added, "I have a couple college buddies who belong to a paragliding club in Colorado. I woke them up. We've calculated with wind speed last night and the upward draft from the valley on the virtual computer. There was only one area they could have launched from and gone far enough. Closest to the border, at thirteen or so hundred feet. Right where the bike trail stops."

How they got on the mountain would tell them more. "They drop in from a plane?"

"We've checked the local airports. But our experts say that all it would take is a small Cessna and some guts, but no flights were scheduled over the area. And nothing took off that headed in this direction. The trails are clear and there are no chutes, though the chute pack was empty and with forensics. It has enough leather on it that they might get a print. And it smells."

"Explain."

"An astringent, maybe. Like alcohol, but not as strong."

Cisco stuck his head into the tent and addressed the coroner. "Find anything odd smelling?"

"Other than the decay?"

Cisco narrowed his eyes. "That wouldn't be odd to you, now would it?"

The coroner made a face. "I'll draw samples from skin and hair, the usual."

"Anything else?" he said into the phone.

"Dr. Hale's ID tag is still missing, but we located her jacket button."

Thorough at least, he thought, especially at this time of night. She'd had the tag going into the Cradle, otherwise she couldn't enter the lab, but she was outside for at least thirty minutes, and could have handed it over to one of the attackers. If volunteered, her palm print wasn't hard to duplicate with latex sealers, but her retinal scan was. She'd have had to run like hell to get from the emergency hatch to Tatiana's Veil and back to make this look good. Doable. She was in good physical shape. But it weakened his case against her.

"I've got an APB out on the motorcycles. Maybe someone else picked them up. But considering how fast they were moving, they'd ditch it fast and change methods."

"Agreed. Excellent work, Wick. Surveillance on Hale?"

"Combs checked in an hour ago. Hale was listening to music and he was going in to check on her. At last check in, the replacement team is stuck on the highway eighty-one in gridlock."

"Use the shoulder and bypass it all."

"That's what caused the gridlock in the first place. That, and us closing down the park, the mountain, and anything else for five miles. I could send the chopper."

"Discretion, Wick. Find a better way." Their job was not to bring attention to themselves. Fade in, do the job, fade out. "Tell Combs to check in every fifteen minutes till the relief shows." He cut the call, still gripping the bullets as he walked toward his car.

Twenty feet from the tent, he stopped, stared at the bullet in his hand, then turned back, ducked inside and went to the equipment table. The coroner frowned at him as he lifted out the dead man's liver, then slid it into the scale pan like a wet fish.

Cisco examined the Marine's hunting rifles, taking a bullet from each. All thirty-thirty's. He looked at the squashed bullet extracted from the attacker's body. Forty caliber.

He went still.

Oh, hell.

A fourth man.

He stood in the shadows, watching, waiting for that moment when his presence would be felt, scented. He intentionally wore aftershave just so this would go faster. He'd been hidden in the corner near the window for nearly a half hour.

The ranky bastard didn't even know. Then he did and the pleasure of his quick fear gave him a hard-on. He stepped into the light, just enough to show his outline, and enjoyed the flare of his eyes, the way his gaze shot around the room for escape. But he couldn't and he knew it.

"How the hell did you get in here?" He said it softly, with a glance at the office door.

"The products are in my possession."

"All of it? Everything?"

"You doubted me?"

"No, of course not. Give it to me."

"It's not done. When it is, I decide." He could tell the man wanted to say more, object, but he wouldn't. *He's at my mercy now.*

"Then why are you here?"

"Find out who this is, everything." He moved a single step forward and tossed a piece of paper on the desk.

His employer didn't pick it up. "I can't. It could bring attention to me."

"You can and you will. You have one hour."

"Is she dead?"

"Not yet."

"Then you failed."

"Is that so?" He came into the light, looming over his employer, and gripped his jaw until his mouth opened. He heard the joint pop. The man whimpered. Pussy. He shoved the micro CD between his teeth, then thrust him away.

The employer pulled it out, immediately wiped it off, then put it into the computer. He opened the files. He sat back, smiling to himself, his gaze on the data rolling up the screen. "We want it all. In twenty-four hours as promised, or the price goes—" He stopped, leaping from the chair when he realized he was talking to air. He glanced nervously around the room, to the darkened corner. Empty.

Then he looked down at the photo. "He's mad."

Cisco sat in his car, working his computer. He searched the Department of Natural Resources. The Marines were listed as safety instructors for a hunt club, along with the area assigned to hunt yesterday. Never trust information when it comes secondhand, even from government people. A fresh name came up on the list.

He muttered a curse as he dialed DNR, demanding a list of all hunters in the area at that time. The fax spit out of the small printer beside him and he snatched the pages. With Lyons, Martinez, and Decker was another.

Jack Wilson.

He threw the paper aside and on the laptop anchored to the dash of the car, he searched restricted files for anything on the man. When he had to enter his codes to get them, Cisco knew they were screwed.

A military photo, stats and career history scrolled past. The dossier was impressive. Four combat tours, a half dozen CIA and DIA sanctioned missions, including participating in the capture of Saddam Hussein. Wilson had been in the U.S.

for only five months. He caught the names of the dead Marines in the mission reports.

A highly decorated Marine with a security clearance that meant big trouble.

Cisco hit the print button with more force than necessary, then lit a cigar, and took a long calming drag. Wilson was on the mountain and should be dead, but saving Hale's life caught him a break somehow. Wilson killed the attacker, evaded the rangers, cops, and the roadblocks. *And any notice by us.* Cisco didn't need any more proof that he was dealing with a well trained, resourceful professional, and that meant that Jack Wilson, USMC, knew more than he should.

We'll be floating body bags before this is over.

Cisco stubbed out the cigar and rubbed his face. He wondered how much personal information on Wilson he could get. Address and vehicle were all he could pull up. The man was clean, almost nonexistent. Stonewalled with delays on classified Intel wasn't helping his case. If they wanted him to find the vials, the director had to back off and give him rope. He closed his eyes and was out cold in seconds, only to be rudely awakened by his cell phone.

He tapped the speaker button. "Yes." He checked his watch.

"Combs is dead."

Cisco sat up. "What?"

"We found him in Hale's house. Shot in the chest. He was wearing a vest."

Teflon tipped. Shit. "And Dr. Hale?" But he knew.

"Missing, sir." Wickum gave him his best scenario. "A struggle, little damage, TV volume loud. No struggle with Combs and one shot fired from his gun. Combs came in through the front."

"Tell me you have more."

"Neighbors report a van parked up the street all night with two flat tires and a pizza delivery boy heading to Hale's safe house was detained and sent off by a man flashing a badge. The kid's seventeen and the description is vague. A black Ford truck was seen behind the house this evening. I have a partial plate."

Cisco's scowl tightened as he worked his computer, scrolling for the information. Wilson owned a black truck. Did he kidnap Hale for revenge? As much as he wanted a pat answer, Cisco couldn't wrap his brain around Wilson killing the agent in cold blood, and not with Teflon bullets. But then, three of his friends were dead. He was cruising for justice. "Find the truck. It's got a LoJac."

He gave Wickum the full license number, then ended the call, and started the engine.

"You're kidding."

"I never joke about my work." She popped out of the chair, nearly tripping over the ropes. She gave him a funny little smirk as she tossed it in his lap, then moved around the cabin, searching in the cupboards.

"What are you looking for?"

"Food. *You* left the pizza behind. I'm starving."

Jack went to her, opened the compact fridge, and waved. She pulled out the makings for a sandwich.

"Please continue, doctor, you have my undivided attention."

She met his gaze. He was leaning against the door frame to what had to be a bedroom, looking so freaking handsome, and the intense way he looked at her just made her melt. As if she were the only person on the planet. But then, since he needed her information, for him, she was. "It's called the Cradle. It's an acronym for Chemical Research And Development Laboratory Environment." She opened the bread bag and started making sandwiches. "It has several levels and it's been in operation for three years. The entrance is through Tatiana's Veil. Between the tourist hours. Once inside, you're there for the shift."

"Lock down?"

She nodded. "No one leaves while the tourists are near."
When he reached to help, she said, "I can do it, please; it
relaxes me and short of a deep tissue massage, I need it." She
smeared mayo and Jack found plates. "The Cradle has everything you need—temporary sleeping quarters, showers, a cafe-
teria. The other floors are the labs. One is solely a cold room
storage for the gas vials. Four . . . well three now. I used
one." She handed him the plate full of sandwiches, then
snatched a half for herself. "But the binary agents are kept
separate by glass, and it's in a metal casing." She ate, chewing fast and waving, using her free hand to sip coffee.

For reasons Jack couldn't name, her animated gestures
made him smile.

"We used the components to test; they're volatile enough
for the process and only the roaches or mice in a vacuum
sealed room were used for a final testing."

"Jesus, what did you create?"

She stilled, met his gaze, and swallowed her food. "An implosion bomb, resistant to IMPF, isoproposaymethylphos-
phoryl fluoride."

His head was starting to swim. "Sarin is odorless, taste-
less, and colorless. How is that possible?"

"It's a Freon-packed bomb about the size of a softball. It
has a light metal alloy casing and can be safely detonated
without volatile blasting material." Syd popped in the last bit
of crust and dusted her fingertips. "The project was to find a
way to make it visible to neutralize it. The bomb ignites and
pressurized Freon is released. It coats the gas and to our surprise, gives it substantial weight. With the Freon, it suspends
it. The ignition of the charcoal mix to neutralize it is instant,
one-sixteenth of a second."

Jack let it sink in. "They attacked for the bomb or the
gas."

She got busy cleaning up, not looking at him. "Mother
should have alerted us and locked the place down. You going
to eat that?" She pointed to the sandwich half.

He shook his head. For a little thing, she sure had an appetite.

She grabbed the food and told him about Mother. "It's the Mommy Dearest of systems. It controlled all the sensors, air content and recirculation, electricity, computers, everything."

"Yet it didn't alert you to intruders."

She still didn't get how they did that. "Not until it was too late, but I was above-ground." She told him about returning to find the Cradle filled with smoke, and she was in tears as she relayed the young corporal dying in her arms. "Oh, hell. I'm usually not this emotional." She swiped her eyes and sniffled. "No, that's a lie, I am. But I've never seen anyone die before."

Jack moved in closer. "Take it easy, Syd."

She lifted her gaze, her lip trembling, a half a sandwich still in her hand. "I want someone to hurt for it, Jack. *Really* hurt."

His heart twisted in his chest. She looked so frail. Not the woman who'd demanded the gun on the mountain. Then he reached for her and she was against him in a heartbeat, groaning when his arms closed around her.

Syd let herself be held, her head on his chest. "This shouldn't feel this good."

"Feels great to me."

She laughed shortly. Typical man. "I meant that you were a tyrant an hour ago." His hand swept up her back, plowed into her hair, and pressed her closer, making her feel wrapped and protected.

"That was interrogation."

"Oh." Amazing how life changed with a little trust. But she wasn't giving him all of it, or anything else.

"I would never hurt you, Sydney." His men were dead because of that implosion bomb, but he didn't point that out.

"After you saved my life, it'd be sorta wasteful, don't you think?" She munched on the sandwich she still held.

Jack looked down and smiled to himself.

Sydney tipped her head back. Her expression went serious. "I'm trusting you, Jack. For now."

His smile fell.

"Betray me and I'll learn how to use a gun."

Jack felt oddly gifted by that. If she thought she was coming along, she was wrong. He'd intended to get what he could from her, then plant her right where he'd found her. She didn't need to be involved any further. And he planned to piss off a lot of people before he was done. "I stand informed and advised, ma'am."

She nodded, and opened her mouth to take a bite of her sandwich when the sound of breaking glass forced them apart. Her gaze went past him to the spot behind the tiny sink. "Isn't that a bul—?"

He was already yanking her to the deck as bullets raked the hull.

Eight

The portal behind them exploded, spraying glass.

"Jack!"

The panic in her voice, in the one word, made him look at her. "We'll get out of this, Syd, I swear."

She nodded, then absently glanced at her sandwich covered in glass, and tossed it aside. "You're the expert. Tell me what to do."

"Stay low." He pulled his gun from his jeans. "Grab that bag." She slung the heavy duffle onto her shoulder. "We're going topside." He checked his weapon.

"Oh, jeez. At least down here something's stopping the bullets."

"He's aiming for the gas tanks. Follow right behind me." He met her gaze. "And I mean *right* behind."

Use him for cover, he was saying and Sydney nodded, then flinched when the spray came again. Hard thunks in the hull. Jack was over her, shielding her, as he moved fast to the vertical steps. Sydney stuck to him like glue as they climbed.

Topside, the sky was pitch black, the air icy cold and stinging.

Crouched, she dropped the heavy duffle on the deck. Jack pulled night vision goggles from the bag and scanned the water. "I can hear the bastard." Engine on, but idling, the sound distorted over the water.

"See anything?"

"No foam, no lights, nothing."

"Who do you think it is?"

"We aren't sticking around to find out." He turned over the engine, checked the gages.

"Shouldn't we radio someone?"

"Not a chance. If it's NSA, they *shouldn't* be shooting at us. They already have you on the suspect list, and if they found the boat, they sure as hell just found out about me. I kidnapped you. How's that going to look for both of us?"

"Okay okay, I get it." Conspiracy, obstruction of justice. God, the poop just keeps getting deeper. Then she heard that odd noise, gusts of wind before the thumps. She ducked low. Wood chipped in the small cabin cruiser's bulkhead. *Same sound as on the mountain.*

On his knees in the wheelhouse, Jack shoved the throttle forward. The speedboat, stationary as it hosed them with ammo, now gave chase, weaving closer to their side.

Jack would barely see to steer so Sydney took the NVGs.

Bracing her knees on the slippery deck, she sighted over the edge. "I can't tell what's what out there, wait . . ." The green glowing NVGs came into focus as the low-slung speedboat churned up white foam and headed toward them. "Oh, God, he's wearing a mask! And he's aiming!"

The shots came again, rapid and quiet. Some plunking into the water. She fell to the deck, gripping the goggles. "It's him, it's him. The guy who shot Chris!"

"You can't be sure."

"Dammit, Jack, it's him!" Although she couldn't see his face, she *knew.*

Jack grabbed a gigging pole and broke it across his knee, then jammed it under the wheel. It was slipping and he'd meant to fix that. "Come on."

"Where? We're going too fast." Then her eyes went wide. "Not that rubber thing, are you crazy? He's in a racing boat! He'll run right over us."

"Then we better get moving." Jack would rather turn and

fight, but with Sydney along, he couldn't. She was here because of him, and he was responsible for her safety. He pulled her with him toward the back of the boat, dragging the duffle, then hurled it in the rubber outboard boat. "Can you swim?"

"Yes, of course, but that water is freezing."

"You're not going in the water." Hunched to not expose himself, he scooped her up and tossed her. Sydney screamed, the sound cut short when she landed in the bottom of the rubber boat.

Jack jumped, his legs going in and he grabbed the towline. The cruiser pulled them at top speed, bouncing the *rubber inflatable boat* on the water like a skipping stone. He severed the line, the RIB slowing away from the cruiser as he rolled into the craft. Crawling to the rear, he pulled her low. "Are you okay?" Hurriedly, he turned over the hundred fifteen horsepower engine.

"Fine, fine." She watched the other boat. "He's not stopping. He's gonna ram us!"

"Here." He pushed his gun into her hands. "Shoot back."

"This might not be a wise thing," she muttered as she clasped it with both hands, and fired. The kickback threw her into the bottom of the boat against a seat. "I told you!"

"Hold on to something, this will be fast." He pushed the gas to the max and the rubber boat leaped a little, then sped across the water. The bounce was bone jarring, yet it wasn't enough. The slick turbine racer turned to cross their path.

"Jack!"

"I see him, I see him." She latched onto the ropes running around the edge of the RIB as he yanked the rudder. The craft turned so sharply, Sydney fell in the bottom again. Shots whizzed overhead.

"Fire back, woman!"

Pissed off, Sydney scrambled to her knees, and cracked off three shots. The report vibrated up her arms and rattled her teeth. "I don't think I hit anything."

"Trade with me. Stay low and hold that down, head east."
He put her hands on the controls.

"East? It's just plain black out here, how can you tell?"

Jack pointed as he crouched in the boat, firing, then re-
loading. His bullets hit the speedboat's hull, but missed the
gas tanks. Then he stilled as the turbine boat rode the curve
of foam close to the abandoned cruiser and sped away.

In between, something went airborne. "Get down!"

Seconds later, the boat he'd shared with Lyons, Martinez,
and Decker exploded, orange-red fire reaching into the night.

"Oh, Jack."

"Crap, I liked that boat."

The speedboat barreled toward them again, and Jack
knew they wouldn't make it. The other was ten times faster,
more agile on the water than the hundred fifteen horsepower
dive boat, and the bastard had a machine gun. He gripped
the pistol, nearly out of ammo, and thought of two things;
safety and evasion, in that order. Moving across to her, he
grabbed the wheel and turned the rubber boat directly into
the other's path.

"You're insane!"

"The wake will destroy his aim."

"I'd rather destroy him!"

Then he heard it. The familiar sound of a chopper, the
roar of boat engines. His head whipped around. "We have
company."

"What?" She rose up to look. "That's a big one, looks like
police." Thank God.

The airboat shot over the water, gaining speed and barely
kicking up a wake. A voice on a bullhorn ordered them all to
stop. The man in the turbine cut between Jack and the police
and fired. Jack instantly changed tactics, and turned to the
left, toward shore. Out of the corner of his vision, he saw a
bullet strike the rubber hide. *We'll be sinking in seconds.* He
gunned it.

The second boat, loaded with men in black, swept near,

and fired a high-powered spray of ammo. Above them, a chopper swooped over the water to hover and shine a light down. Jack quickly maneuvered the RIB away from the lights.

Sydney sighted in on the airboat. "Oh, God, Jack. It's Cisco."

For a moment, a breath, her world went still. She met his gaze.

"You want to go to him?"

A dozen reasons to go flooded her mind at once. But only one contradicted, Cisco would charge her and lock her up. "No, I'm sticking with my best weapon." And her only ally.

"Ooh-rahh. Let NSA deal with the masked man. We're outta here."

She didn't even know where *here* was, for pity sake. Jack steered the boat toward a shoreline she couldn't see, pushing the engine hard. She hoped he had a lot of gas. This is all my fault, she thought, sinking into the bottom, soaked to her skin. She rolled the warm gun in her hands.

And I've just turned us into Bonnie and Clyde.

In the black speedboat, he taped the throttle down, then moved swiftly to the rear, set the timer on the detonator and left it on the seat. He sat, pulled on the air tank, then quickly secured the straps and extra weight belt. The speed of the engines shook the boat and he knew it would overturn soon. It was a matter of hitting the right wave at the right height. And they were coming fast. Clever man, he thought.

He pulled on fins and adjusted the dive mask. Popping in the regulator, he gave the scene one last look. An airboat raced across the water as if floating above the surface, heading right toward him. The other with Hale aboard was only a couple hundred yards to the right. He glanced at the timer, the numbers glowing red in the dark, and he waited; ten, nine, eight, seven, six . . . he leaned back, falling into the river. The boat kept going.

Black water closed around him, the turbine's backwash

spinning him like a blender. He didn't fight it, and let the weights equalize him, then drag him deeper. As he descended, he tipped his head back to watch the bright flash of orange and white as the bomb ripped apart the Eagle boat. The percussion vibrated down to him twenty-five feet below the surface, yet the flames were only blurred fractures of light.

He dropped the extra weight belt and looked at his compass, checked his air supply, then finned toward shore.

Cisco said nothing, his expression flat as the explosions lit up the sky. "Get me in the middle of that." Then into the hand radio, he said to the chopper pilot, "Maintain position over the explosion area, then toward shore." He changed the frequency and barked at Wickum, "I want to know everything about that turbine and I want it ten minutes ago!"

But how did that attacker find Hale and Wilson before he did?

That Jihad on the water didn't fool him. The bastard in the turbine was still alive, and closer to Hale and Wilson. He couldn't see shit from here.

He signaled the chopper to meet him on shore. "Put us on land, now."

Jack glanced back as the turbine exploded, then faced the shore, wishing for more horsepower.

Sydney smiled. "Yea! The good guys win."

"It's a ruse. But keep up that positive attitude, Syd, we're sinking." He drove the boat right on shore. "Get out, hurry."

Sydney grabbed the bag, galvanized by his tone.

Out of the boat, he pushed it into the water, his gaze flashing to the chopper and the airboat near the last explosion. Thigh deep, he withdrew his K-bar knife and stabbed the thick rubber hide, pushing the deflating crafter farther out. The weight of the engine would take it down. Jack waited until it was nearly under, thinking he was still paying for the damn thing, then hurriedly sloshed onto shore.

He grabbed her as he took off. "Keep moving, this isn't over."

The airboat was moving closer, the noise like fangs snapping at their heels. They ducked under branches, feet sinking into the wet earth.

"He's right behind us."

"Don't talk. Keep running."

Sydney obeyed, struggling to keep up with his ground-eating strides. The chopper swept near the shoreline less than fifty yards down river, the spotlight glazing over the darkness and moving toward their position.

Jack grabbed her and went to the ground. His dark clothing shielded them, and over her body he sighted through the NVGs. The airboat landed, men climbing out like ants over a cake. Ponytail was in the lead, heavily armed and flashing a light over the ground. Four men spread out in a search grid, the chopper spotlight above giving them a daylight view. He heard the static voices on the radios, yet couldn't decipher any of it.

Sydney shifted and Jack put his lips near her ear and whispered, "Don't move."

Footsteps cracked twigs, scuffed leaves. Night dew left everything wet and musty. Dampness soaked his jeans. Sydney must be marinated in it. Slowly, he brought the NVGs to his eyes again. They were down shore about thirty yards. That meant they didn't see where he and Syd had come on shore. To his right, Jack heard something. A swishing. Then he recognized it. The shunt of compressed air.

Cisco approached to his left, but his attention was to his right. Less than twenty yards. The mercenary. He was a shapeless form, a big black creature against a pithy night. Jack wanted to kill him with his bare hands, watch his life flick out, but he had to keep Sydney safe. Then the guy was moving, the glint off glass let Jack pinpoint his location. He looked at the agents headed in his direction, away from the shore. They'd find them in a minute, and they couldn't run.

Jack moved off Sydney, covering her mouth and pointing.

She could barely see him in the dark, yet his breathing was slow and calm, a comfort when her heart was racing. He pointed left and right, then handed her the NVGs. Sydney saw both, Cisco and his agents, and the black figure farther upshore. She looked at Jack and he made a motion, two fingers crawling and she nodded.

They moved slowly over the ground, covering no more than a few feet or so without noise. Jack paused to sight, then took a chance, rose up, and threw a rock toward the diver. Before it hit, he was flat on the ground again, Sydney beneath him.

The stone dropped hard enough to let them know it wasn't a snapping twig or a falling branch. NSA hurried toward it, the chopper moving over the location. Jack pulled Syd off the ground and they ran in the opposite direction.

He heard wet, hard footsteps. The mercenary. He'd come to finish what he'd started.

He's got to get past me first.

Cisco could feel the man's presence, moving as they did, pausing when he did, yet he saw nothing. For all he knew, he was walking right past the son of a bitch.

"Light a candle," he said softly, and an agent shot a night illumination rocket into the sky. It burst, showering the area in a white glow that grew brighter by the second.

Movement grabbed his attention. Cisco saw a single figure and fired, then ran close. The muffled grunt said he met his mark. The sun was coming up, the illumination candle clearing the darkness, yet when he reached the spot, there were only footprints. He grabbed the small tank and dive mask. Clever bastard. A few feet farther up shore, he found more prints.

Cisco spoke into the radio. "Block the roads in a five mile perimeter. Wake people up, I want teams at any access into the towns, schools, churches. I want this fucker. Bag the gear."

Cisco kept moving, following the tracks. Agents split and fanned out.

"Hale and Wilson?" An agent rushed up to him.

Cisco eyed the shoreline. The forest was dense and wet. Excellent cover, and Wilson was skilled at evasion. But that Hale was running with the Marine told Cisco she'd betrayed her oath.

"They're secondary. Retrieving the vials and prototypes are number one," he reminded the agent. He tossed the dive mask at him. "And this bastard has them."

Raymond Bertrand gazed out the window of his plush office. While the east view was of the acreage surrounding the Chem–Loc laboratory and plant, the west window offered a bug's eye glance into the lab. Surrounded by concrete and steel, it was a sea of clear glass, the partitions pressured and chemical-proof against the most fatal elements. At four in the morning, there was only one man in the lab. Montoya was the smartest chemist in his employ. If anyone could make the formula work, he could.

He flinched when the phone buzzed, and moved to it, glancing at the number before answering.

"We're running out of time."

"I'm aware of that. You called just to say so?"

"No, to keep you on your toes."

"Fuck you."

"Nice mouth for a CEO. Is it working?"

"He's had it for less than ten hours, what do you think?"

Through the optic wires, he heard a tired sigh. It made him smile. Pompous ass.

"You're a scientist, you should know the routine."

"I do. And the stakes."

"Remember that."

And that if I go, you go too, he wanted to say. But Raymond knew if this came to light, he'd be the one to go down in flames. But it didn't pay to anger his partners. Not when they'd risked everything for this. He hung up without comment, pressed the stop tape, then went to the glass window. His attention followed Montoya as he preformed the experiment.

Montoya would run it through a computer synthesis first, making sure that Hale's notes were correct, then do a physical experiment.

The camera inside the lab panned movement and Montoya looked up as if to say something, yet didn't, turning back to the lab environment. The scientist couldn't call in the hazardous material teams and had to do the cleanup himself, a high risk in itself. When they had the proven data, any experimentation would be illegal, to be conducted by none except the U.S. Army Chemical and Biological Defense labs.

It was, he thought, an act of treason.

Sydney clung to Jack's side, exhausted; the sun was nearly up and they'd been moving for hours. Probably not, but her legs were screaming as if she had. "Jack. Please."

He slowed, wrapped his arm around her waist and pulled her along. "We can't stop, Syd, Cisco might be right behind us, and I know that killer is."

That pushed her on.

"Cisco will have roadblocks and search teams moving into position."

"How did he find us?" she said softly.

"I have no idea. I was good about covering my trail." He focused on the ground, each lump in the earth, any paleness in the dark earthen floor. Jack could put on a Gilly suit or his uniform and blend in. It was his job, his training. But this merc or whatever he was, had the same education.

"So what's the plan, pathfinder?"

He smiled to himself. "We're actually safer in a town, in a crowd, then maybe we'll catch a break."

She stopped. "You have no idea, do you?"

"Not a clue. I'm improvising."

She trudged on. "God, I hate honesty in a man some-times."

Cisco was like a dog sniffing a trail, his steps long and biting as he combed the woods, tracking the diver and looking for signs of others, his partners. The rising sun bled through the trees as he followed the shore. His boots sank deep in the mud behind the prints of the dive boots. And without pause, he kept going, sloshing up the shore, and sighting through binoculars. He's walked the shore-line, covering his own tracks back into the water, Cisco thought.

He radioed the chopper pilot.

"We got nothing, sir, lots of debris, and a man in a small John boat."

Cisco scanned the surface and saw it. A partner. "Get on him and take him out."

"Sir?"

"Take him down!"

Cisco ordered the air rescue boat to his position as the chopper sped toward the John boat, guns locked and loaded.

Jack grasped her hand, helping her over fallen logs. Her fingers were small and cold in his, their clothing wet and making each step a labor. The trees still had their leaves, green and yellow gold, yet it wasn't enough to keep them completely hidden. His mind worked over where the attacker could have gone. He'd escaped with a plan, Jack didn't doubt it or they would have heard something more. Or taken a cou-ple bullets.

Jack stopped, twisting, scanning the terrain. He pulled out a GPS and locked it in. The map came up in seconds with their location. "We're farther north than I thought. That way." He gave her the duffle. "You go straight till the ridge, then right."

She hoisted the heavy bag. "Alone? Where are you going?"

"To cover our tracks. Go, Syd. Trust me, I'll find you."

Before she could say more, he turned back the way they'd come. Fear kept her riveted where she was. Jack, what she could see of him, looked like a kid playing "don't step on the crack" as he stepped on logs. Then she couldn't see him anymore.

With only his knife, Jack stirred their tracks, then shifted dirt and moss over the depressions. He swung from branches, used the thick beds of leaves to cover his footprints. He could see the movement of the agents near the shore, the sound of the chopper muffling his own, but the night illumination candles threatened his position. With a dead branch, he swept the forest floor, then marked their tracks in a different direction.

Sydney made it to the ridge and climbed, obeying Jack to the letter. The last time she went walking in the forest people died and the eerie quiet danced along her spine. Minutes passed with no sign of Jack, nor animals or the wind in the trees. Her vulnerability tasted foul, the insular world she'd once had dissipating rapidly.

Images flashed in her mind, overtaking her with their vibrancy; Chris Tanner dying in her arms, the man in the mask stepping over the bodies of her friends and aiming at her. She tried shaking them loose, but what she didn't know then, now made her nerves twist and pull. With every step, her gaze shot around the woods, the uneven ground reminding her she was alone. *He's out there.*

Suddenly a hand closed over her mouth. She went rigid, a scream rising from her throat.

"It's me, it's me. Relax, Syd. Relax."

She hadn't even heard him coming!

Jack eased his hand from her mouth, and she turned sharply, her stare so wide and stricken he frowned. "Syd."

"I thought—I was afraid you'd—"

"You thought I left you out here?" Jack couldn't be more stunned. She nodded. "Damn, Syd." Jack embraced her and she clung to him and buried her face in his chest.

"I'm a wuss. I know."

He passed his hand over her hair, pressed his lips to her forehead, then made her look at him. Christ, she was shaking. But he couldn't force her trust; she had to come to that on her own. "Want my oath in blood?"

"God no, ick. Germs multiply at a rate of—" She smiled and shut up.

"We have to keep going."

She glanced at the forest, the flash of lights in the sky. He took the duffle, and urged her ahead of him, doing what he could to destroy their trail.

After a while she said, "I hear cars." The thought of civilization buoyed her.

"Should be a four-lane road ahead."

"Finally, people without guns."

He moved ahead, shielding her. "Don't count on it."

Nine

Bullets from the chopper plunked in the water with the frenzy of angry fish, yet missing the man. When the airboat skidded over the water, bumping the fishing boat, the man's terrified stare told Cisco he was wrong.

He sighed and growled into the radio to the pilot. "Good call, Magus." Christ, he was losing it.

He stood in the airboat, feet braced and watched his agents swarm over the man, search, and yank his hair to be certain it wasn't a disguise. They questioned him. Yes, he'd seen the explosions. No, he didn't see anyone else. Too much fog.

Releasing the old man, Cisco ordered the boat to shore and the chopper to continue circling the area for debris or proof of life. His phone had been going off in five-minute intervals since they had discovered Combs's body. It was a half hour to reach the shore, and when he stepped onto the dock, he looked at the list.

Wickum and the Director. They were dead even with calls. He called Wick first. "Just how screwed are we?"

"Big time."

A half hour passed before they could see the road and vehicles. Another twenty before Jack was certain NSA hadn't posted men this far. He wasn't positive, but they didn't have a choice. Leaving the woods, they stepped into a parking lot near a Wal-Mart. The lot was empty, the streets barren except for the occasional car speeding past. It was barely sunup, the stores locked tight.

Jack spied a run-down gas station across the street. "Excellent." It was dirty, the drive unpaved, and littered with barrels, but his attention was on the row of junk cars sandwiched along the left side and back of the building. They crossed, and he pulled her beyond the wall, then checked behind them.

"Tell me we're not stealing a car."

"No, we're stealing a piece of junk." He walked behind them, eyeballing each.

"And you thought we needed yet another government agency tailing us?"

"My truck is back at the marina, probably impounded by now." Tracked by the damn LoJac, he thought, squatting. It was the only way Cisco could have found him so fast. "We need wheels."

"Then what does checking the ground have to do with anything?"

"Looking to see which one was driven recently. It's a good chance it operates."

She blinked. "Oh." Then she frowned. "You've done this before."

He admitted nothing and said, "Watch the road. Especially for a black SUV."

For Cisco, she thought, and moved to the edge of the building, peeking out. Her heart still pounded so hard it ached; the memory of bullets and the guy in the turbine made her recognize her mortality. Her lifespan was looking pretty short right now.

What would killing her accomplish? She hadn't seen any faces, so there was nothing to identify. And if someone wanted her to take the blame, then dead, she was useless. They had the implosion bomb and the gas. Well, that wasn't for sure; Cisco hadn't had proof as of last night, since they couldn't get inside the Cradle.

She heard Jack grunt and glanced over. He'd wedged himself into a car, getting under the steering column. So much for her degrees coming in handy in a tight situation she thought and turned her attention back to the road. Her body clenched as a police car zipped past, and she leaned out to watch until it disappeared. The engine had started, and she spun around.

Jack was pulling it out of the line of wrecks. "It's even got some gas. Get in."

She ran to the passenger side, but the door wouldn't open. Jack leaned and rolled down the window. Sydney slid in, plopping on the seat and sending up a cloud of dust.

He put it in gear, easing it out of the lot. He didn't drive out the side where they'd come in, but pulled around back, turned left onto a residential street, then after a block, pulled onto the highway.

The car kicked up a trail of smoke. "It won't last long."

"I've never stolen a car before. I've never stolen anything," Sydney said.

"You're a badass now, Hale. Your clean record's gone straight to hell." Though he teased, Syd noticed his gaze move from the rearview, side view, then to the road ahead in a dance that was anything but calm.

She made a face, plucking at the leaves from her hair. "How can you be so laid-back after what we just went through?"

He gave her a deadpan look. "Because whining doesn't help?" Yet he reached over and grasped her hand.

She flushed. "Point taken. We've broken about five federal laws already, I guess one more won't matter."

"That's the spirit. Because if we get caught, we're going to jail."

"Then don't get caught, because I'll look fat in prison jumpsuits."

Bertrand snapped awake, and looked frantically around. For a moment, he thought the guy was back—to kill him. The man was plain scary, yet the office was empty, daylight streaking through the bank of windows. He pushed out of the chair as the intercom buzzed. He rubbed his face, moving to the window and stared down at the glass ceiling to the lab. Montoya was below, looking into the camera lens.

He tapped the intercom. "I'm ready to start."

In a full hazardous material jumpsuit to protect him as well as the clean room, Montoya moved to the vacuum-sealed cubicle. He placed the small sealed glass container on a pedestal, stepped out, then pushed the automated controls. He let in the rats, then a robotic arm extended from the housing to the left, grasped the container and punctured it. Exposure took seconds, death was ugly and swift. After venting the room and hosing it with water, Montoya entered and injected the dying creatures.

He waited, and Bertrand tapped the keys on his computer and brought up the camera, focusing on the animals. Some rats continued to writhe; five out of ten were dead already. For another ten minutes, they watched, waited for life to return. Then Montoya looked up at the camera, and shook his head.

Bertrand hit the speaker button. "You're misreading something. Start over."

"I'm telling you, it's worthless. It's incomplete."

"She made it work. Are you saying you can't?"

"No. Something is missing and I'll find it."

Bertrand knew Montoya wouldn't give up because that meant he'd have to admit Dr. Hale was smarter. He turned from the window and picked up the pre-paid cell phone. He hit speed dial. "The data is incomplete."

"Not my problem."

"You won't get paid for retrieving half a product. Hale is the only source. I need her brain."

He snickered. "You want that still attached to her body?"

She was in the news.

Sydney stopped short in the electronics department of the super store and just stared.

Jack took several steps before he noticed she wasn't beside him. "Syd?"

She turned her head slowly and something clutched in his chest when he saw her glassy eyes. He looked. "Shit."

The convenience store video tape replayed on the news broadcast, the anchors picking apart the scene. The film was a bird's-eye view of the store. Sydney walked in, the blood on her hands and shirt clearly defined in Technicolor. She went to the bathroom and her nervous demeanor was dissected in the broadcast. It showed her on the phone.

The anchor reported over the film. "A body was discovered near Skyline Drive. The suspect is a woman, early thirties, yet names and details are being withheld pending an investigation. Shenandoah police are searching for the suspect for questioning."

Christ, there was a hot line number under it.

The anchor went on to report a missing person.

"One body, not your friends. But you said Cisco took the tape?"

"He did. We have to get out of here."

Jack pulled her away from the TV, his arms full of clothing. He took the shopping basket Sydney held and moved to the checkout. The cashier gave their muddy clothes a passing glance as she chewed gum and rang them up. Jack glanced around, shelling out the cash and wishing he could use a credit card. But it could be traced. With his purchases paid and bagged, he gripped the sacks and her hand and left.

Sydney stumbled numbly alongside him, and he paused and hissed, "Snap out of it."

She looked around them, then whispered, "They've accused me of murder!"

"No, sought for questioning. They have no proof, Syd, Cisco saw to that."

She was suddenly aware of his anxiousness as Jack tossed the bags into the car and started it. They drove out of the lot, and were back on the highway within minutes.

"My mother is going to see that. My reputation, my work . . ."

"—has nothing to do with this."

She turned on the radio and heard the same report again. "It's not you in the news hunted by police."

"Shenandoah police should be looking for me, not you. I left their custody." It didn't make sense. "Cisco might have let it leak, thinking it will force you to come in because you'd want to vindicate yourself."

"I do. It's a lie."

"I've got no problem with you bailing."

She frowned. "Excuse me?"

"I'm going after the son of bitch who shot my friends . . . with or without you."

He was speeding, gripping the steering wheel. "Jack. What's wrong? You're scaring me."

He did a double take on her, then sighed and slowed the car. When he spoke, his tone was calmer, but still had an edge. "This news shit will just get in my way. More eyes on the lookout, and the guy in the mask will see that broadcast. He could get information, but that's not our problem."

"How can you say that? He tried to kill us!"

"Yeah, *us*. And if anyone's guilty, it's me. I killed his partner." He paused for a second, then said, "I can get you to protective custody, if you want. The choice is yours."

"I already made that decision in the boat."

"I won't hold you to it."

"Go to hell."

"Gee, honey, is this our first fight?"

She gave him a snide look.

Jack drove past a motel, doubled back, then pulled into the rear lot. It was a one-story, a line of rooms facing the lot, run-down and a little dirty. Perfect.

Syd took one look at it and muttered, "Gross."

"Fugitives can't be choosy." The seediness of the place was obvious with the desk clerk behind glass, grabbing the cash and shoving the keys at him. He returned to the car, opening her side. When she didn't get out, he frowned.

The radio was broadcasting the same report over the airwaves. Roads were blocked and now she'd be blamed for the lack of tourist trade. She grabbed the keys, climbed out, and slapped them into his hand.

She met his gaze, a stretch of tense silence before she said, "Jack, those families, they'll think I did that."

"Nothing we can do about it." He moved around her, gathering his gear and the shopping bags. "Their phones are likely tapped." He pulled her toward the room door. "NSA's already aware of my relationship with my men. Or they wouldn't have found the boat so fast; we all owned it. They're watching your colleagues' families, too." He shoved in the key and popped the lock. "We can't risk it."

"Maybe we should arrange a meeting, in secret with NSA, or the local police? FBI?"

"Jesus, haven't you been listening?" He practically pushed her in.

She turned on him. "But it will bring it out in the open, intra-agency, at least!"

"No." He slammed the door. "NSA can supercede the FBI, and no, Syd, the American public *cannot* know that you were mixing Sarin gas under the Luray Caverns." He flipped on the lights, tore off his jacket. "Jesus, the danger of that alone will have the environmentalists on a warpath. Fucking stupid place to put a lab, around tourists? What were you people thinking?"

"I didn't make that choice!" She ripped off her jacket and threw it at a chair.

"Well, you're going to pay for it. It was your project, you were in charge, and you had the access. Everyone is dead except you. They will accuse you of selling it to the highest bidder."

"Why, thank you for blaming me for everything, Jack." Her voice broke.

He stilled, his features pulling tight. "Shit. I didn't mean—"

"It doesn't matter." Her muddy sweatshirt joined the jacket. "You might not give a damn about anything but your revenge, but I do. I worked damn hard to get where I am. They're shredding *me*. I created that implosion bomb to save people in combat." She poked at his chest. "Men like *you*. Now it's on the loose, they have the disease *and* the cure. So don't go all 'I'm going this alone to avenge my troops' crap. I already know you better!"

"Is that a fact?" Jack watched her pace around the small room, listened to her browbeat herself. "You need to calm down."

"You need to stop patronizing me! My career is over! Who will believe I'm innocent even if I'm cleared of this? It'll linger and I'll never get another job or get to finish the project." She turned on the TV. "Look at that. They're making stuff up. This will never end, and I'm so over being a patsy for NSA crap!"

He shut off the TV and when she started to push past to turn it back on, he grabbed her shoulders. She shoved back, the same rant spilling until she didn't know which end was up.

Then Jack showed her, laying his mouth over hers in a deep hot kiss.

She opened for him, unleashing a flood of emotion and want, as she drove her hands into his hair and gripped his skull. Angry, passionate—needy. She massacred him, twisted his insides as her mouth twisted over his.

There was no talking, no softness or tenderness. Her energy pored through her—so thick he could taste it on his mouth. She pulled his hand to her breast, under her clothing and he cupped her, pushed under her bra and enfolded skin. It made her moan and she reached for his fast growing erection, massaging him through his jeans.

"Touch me, please."

His hand slid down her stomach, making muscles jump and when he opened her jeans, she whimpered, hurriedly pushed them down. Then he was there, long fingers diving into her, slicking her deeply, and Sydney did the only thing she could—she took it. Eager and pulsing for that end, that sharp edge she hadn't had with a man in a long time.

Jack stroked her, plunged in another finger. She didn't say a word, her kiss eating his mouth, and he could feel her body clench wetly. He pushed his knee between hers, spreading her, and he quickened with her, a wild thrust of hips and tiny sounds that seeped beneath his skin. She came hard, on him, shrieking against his mouth, and digging her fingers into his shoulders. She rode his fist and he kept playing, dragging it out until she collapsed against him, her forehead on his chest. After a moment, she tipped her head back, breathing hard as she met his gaze.

"That take care of everything for you?"

Any cover we had is blown to hell.

From inside his car, Cisco watched the news report relay. He had Wickum on the phone at the same time. "Who the hell got ahold of that tape?"

"Isn't the copy still in your vehicle?"

Cisco leaned over the backseat and searched, came back with it. He threw it on the floor. Obviously, there was a duplicate.

"The Shenandoah Police found a man stripped of all clothing and hanging from a tree, a single shot to the head. I can't tell if it's one of the attackers. Could be isolated."

"Not hardly. I want that body. Someone used that tape for tabloid attention, or to force Hale and Wilson into the open."

"Well they aren't, we have searched a ten mile radius and no one has seen anything."

"He's too smart for that, Wick. He was in a tribe in Afghanistan for three months before his cover was blown. He can hide." Cisco mentally ticked off scenarios, options. "We need to leak more to the press."

"And say what?"

"Our security on the murders isn't completely trashed. Nor on the Cradle. It's still a gas leak. But I want an official report to get in the hands of that TV anchor. Nothing to national news yet. They'll pick it up if there's more to go on. There won't be. We have to make certain. Tell them Dr. Hale was taking a hike and discovered the bodies. She tried to revive them. When she couldn't, she phoned the police and is now in protective custody."

"That's weak as hell. The video shows she was wearing a skirt."

"But it's plausible and that's all we need. Hale's house and phone aren't listed anywhere so we're covered. Press won't find it. Unless we have another leak. I want you to wait twelve hours to release that, too. Maybe Hale will come in. I'm sure the old man on the fishing boat and the explosions will be next on local channels." As long as it didn't go national, they were okay for now. "Lock down the police, Wick. National security takes precedence and make sure they know it. Threaten them with charges. This is bigger than the death of the Marines. Or the tourist trade."

"Marcuso's got some data from the elevator."

His brows shot up.

"I sent it to you."

Cisco tapped the computer keys, then watched the recording play out in Real Player. It was exactly as Dr. Hale had said. "At least she didn't lie about that."

"I don't think she's lying at all."

"How'd you get in the service with that attitude? Do not trust the woman. That could all be for the sake of that camera."

"You're the most cynical bastard I've ever known. She defended, she returned fire. Hell of a lot to do for a lab rat."

"Can you lift that pedestal any higher? She had the codes, lost her tag and she ran with Wilson."

"You don't know that for sure."

"She would have called out, would have done something."

"If she couldn't?"

"Then the discussion is still up for debate."

"You're just trying to get out of paying up," Wick groused, then added, "That racing boat was stolen, by the way. The owner filed a report this morning. No witnesses. And of course, nothing left of the boats."

Another dead end not worth pursuing. His second line buzzed. "Christ," he muttered.

"That would be the director. He's phoned several times."

"I'm still thinking up a good lie."

Wick snickered, then cut the line.

Cisco answered the director's fifth call. "Sir?"

"My office, one hour."

"At this point, sir, leaving the area is unwise. We are—"

"The USD wants to speak with you." The line went dead.

The Under Secretary of Defense. Great, an ass chewing in the middle of a terrorist threat. He reached in the glove box for his electric razor, grabbed his jacket, then left the car, hurrying to the chopper.

She smiled grimly. "How like a man to think an orgasm fixes everything."

"It didn't?" His fingers were still inside her, and he pulled and pushed, loving her gasp of breath. "You were pretty wound up."

The reasons why hit her again and she moved out of his arms, walked the two steps to the bed, and fell face first.

Sydney threw her arms over her head. "Oh, God," was muffled in the spread.

Jack frowned as he knelt on the mattress. "Sydney?"

"I've been accused of murder, my team is dead, my career is over and to solve it, I just had sex with a stranger. It deserves some *how stupid can you get* moments. Please, humor me."

All that was muffled. Smiling, he leaned down. "If you think that's sex, then you need some."

His deep voice drove a chill over her skin. "I'm embarrassed. It was so *not* me."

"Lack of opportunity or desire?"

She was quiet for a second, squirmed uneasily. "Both. It was just too easy for you." *To rip me apart and make me come like a hurricane.*

"Hale, with you, nothing's been easy."

His deep voice was near her ear, and her body humming with the rage of desire made her want to roll over and beg him to give her some wild monkey sex. Men being men, she wouldn't get an argument. Instead, she pushed off the bed and with her back to him, said, "I'm taking a shower. God, I smell like the river, how could you . . . never mind, you're a Marine, you probably enjoy the scent of mud."

Jack chuckled softly as she took the shopping bags with her into the bathroom. He rolled off the bed, groaning when his erection reminded him only one of them was satisfied, then pulled out the gun still wedged behind his back. He grabbed his duffle.

Time to get busy.

When Sydney came out, she stopped short in the alcove by the bathroom. She half expected Jack to be asleep, secretly hoped that, so she wouldn't have to look him in the face; but fortune wasn't her buddy this week. Just looking at him brought on a delicious shiver. The man knew a woman's body, but then, *any* climax lately was a good thing. She really didn't have a problem that he was nearly a stranger. Fingers inside her sort of broke that barrier, but it was how easily she let herself go that had her tied in knots. And she wanted more.

Her gaze moved over him where he sat at the round table with an amazing array of weapons and commando stuff laid out in front of him. There was so much power in the image, she felt her insides clench. Jack would never let her down, it just wasn't in him to do anything half measure.

He glanced up, frowned slightly. She knew her eyes were red. She'd had a nice pity party in the shower, but it was over.

Two to a customer and he was right, whining didn't solve anything.

"You okay?"

"No, but I'll work it out."

He stared at her, debating, then went back to cleaning a gun.

At least she thought he was cleaning it. What did she know? Strolling closer, her gaze floated over the gear. "Tools of the trade?" No wonder the duffle was so heavy.

"Some."

He must really believe they were in for trouble to have all that.

"There's food."

She glanced and grabbed the greasy bag off the night-stand, and sat on the bed. "You left?" She dug in, jamming fries in her mouth.

"I called room service," he offered dryly.

She made a face, then smiled.

Jack liked teasing her. She was so damn gullible for a scientist and right now, she looked cute in the cheap, gloriously thin nightshirt, her hair wet and curling. She moved to him, giving him a whiff of freshly washed skin and the sexy details of her body as she offered him a burger, then sat in the neighboring chair.

"I want to see the news and I don't want to."

"No point in it, Syd."

"My mom is probably frantic."

Jack held out his satellite phone. "Call her if you're worried."

"What do I tell her?"

"Only what will comfort her."

She grabbed it, dialing. "Hi, Mom. Yes, I saw it too. Of course, it's not true. It's not me in those pictures. I know it looks like it, but it's not. Yes . . . what?" She tipped the phone away. "Lila Handerson came to visit to see if she was okay."

"Damn."

"Jack, her husband was killed in the attack. She's very sweet." She listened into the phone. "Okay, yeah. I'm fine. It's all fine." She gave Jack a wide-eyed 'I hate lying' stare, said good-bye, then cut the line.

"Who's Handerson?"

"My project assistant. His wife is a pretty blond and very kind. She brought her some dinner."

"Does she do that often?"

"No."

Jack frowned, stopped working. "Just how old is your mother, Syd?"

"In her eighties." At his surprised look, she added, "I was a late in life baby. Very late. My father's dead. Probably from the embarrassment of the world knowing he had sex in his golden years."

Jack heard a lot in that statement. As if she had to make up for it with more brains than the average Joe.

"Mom's been a little forgetful lately. I hope she's okay."

"The quickest way to get to you is to threaten your family."

She rubbed a chill off her arms. "Lila wouldn't hurt her, God no. The woman is deathly afraid of spiders, for pity sake. Besides, helping others helps the grieving process. Even though Lila wouldn't say a word about her husband's job."

Jack kept his mouth shut, and despite his doubts, he admired her optimism. He'd lost that in the past years, some faith in human nature. Right now he didn't have the luxury and privately stuck to his theory.

She reached for the curtains, and he barked, "No!" She jerked back hard, wide-eyed. "Don't touch the door or the windows. They're rigged."

She looked at the door, but didn't see anything. "With what?

"Electricity."

"Is that really necessary?"

Only his gaze shifted up. "We have no friends, Syd."

She inched the chair away. "You think of everything."

"Apparently not enough food for you." He took a cluster of fries.

Syd finished off the burger, then looked around for more. "Food is my vice, and I always eat when I'm nervous. Never seems to be enough. I should be the size of a horse when this is over."

Over? Somehow, she knew, it had just begun.

Pentagon
Washington, D.C.

Cisco fingered the bullets in his pocket as a well-dressed man opened the door and simply gestured inside. Cisco had been here once before and while he wasn't intimidated by the surroundings, the Under Secretary of Defense was a formidable man. The director of the NSA was no slouch either. A three star general. That both were in the office at this early hour warned him that this would not be an easy chat.

"Under Secretary," he said to the USD, then looked at his boss. "Director."

"Brief him. In detail," the director said, and the USD sat back in his leather chair, and met his gaze dead on.

Cisco gave him a detailed rundown. Jack Wilson's name he kept to himself. He'd examine his reasons later. When the USD asked if he had a dossier on suspects, he said plainly, "I can't respond Sir; we don't know the identities of the assailants."

"Nearly twenty-four hours and this is all you have?"

"Not including my dead agent?"

The USD bristled.

"Agent Cisco," the director warned, "*I'll* cut you slack, but he won't."

Cisco met the director's gaze. "Forgive me, sir, but I can't fight if I don't know everything. You tie my hands with bureaucratic access to level five. Slow response to imagery and satellite surveillance. So if we're going to continue to make nice and act like this isn't a grave threat, then I'd like to get back to Virginia."

"Are you always this blunt?" the USD said.

Cisco looked at him. "I'm tasked with preventing foreign adversaries from gaining access to classified national security information. Despite our every precaution, after yesterday morning, they have. Yet I've waited half the day for Intel, infrared, and satellite photos."

"You don't have any suspects?"

Cisco felt a headache brewing behind his eyes, his patience stretched thin. "Every member of your staff and anyone within reach of this project, including Dr. Hale, is a suspect."

"You're accusing the most trusted senators and scientists in our country."

"I can't uncover the source if there are limits, sir. I've ordered a deep probe into everyone's background. Let me have it all. It will be kept eyes only," he assured when the USD looked to protest. "But we have a traitor."

The USD arched a brow. "Don't let that stop you from looking outside my staff." The USD stood and moved around the desk, folding his arms and regarding him. "You're tasked with finding the gas, first and foremost."

"But Dr. Hale is—"

"The greatest threat to this nation and its citizens is that Sarin gas is in the hands of terrorists." He waited till Cisco acknowledged that. "They have it all, which makes them immune when they use it for attack on this country."

Cisco ground his teeth. "Yes, sir."

"You want to be informed, Agent Cisco, then what I'm about to tell you cannot be shared with your people."

"It's difficult to ask them to risk their lives without all the information."

"Too bad; make it work. Any help will be granted to you,

and any access." The USD gestured and the director handed
Cisco a black plastic card.

Access codes to every aspect of NSA and the Central
Security Service. All communications, computers, and intelligence, SIGINT, Signals Intelligence, which intercepted cells
and satellite phones, computer traffic. He had clearance for
most, but not carte blanche. God dammit, why did they wait
until now? And all this said he was stepping into a mess and
he wondered when they were going to unload the really
smelly parts.

He slipped the card into his wallet, then inside his jacket.
He wouldn't thank him and the USD knew it.

The Secretary hesitated, clearly debating what he needed
to reveal. When he spoke, Cisco was floored.

And everything else, including Combs's death, became in-
significant.

Ten

In the darkened room, she was sprawled over him like a limp dishrag, sound asleep.

He wished he'd gotten more rest himself, but she was one of those women with flesh and curves, and what man could sleep with all of it wiggling against him and leaving him with a hard-on the size of a cannon.

His gaze flicked to the curtains. Sundown, time to get outta here.

"Come on, Syd, wake up." Not a muscle moved and her bare butt was too tempting. He gave it a soft pat.

She flinched and into the pillow said, "Haven't you heard about personal space?"

He chuckled shortly. "You're in mine."

She lifted her head, her insides already dancing before she met his gaze. God, he looked so yummy right now.

He glanced meaningfully down to where her hand lay just above a ferocious erection pushing against his jeans.

Her gaze flipped to his. "Is that one of those *morning* things guys get?"

"I've been awake for a couple hours."

She slid her hand upward over his abdomen.

"That doesn't help," he groaned.

"You're attracted to me?"

She said it with such disbelief, Jack rolled her on her back, hovered over her. "Want me to prove it?"

She smiled, wondering what got into her. Must have been the good dreams and spectacular hand sex. "Is this why you woke me?"

He thought for a second. Considering his brain was somewhere between his legs, it wasn't easy. "No, we gotta go."

Her brows knit. "It's just getting dark out."

"And we won't be seen as easily." He rolled off the bed and stood. "Five minutes."

Her gaze went to his bare chest. "Jack." She scooted off the edge as he turned toward her, a fresh shirt in his hand. "I hope you got medals for those." His skin was carved with scars, one she knew was a bullet hole. Her fingers slid over the pink jagged rip near his ribs. He flinched a little.

"Tickles," he said.

"That looks fresh."

"A couple months, yeah."

"How'd you get it?"

He tensed. "I can't tell you that, Syd."

"Or you'd have to kill me?" But she was already bending, brushing her lips over his wound.

Jack slammed his eyes shut. "Something like that." Then she kissed another. And another.

"I could be here all night."

He gripped her waist, pulling her close and she looked up. He stared down into her pretty whiskey colored eyes, and she reminded him of a wood elf or a fairy. She was a head shorter than he was, and her hair was wild. "This isn't what I ever intended," he said, lowering his head, his gaze on her mouth.

"Yeah. I know, me either."

He laid his mouth gently on hers, his kiss soft, but only for a moment, like testing the waters. Then it blossomed, and he kissed her as if the world was coming to an end, rolling his mouth over hers, his hands bunching in the nightshirt and pushing her into him.

Sydney knew Mecca, paradise, her head was swimming,

her body lit up and danced the happy mambo. *Damn*, he was good at this. She wanted it to go on—would have, at that moment, risked her life to stay right there and let him take her like some conquered princess.

But he was smarter.

"We have to leave," he said between devouring her mouth and damn near making her climax with a kiss.

"I know, I know. I barely know you."

"I know enough." He kissed her again, harder, deeper, lifting her off the floor and molding her to him. Sydney felt the powerful push of his erection, and every inch of her throbbed from the inside out. Unfortunately, he set her down, forced himself to stop.

A better man than she, she thought. His breathing was as labored as hers, thank God. It would be a shame if this was all one sided.

"Christ."

She could see his struggle as his hands slowly left her and he stepped back. He stared, so perfectly still.

Jack had to be, or he'd snap in half. "Pardon me while I jerk off in the shower." He turned a sharp right and went into the bathroom.

Syd laughed, feeling kind of powerful, then she reached for her clothes.

Cisco climbed the final stairs to the Pentagon roof as his cell went off. He hoped this was good.

"The Cradle is open," Wickum said.

He stopped on the staircase, the chopper revving up and growing louder by the second. "Chemical levels?"

"Nothing that isn't within the safe zones. And Dr. Hanai is still alive, Gabe."

Cisco stopped short, wind kicking through the open stairwell.

"But not for long."

"Wick," he warned.

"It's gone, all of it. The computers destroyed, the cold

room blasted open, and everything is burned or full of bullet holes."

Something settled over Cisco, all doubt erased.

"Marcuso's trying to retrieve data. The scientists were executed, some with their throats cut. So fucking unnecessary. Corporal Tanner was the only one to take it in the chest; the rest got it in the head or face. Tanner got one terrorist, no ID on him yet. The bullets match. Three shooters I figure, same weapon. And they took souvenirs, for Crissake."

"From who, what part?"

"Fingers, ring or pinky, left hand. On everyone."

There was a purpose behind that. "Mother?"

"Still not responding. But we have the last bit of data she pulled. Nothing earth-shattering. And that scent on the chute packs was witch hazel, by the way. It was soaked with it."

"Hale?"

"No sign of her or Wilson since the boat explosion. They've vanished."

"Time to call in the locals, put out an APB on her and Wilson."

"And the wisdom in this? Unless they had a car stashed and knew of the explosion beforehand, they're walking."

"Wilson will find a way."

"If the Shenandoah police are looking for him, they have nothing to go on."

"Don't give them anything. Apprehend only, no questioning. We have to get Hale in before there's another attempt on her life."

"I feel silver gracing my palm. Sounds like you're changing your tune."

"Forget it. Until I know who gave up the codes, she's my prime suspect." And the killer's prime target. "Any hits on CODUS on our man from the mountain?"

"Not in our system."

"Open all channels everywhere, Interpol, Mossad, MI-5, Russian Intel, get me something more on that man on the slab."

"I don't have that kind of access."

"I'm giving it to you." Cisco paused in the stairwell, looking below for anyone within hearing distance. He gave Wick the access numbers. "Erase the path when you're done, got that?"

"Will do. Where are you going?"

"To call in a marker."

He pulled the mask over his face and kicked in the door. A woman screamed. He aimed the rifle at her head. "Shat the bladdie hell up!"

The female dropped into a chair, grabbing her kid. He moved toward her, slipping out his knife. She shrieked again, covering the little girl. He brought the knife close to her head as if he'd pare her down the middle, looming over her, and liking the spark of defiance in her eyes. Then he severed the phone lines behind her. She sagged into the chair, sobbing. He tied her and the kid up, stuffing rags in their mouths, then went to the balcony, and pushed open the sliding doors. He knelt, adjusting his scope, then affixed the silencer and sighted for three locations. He had a lot of room for error up here. He didn't plan on needing it.

He could hear the woman whimper. "Shat up!" Bladdie whore. He hated the poor, didn't want to be near them, their stench lingered with reminders. But there were exceptions—like when they were useful. He pulled off the ski mask and rubbed his hand over his hairless head.

Then he sighted.

He could see her in the old car; too bad he needed her. He had a clean shot to her head.

Then the man came out, his body a shadow blinking in and out of the light from the store. The sun just past the horizon, everything purple and hazy.

"Turn to the left a bit, chum. I got one just for you."

Fluorescent lamps blinked on and spilled light over the rain-soaked parking lot as Jack left the store and walked toward the car. When Syd started to get out, he shook his head.

His gaze flicked over their surroundings, noting any cars that moved slowly and passed parking spots, the roofs of buildings across the street. He felt like the prey in the crosshairs as he opened the car door, handed her the bags, then gave the area another glance.

"Jack, what do you see?"

"Nothing." Yet he felt it, like in Afghanistan, the sensation of a scope zeroing in on the back of his head.

"Well, get in, then."

He did, turning over the engine. He put the car in gear, easing out, turning to look behind. He could find suspicion in everything today, but nothing concrete. He paused at the exit to get onto the road.

He leaned forward to see if it was clear. The window glass beside his head exploded. Syd screamed as he stepped on the gas and cut across the road; drivers slammed on brakes, horns blasted. "You okay?" She didn't answer. "Syd!"

"I—I . . . am—"

"Talk to me, Einstein, I can't look." He drove defensively, on the road, then off, and headed away from civilians. Through the rearview, he looked at the rooftops and glimpsed movement on a balcony of an apartment, but nothing else.

Finally, he looked at her. The bullet was imbedded in her car door under the window. And her thigh was bleeding.

"Oh, damn. Hold pressure on it." She looked from the wound to him, dazed. "Now, Syd! Do it now!"

Jack pushed over the speed limit, the car rattling. When she didn't move, just staring at it, he grabbed her hand and smashed it down on her thigh. It shook her loose and as he drove onto the highway, he undid his belt, then slid it off. "Strap this right over it and hold it tight. Release it every ten minutes or so."

She took the belt and obeyed. "This is a really bad week, you know? I didn't even feel it."

"I know. God, I'm sorry."

"You didn't shoot. Stop blaming yourself."

"It was meant for me."

"How can you tell?"

"The shot came from above land level. If they wanted you, they'd have shot through the back window. At least, I would have. Jesus H., how is he tracking us?"

"You can't be all things everywhere, Jack."

"I fucking need to be, or we're both dead."

"You couldn't lie to me, just once?"

He wanted to pull over and hold her, stop the bleeding, but he couldn't. If that shooter wasn't above sea level, then he was behind them.

"Slump in the seat, but raise your leg a bit."

She obeyed, the sight of her own blood making her woozy. "It burns."

"Just keep the pressure up." He glanced, seeing only the blood oozing between her fingers. His heart jumped in his chest and a cold tingling sensation radiated out to his arms. What's with him? She'd be okay, and he'd had men shot before—hell, he'd taken a bullet, and he never felt this kind of panic. Men, he reminded, men who'd made it part of their career choice, not some egghead scientist who was an innocent target.

"It's not that bad, just skimmed the top of my leg. If I were thinner, it would have missed. How's that for diet motivation?"

"This isn't funny, dammit. You shouldn't be in this situation or here with me."

"Let's not start that bad choice-good choice hypothesis. You won't win. I'm an expert at theories. I'm seeing this through, so buck up and deal with it, Marine."

He couldn't help the smile twisting his lips and relaxed. If she was coherent and sassing him, the wound wasn't too bad. "Take your pants off."

"Excuse me?"

"What's your problem? I've touched all those jeans are hiding." He winked at her startled expression. "I need to see the wound." She unfastened her jeans, wiggling on the dirty car seat to get them down. Jack leaned and squeezed. Fresh blood poured. "It needs stitches."

"No, it does not, and who's the doctor here?"

"Chemistry and microbiology do not make you a medic."

"Microchemistry and immunology, too," she corrected. "And I have minors in anatomy. I know the human body or I'd be useless in my field. It's a graze, a flesh wound."

"You watch too much TV. There's a kit in my gear bag, it will have to do for now."

She crawled over the back, her panty-clad butt nearly in his face.

"You might want to pull the jeans up; you're giving every other driver a good look at your sweet behind."

She plopped down, then winced, then shimmed her jeans back up. She waved at some guy beeping his horn at them. "Gosh, he looked so thrilled."

"He'll probably be having fantasies all night." Jack wished he had time to make some of his own with her, and glanced in the rearview mirror, suspicious of every car trailing them.

Syd noticed. "Anyone there?" She got the kit.

"Probably. But why are they still chasing us? They have the gas, and the prototypes. Why risk taking out the last witnesses when they hold all the cards?"

Syd looked down at the small, olive-green plastic kit and experienced something she hadn't in a while. Guilt, full out, skin tightening guilt.

"Criminals don't risk that much and terrorists are unpredictable, but they know after the attack, every authority in this country is on alert status now." He shook his head. "Why not go deep underground and stay there? I don't get it."

"I do."

He glanced, frowning. "Say again?"

"I think I know why they're still hunting us."

"Yeah? So give, Einstein."

She didn't speak, and he glanced her way. Her expression told him everything.

"Shit. I'm going to be really pissed, aren't I?"

Caracas, Venezuela

Cisco stood at the wide French doors, watching the child play in the backyard. The setting sun glistened off the pool, liquid spilling from a rimless waterfall. He tipped the crystal glass to his mouth, thinking that some people really knew how to live.

At the sound of a door opening, he tossed back the twelve-year-old scotch.

Heels clicked on the tile floor and he knew the instant she recognized him. Her short indrawn breath echoed to him as if it were in his ear.

"What are you doing here?"

He didn't look at her, knew what he'd feel when he did. "Good scotch, Saroan. But then, it's probably contraband."

He heard the rapid click of heels as she crossed the room and shouted. "Alainia! Alainia!"

"She's fine." He gestured with the glass to the backyard. "And lovely."

She rushed to the doors, pushing him aside and out into the backyard. She went to the child, hugging her till she squirmed, then put her down. The nanny came close, both she and the girl glancing at him. Saroan put on a good front, stroking her daughter's dark head, then smiling assuringly. She didn't look his way.

For a fleeting moment, Cisco wondered what it would be like to have that. Someone who gave a damn. Then, an instant later, the thought evaporated and he focused on his purpose. He was here to collect a debt. Or rather, use it thoroughly until he needed her again.

Saroan turned toward him and Cisco felt his chest grow

snug. Her strides were short and quick, pulling the narrow beige skirt and defining the curves. She was still breathtaking, he thought, and rarely awarded that praise to many women.

Saroan Kasminova was different.

She wore her beauty well. Just as she could an AK-47. Chechen born, she was well connected. Still well connected, he thought with a glance around the large house. Their paths crossed several years ago, in another lifetime. Another agency. She was running guns to the Serbian rebels. When Cisco caught her, she instantly turned over. Cisco cut her a deal and orchestrated her death in an assassination. Saroan was clever enough that he'd kept tabs on her since. The reason she turned so quickly was kicking a ball in the backyard.

Saroan slipped inside, gave her daughter a last look before she faced him.

"You've risked my life and hers coming here. I was dead to you, Gabriel."

"We need to talk."

"Go to hell."

"You owe me."

Saroan hesitated, then went to the bar, splashed liquor in a glass, and drank it all in one shot. She slammed the glass down on the mahogany surface. "You swore you'd leave me alone." She opened a small drawer at the bar, slipped her hand in. It was empty. Her shoulders fell and she faced Cisco.

He dangled the gun, then popped it apart and tossed the pieces on the sofa. "I'm not here to resurrect you." If anyone knew she was alive, his own life and reputation would be worthless.

A single tapered brow shot up. "How did you find me?"

"It doesn't matter. But if you want to stay hidden from the rest of the world, you'll help me."

"Do what?"

Cisco strolled closer. "Who made this?" He handed her the silencer.

Saroan took it to the window, turning it over in her elegant hands. "Custom made, longer barrel, solid cushion insulation." She tipped it to view the threads. "Rapid fire, yes? Interesting."

"Not what I want to hear."

She handed it back, folded her arms.

"Don't even think about cutting a deal. One to a customer. And I still know where your past lies."

Cisco could almost see the chill run over her skin. He glanced to his right, out the glass doors at the child. "She looks like you, Saroan. Does she know about her father?"

Beside him she tensed, her breathing quickened briefly, yet she showed no other sign of her distress. And he knew exactly how deep it ran.

"No, you bastard, and she never will."

He turned his head. "Am I the only one who knows?"

The threat lay between them, soft, like a layer of silk sheets.

Her gaze darted to her daughter, then back to him. Her lips were pressed tight, the only sign of the anger boiling inside her. She gestured to the silencer. "He's one of yours. An American."

"I need more than that." Her perfume was intoxicating and giving him vivid memories he didn't want.

"He calls himself the Clockmaker."

"Saroan." The warning hit the mark.

"I've never seen him." She shrugged. "No one has. Everything is moved by a blind carrier."

It was a trick of the terrorist trade. No one group knew too many details about the others. Transactions were done by mail with post office boxes, calls made from cheap cell phones that couldn't be traced as quickly as land lines, then discarded. The buyers and sellers often used vagrants or addicts to make the drops and deliveries for them. Someone desperate for quick cash. It kept the negotiators clean if it went sour.

He offered the bullet that killed one of the Marines. "Tell me about it."

Under the sunlight, she examined it. "It's one of the Clock-maker's. I have a few of them left."

He looked at her sharply. "Get them."

She strolled to a hall closet, opened it and pushed back the coats, then gave the wall a kick. It sprang and Cisco saw the cache of weapons, cleaned and shelved.

"Expecting another coup?"

"I have a child to protect." She withdrew a box, closed up the closet and brought it to him. She offered one, pointing to the base. "See the marks, like hands on a clock."

He compared it to the spent bullet. It was destroyed beyond recognition, but forensics could lift it.

"He marks everything like that. His only signature. I don't know the significance of the different positions of the hands, but they're always there. Even on the silencer." Palm out, she wiggled her fingers, and he gave it up. She pointed to the faint marks near the screws of the silencer, then she took a bullet. It slid perfectly into the custom silencer.

Cisco pocketed the stash. "Anything else?"

"No. I kept my end of the bargain."

He didn't move. He had nothing to say to her, nothing to discuss. They'd made the pact years ago and he'd broken it. Yet his hand rose, almost without control, to push a strand from her cheek. She went rigid, her eyes flaring, almost begging him not to touch her.

He withdrew, releasing a slow breath, then headed for the door.

"Gabriel," she said, her accent heavy and seductive.

He looked back.

"The next time you come near me or my child, I *will* kill you."

His gaze wandered over her for a long moment, and he knew she meant it.

"If that look is any indication, I'm already hamburger."

He schooled his features. "All right, give it to me straight and simple."

She released a slow breath, and said, "I was working on a project alone. None of my team knew what it was and they were so busy with creating the secondary implosion bomb, they hardly noticed. After the first was successful, we were to enlarge it."

He sent her a look that said this was not the short version.

"I worked to find an antidote for Sarin exposure."

"There's atropine."

"Not good enough. Sarin kills so fast and if one survives, it leaves a lasting impression on the nervous system, resulting in complications for the rest of their lives."

"I've seen it firsthand."

That made her wonder what he did for the country. "Then you understand that something had to be done. This nerve agent can be easily created like mustard gas, and my goal was to create a fast-acting serum for Sarin gas that will halt any progression into the nervous system. Maybe used as a preventative serum. Like polio shots."

"You didn't trust me to tell me this?"

"You kidnapped me and took out my guards, dragged me all over creation, got me shot at, why should I have trusted you? And well, then . . . I didn't have the time."

"How about when we were in bed together?"

Her features tightened and she snapped, "I was thinking of other things at the time, thank you very much." Like how fast she could have some monkey sex with him?

"God dammit, Syd, I'm walking blind in this already. I can stop an enemy I can see, but with this—!"

"Do I need to do something to you to make you calm down?" she cut in.

His expression froze, and he blinked. "Don't change the subject." But his temper simmered. Then he thought of what she'd created, the ramifications. "Man, oh, man, no wonder they won't let up." He rubbed his hand back and forth over his head, then gripped the wheel. "Do you realize how valuable that is? Billions of dollars for the fear factor alone. Every nation, every person would want it."

She shimmied her jeans down to her knees, then opened the kit. "I was being paid a salary, no profits. Besides, I didn't do it for the money. With a workable serum, we at least had a good countermeasure to help the victims. Better than the implosion bomb, which only works in close quarters. It doesn't have a name yet but the serum, I called it Kingsford for its charcoal properties." She cleaned the cut, applied an ointment. The bleeding hadn't stopped completely, turning the salve a bright pink. "We'd have a serum that would save them and not just prolong a miserable life after exposure. We had to make Sarin obsolete."

"Does it?"

She cut gauze and tape, her moves efficient. "According to my last test results, yes, but I haven't done a final rodent test to document my formula and be absolutely certain."

"Could they have taken it from the Cradle?"

She stilled, thinking. "Yes. It wasn't in the main computers, only mine." She taped the gauze. "And they'd have to know what to look for, too."

"Who knew about it?"

"NSC and the Under Secretary of Defense. Not even Cisco knew. Though he probably does now."

The list of suspects just got smaller. If they had her serum formula, then they were trying to kill her so she couldn't recreate it. Or because she was the last link? Either way, it put her life in greater danger. Jack said nothing, his pulse quickening, then settled when a dose of reality finally hit.

"This doesn't change anything. They have it. We don't. Our only trump card is that formula and it's buried under six hundred feet of rock."

"Not exactly."

Eleven

He didn't pursue a losing situation. He'd cut his losses fast and try something different. Disgusted that he'd almost killed Hale, Van Meer opened his hotel room, threw off his jacket as he walked the short hall to the living area. He stood still for a moment, letting his gaze roam the luxurious suite. *Worth every rand it cost me.*

He walked to the bar, poured a generous glass of gin, and drank half without stopping. It hit his stomach and pooled, the booze spreading its effects through his limbs.

Not enough to drown the small sound.

He drew his weapon as he turned, aiming at the door. She inhaled, her pretty blue eyes going wide. It made her look more ripe and innocent. His dick went hard at the sight of her. "You push me, doll."

"I can leave, if you want?" Her little pout was practiced, but he let her live the fantasy. It was his too; an angel with long blond hair, sweet pale skin.

"Put that away please."

He pointed the gun to the ceiling.

"Where is it?"

He inclined his head, then holstered his gun, watching her lithe figure move to the fridge in the small kitchen. She wore a dress, soft blue and frilly, making her look like a girl instead of a woman. He met up with her, watched as she opened it, stared at the sealed bloody bag. Her features slackened a little.

"Take it."

"God, no, I just wanted to see it. To be sure."

His dark brows drew down. "You're a strange little bokhie, aren't cha?"

She looked at him, eyeing him from head to foot. He liked when she did that. She shut the door and moved toward him, her sly smile saying much. Within inches of her, he scented the clean fragrance of her skin, and let it wash over him as he slid his arm around her waist, pulled her against him. She let out a gasp, a little strike of fear. It made him hot, and he towered over her, swallowing her in his arms. She stared up at him, her eyes going soft and kittenish. Then her tongue slipped between her lips, snaking to lick his tattoo, following the curves of the black snake wrapping his bicep.

He'd have her again, until he was done with her. Till she was no longer useful. She was beautiful and clean, but merely a functional part of his mission. An element he needed. Her purity was tainted, well used. Like everything in his life. A reminder that he'd grown up dirt poor and unwanted; his father dead in an uprising when he was a kid, his mother shoving a gun in her mouth because she was too weak to deal with anything more. That the bitch waited till he walked in the door to the hovel she called a home to do it made him hate her still. Her deed tainted him, ostracized him from the church, others, taking away his choices and left him to make something of himself alone. He was glad for it, the freedom, watching out for himself. It gave him back control, his choices, yet his stint in the military took that again. Following orders was a joke. He knew more than his commanders could ever learn in some tactics class.

So he left to keep power in his grasp. His reputation earned him respect and money. Money was the great cleanser. When he had what he needed, he'd wipe out all traces to his past, and leave it all behind. Including her. Yet right now, as her hands slid over his erection, she still had value.

Tomorrow—was another matter.

As the jet headed back to the U.S., Cisco sipped water and fingered the silencer. The two fingers of scotch buzzed through his brain, loosening his muscles, making him think of Saroan in ways he'd hadn't in years. Around him, six agents on different computers worked to find any reference to the Clockmaker. He hadn't slept in forty-eight hours and stole only fractures of rest. As he waited, his eyes drifted closed and for a moment, he could almost feel Saroan's soft mouth beneath his.

"DNA from CODUS on your mountain men," an agent called out. "We've got photos."

Cisco was awake instantly, demanding coffee and attacking his computer. "A registered offender?"

"No."

Cisco glanced up, scowling.

"A link to MI-6."

Good boy, Wick. The picture and file downloaded. The dead man on the mountain. British born, Royal Marine training. Allan Boatwright. Dishonorably discharged for theft of a weapons cache. Did some jail time. Cisco scrolled to known associates. It was a long list. He narrowed the field to men who'd have training to get into the Cradle and disable Mother.

Winston O'Hurley, Irish born, IRA. Demolitions expert. He recognized him from photos of the body in the Cradle. Sought for three Belfast bombings, one at the British consulate. Another in Dublin near a church. Suspected to have assassinated a member of parliament by wiring his morning teapot.

These were some pissed off men, he thought.

Thomas Maitland, British Army. U.K. Special Forces training, electronics expert, Fifty-first Scottish Brigade, MI-6 most wanted. Location unknown. Henri Mautier, French, dismissed from DGSE. Directeur Generale de la Securite Exterieure. Great, French Secret Service. The man had intelligence that could screw every nation. Charged and tried, but escaped from custody. Four men died trying to recapture him. Heavyweights, he thought. Martin Van Meer, South African born, British trained, same unit as Boatwright. Location unknown. U.K. Special Forces, tactics and assault, SERE training, Search Evasion Rescue and Extraction at Coronado. *Christ. We trained him.*

The Intel ran for pages. The last dozen never apprehended, but suspects in several attacks with rebel factions in Central America, Asia, Ireland, and the Middle East. His attention slipped back to Van Meer, Aka *Judas*. He searched for any connections to the man. Same circles as Boatwright, Maitland, and O'Hurley. Seen with Mautier, and MI-6 believes he orchestrated the jailbreak.

Cisco stared at the photo shot at long distance somewhere in Libya. Bald and big, Van Meer's tank shirt showed thick arms and shoulders covered in tattoos. There was one on his throat but he couldn't make out more than a blur in the picture. The elevator tapes gave them a good contour of the man's face. Cisco ordered his experts to try to match it with the MI-6 photos. It wouldn't give them more than a mild connection if it matched.

He kept reading, plucking details from each file. One name reoccurred. Nathan Hoag, an American. Served a few years in the Army, discharged. Did five years jail time for explosives and weapons contraband. Since then, he'd been clean. Cisco pulled up his military record; nothing stellar, no combat, but he was an armorer, cleaning and refurbishing weapons. The picture was fifteen years old.

He hit print, then checked his watch. "Tell MI-6 we have Boatwright and possibly O'Hurley on a slab. Send them everything and ask them to please return the favor. I want pictures on the DB on the Skyline Drive a-sap."

If he was anything like the two dead they had, Shenandoah Police wouldn't pull a print on the bodies, but Cisco could get a blood type and DNA match. All this meant that he had one less SOB to chase and Judas was more volatile than his file was telling.

"We got a hit on the Clockmaker from a contact in Colombia!" Agents howled and grinned as one handed over a photo. Cisco studied it, then glanced at his computer screen. Younger, trimmer, still butt ugly. "That's Nathan Hoag. Where is he?"

"Utah."

Cisco picked up the cabin phone and gave the pilot new orders.

"*How* not exactly?" Jack said. The edge to his voice made her talk fast.

"Okay, okay, the paper I burned, it was my latest test results, and I knew before the attack that I'd succeeded."

"And you destroyed it. Why?"

"I didn't trust you. I thought you might be after it."

"Oh, hell." Serves him right, Jack thought.

"This is a blessing in disguise; the bad guys don't have it."

"And when they figure out that they have an incomplete formula, what do you think they'll do?"

She was shimmying back into her jeans when that sunk in like icy water over her head. "Oh, damn." She plopped on the seat, then winced.

"Yeah."

"I still say this is good." She gave him a superior *I'm right, you're wrong* look. "I didn't update my data on the computer. I do that after I've run all the tests and mostly use pen and paper. I work better that way. They stole day-old data, baseline testing sequence, blind rodent tests, but I had another sequence to add to the computer files and hadn't done it yet."

"But you burned it."

"I remember every detail, Jack."

His look was full of skepticism. "It's got to be complicated."

"Yes, it is. The molecular structure sequence eradicates the rapid cell lysis—"

"Spare me, baby, I get that you're smart." She blinked, then smiled. "Can you reproduce it?"

"Sure, give me some paper—"

"No, Syd, can you reproduce it, physically."

Her brows shot up. She'd never considered that.

"We have to make the theft obsolete."

"That's three years' work to make that implosion bomb and I'm telling you now I'm not a metallurgist. I can't make the housing."

"Just the serum. It's our only weapon. Can you do it?"

"Yes, of course I can, but it's not like mixing a cake batter in a kitchen."

"What do you need?"

"Chemicals, medications really, and a couple other elements. Scales to make correct measurements, a centrifuge, a microscope, vials, and syringes, why?"

He pointed and she saw the sign for the University of Virginia.

"You can't be serious? We'll never get in there."

"Anyone tell you that you're a pessimist?" He turned off the highway, heading toward the college.

"This is pointless. Not to mention dangerous. The elements are drugs, Jack. They won't have them at a college, and if they did, it would be under high security."

"You're a doctor, can't you write a prescription?"

"Certainly, *if* I had an ID, but that's back at my house." With some gauze, she blotted at the cuts on his cheekbone. He flinched, surprised by it, then looked at the cloth and let her clean him up.

Jack's mind went over strategies to get what she needed; breaking and entering in a pharmacy wouldn't do it. The police would be there before they got what they needed. He had to get her an ID, something that would pass so she could get the chemicals she needed.

He was quiet while she played nurse, then said, "You're

right. The risk of getting in the lab and not having what you need would be a waste." Back up and regroup, he thought. Who could he trust to help them? He turned the car and headed north.

"Even if we did get the elements and lab, how would I test it?"

"Do you need to?"

"It works, but I have to be certain."

"We don't have that luxury. If you can recreate it, then we'll have some bargaining power if we need it. Because if Cisco doesn't find who started this mess, then one or both of us will take the fall for the murders and the gas."

She sat back and said, "Your honesty can be so annoying sometimes."

Nate Hoag was a short, tubby creature with Friar Tuck hair and large eyeballs that protruded from the sockets. Around sixty, he was cocky for an ugly man, offering little resistance and opening the gate without a fuss. When they entered the mansion, he was feeding caged birds and ordering servants to bring coffee and pastries.

Cisco's team detained the servants in the kitchen and he asked Hoag to stand, then waved to an agent to cuff him.

Hoag took it in stride, asking an agent to close the bird-cage for him. "My attorneys will rip you a new one."

"You don't get to phone one."

"I know my rights. I'll turn state's evidence, cut a deal."

"I don't work for the state." Cisco showed him his ID and he took sadistic pleasure in seeing Hoag pale. "You have no rights when national security is at risk." Cisco pushed him into a chair. "Search it."

Clocks ticked and chimed as agents combed the premises. Cisco remained with Hoag, lit a cigar, and watched him. Hoag warned the men to be careful with his things and the longer he sat the more he sweat. It was repulsive. It took about ten minutes of staring for the shield to crack.

"What the fuck do you want?"

"What do you think I need, Hoag?"

The man frowned, looking much like a shriveled mushroom. "You don't have shit. I let you in without a fight, you didn't read me my rights, you didn't have a warrant. Nothing you do will hold up in court."

Cisco slipped his hand inside his jacket, and shook out the warrant. It was signed by the Under Secretary of Defense. "Shall we talk now? Or wait for the experts?"

"Experts at what?"

"Extracting information."

Hoag scoffed. "You'll never get away with it."

He would, and the doubt colored Hoag's features. "Who did you sell these to?" He showed him the Teflon bullet.

Hoag didn't say anything, plopping back in the chair. He reminded Cisco of Jabba the Hut.

"You can give them up now, or later. But it will happen."

An agent came in from outside. "There's a cellar in the base of the garages, under a trap door of concrete and full of these." He put the altered Russian weapon on the table. "And a safe."

The little weasel was going to spend a lot of time in a federal pen. "You know the drill," he said to the agent. They'd get photos, prints, crack the safe and confiscate it all. He looked at Hoag, arching a brow.

"I'm not talking to you, so you can just kiss my white ass."

Cisco moved closer, staring down at the man, then blew on the tip of his cigar. "You're under the impression that your country is *asking* for your help, Mr. Hoag."

He brought the glowing red tip closer to those bulging eyes.

Jack glanced in the rearview enough that Sydney knew something was wrong. "You see someone?" She resisted the urge to look out the rear window.

"There's a cop following us."

"Cisco wouldn't have called in the locals. Not if he wants this kept quiet, and he does."

"He's NSA, he doesn't have to tell them anything, just to apprehend."

"Oh, no."

"Don't look and don't panic." He drove for another mile watching the police cruiser gain speed. He shifted lanes, and exited the ramp. "We have to ditch this car."

"And steal another?"

"Not quite."

Jack made several turns. The cop followed. He cut behind the main roads, taking side streets and getting behind the cruiser. Jack thought they'd been made until the cruiser switched lanes and jumped off the highway. He drove to a suburban area with strip malls and gas stations outside a residential community, then parked in a mall lot, and shut off the engine. He got out, gathered everything, then came to open the passenger door.

He offered his hand. "How do you feel?"

Her fingers slid into his and she hung on, thinking he was a real gentleman under all that gung-ho stuff. "Since we're being so honest, it hurts like hell."

"Lean on me, then."

She did, and his strength and solid muscle felt like an anchor. "Want to tell me what we're doing?"

He walked to the corner, raised his arm and hailed a passing cab. "Getting out of sight."

The cab rolled to a stop, he opened the door and as Syd climbed in, he looked around for the cruiser. Satisfied, he got in and gave an address. When she started to talk, he shook his head, holding her to his side. The cab pulled up in front of a small house in an old neighborhood south of Woodbridge. He paid and they got out.

"Your house?"

"No, it's a friend's. He's in Iraq. I check on it for him."

They were nearly to the door when he heard, "Well, hello there."

The singsong voice made him freeze and he turned, plastering on a smile for the older woman. Brandishing a flashlight like a weapon, and wearing a jogging suit not meant for a real workout, she held a leash, at the end a tiny, hairy dog that shook even as it stood still.

"Hello, ma'am, how are you?"

"I'm fine, but you don't look well." Her gaze flicked to the cuts on his face, then went to Sydney, intent on her bloody pant leg. She walked closer, peering at them under the streetlight.

"We had a car accident, ma'am. Rick's place was closer and we've been with police all night. Besides, I need to check on things for him, water plants, you know."

She stared at Sydney for a long moment and Jack shielded her.

"If you'll excuse us, good night ma'am."

Sydney tried not to hobble, but it was useless. Jack was almost forcing her to look more lame than she was. He flipped out a set of keys.

"When you speak to Rick you tell him he's in our prayers," the woman called.

He looked back and smiled genuinely. "Yes, ma'am, I will." Jack opened the door quickly, ushering her inside and sealing them in.

"You're so slick."

"We aren't safe here—Mrs. Whatsherface is too nosy." Rick had complained about the woman's comments when he brought women home and they were there the next morning. The woman was the moral majority for the neighborhood. "We can take Rick's car." When she looked to protest, he said, "If he knew about this, he'd be here with us."

"You know him that well?"

"Yeah, sure."

"I had my hair done and nails manicured with my best

friend, Tish." Her throat tightened. *Tish was dead.* "She is—was—an entomologist, studied bugs. The bug bitch I called her. But I wouldn't ever have said for certain she'd risk her life for me."

"Would you for her?"

She thought for a second. "Yeah. I suppose so."

"It's a lot simpler than you think." He checked the house, flipped on the heat, then searched through the cupboard and closets. She stood in the living room, feeling weird about being in the house without the owner, then noticed Jack coming back in with armloads of stuff.

"What *are* you doing?"

"Supplies."

She glanced at the sleeping bag, jackets, and clothes. "Are we camping?"

"You never know."

Jack hooked up the computer and had to use dial up since Rick had the DSL cut off when he deployed. Then he pulled paper from the printer, slapped a pen on top and said, "Tell me what you need. Everything."

She eased into the chair at the desk, getting busy.

He went to examine the fridge, grabbed two beers and came back to her. He handed over one and popped the top on his own, taking a huge drink. She had two sheets spread out; on one she wrote, very fast. The formula, he thought. Looked like hieroglyphics to him, but with every couple of lines, she'd jot something on the extra paper.

After a minute, she sat back, and held it out. "There you go, those are the elements." She opened her beer and sipped.

He pointed to the remaining paper. "That one is the formula?"

"Yes."

He took it, turning on the shredder.

"Jack! Wait! Now that I have it written out, I should probably—"

"No. It will take some major screw-up to get you away from me but if that should happen, we don't want them to have it." He sent it down and the shredder chewed it.

"Whoever *them* is," she said sullenly.

"I also need a list of people involved with the Cradle."

"That's a lot of high level senators, chemists, military, Under Secretary of Defense, his staff."

He was thoughtful. "Anyone could be involved in this. There are a lot of gophers for people like that."

"They're the most closed-mouthed, trusted people in the capital."

"Then how did those killers succeed so easily?"

She made a face, not liking that the people she'd trusted and what she believed in was crumbling around her.

He saw it, the flash of sadness, when a truth you didn't want to see showed its ugliness. He tipped her face up and bent to kiss her softy. "You need to come out from under those rocks, honey, you're so naive." He liked that about her. "There is a traitor somewhere in the hierarchy. Someone with power."

He didn't have to say it. Find them—*before they find us.*

"You want this back?" He held out her ID card.

She snatched it. "Oh, thank God. It's proof I didn't give it up. This is how you found me? Why didn't you give it back?"

"Trusting you wasn't an option then either."

Syd frowned, and wondered what else he was hiding as he pulled her from the chair and sat at the desk. "Why do you need a computer?"

He typed. "To find out where your supplies are and how I can get them."

"You can do that?"

"I don't have official authorization, but I'll try." He typed, his fingers flying over the keyboard. Pages came up, not Web pages, but something else, and she looked closer. Inventory, pharmaceuticals. College thesis experimentation.

"How did you do that?"

"Classified."

She took a step back, staring at him. "Just what do you do for the Marine Corps, Jack?"

He stilled, met her gaze, then looked back at the screen.

"You can't tell me?"

He shook his head, keying up chemical sales, other government laboratory facilities, then medical colleges in the area that would have what she needed. He glanced at her list and typed.

"Even a hint?"'

"A hint would be revealing classified information, an oath I swore to uphold."

"So did I and I told you."

"Mine didn't get people murdered in cold blood."

She stepped back, horrified. "You blame me?"

His gaze snapped to hers. "Oh, hell." He stood, reaching for her. "No. I don't. Of course not."

She backed away. "Kingsford is the cause of all this, Jack, I know that. Don't you think I know that? I made it, I knew when I did that people would kill to get it, but I was finally creating something worthwhile and I thought I was safe down there."

"Sydney, I don't blame you." He tried to hold her, touch her, but she turned away from him, hugging herself.

"I lost friends, too, Jack. Good people. Very good." Her eyes filled with angry tears that never fell.

"I didn't mean that they were any less valuable than my Marines."

"They aren't. I'll make the damn serum." She looked at him sharply, fury rampant in every fiber of her body. "Then I'll do something so no one will ever die for it again!" She limped past him.

"Syd?"

"I need a shower," was all she said.

Jack dropped into the chair. Damn. *You can be a perfectly insensitive jerk sometimes, Wilson.* He'd been able to handle just about any tough situation, but Sydney was a new breed of trouble. She'd just proven he'd been in the field far too long. He'd lost something of himself out there. He wanted it back.

Unsure of what to do about it, he refocused, and grabbed the SAT phone. He punched the numbers, his gaze on the hallway and he expected her to come back out. She didn't.

Hutch answered with a yawn, then instantly perked up.

"Sherman and Peabody still where I left them?"

"Yeah. You okay, pal?"

"Got a posse closing in, Hutch. Stay clear."

"I don't like the sound of that. Are you safe?"

He glanced up the hall, and expected to hear the water running, yet didn't. "For now, yes. Don't tell them I'm coming. They work better under the threat of bodily harm."

He ended the call, and turned back to the computer, yet his concentration was overshadowed with Sydney, the pain in her expression, the blame she shouldered. He rubbed his eyes. You bull-headed ass, he thought, and pulled out the crumpled picture of his friends. Decker would remind him that women were ruled by their hearts. Lyons would say *leave work at the door, Capt'n, they don't need to see it,* while Martinez would insist his lack of Latin blood in his veins kept women away. But Jack knew it was easier to force them back than let them in, and he was so hard charged to get the bastards that he hadn't truly considered the emotional thrashing she'd taken. And he'd just thrown salt in the wound.

Jack pocketed the snapshot, then pushed back in the leather chair, and stood.

He rubbed his face, then headed toward the bathroom.

Twelve

He stood outside the bathroom, removing his clothing piece by piece and, dropping them on the floor. He could see himself in the mirror inside the bath, bright splashes of blood slashing his face and mixing with sweat and dirt. The trail was dead again. Images came, and went, the effortless death, and he smiled, stepped inside, and turned on the shower. He didn't wait for it to heat up before he stepped under the spray.

He took up the bar of lye soap, and a scrub brush, lathering it up and raking the boar's hair bristle over his skin. It turned red, blood rushing to the surface and bleeding where he scrubbed too hard. He didn't feel it, his skin gone hard and leathery years before.

As always, images of his boyhood flashed, and he could see himself staring at his dirty feet sticking out from under a shabby quilt someone had thrown in the rubbish. He'd look at his fingers and toes and wonder what it was like to be clean. To have new things, to sleep on fresh sheets. Even in his state, his skin raw and burning red, he knew this wasn't normal, that he'd taken his own need to cut away his past, the people who'd shaped him into what he'd become. He dropped the scrub brush and braced his hands on the wall. He let his head fall forward, for water to beat on his spine and rinse him.

The pink tinge of watered blood swirled around his feet. He watched it circle the drain, slide across his toes.

When the water ran clear, he shut it off.

Then he reached for the plastic bottle, popped off the cap and closed his eyes. Like a ritual, he poured the clear liquid over his head. It was cool as it slid down his back, the witch hazel stinging—and cleaning him perfectly.

Panama

Heat rippled up from the floorboards, thickening the air till it hung like a spongy curtain, lifeless and still. Cisco leaned back against the wall, and wished for the cool clime of Virginia as sweat pearled on his forehead, dripped down his back and ruined his last clean shirt. The safe house wasn't safe, just a small two bedroom near the airport that was vacant for their use. A staging area for bringing treasonist bastards like Evan Pontelli back to stand trial. With or without extradition papers.

Pontelli was smart to leave his home country. His biggest fault wasn't in dealing with a weak man like Hoag, but in his confidence. Agents had picked up the sharpshooter before Cisco landed, in a bar and telling tales out of school. Unfortunately for him, there was a female undercover CIA agent tailing him and within hearing distance.

Cisco watched interrogators work on the sharpshooter. They were being too gentle, he thought, and after two hours of this, he pushed away from the wall and strode closer. The Under Secretary of Defense took away any restraints, and he was pissed enough to use his advantage. "Out, all of you."

"Sir, we are—"

"Under my orders." The room emptied and Cisco turned back to the man. He was former army, sniper qualified. The raid on his apartment got them enough evidence: the weapon he used and bullets. But that's not what he wanted. He wanted names. People.

"You know you'll get life for engaging in a blatant act of treason and murder, Pontelli."

The man's expression didn't change, staring straight ahead.

"Those weren't good old boys you picked off, they were Marines."

His prisoner's features pulled with the realization, yet his gaze never flexed.

"You were military; you know what will happen to you if you make it to Leavenworth? They'll all know . . . I'll make sure of it."

Pontelli understood. The color draining from his face was a giveaway. Cisco didn't have to explain that his fellow prisoners would shred him the minute they learned he'd committed treason. While there were thieves, dealers, and killers in Leavenworth, there was still a code. The brotherhood protected their own—and their country.

Cisco slipped out his own butterfly switchblade. He toyed with it, flipping the razor thin blades in and out of the handle. The scissoring sound made Pontelli flinch.

Pontelli watched him, watched the blade. "You don't scare me, agent man."

Cisco flicked the knife at him; the man howled. He stepped back to watch him bleed. There were two thin slices through his shirt, enough to sting and bleed, but not life threatening. Yet.

"Do you know the bacteria and disease running rampant in this country? An open wound is just asking for it." He flicked and made two more cuts.

Pontelli stared at the far wall, his craggy features tense. "Fuck you."

He flipped open the blade and held it to his cheek. "Ears come off so easily."

Pontelli jerked his head aside and glared. "What good will it do? They covered their asses."

"Who?"

He didn't respond.

Cisco made another cut. Pontelli sucked in a sharp breath. "Who gave you your instructions?"

"He didn't leave his name."

"Who was your partner?" But Cisco knew, intelligence agents were swarming over the country looking for Keith Sagnier. Cisco hoped he got two in the head before he could question him. He made another cut, near his throat.

"Fuck fuck!!" Sweat rivered down his face and chest, melting with his blood and dripping on the floor. "I never saw anyone till we got on the mountain! The other guy was already there. You can't pin anything on me, man. Paid in cash by mail to a P.O. box. Maps, times, instructions, and nothing more. I burned it all."

He was too damn smug. Cisco cupped his hands and popped Pontelli on the ears. His eyes rolled violently.

"*What* were your orders?"

"No one gets off the mountain alive!"

"You failed."

The man looked up. Blood trickled from his ears. He didn't hide his expression soon enough.

"You should have gotten them all, Pontelli, because there's a highly trained, highly pissed off U.S. Marine looking to put two in your head."

"Like he could," he scoffed. "You have to protect me, anyway."

"Says who?" Disgusted, Cisco walked out. Agents converged on the porch, looked beyond him to the suspect and back. "Patch him up and take him home. We're done here." He felt no guilt over his methods. It got him what he needed fast, proving Pontelli was just an appendage in the operation, a greedy fool with a blind as a bat mentality.

Cisco slid into the waiting car and headed to the airport.

Whoever planned this attack was thorough and cunning. He suspected the South African, Van Meer, but had no direct connection to the man. Being associated with idiots like Pontelli wasn't enough for a conviction. Associating with anyone on the NSC, was.

Regardless of the USD's orders, he would dissect the private lives of anyone involved. The truth was there, he just had to keep digging. Fast.

Peter Wickum stood by as the coroner lifted the black body bag into the wagon, transferring it into Federal custody. The bullets and lack of fingerprints said the body was one of the men who'd attacked the Cradle. From the MI-6 files, he knew who the man was: Thomas Maitland. And he was fresh.

"He's ours, dammit, and we need to find out who killed him. It's our jurisdiction," the police officer said.

"NSA supercedes, and right now, officer, you're lucky we don't charge you for withholding information on the hunter." Pete believed he could have prevented Hale's kidnapping if they'd known about Wilson sooner. Cisco didn't want to believe Wilson killed Combs, but finding him with Hale was proof enough for Pete. She would never have gone with him if he'd killed the agent.

"You people didn't give me a chance, took the tape and left. He was long gone anyway."

"Stay clear of this," he warned. "You don't want to deal with my boss again."

As the wagon pulled away, Wickum climbed in the SUV, drove back to the kill site. He parked and left the truck, walking with a fellow agent up the hillside. He stopped beside the yellow tape and used night vision binoculars again to see the view from the kill zone. Only the tops of the tents weren't in range, the trees blocking most of the view. That the body was dumped so close to the crime scene compound sent a message Pete understood.

He's still here.

He had what he came for, why risk capture? It was a taunt, he realized, and he moved down the mountain, and stood under the trees, hoping the tree trunks were less ob-structive than the branches. They weren't. A branch cracked, and he lurched out from under the tree before debris hit. The agent with him shone the flashlight over the broken wood. It was a live branch, not rotted, and attached to it was a sev-ered hand. Instantly, he stepped back and flashed his light up-ward.

"Good God."

Crucified to the thick trunk by wires was a man's body, in street clothing, yet masked. It was folded to the right, dan-gling from one arm, the severed wrist dripping blood. The feet were bound together, yet suspended in the air.

"Get a forensic team up here."

The other agent spoke into his radio as Pete searched for footprints. His presence probably destroyed most already, yet he walked the surrounding area, wondering how the killer got the body up there, then noticed scrapings on the far side of the tree, grouped holes in the trunk. Boot spikes, the kind tree climbers use, Pete thought. He bent, pushing leaves and pine needles aside and he found impressions. Nothing deep, clearly destroyed to hide the prints, yet he squatted for a mo-ment, taking note of a faint heel imprint. He followed its di-rection.

Another fifteen minutes passed before he located exactly what the killer wanted him to find. Agent Combs's badge and wallet. Cleaned of prints, no doubt. Then he experienced ex-actly what the killer intended; humiliation that they'd been chasing suspects they'd never find. This deadly display also meant the killer was on the mountain while NSA and CBC teams were scrambling to figure out what happened.

Fury stirred in him. He wanted this SOB before, now he wanted to be the man to kill him. He left the scene untouched and returned to look up at the body. He inspected the boot sole. Large, and familiar. If they matched the tracks they found outside Hale's house, he could surmise that these were the killers.

Whoever did this was either laughing at them, or apologizing by murdering Combs's killers and handing them over. Sick.

Yet this display was a statement; *nothing can touch me and I'll kill everyone who has.* It made the leader all the more elusive.

The position of the body said something religious. He'd let the psychologists deal with that; the least of his problems now. He withdrew his phone and hit speed dial, then put it to his ear. Cisco was going to be really pissed.

Cisco was on a secure line as the jet landed, a door between him and the other agents closed. He knew they were wondering what was going on but when the Under Secretary of Defense called you, everything stopped.

"Sir?"

"I wish I had better news, but we had army CBC test Hale's formula from the data she entered before the attack."

Okay, he thought. This was a wise move.

"It doesn't work."

"Hell."

"It's close, they tell me, but not close enough. Something about convulsions."

Clearly the USD didn't know anymore about chemical reactions than he did. "Then whoever has the data, knows that, sir."

"You're one ahead of me, Agent Cisco. Explain."

"They are still hunting her for one of two reasons; to stop her from recreating it again for us, or because they need her. If what you say is true, it's the latter."

"I agree. *We* need her now. They have the gas and could use it. We have no defense against it."

"When I find her, I'll bring her in."

"Let's hope you do that before someone dumps this crap on us."

"Yes, sir."

The USD ended the call, Cisco rubbed his mouth and stood, then moved to the door, and threw it open. He was sworn not to reveal a word about Hale's formula. He couldn't tell them why, only give orders.

"We need Hale, Wilson has her. I want ideas and don't wait for my approval to use them."

Jack rapped on the bathroom door. She didn't answer. "Syd, I'm sorry." He heard a sniffle and it sliced through him like a blade. He rubbed his mouth. Man, he really needed to learn to think first, speak second.

"It's for your own safety, baby, the less you know the better."

She threw open the door, her eyes red and her face flushed. "You think I'm impressed by all this cloak and dagger crap? I'm not." She scrubbed a towel furiously over her bloody jeans, then threw it down and pushed past him into the hall. She stopped, delivered a chilling glare, and said, "I've trusted my life to you, Jack. I broke my oath *for you*. I deserve to know more about why I should keep blindly trusting you."

"You won't like it." That he was even considering it was madness. The knowledge would scare her, leave her vulnerable. What he did was sometimes very ugly. Then her loss struck him again; her trust, security, the friendships she'd made in the Cradle, her credibility, it was all gone. She was alone, innocent, and the danger to himself could never compare to destruction of her life.

But secrets drive women away.

"Please, Jack, I need to know." Her lip quivered.

Jack could have taken just about anything but that. "I'm part of special teams." He advanced, crowding her, his gaze locked on her like a target. "I go where I'm needed at a moment's notice and for however long it takes. Hell, I've been in the U.S. for only eight months in the last three years." He kept moving as he spoke, forcing her to retreat, wanting her to hear every word and be very clear about who he was.

Suddenly, it was all that mattered.

"The scar on my side? A Taliban soldier gave that to me and left me for dead in the Kush Mountains."

The backs of her legs hit the bed. "Taliban?" Her mind instantly tumbled with what he had to do to get to that point, what that truly meant.

"I'm authorized to steal, capture or kill threats against America and its citizens."

She blinked, wide-eyed with shock, his brutal honesty impacting hard.

"And I'll do anything in my power to see the mission succeeds."

She dropped onto the bed. "God, you almost sound like Cisco."

His features pulled taut, the comparison stinging. "I warned you." He spun on his heels and quit the room.

Sydney watched him go. He was one of *those guys*, she thought, the ones you know might exist but people never wanted to know for certain. The average person, she supposed, would lump them all together in the battle against terrorism, never thinking of the risk, the length they'd go to to crush it. But Jack had dismissed everything, left it behind and faced the real human threat head on.

Close enough to be stabbed.

She'd bet the men murdered on the mountain were just like him.

Suddenly, she hopped off the bed, and limped after him. "Jack, wait."

He went still in the hall, his back to her. His rigid spine spoke volumes. He didn't know what was coming, yet he awaited the blow, for her to accuse or defame, then turn away from him. She couldn't, and as she closed the distance behind him, he knew she never would.

She felt lost, alone as he was. She started to touch him, to make him look at her, then she simply slid her arms around his waist and laid her head on his back. "Thank you."

Jack slammed his eyes shut, tipped his head back, and for a moment he held his breath in the stillness. Then he covered her hands. "For what?"

There was an odd catch in her voice. "For being who you are, for doing what you do." His courage alone was almost unfathomable.

He pried her hands off and turned to face her. "You've got to swear that—"

She held up her right hand. "I do. I swear. Not another word." She laid her hand to his jaw. "Ever."

Jack turned his face into her palm, brushed a kiss there as he drew her into his arms. "Thanks." Without her shoes, she felt even smaller in his arms and he held her tightly, aching inside. He'd never trusted a woman enough to reveal even this much and Jack knew he never would again.

He felt her fingers dig, and she nuzzled her head and shoulders to fit snuggly in his embrace. It brought a smile, and he was strangely touched by the comfort she found there— and how good it made him feel. He pressed his mouth to the top of her head, rubbing her spine.

She let out a long sigh. "Can we seal this new oath with a kiss?" She looked up at him. "Maybe, huh, huh, maybe?"

He smiled slightly as his gaze traveled over her face, the fall of her dark hair, just noticing the gold flecks in her brown eyes. Her expression was at once innocent, and sexy. A hell of a combination. Jack wasn't much on centerfold types, pretty was good but most times, after a couple months, he didn't like what he found beneath. With Syd, he already knew what lay beneath, aside a wicked sense of humor.

"Well, don't just jump to answer. Take your time."

"I'm thinking, a kiss will never be enough," he murmured, lowering his head.

"I'm so wide open to suggestions it's pathetic."

His dark chuckle rumbled in the hallway an instant before he laid his mouth over hers. Something unfamiliar crackled through him. It wasn't instant, it'd been there, waiting—in that place he'd packed away most of his emotions, the need to link himself with her when he'd been solitary for so long. He kissed her and kissed her and somewhere in between, the barrier broke, poured like water from a shattered dam.

Sydney felt it, a difference in him. Patience turned possessive, as if he was staking claim, that he knew she'd deny him nothing of herself. She wouldn't. His hands splayed her back, driving up her spine as his warm mouth rolled back and forth over hers. She felt his restraint, his need to crush and take. Her brain went fuzzy, her thoughts centered on only one thing. *More. I want more with this man.*

Jack gave. "You know where we're going." It wasn't a question.

Yet her answer spoke when her tongue slid into his mouth, in her hips rising to mesh with his. Jack nearly roared, letting go a little more. His hands mapped her contours and she moaned, a delicious little sound that nearly tore through his restraint.

Impatiently, he backed her up against the nearest wall, devouring her mouth as his hands plowed over her body.

She winced and jerked back. "Ow, sorry, oh, that stings."

He looked down at her leg. It was bleeding again. "Oh, hell. Sorry, baby. Let's have a look now. Have a seat in the kitchen, the light's better."

Almost robotic, he turned away, and went deeper into the house. She stared at his back for a second, too turned on to move.

Then he called out, "And take those pants off, too."

She smiled. "You're always telling me to do that." She went into the kitchen and slipped her jeans off.

He came back with a large plastic toolbox. "And you keep doing it. What's that say?"

She sat at the kitchen table in panties and a T-shirt, peeling the layers of gauze. Her breath hissed.

"Stop that before you tear the skin," he said, and she looked up. He tugged her to her feet, gripped her at the waist, and lifted her to the counter. She gasped at the cold stone under her bare skin.

"Do you always just do what you want without asking?"

He looked chagrined. "By your leave, ma'am, I'm not used to waiting to take action."

"That just excites me all over. Bossy men, who'da thunk it?"

He snapped on latex gloves. "Wiseass." He carefully cut the bandage away and started cleaning the wound. It was bleeding at the point of impact, but the rest was dried and sticky.

He wasn't all that gentle and Syd smacked him on the shoulder when it hurt too much. "Ease up. I'm not a Marine, ya know."

"Oh, I know." He winked, then rummaged in the large kit. He snapped the cap of a small plastic tube with a needle on the end. "It's Novocain."

"Is that necessary?" Though the leg felt on fire right now.

"Unless you have an amazing pain threshold, this is really gonna hurt. Too much blood is caked on the wound. There could be fibers from the jeans in it, glass. It did pass through the window. And who was telling me about how fast germs multiply?"

She gestured for him to keep working. "You could have stopped at fibers."

"I have to open it back up."

"Gee, no stick to bite and whiskey?"

"I have morphine."

She shook her head. "Go ahead." He injected the topical Novocain, then while he waited for it to take effect, he laid out his bandages.

Syd grabbed a stack and with some antiseptic, cleaned the couple of cuts on his jaw and neck. "They aren't bad. But you have flakes of glass only a shower will clean."

"We can try that later."

"We?"

He slid her a dark sexy look that liquefied her muscles. "Nothing gets past you, huh, Einstein?"

"Not unless I want it to. And I could jump on you right now, boo-boo an all, like an undersexed teenager."

"Undersexed?"

She lifted a bottle from the kit, read the label. "Antibiotics? Prescription?"

He got the message. She didn't want to discuss her sex life. Fine with him. His mind was already on that lacy bra he'd bought and how it looked on her—because the transparent panties were just about driving him nuts as it was.

"Rick's a corpsman, Navy."

"I thought he was a Marine."

He soaked a cloth in the sink. "Might as well be." He hesitated for a second, in voice and moves, then said, "He found me in the mountains."

Sydney felt oddly privileged. The tiny piece of him made her feel closer to him. Rick had saved his life. "I should thank him for that. But I swore an oath."

He glanced, flashed a smile, then applied a wet cloth to the wound, softening the dried blood. He blotted and rubbed, taking tweezers to pluck out debris. "This will burn," he warned and drizzled hydrogen peroxide on it. He blew and blotted again, but when she didn't utter a sound, Jack looked up.

She sat perfectly still, gripping the counter ledge, her lips tight. Yet tears cascaded down her face.

"Aw, honey I—"

"Keep going, please."

He felt helpless, a first in about a dozen years. Silent tears were a powerful thing to see, and he hated causing her more pain. She'd had enough for someone who didn't wear Kevlar to the office. She bit her lip, swallowed hard, trying so hard not to sob, and Jack leaned in and kissed her, focusing everything into it, a slow molten roll of lips and tongue. She responded instantly, and he felt a tender ache in his chest when she cradled his jaw and took control. It was an eating kiss, as if her pain flowed through it, almost dark and ravenous, and when he pulled back, she looked more exotic than before.

"It still hurts like hell." She sniffled.

"I was trying to take your mind off it."

"And that's all you came up with?" Her fingers dribbled down his chest to his jeans.

Christ, the woman was going to make him an idiot. "Give me a minute, I'll think of something else." Jack went back to cleaning the wound down to the tissue. It bled again.

Syd wanted to cry like a baby, but what good would it do? She stared at the long, narrow gouge, seeing exactly how close they came to dying today. She'd have a permanent reminder of how precious life had become.

"I know it looks bad," he said, "but it has to heal from the inside out. It's broad enough that stitches would just make the scar worse."

"The scar's the least of my problems."

He covered it with antibacterial ointment, then bandaged it. He sat, and propped her leg on his shoulder to wrap the Ace bandage around her thigh. "Bad fashion statement in a bikini?" He secured it, then pulled off the surgical gloves.

"As if. You do not want to see this body in a bikini." She was glad to think of anything but the pain right now.

His gaze lingered over her. "You underestimate yourself, Einstein." He kissed her bandaged leg.

"I rarely do, Jack. I know my weaknesses." She slid her leg off his shoulder, and for a moment she just stared. "Algorithms, English Lit, loading i-pods . . ." Suddenly, she gripped handfuls of his bloody shirt, yanked. "And right now—you."

Her mouth covered his in a swoop of heat and she put every seductive nuance into it. There wasn't much information in her past to gather. She'd spent her adult life getting her doctorate or using it. But she tried.

And she was winning.

Jack felt like a puppet being played and he let her. Her life was in shambles and she wanted control, wanted to command something and he let it be him. She teased, drawing back and making him chase her, then erotically licked the line of his lips before she pushed her tongue between. A hot, desperate need riddled him down to his heels as she kissed him. He wanted her, right now, on the counter, and the image made his dick like lead in his jeans. When she broke the kiss, it was to peel off his shirt. Her hands scraped over his skin, and she dragged her tongue across his nipple, then suckled.

It left him trembling, his head thrown back, and he gripped her hips, wedging closer. His hand slid upward, under her shirt, along her ribs, teasing the underside of her breasts cupped in a lacy bra. Her kiss intensified.

"Keep that up, Marine. Please."

He drew off her shirt, his lip quirking at the pink lace bra. A quick flick and it was falling. Jack swept it away. His gaze rolled down her body, and everything between them seemed to go still for a moment. By increments she leaned closer, her nipples grazing his chest. That first press of flesh to flesh held a sort of euphoria, crossing the line of intimacy. Jack had helped a lot of people, rescued many, killed to save them, but nothing compared to the single moment when you invited someone this close. He fought for patience when he was craving her like air, his body flexing with need. Although Syd might have a mouth on her, he sensed this was a brave thing to do.

She was still, waiting for his touch, watching his hands come toward her and when they did, Syd experienced something close to nirvana. She covered his big hands and arched and Jack kissed her and kissed her, loving her moans, her eagerness.

He wouldn't last long.

Not with her touching him like that, her small hands mapping his shoulders, sliding over his hair. He bent, his gaze locked with hers as he closed his lips around her nipple. She watched it, the erotic slip of his tongue over her flesh and her muscles tightened. The need to stretch was nearly uncontrollable. She had always had sex in the dark, never in broad daylight and certainly not on the kitchen counter. It was exciting, daring, and when his warm hand cupped her breast, thumbing her nipples as he tasted the other, Sydney went lax with desire, feeling every touch build toward the eruption. The anticipation was killing her.

Then he moved lower, across her stomach; carefully he spread her legs, moving between.

"Hurt?"

"Not where you think."

He held her gaze as his finger followed the edge of her panties, then tugged them down. He found her and her gasp tumbled into his mouth as he stroked her. At eye level, he missed nothing. Her panting, the way her hips started to move with him, her scent.

She hung on. "Jack, please."

He thrust his fingers inside, and she came off the counter, but he pushed her back till she lay flat, gripping the edge of her panties and pulling. Then his mouth was on her, tongue digging, and Sydney shrieked and squirmed.

"Oh, Jack. Oh, my God."

"Like?"

"Next week you can stop that. I want *you*."

"You won't make it that long."

"Says who? Jack!"

He flicked her clit, then circled it, over and over as his fingers slid in and out. He watched her writhe, draw her legs up and buck. He wanted to be there, and he would, yet Jack held her there, a testimony to his will when he wanted to slam into her and fuck her silly. But this was different. She was. The desperate situation or something else.

Right now, it just didn't matter.

She sat up and climaxed in his arms, clinging to him, her hips thrusting, her expression startled and so unlike any before. Transformed in ecstasy. A little wild, a little innocent. And he held her as she rode the wave of pleasure. Jack almost came just watching it.

When she settled, she went limp. Jack wrapped his arms around her.

"I won't ruin this by saying anything like wow, that was amazing and what's next."

Jack smiled to himself, and instead of talking, he cupped her behind and pulled her off the counter. Her legs went around his waist and she met his gaze, blushing a little. He felt the heat of her through his jeans as he walked, taking her where he wanted. To the bed. He lowered her legs to the floor. Her hands splayed over his chest, and Jack knew what he looked like. He saw it in the mirror every day. A train wreck. Yet she kissed old wounds and new scars as she opened his jeans wide.

She met his gaze, smiling smugly as her fingers dipped inside and wrapped him. His eyes slammed shut. His chest rose and fell hard.

"I should probably mention"—his lips coasted across her mouth, his hands sweeping over warm flesh—"that I haven't been with anyone for a very long time."

"Are you saying this might be a bit . . . brisk?"

"Probably."

"Then we'll just have to keep at it till we get a little patience."

He crushed her against him, burying his face in the bend of her throat. "Jesus," he murmured. "I've waited a couple decades to hear a woman say that."

Thirteen

"You're showing amazing restraint."

Hurriedly, he toed off his boots. "It's gone, all of it. I want to toss you on your back and go to town. Jesus, I feel like I'm seventeen."

She laughed and couldn't help touching him, finding new scars and tight tanned muscle as he shed his jeans.

She took a long look, letting her hands follow her gaze over ripped abs and broad thighs. He runs a lot, she thought, and when she wrapped his erection, he groaned. That perfectly male sound she hadn't heard in a long time.

"You're making me insane," he said, pulling her hand free, and she wrapped his neck, giving him free reign over her body. He took it, feeling the sleek turn of her hip, the soft warmth he wanted to enfold him. He insinuated his knee between her thighs, teasing her, rubbing and thrusting till she squirmed with need. Then he eased her back, one knee on the bed, then with a thrust of his leg, pitched her in the center of the bed.

Syd grinned, watching him come closer, all ropy and tanned, and he tossed the packet he'd had in his wallet. "Always prepared?" She pushed him back on his haunches and straddled his thighs.

"You never know when opportunity arises." The heat of her sex burned him.

She rolled the condom down. "Well, it's rising." He smiled, smoothed his hand over her hair and kissed her.

Anticipation rocketed through her, and she couldn't remember when she was this excited about a man, this fascinated at the play of skin as he moved.

"Your leg okay?"

"What leg?" She pushed his erection down, the tip teasing, and Jack gripped her hips, dragged her close, and slid into her in one smooth stroke. Eyes locked and they both breathed hard. The solid length of him was heavy and warm, and Sydney felt a little pain in her thigh, but the intense feelings rippling up her body overshadowed it.

Her nipples barely touched his chest, and he cupped her jaw with one hand, driving his fingers into her hair and tipping her head back. It was a possessive move, capturing her, and when she rocked, his kiss deepened. His hand slid down to close over her breast, his thumb making lazy circles while his other hand guided her, urged her. She never broke eye contact, her body undulating like a scarf in the wind.

Jack swallowed, glancing down to see himself disappear into her body. He slammed his eyes shut and fought for command, to keep words he probably shouldn't say from spilling, but planted deep inside her, his body wasn't listening. He leaned in, kissing her, easing her to her back. He withdrew and thrust, and Sydney bowed beautifully beneath him. She begged him to come closer, but he'd crush her so he grasped the headboard, one hand under her hips, giving them quick motion.

"Oh, yes, Jack. I want it faster."

"God, Syd," he groaned. "I'm barely hanging on here."

"Then don't."

It was a crack in the dam, a flood of energy and his hips pistoned. She met and matched, drew her knees up, planted her feet flat, taking him in. She whispered his name, what he was doing to her, how she felt—and her lusty words pushed him to the brink. Then he felt her tense, quicken, captivated as she reached between them to feel him slide wetly into her, then retreat. Her touch was heavy and bold, and he loved this side of her. Hidden under the scientist, sexy and daring. A little brazen. Her soft flesh hardened around him, trapped him in a throbbing flex of feminine muscle and slick skin.

Jack wanted more, to connect when he hadn't—wouldn't—allow himself to have more than casual and quick sex till the next call, the next mission. He laced his fingers with hers, trapping her, spread under him like a sacrifice. Hovering on stiff arms, he held her gaze. Waited for her to object.

She didn't. A tiny smile fluttering through her gasps. "Go to town, Jack. I won't break."

"Oh, Jesus."

His control severed, and Jack cocked his leg and thrust, driving her across the bed, a primitive roar climbing up his spine. He muttered an apology and shoved and shoved, and yet she still took him, her hips rising to grind to his.

Her breath hitched. Pale innocence met seasoned and scarred, his possession raw and savage. She came and held nothing back from him, whispering her satisfaction. A flex of twisted muscle and slick bodies meshed as his climax joined hers. And she felt it, accepted the power of this man, the brutal honesty in the moment.

Jack threw his head back, suspended, the wild grip of her flesh wringing him. Splintered rapture shredded his composure, swelled and ruptured. Yet in the deep throes of release, he noticed things. Every inch of her skin melting to his, her little tremors, the flare of her smoky eyes. "Ahh, Sydney," he whispered, driving his arms around her, the last threads of passion dissolving under a slow, thick kiss.

He rolled to his side, gently pulling her injured leg across his and watched her world come into focus. Her lashes swept up, her eyes soft and feline sexy. Her lips curved gently and Jack felt air lock in his lungs. Flushed and rosy, she was incredibly beautiful right then. More than a big brain and a list of degrees, he thought.

Needing to touch her again, he brushed her hair back, tucking it in behind her ear.

The gesture was so endearing, it made Sydney's heart clench. Her hand on his chest, she leaned in and kissed him. The move thrust her hips to his and he moaned, squeezing her.

"So." She nipped his lips, and his indrawn breath made her feel powerful. "You think Rick has more condoms around here?"

His smile was slow, then he laughed. "God, I hope so."

The nerve agents hadn't surfaced. Cisco had gone so far as to strip himself of any government markings, put on jeans and leave his face unshaven and hair out of the ponytail before he flew to Miami to meet with a DEA field operative and moved into deadly company. But he'd heard nothing, no matter how much money he'd spread around. No rumors, no intel, not even a peep. None from the FBI people who were damned pissed they hadn't been kept in the loop as the CIA was.

The lack of knowledge amongst Mafioso's and cartels told him they were keeping a tight lid on it, or it hadn't left the country. He'd put a lock on all air, sea, and auto travel, alerts on the most watched list of terrorist threats, and the TV networks issued a heightened terror warning to cover the upscale in manpower. Hundreds of agents were searching, busting ass in airports and at borders.

The media leak was contained for now. Local police were pissed, but cooperating. He just wished he could find Hale and Wilson. His gaze shifted to the computer screen, his hands cupped around a paper cup of coffee. Martin Van Meer glared back at him, looking mean and violent from his Royal Marine photo.

MI-6 insisted he was in the U.S. They were glad to know that Van Meer's usual team was dead. They weren't surprised. Cash would get him interested, but he murdered at whim, when it suited, threatened and often for the delight in the power of taking a life.

He'd gone from hired killer to mass murderer.

"Yes, darling, late again. Forgive me?"

He listened to his wife, her energetic encouragement though she'd no idea what was happening to her family fortune. Wealth she'd entrusted to him. His children's inheritance. Her whole world centered on catering to him and the boys. She didn't think he realized that everything she did in some way benefited him, his image, the people who worked for him, but he did.

He said good-bye, hung up, yet couldn't take his hand from the receiver. He would much rather be with her, knowing she was curled on a sofa, reading, or writing notes to people.

Bertrand twisted at the soft call of his name.

"You shouldn't be here."

"Probably."

"He's watching."

"No doubt." She strolled across the office, removing her coat and throwing it on the sofa. She unbuttoned her blouse as she came toward him, her skirt sliding down. She stepped out of it, naked beneath. Her boldness always took him by surprise, slamming heat through him.

She hopped on his desk and with her foot, pushed the leather chair out. His gaze lowered over her lush body, and not once did the plump figure of his wife come into his mind.

Nothing shadowed this woman. "You want something?"

"Fuck me."

That shocked him.

"Right here, right now."

"This is a business. My office." Yet he gravitated toward her, his breathing labored and making his head light. He knew what would come and it made him hard. She intoxicated him.

She slid her foot over his crotch, her toes wiggling, then, when he was close enough, she gripped the waist of his suit slacks and pulled him the rest of the way. He could feel her sex through his clothes, the heat of it. She opened his belt, his zipper, her hands were inside, warm and molding him.

He stared down at her. "You're fucking him, aren't you?"

"You want him in line, right?"

"You're dealing with a very dangerous man."

"That's the excitement." She stroked him harder and harder, bent and licked him like a lollipop till he was arching back. Then she shifted on the desk, her elbows on the surface, and let her legs drop wide. He came out of his stupor to see her drag her fingers across her slit and show him the wet pink flesh.

Her gaze dropped to his crotch. "You have a problem I can solve."

Without any words, he pushed her flat on the desk and thrust into her in one powerful push. He didn't hear her moans, didn't kiss or fondle her, and simply hiked her legs around his hips and pumped into her. Her breasts bounced and she laughed, laughed! the entire time. He blocked her out, fucking her like a madman and when he came, it was heavy and quick. Nothing lasting, nothing profound. Just a fuck.

It was a couple minutes before he rallied his thoughts and he realized she'd come too easy. *She's been with him.*

He left her, turning his back.

"Don't come here again."

She sighed, pouted a little, then started to dress. "I come every time I'm with you, honey."

She was so easily had. But if she had thoughts of him leaving his wife for her, she was dreaming. His wife might not be young and sexy, but she was loyal, which was more than he could say for either of them.

And the last person he trusted was the one slipping into her shoes in his office.

"I need it. Now."

She glanced up, her expression sharp, the sweetness gone. "I know."

"No, you don't. I've got everything riding on this."

"Has he recreated it?" She gestured to the glass ceiling out his window.

"Not yet, but he will."

"Then we'll talk when he does." She grabbed her coat and purse, then left.

Pete Wickum knocked, then stuck his head into the room. It was a storeroom in a small warehouse, west of the Cradle, cold, drafty, and now filled with desks and computers, men and women using it for a field office.

Cisco typed on the laptop wired ten ways till Tuesday, and paused long enough to gesture for Wickum to close the door behind himself. Pete did, then took a seat and slid a bag across the surface.

"You look like shit, Boss."

"Thank you, Wick. I can always appreciate your honesty." He sat at a makeshift desk, interested on what scrolled up the screen.

"When did you sleep last?"

"I caught a nap on the plane. Something I need to know?" Cisco typed and read.

Wick pushed the bag a couple inches closer.

Cisco looked up, opened the bag, pulled out a wrapped sandwich. "Thanks." Without even looking at what he ate, he chowed down. The heavy drop of food in his stomach made it clench.

He kept reading reports. Bodies had been taken out of the facility while he was gone, the coroner doing his job. It wasn't hard to tell how they were killed, but the missing fingers gave him pause. Guerilla fighters often took souvenirs from their kills—jewelry topped the list, sometimes ears, but fingers were cumbersome, identifiable, and after a couple days, they'd rot and smell.

Cisco sat back, wiped his mouth with a napkin, then looked at Wickum.

Pete took it as a signal and read from his notes. "Both bodies on Skyline were positioned like a crucifixion. One in the tree, the other on the ground. I don't know the significance of that. No time to string them up, maybe." He tossed a wallet on the table.

Cisco opened it, his features pulling tight. *Combs.*

"Wilson didn't do it."

"I know. I knew that I think," he admitted. "The man pisses me off because he knows he should bring Hale in."

"All the shooting going on at the boat, I'd say we broke even more trust."

Cisco sneered.

The man never sneered, Pete thought. He was usually impassive, holding back emotions. This was getting to him, he thought. "Forensics found traces of blood on the chute packs, old, maybe three days longer than blood samples in the Cradle. We have matches all around with the heel prints on the mountain, with the bodies on Skyline. Face matches, according to MI-6 and the blood type matches Van Meer; but since they don't have a sample, and DNA marking for military is with our government, not theirs, we're not going further with that. And the FBI is really pissed at you."

"I'll live."

"The access you gave me . . ."

Cisco perked up, willing anything to come his way.

"We could be hunting for weeks. I mean, this project is committeed to death. One for finance, one for research and development. Some serve on both. The finance committee consists of several high-level senators and scientists. Two of which are directly associated with Dr. Hale. A couple senators gave her glowing reports on her progress with the Implosion bomb. Other than that, no personal connection. Though

Senator Mackelson is related to her assistant, Handerson, and yes, he was one of the attack victims," Pete said when Cisco scowled.

He jotted the name down. "I don't want association. I want the people who'd have access to classified Intel and a reason to steal."

"All of them have access to documents. No one had access to the Cradle's data without USD's authorization, which he did not give as far as I can tell."

"Crap."

"Once cleared for the NSC on this, they shared information. Too many cooks, if you ask me."

"And they expected it to remain secret? Christ."

"If you want to narrow it down, Gabe, no one had the access codes to get inside except Mother, and the scientists. So this brings us back to your theory of who gave them up."

"They're all dead except her."

"And the scientists not on duty that day?"

"We have surveillance on them, but so far, they're taking it like a vacation. You'd think they'd be upset they're out of a job and all their friends are dead."

"They don't know that, Wick."

"How could I forget?" Man, it was tough keeping track of who knew what. "According to Mrs. Hale, Lila Handerson visited her just after the attack, however Handerson has disappeared. We've searched her home and haunts, nothing. She had a trip to the Caribbean booked with her husband before the attack but hasn't used the tickets."

Cisco frowned. "We have an agent on Hale's mother?"

"Only recently. The female agent is in the house next door."

Cisco nodded, and Wick glanced at his notes. "One connection I have is that a member was Dr. Hale's graduate studies professor, Daniel Kress, another was her boss for a while, and recommended her for the position based on her theories for the implosion bomb." He flipped a page in his notes. "Professor Jabez Nazier. Both are now on the finance committee."

"Could be one hand greasing the other in Washington. Dig deeper."

"I've looked into personal attachments, and I'll have something on personal finances that's more than a D.C. bank account in a few hours, maybe less."

A sharp knock rattled the thin walls, and Marcuso stuck his head in. "I've got something." Cisco waved him in.

"Captain Wilson has no listed phone numbers, and I mean, not anywhere."

"How is that something?" Cisco snapped, then rubbed his temple, the constant throb stung his eyes.

"Eat something else will you?" Wick said. "You're a crabby bitch today."

Marcuso's brows shot up at that.

Cisco slid him a narrow stare, yet worked on the second sandwich. It tasted like fried grease, but he was too hungry to object. "Go on."

"Everything about this guy is pretty much low key. At first look, he's got normal stuff, house, truck, phone. But he has a satellite phone."

Cisco's head jerked up. "I knew that; he's not answering because we found it in his house."

"Yeah, but Wilson's been on foreign soil a lot. Cells don't work where this guy's been, undercover; can't have stuff marking him. So I'm thinking, maybe he gets issued a satellite phone for the field. I checked. He still has it."

Cisco leaned forward, waiting for the rest. There had to be more; his days were just going downhill too fast not to have more shit hit the fan at least once an hour.

"Not the kind you can buy in a store. He wouldn't use telecommunications satellites; someone could intercept that. This one bounces off of surveillance birds. Strictly military frequency."

"He's on call twenty-four-seven," Pete added. "No matter what, he wouldn't shut it off."

"Technically, he's on leave."

"But he doesn't have to turn it back in."

"God dammit, how come we didn't know this two days ago?"

"Other than we didn't know Wilson even existed and was on the mountain? And we didn't have access to that kind of Intel. It's clandestine. This guy is hot shit. A little scary. No matter what you think you can do to him, his record will stand up against you."

"Yeah, we'll see." Cisco pulled out his cell phone and dialed.

Syd had more energy than a platoon, Jack thought. He could sleep for a week right now. He smiled as she jammed the last of a sandwich in her mouth, then eyeballed the food spread out between them. Her appetite was astounding, he thought, his gaze trailing over her. She'd showered, or rather, they had; her hair was still wet and she wore an old olive green T-shirt of his. He didn't know what it was about women and wearing men's clothes, but he understood the attraction. The shirt was too big, tissue thin from so many washings and left nothing to his imagination. Not that he needed to stretch it. There wasn't a part of her he hadn't explored. Thoroughly. He actually knew what it was like to ravish a woman.

"Did you make your list?"

"I was having some wonderful sex, so no. Sorry."

He smiled. Yeah, the first time was great. After that, it just got better. Damn if the little egghead wasn't a wildcat in the sack.

"You look so different when you do that," she said, and leaned in to kiss him.

Her lips never met his. She sat up, frowning. "Do you hear that? It's a buzzing."

Jack dragged his attention off her, then leapt off the bed, grabbed his jeans and shoved his legs into them before he raced out of the room.

Sydney dusted her hands, then followed. He grabbed that weird phone off the desk.

"It's an Autovon line."

"A what?"

"A government line." He answered. "Who is this?"

"Special Agent Gabriel Cisco. Don't hang up."

"Give me one reason." Jack grasped Sydney's arm, pulling her with him to the bedroom. He covered the phone. "Dress, now. Cisco."

Sydney's eyes flared wide, then she immediately searched for her clothes.

"We can protect her," Cisco said.

"Not good enough."

"He's looking for you, you know that."

Jack said nothing. This wasn't news. Jack's goal was to avoid him and go right to the top to the one who gave the orders.

"You put her life in danger, Wilson."

Sydney rushed up to him, tucking in her shirt.

"And you used an innocent woman as bait. There were men watching her place, a van outside, and you leave her with one man?" Jack clamped his mouth shut. Debating security now wouldn't accomplish a thing. "Christ, Cisco, you'll use anyone, and I'm not letting you do it to her." He let her listen in.

"I'm actually grateful you took her when you did. My agent is dead."

"Oh, God, Combs," Sydney whispered.

"I knew I should have ghosted those two," Jack muttered.

"Then you'd be charged with manslaughter."

Sydney leaned in to say, "So would you, Cisco. You let my team die down there."

Cisco hesitated, and Jack knew she'd hit a mark. "We need Dr. Hale to finish and create her formula."

Jack went still, silent.

Cisco pressed. "The vials are still missing and could be used."

Syd covered the phone. "They don't know I completed it."

"And we don't want him to know. Not yet."

"But if Cisco wants it, he'll ruin you to get it, Jack. You're risking your career for me. This is out of hand, maybe you—"

"No. We finish this. And I'm damn sure not leaving you to the wolves." He clutched her, pressing his lips to her forehead. "We're a team, Einstein. I've already lost one and I'm not losing another. Especially not you."

Then in the phone he heard, "I could charge you with kidnapping, and I'm sure you know obstructing a federal investigation is a crime."

"So is covering up *murder.*" He cut the call.

Jack started to put the SAT phone down, then went still. "Oh, damn." He looked at her. "This is how he's tracking us."

"Who, Cisco?"

"No, the shooter. Man, how did he get the frequency? It's classified."

"But isn't that one of the militaries?"

"Yeah. Jesus, that took some doing."

"NSC you think? Or Cisco?"

"Not Cisco; he would have used it a long time ago if he knew about it." Jack was already walking to the garage, and Syd followed. He grabbed a hammer, and put the phone in a vise on a workbench. "Stand back." He smashed it, and kept hammering till it was nothing more than tangled wires and chips.

"Do you feel better now?"

He sifted through the pieces. "There's a locater chip." He found it and dropped it to the floor and ground it beneath his heel. Then he trashed the rest. He grasped her arm, pulling her back into the house.

"Jack?"

"We need to leave. Now. Clear everything, Syd. Stuff it in a trash bag, we'll take it all with us and dump it." He sat at the computer, clearing the hard drive. Done, he grabbed his gear bag, refilling it.

Sydney gathered the sheets and started to put them in the washer, then opted for the trash. Jack pulled on a shirt, then his boots, racing to throw their things into the black Escalade. They did all they could to destroy or remove any evidence they had been there, but they couldn't get it all.

"I've got the medical kit," he called and loaded it in.

She rushed into the garage. "Okay. I'm done."

"Let's go." Jack went back for a last look, then slid into the driver's seat and hit the garage door opener.

He was furious, she could feel it in his stiffness, see it in the tight press of his mouth. She reached over and touched his arm. "You couldn't have known he'd get the frequencies, Jack."

"I know," he said through gritted teeth. "But this guy has an inside track and I underestimated him. I led him right to us!"

"But he can't now, right?"

"No, but given his performance so far, he's on his way."

He drove out into the open, a loaded gun on the console between them.

Fourteen

Cisco ended the connection, tapping the phone against his mouth.

"Must be really hard for you when they don't do as they're told."

He looked up at Wick. "You're awfully smug." He redialed and got nothing, then laid the phone aside.

"You can't threaten him. That's what bugs you. He's the only reason she's alive."

Cisco waved that off. "Where would he go next?"

"That depends on what they know."

Marcuso stepped inside without knocking. "They were in Annandale. A house belonging to a Navy corpsman who's in Iraq. Who, by the way, won the bronze star for saving Wilson's life. But you didn't hear that from me."

Because it was classified.

"*Were* in Annandale?" The team was zeroing in as they'd talked.

"We weren't fast enough."

Cisco wasn't surprised. Convinced Wilson would keep Hale safe, he still needed her to do whatever she could to this formula. That, according to data, didn't work yet, but didn't mean it couldn't work. A hell of a lot to ride on one woman's brain, he thought.

"Put an APB out on the corpsman's vehicle. Tag them; we need her."

Wickum frowned, but Cisco couldn't explain. Hale's Kingsford serum was more than classified and he'd already broken a couple rules by giving Wick the USD's access.

He turned to what he knew. "Van Meer's been wounded, that's for certain, since it was his blood on the elevator doors." They had a DNA blood match from a bombing in Ireland, the U.S. embassy had sent by Interpol.

Wickum's phone rang and he answered, spoke, then handed it to Cisco. "MI-6 and you're not going to like Van Meer's recent M.O."

Black market weapons. He had the contacts to sell.

Jack took surface roads, intentionally putting them in heavy traffic. The more people around the less chance of a hit, he'd said. It wasn't comforting.

"You really think he's near?"

"He'd had that frequency for a while." For good measure, he'd disconnected the GPS in the car. "He was probably very close when we were in the house."

"That just gives me the creeps." Sydney looked around at the other drivers. "I wish I knew what he looked like." Big, was all she remembered, crazy blue eyes. Between them were two prepaid cell phones, activated and with a walkie-talkie feature. It was the last of his cash and Sydney wondered what they'd do next. They couldn't use credit cards or even the ATM. All traceable. Avoiding capture was a careful game of chess.

Yet, right now, they had no one to turn to and no place to go. Almost everyone she knew was dead, and they both knew their only chance of survival was the formula. Syd almost wished she hadn't created Kingsford. Wished it had failed and she was still in the Cradle.

"What if this is a ruse?"

"Huh?" He changed lanes.

"What if this getting the formula is a ruse and what that guy really wanted was the gas vials."

"Possible." But Jack wasn't biting. "The gas could be made outside the U.S. in a country with less restrictive regulations."

"But that means we're chasing a ghost."

"We already were, honey." He reached, grasped her hand. "And it doesn't change anything. We still need your Kingsford."

After a stoplight, Jack turned left into a large empty parking lot. At the far end was a huge warehouse that looked abandoned.

"Hotel accommodations?"

He smiled. "God, I love how your mind works. No, I have some people who owe me a favor and I'm cashing in."

There was a small sign on the front right, the name faded. Something about distribution, though it lacked a storefront or trucks. Jack drove around back.

"Are they trustworthy?"

"Yeah, a little odd though."

"You've never met many scientists then. Our metallurgist, Ron Wagner, had purple hair at his temples and a nose piercing."

Jack made a face. She knew that was coming. He was mister conservative. Except in bed, she thought, smiling to herself. "Ron was having an affair with Lori McKeen, his data analyst."

"His?"

"She'd input his data, double-checked it. They were of like minds. But some of the team didn't approve of their relationship."

"Why not?"

"Jealous, I guess. It was clear when they were together that they'd had sex and it was mutually satisfying."

"I hear ya." He winked and loved her light blush. "What about you, Einstein? Any affairs with the other scientists?"

"My work took up most of my time."

"That's not what I asked."

She looked him dead in the eye and could see a little jealousy bloom. "No. I wasn't interested, though I got hit on."

"By whom?"

"Tanner mostly." She looked away. "God, I liked that kid." She sniffled.

"Tish was the bug girl, what about the rest?"

She was grateful for the distraction. "Piccolo was a real geek, a biohazard specialist, small, had a couple of nervous ticks. Corporal Tanner enjoyed rattling his cage when he checked on the security. Pic could handle the most dangerous chemicals, but a man with a gun intimidated him. He was a weenie."

"Who could have betrayed the team, Syd?"

She scowled, not liking that line of thought one bit, then sighed. "Anyone, though none of them had a single stake in it. We all worked together, all of them benefited as the project did. Since the first implosion bombs were successful, the next step was to develop a larger one. We'd just started the schematics. We had funding for extreme measures, high risk, low return. I'm the only one who had work that didn't include them. Handerson was second in command; he only assisted me when I asked."

She stopped, frowning to herself.

"What?"

"Matt Collier called me the morning of the attack. Ransley, Cooper, and Spellman didn't. But Mac said they'd been questioned."

"Handerson was inside?" She nodded. "And his wife went to your mom's right?"

"Yes." It came out warily. "She probably knew of his death by then."

"And went visiting? Not likely."

"Then why?"

Jack didn't want to worry her, but had to be frank. "Hurting your mother would serve a purpose, force you to do what they wanted."

"You're scaring me."

"Maybe Lila just needed to get out. She have anyone close?"

"Not that I know of, but we didn't socialize. Discussion of the project outside the Cradle was forbidden."

"But you did with Tish Bingham."

She felt unreasonably defensive. "She's dead, what does it matter?"

"I'm just trying to get the big picture."

"No, neither of us wanted to talk about work. She was a good entomologist but she wasn't as committed as I was. We did the shopping and nails thing, but I hadn't seen her in a week or so. We worked a different shift." Sydney worried the edge of her jacket, her mind coming back to her mom. "My mom's old Jack, and kind. She'd give a stranger a hot meal. She wouldn't even know she was in danger till it was too late."

"I'll think of something, I swear. Even if I have to call Cisco." Right now, Jack put faith in Cisco. It was all he could do.

He parked out of sight of the street, then got out, coming to her side. She swung her leg out, then groaned. "Easy baby, it'll be stiff."

"It wasn't before."

"You gave it a workout."

She flashed him a superior look. "Me? I had help."

"And I'll be happy to make you tired and stiff again, ma'am." He encircled her waist, kissed her once, then helped her to the door.

She leaned into him. "I wish we were back there, alone, shutting out this mess."

"And doing it outstandingly well," he murmured in a voice that made her melt.

She turned her head and he did what she wanted. He

stopped everything to kiss her. A delicious reminder of the few hours past. "So what was Handerson like?"

She made a sour face, telling him she'd rather keep kissing and get busy somewhere private.

"Happily married. He was a good guy, but he liked the team to know he was second in command. I assigned him the tour for the finance committee the—"

He stopped short. "What tour? When?"

"I thought I told you. The morning of the attack, the finance committee was supposed to arrive for a tour at seven-thirty A.M. They'd done it each year since the Cradle was in operation. They go through files, watch, listen, question. They're the money magnets, and come to see how it's used. They're condescending and my temper gets me in trouble, so I gave it to Handerson. He's pretty much a butt kisser and likes showing off his work."

"Did Cisco mention the committee?"

"No, they must have turned them back when Mother didn't warn them. They weren't due for another half hour or so." He had that dark familiar look that said he was pulling everything apart and dissecting it quickly. "What are you thinking?"

Jack tried to make a connection and failed. "If they never arrived, then they probably never left."

"If the warning system worked. It didn't."

"So why didn't that group get caught in the middle of it?"

She stared at him. "I don't know. Maybe they were radioed to turn back when Mother went down?"

"I was there at seven-thirty, and I didn't see anyone. I didn't see Cisco till I was in the ranger station a couple hours later."

Jack kept the thought in the back of his mind and was reaching for the button when a buzzer sounded.

Sydney flinched. On the wall of the building was a camera like a big eye staring back at them. It moved.

"We're not a public facility," came through a speaker.

"Open up, you apes."

"Who are they?" she asked quietly.

"They go by Sherman and Peabody." She chuckled to herself as he hit the buzzer, and said, "I can get inside, and you know it. Open up."

The locks instantly clicked and the door swung open. But there wasn't anyone there. Jack moved ahead, leading Sydney down a black corridor. Black lights shown down at the end, and when they reached it, a dark-haired man in a chair on casters shot across the room toward them.

He was young, a little plump, wearing black glasses, and looked as if he never left the chair, it molded his body so well. He stopped the chair in front of Jack.

Jack stared down, fists on his hips. "Christ, you're an ugly son of a bitch."

Sydney blinked. "Jack!"

The man grinned and came out of the chair, grabbing Jack in a bear hug. She let out a breath, smiling as Jack clapped him on the back, then pushed him off.

He turned to Sydney. "Doctor Sydney Hale, this is Sherman."

She shook hands, and he looked her up and down. "I didn't know you had good taste, Jack." He bowed and kissed her hand. "My lady."

"Cut the crap and let her go."

He did and stepped back, grinning.

"That one"—Jack pointed—"is Peabody." The other man tapped a key, then shot across the room, spinning the chair before stopping it. He took one look at Syd and whistled.

"Oh, you guys need to get out more," she said on a smile.

"When everything comes to us? Nah. Nice to meet you." He looked at Jack. "So what can we do ya for, Jack? You aren't here to visit." Peabody stood, checking out the cuts on his face.

Jack stepped back. "I need your help, and it's not all that legal."

The pair looked at each other and grinned. Back in the chairs, they spun and pushed across the room.

"I told you, odd," Jack whispered to the side.

"They look rather normal." Though the brow piercing was a bit much. And Jack was friends with them?

The two young men, no more than twenty-three she'd guess, sat at a massive workstation. It reminded her a little of the Cradle. Sherman and Peabody manned computers just as large, a server, and the two workstations each had about five flat screens at different heights with just as many keyboards. One was running a War Craft game. Above them on the cinder block wall painted black was an array of medieval weapons and a couple cloaks. Reinactors? These guys were so pale they looked more like vampires.

"What do they do here?"

"We debug systems for several companies and the government," Sherman answered.

"It was either that or jail."

Peabody glanced over his shoulder. "Jack caught us, Dr. Hale."

"They hacked into DOD files and made a mess of the phones, troop allocation. Even sent themselves a couple fat government checks."

"Then why aren't they in jail?"

"They were only sixteen at the time."

Sydney looked back at Sherman and Peabody. They slid from terminal to terminal, pausing to sip a Coke or grab a handful of some junk food from the many open bags before tapping on the keyboards. Sherman typed on two different ones at the same time. Impressive.

"Okay, we're in and rolling."

Jack moved in closer. "Make the ID for her."

Sydney watched. It was almost like a dance. They rolled between the computers, the chairs slipping over the concrete floor that had been coated with wax. "Dr. Hale, please stand by that wall." Sherman propped a camera wired to the computer on a pedestal.

Sydney smoothed her hair and clothing. "These clothes don't look proper."

"I can change that; a suit?"

She blinked. "Well, yes. Preferably one I can't afford."

Jack stood behind them as they took her photo. She came to him as they loaded it up. Peabody went to town, smoothing her hair, giving her lipstick and a little makeup, then changing her T-shirt to a lovely Ralph Lauren suit. Charcoal gray with a pale lavender shirt.

"*Good* taste, you guys."

A sheet printed out and Sherman cut it, then put it through a laminating machine. He handed it to her. It looked like the real thing. It even had the watermark on the laminate. God.

"What next, Jack?"

"She needs these chemicals."

Sherman took the list, glanced between the two, then gave it to Peabody.

"You going into the drug business, Wilson?"

"No." They waited and he didn't speak.

"Suit yourself."

"They're here, at this supply facility."

Sherman worked the keyboard. Syd saw screen after screen blink in, then code, in nothing more than zeros over the monitor.

"You two might want to take a load off; this will take a while. Mega huge encryption coding. Echo block. Cool."

Jack guided Syd to the kitchen nearly half a block away; she slid into a chair.

She inclined her head to the boys. "Fill me in."

"I'm trying to get you everything you need."

"They can do that?"

"Yeah, good kids. Except near a computer that's unsupervised."

"They aren't monitored?"

"Sure, but I'm betting they've routed it so it's monitoring a daily work pattern and not what they are doing now."

"Clever."

"I'm in!"

Peabody cursed, and sat back as Sherman typed wildly. Jack and Syd hurried to the console. "You can pick it up at this address." He reached for the printer, his fingers wiggling as if that would speed it up.

He handed the sheet to Jack. Syd took it, checking the list. It was a computerized order, routed through a college Chemistry department. Whoa.

"Now we need access to a lab."

She tugged on Jack's arm and he bent. "Why not go to Johns Hopkins? I did my graduate and doctorate studies in immunology there and I could get us in."

He shook his head. "That's exactly why we can't. People know you and could spot you. Not to mention with your name in the news, the press are probably camped out."

She'd forgotten about that. "Yeah, it's not as if it shuts down at night, either."

"We need a lab that closes its doors after six."

"You're going to get us into some major trouble, aren't you?" Sherman said, and Jack turned back to them.

"No, wipe your trace. I take the blame for anything. I need credit cards, and cash."

"That's it?"

"It's enough for now," he said, giving Sherman a light shove. "Move the cash out of my own accounts too." He pulled out his wallet, slipping the bar code card free. "Can you tell me what this is used for?"

"Where did you get that?" Syd demanded.

"Off the guys staking out your place."

She took it, turning it over. "And the reason you didn't tell me was what?" She shoved it back, and glared up at him.

Jack escorted her a few feet away and said softly, "I couldn't do anything with it, so what's the point?"

"Honesty." She punched him in the side.

He leaned down. "Like you and Kingsford?"

"Okay, we're even."

"I didn't know I was competing."

"Shut up, Jack." She popped up and kissed him. Jack seized the opportunity and made her pay for her doubt.

"If you guys are going to keep that up, there're five bedrooms back there," Sherman called and pointed.

"That's good to know."

Syd blushed as Jack forced himself to let her go, then handed over the card. From under the desk, Sherman drew out a credit card scanner. These two could be dangerous if their talents were given free rein, she thought.

Sherman swiped it through, loaded, then brought it up on screen. Syd grabbed an open bag of chips and munched. Sherman glanced, then went back to work.

"It's an entry card. For some place called Chem-Loc."

"Oh, hell."

Jack snapped a look at her. She drew him away from the boys. "Our blood was tested, anonymously. I bet that was the chemical company that did it."

"Did they get anything tangible? Samples?" He was thinking someone had been inside the Cradle to get it.

She shook her head. "All done inside the Cradle and an information relay. Even I wasn't told what or who. It was unspecified, with only a number identification. They were not to know who they were testing or from where."

There went that theory, he thought. "Yeah, and the Cradle was supposed to be secret, too." She sent him a bitter look. "Sherman, get me what you can on Chem-Loc."

"How deep?"

"Deep six, buddy."

Sydney wasn't even going to ask what that meant. That they could get more than was published by the company said a lot about their skills.

Peabody spoke up. "I have a lab, a community college campus; it's minimal."

"I don't need much."

"Security?"

"Night watchman with a weapon. Hum?" Sherman peered at the screen. "It doesn't have motion sensors, but it's wired with alarms."

"Excellent."

She looked up at Jack. "When do we go?"

"Tonight."

"You want them in, get me the new frequency!" The jig was up with Wilson, Martin figured. He hated needing help to find the son of bitch.

"We can't—I can't, not anymore. Do you know what he had to do to get that? They've probably traced it to us."

"No they haven't. Stop panicking before I have to shoot you too."

He was silent as that sank in.

Van Meer smothered the urge to chuckle.

"Bring me the elements."

"They're safe."

"Do you know anything about storing those chemicals?"

"Don't speak to me as if I'm stupid," he warned. "I'm not."

"Sorry. Forgive me."

Van Meer settled back in the chair, flipping through channels, looking for anything on the bodies he'd left behind. He liked seeing his kills on the news. Almost like an ethnic cleansing.

"You're certain you haven't left . . . evidence around."

He glanced toward the bedroom. If he did, it was intentional. "When I get my money, I'll clean the rest up neatly." He shut off the TV, and stood, tossing the control aside before he walked toward the bedroom. "Get me what I need."

"I told you, it's not in my power."

"I've killed a lot of people for your deal, Bertrand; do it, or that round little woman of yours will be added to my collection."

"You touch a hair on her head and I'll—!"

"Shat up. You have no power over me, you greedy little fucker."

"I have your money."

Van Meer stilled, his eyes narrowing. "And I have the gas. Which do you think will be more effective in a standoff?"

He cut the call, pocketed the phone, and walked to the bed. She slept beautifully, almost as if she'd poised herself before nodding off. Probably did. He stripped, and climbed on the bed, waking her. When she turned to him with a moan, a stretch, he moved over, pushing her thighs apart.

"Martin?"

She sounded annoyed. He didn't care.

Bertrand discreetly slipped the phone into his jacket pocket, then rubbed his eyes. He was the wrong choice. Hadn't he warned them, he was the wrong choice for this?

He walked back into the living room and his guests. His wife buzzed around the room, chatting with each person, making certain they felt welcome. He was the one who shouldn't be here, but staying at the office, hovering over Montoya, wasn't making progress. Judas wanted what he couldn't deliver. Not anymore. They'd risked being revealed by getting into those classified files and while there was no connection to him, if this fell any farther apart, it would come to his door.

He needed the gas to destroy it properly. They'd had to take it with the formula, to cover the true theft and to give themselves time to duplicate it. The feds knew now, he thought. They had to. Too much time had passed. This was supposed to be done within twenty-four hours. Make the exchange and Judas would disappear. But nothing had gone right and as Bertrand accepted the dry martini from the caterer, he wondered when his world would crash.

Wickum entered the office. "Coroner says he wants overtime pay."

Cisco scoffed, his palm shielding his eyes. They'd only recently removed the last bodies from the Cradle and the coroner was busy, though the cause of death was obvious. Wick rolled a bottle of Tylenol across the desk. Cisco snatched it up, flipped the cap and poured some into his mouth. He swallowed without water.

"Tell me that smile means something," Cisco said.

"I looked into the personal finances of everyone with a link to the Cradle. Everyone's aligned with his or her salary but we have some rich people on the council. Really wealthy. Only one thing connects outside the council. What's Chem-Loc Corporation got to do with the Cradle?"

"They tested the blood of the Cradle scientists and the guards, all done anonymously," Cisco said, then turned to the computer, tagging up Chem-Loc in the DOD files and refreshing his memory. "The blood sample is read at the Cradle, nothing sent out physically. The inhabitants put their finger in a slot, got a small prick, and the data instantly went to the chemical company for analysis. No one knew which company it was and the company was not aware of whose blood they were testing or from where. Just what elements to search for, and deterioration."

"Why didn't Mother do it?"

"She did. Mother was the relay through Langley. Cradle computers had no outside link, except to Mother. But the analysis had to come from a secondary source. Double blind they call it. Eggheads insisted."

"Why not use the Army?"

"Because the Army didn't know about the Cradle, Wick. I don't make the decisions, I just enforce them." Cisco looked up. "So who are the guilty?"

"Dr. Kress, Senator Mackelson, and Dr. Nazier are major stockholders."

"How major?"

"Fifteen percent."

"Sizable, but not alarming."

"Except that they only recently bought in. Chem-Loc is on shaky ground. Not enough new discoveries. They research and develop, not manufacture. But they hold the patents on what they make after FDA approval. That should be millions but R and D take up the capital. CEO Raymond Bertrand tried to get financing for manufacture but couldn't swing it since Chem-Loc has been the subject of two hostile takeovers in the last five years. That's where Nazier and Kress stepped in. Mackelson was already a shareholder. Probably talked them into it, though who would invest in a failing company?"

"A tax write-off if it went belly up. Is it going under?"

"Not yet. But its teetering."

The ramifications hit him. Hale's antidote could save a dying company. Before he went wild with excitement, he needed proof, and questioning Kress or Nazier would alert them. He opened his mouth and Wick cut in with, "I've already put phone taps on Nazier and Kress."

"Good. Put them on the head of Chem-Loc, Bertrand's home, and all his researchers. And I want video surveillance on Bertrand. And not just outside." That would take some doing, to get cameras inside his offices, but it could be done. Outside surveillance would have to do for now.

"The senator?"

"Yes. No one is out of the loop yet, Wick. But anything comes to me. I want the transcripts."

"The scent on the packs, the witch hazel? It bugged me, so I combed the area for any purchase of witch hazel in large quantities. Three drugstores, and two Wal-Marts. I focused on the drugstores. Someone bought a case recently, but paid cash. It's a store about twenty miles from Chem-Loc. We should be getting the in-store surveillance video any minute."

"I want to see it as soon as it's up," he said, then stood. "Marcuso!" he shouted.

Wick stepped back. Cisco never yelled. Marcuso scampered in, headphones still on his head. "Sir?"

"Just how good are you? Really?"

Marcuso's shoulders pulled back. "Just tell me what you need."

fifteen

Cisco needed to walk, to think, and unconsciously, he ended his steps at the Tatiana's Veil entrance.

He'd seen the photos, the video of everything before bodies were removed. But perhaps seeing what the killers did and saw would turn his brain onto a new path.

With all his resources, he hadn't progressed far in the last forty-eight hours.

Inside the cavern was bright, a generator operating the tour lights and running the elevator. The underground entrance was open. His gaze traveled over the cavern, making certain nothing was left behind to give them away. He didn't doubt that this billion-dollar facility would be put to use again. Especially now that Dr. Hale had created a preventative serum. He needed her to finish it. Moot, he thought, until he could bring her in.

He stepped through, traversing the narrow corridor. The wall scraped his shoulders and he had to turn sideways to get through it. The next area was small, able to house no more than three people at a time. The palm print scanner hadn't been reactivated; fried like the rest of the security measures. There were prints all over, matching the scientists on duty. By the time Dr. Hale was aboveground having her secret break, everyone who should have been there was inside and doing their job. It gave weight to thoughts that one of the scientists let them in. Though he knew Hale wasn't the one. She'd logged in the evening before. She was due to leave as soon as the inspectors departed.

He got on the lift and took it down. The doors slid open.

The scent hit him first. Death. The metallic odor of blood and the burned computers. He stepped out, a steel grid floor beneath his feet sounding hollow. A half dozen feet above his head was a sprinkler system. Both were necessary should the entire facility need to be washed down. But it hadn't come on. The reason and opportunity still unresolved to his satisfaction.

He'd been here during the construction, the testing of security, the first day, Dr. Hale had opened the door. It was nothing like that now.

The walls were splattered with blood, now dried. The floor covered in chalk outlines of the dead. Two Marine security guards were right here. Tanner was on the lower levels.

He didn't know why he was here. Forensics and Army CBC had been through here since it was opened. The last body had been removed only this morning. There was nothing new to learn. But he needed the killers' perspective. It wasn't hard to get. No conscience. No guilt. No reprieve.

Everybody dies.

Several of the team probably didn't know Judas was down here till the killers were in the corridors. From the photos, he mentally positioned the bodies in the chalk frames and matched the room to the photos.

McKeen and Wagner were found in their section, close to each other. From the position of McKeen's body, it looked as if the metallurgist had tried to shield her. The shot went through him and into her. That didn't stop the killer from tapping one into her head. Wagner's first two fingers on his left hand had been severed. Handerson was in the hall, facedown, two bullets, one in the back, the other in his head. He'd fallen to his knees at the first shot, then facedown after the second. His brain matter was on the opposite wall. His fingers were missing as well.

Cisco walked the path of the killers. They'd split up at the elevator, two maybe three going one floor below, two taking the main section. Hale's lab was below this level, nearer to the cold room. Tanner's post. But Hale was already aboveground by then. So they had to look for her, kill anyone in their path.

The man in the emergency elevator got lucky when she came back down, or he'd never have seen her. But he'd have gone to her house, stayed around to search because he'd thought he had time. They didn't count on Wilson. Judas and his men cut and ran then. Pontelli was in custody, and Sangier, because he'd decided to fight back when he was found, was dead.

Cisco entered the stairwell that connected the four floors.

Hale's lab was above the cold room. She had the entire level to herself. As he stepped in, part of it looked as if she'd be right back any second. A small bottle of hand lotion rested on a table near latex gloves and a petite size hazmat suit. Papers were strewn everywhere. There were sticky notes on the stainless cabinets, one to remind her to pick up her dry cleaning by five. The rest was destroyed. He went to the computer, noticing the open drawer of micro disks, a cup of coffee untouched. Cream soured like cottage cheese, floating on the top with specs of dirt. The computer, as large as a chair, had a straight line of bullets through the hard drive. This was the only area without blood.

He exited the level and climbed to the next, walking the long corridor toward the escape hatch. There were guards at each level except Hale's. It wasn't a privilege. Her lab was sandwiched between the cold room below—and the next two levels of labs above. It was enough security and the Cradle wasn't that large. One level took up the commissary, showers, and cubicles with beds, and the electrical housings. Though who would want to stay in a claustrophobic place like this was beyond him.

This level contained four stations, Hanai, a physicist, was found at one end, still breathing. Cisco never had the opportunity to question him. He was dead within hours from blood loss and lack of a functioning liver. Dysart, a chemical engineer, and Piccolo, biohazard specialist, were killed at their stations. Piccolo, a thin shy man, he remembered, unlike Dysart who was much younger, nearly Hale's age, and just glad to be employed so he could buy hockey tickets. For any game, anywhere, he recalled.

The bug woman's lab, he thought, stepping inside a small, contained area. Tish Bingham. The room was a wreck, blood on a lower cabinet, her prints in it. She was knocked down, he decided, and Tish Bingham saw her death coming. She was shot in the face—more than once. His gaze flicked up when cages rattled with several dozen rats and mice. *They miss their keeper.* Nearby glass cubes were filled with roaches crawling up the sides to get out. The fascination with rats and roaches escaped him.

Takes all kinds, he supposed, left, then walked down to the cold room level used for storage and containment and nothing else. The vault was open, the thick steel doors peeled back. The glass shelves nothing more than crystalline dust now. Humidity and water collected in the normally refrigerated room. It took a lot of explosives to get in there, he thought. Maybe two pounds of C-4 at least, and it should have done more structural damage to the floor and ceiling, but it hadn't.

If they had the codes for the Cradle, then why not have them for this room, too? Or had Hale changed them before going aboveground? She was the only one with authorization to handle the deadly chemicals. Without her presence, they'd had to blow it.

He stepped into the vault, and checked the signature list. It was an old-fashioned dry erase board. According to it, no one had been inside for at least two weeks. The Sarin gas would be scheduled for destruction only when they were done testing. Why did they need four vials in the first place? One was effective. Two, three drops would be enough to kill everyone in here. He stepped out, noting that the hazardous material suits were shredded from the blast, only the helmets were still hanging on the wall. He left the cold unit, passing a spot of Van Meer's blood and the outline of his teammate. Tanner had done his job, he thought as he walked to the end of the corridor, where the artificial cement walls were open, the skeleton of the high-speed elevator dangling. The cave-in below it was mostly rock. Blown on a timer when the elevator was already at the top. Or it would have brought the lift crashing down and more steel and rock would be in the mix.

He looked back to the opposite end, imagining as Hale had described, the masked man coming toward her. Tanner had already been shot, the man stepping over the body of Hanai, he decided, aiming. Hale in the elevator, thinking she was safe. The killer following behind—riding up with the dead body.

Cisco frowned, pulling out his notes again. Wickum had said they'd taken fingers from everyone. So if this guy was slicing off souvenirs from all the men, why not take Tanner's, too. Once he was inside, they could have tortured the scientist for anything else they'd needed, but Cisco believed the missing fingers weren't just trophies.

His cell buzzed, the sound loud in the laboratory. He glanced at the Caller ID. It was Hodge. He hit send.

"We know how they fried Mother."

"About time."

"Electromagnetic pulse."

An EMP device emitted short, high-energy pulses reaching ten gigawatts and obliterated the electronics instantly. "Mother is protected against that. And if so, why didn't anything else go down nearby? The ranger station isn't that far away. Nor are the hotels for the tourists. And no one reported downed communications."

"Get up here, sir. You have to see this."

* * *

The man sat comfortably, his gaze on the computer screen. He loved technology. They couldn't see him, but he had to know he was dealing with a reliable source. "I'll accept bids for the next twelve hours. Then we meet."

"Why is that necessary?" a man said, his video-linked picture in the upper right corner of the screen.

"I have it; do you really want to argue with me?"

"No, of course not."

"How much do you have?"

"When you win the bid, you'll learn that. Not before."

He cut the connection, re-routing the signal, and leaving it dangling in Amsterdam somewhere.

He closed the laptop and found her standing to his right, leaning against the wall.

"You can't be serious."

He didn't respond, sliding the thin computer into a bag.

She pushed off the wall, walked to him. "You have no idea how dangerous that stuff is, do you?"

"I know every risk I take."

He spread his legs, pulling her between, his hands under her skirt. Though her expression looked angry, she let him play, let him tease.

"Do you? One drop could kill us both in minutes. And there is nothing that can save you, but maybe atropine to the heart."

"Yeah, yeah."

He wasn't listening, busy opening his slacks, freeing himself. She started to straddle his lap but he pushed her to the floor, cupped the back of her head and brought her mouth to his dick.

Even she thought he was stupid, that he didn't know what he was doing. But she didn't know of the plan he had that would take him to the end of this. To his future. He made his own choices and as she brought him to a climax, he decided, he'd make one for her.

* * *

Jack and Sydney sat on a sofa that had seen better days ten years ago.

Between them were printouts of information Peabody pulled from Chem-Loc. He'd hacked into the mainframe and the printer was still spitting data sheets. Most of it was Greek to him and gave him a headache. Sydney was engrossed in it.

"What do you make of this?" He tossed the sheets into the pile and ground the heels of his palms into his eyes. They had an hour or so before they could go to the supplier. The nearer to closing time, the more likely they'd overlook any odd detail.

"It's development for several new drugs. Only one was successful, but the FDA wants more tests and case studies before approval." She looked up. "That delays production and marketing."

"Meaning they're sinking money in and not getting anything back."

"Yes, but that's how it is with drug companies. They put a lot in and if it pays off, it's billions in revenue. Do you know the hit Merck took from withdrawing Vioxx alone?" He didn't answer and she waved off the train of thought, tapping the papers. "Chem-Loc had a cushion. A government contract."

"For the Cradle?"

"It's unspecified, but the bill is far larger than it should be. Testing blood isn't costly. Not for the deterioration of white cell reproduction and—" She stopped rambling, knowing he didn't want to hear this.

He grinned. "Your brain is amazing."

She didn't blush, but made a face. "I studied to get it, Jack."

He leaned, slid his hand along her jaw and into her hair. "Yeah, but it's a turn-on." He kissed her and she moaned deliciously.

"I think anything would turn you on, Marine."

"I got a thing for women with big brains."

She laughed under the pressure of his mouth as it molded

over hers, then she pulled on his shirt and she leaned back. Papers crushed beneath them and his hand dove under her behind, lifting her to mesh her hips to his.

"God, I want you."

"Where? When? Right now? Oh, yeah, I'm ready." She said it all in one breath. "Screw the mission, take me someplace private."

He groaned, and deepened the kiss.

"Hey Syd, Jack. When you're done makin' out, I've got something you should see," Peabody called.

Jack broke away and buried his face in the sofa arm, breathing hard. She turned him inside out and he wondered if he could get off her without killing himself.

"We have an audience." Though they were in a living room area that looked like a college dorm hang out.

"Damn kids." He eased back. "I should have sent them to jail and made the state pay." She laughed as he stood, then he pulled her off the couch. They stopped by Peabody's terminals.

Peabody leaned back in his chair, stretching, then pointed. "See that?" It was a ticker of data loading constantly. "It's usually imbedded deep. That tells me there's an echo. A computer *outside* the mainframe tapping into Chem-Loc."

"The boss. I'm sure he doesn't want the employees reading his E-mail."

Peabody shook his head. "They've got a staff of computer technicians over there. This one is deep. Someone is watching *them*."

"Can you find out who?"

"Maybe."

"I've never heard that from you before, Kyle."

Peabody looked at him, frowning at the use of his real name. "I tried already. I can get in just about anywhere, Jack. But this has got to be NSA. They are the encryption kings and way out of my league."

"Back off, then. We don't want them to know we're look-ing."

"That, I can do."

Cisco squatted and tipped the box on its side. Dirt slid off. It looked military. "Check the naval yard. Seems they were working on something like this with academy students. Get this to Marcuso, tell him to take it apart. Hodge, find out who bought it, sold it, anything."

The black box was made of high-density plastic, and had been buried in the ground. The only reason they'd located it was because a member of CBC was doing a scan to see if he could pick up a Sarin gas trail and he tripped over it. Christ. Its position was higher on the mountain, and it pinpointed Mother. One was bad enough. He'd bet there were more. He straightened and his gaze traveled over the site.

"Do we have to dig up the entire mountain?" Hodge said.

"Use metal detectors. But this one is small enough to be handheld. I bet this is what they had in the backpacks we found on the mountain."

His cell vibrated. Man, he was sick of hearing it ring every five minutes.

"Drugstore video shows a woman picked up a *case* of Witch Hazel."

Cisco arched a brow. This guy had a thing for antiseptics.

"It's a bad view and she's wearing a ball cap, but it looks like Dr. Handerson's wife, Lila."

"So much for the grief-stricken widow."

"But she bought the witch hazel *before* the Cradle at-tack."

Cisco pinched the bridge of his nose. She could have taken the codes from her husband, the swipe card, and if she was clever enough, a palm print to open the elevators. Shit.

"Nothing in her house has been touched, her suitcases are missing, but none of her family has been in contact with her."

"She could be with Van Meer, or dead." Which was the

same thing. Van Meer swept his trail clean. MI-6 had at least thirty counts of murder on him and he was racking them up here.

Jack was in the back of the car, out of sight. Dressed in a dark skirt and a jacket, Sydney drove. Where Peabody got the clothes, he didn't ask.

"I can't believe some company will hand them over."

"It's on file and people go by what the computer print says."

She was nervous and he didn't blame her. He'd like to be the one going in, but the authorities were looking for two people, not one.

"I can do this. I can."

"You talking to me or yourself?"

"I'm psyching myself up because my stomach is doing jackknives."

"Just act like you own the joint. I'm right here."

"Promise you won't shoot anyone?"

"I think I'm insulted." No, he *was* insulted. "You still take me for some knee-jerk reactionary, following blindly down a path grunt?

"Well, no. You don't follow the rules, and you *are* a grunt, but, well, you fire that thing so easily."

"If you could aim worth a damn, you might, too."

"Jack."

"What?"

The snap of his voice told her his feelings. She slipped her fingers between the seats, wiggling them. "Sorry. I shouldn't judge."

He grabbed them lightly, kissed them. "I have a purpose, keeping Americans safe, me safe, my team. But I won't kid you, I like putting the bad guys six feet under. There is only a cause between me and them."

"I don't think that."

"You did or you wouldn't have asked me not to shoot

anyone. And to protect you I would, but never an unarmed person."

"I just don't want anyone else to die because of me."

"It's not your fault, dammit." Jack rubbed his mouth and understood her feelings too well. They were the only survivors. "None of this is, and how about the guy hunting us?"

"Oh well, he's a given."

"Easy to cross the line, huh, Einstein?"

"Defense of your person is one thing, the intent to kill innocent people is different."

"To him, it's semantics."

"God, you're testy tonight."

Yeah, he was, and he knew why. He was always alone when he infiltrated, relying on himself, his Intel, and his stock of ammo. Bringing in a civilian with no skills was dangerous. He could handle a quick change in the plan. But Syd? He closed his eyes, facing a truth he'd tried to avoid and hoping it didn't creep into his judgment. He was afraid for her and, dammit, afraid for himself. Losing Sydney would leave him with nothing. Again.

The only reason he wasn't doing this himself was she had qualities that would get around other men. "Don't examine me too closely."

"Been there, done that. Loved every second of it."

Jack's gaze flicked to her. From his position, all he could see was the back of her head. "Wise ass." Yet he smiled.

"I know who you are, Jack. I've seen it."

He knew she didn't mean in bed last night.

"Oh God, we're here." Syd swiped her damp palm on her thigh, wishing this was over with. *I'm so not the cloak and dagger type.*

"Calm down. Remember what we discussed. Drive up to the warehouse and offer the invoice. Show them that big brain, the authority, don't take any shit from anyone."

She tried to behave as if she were alone. "It's not a large supply house."

"This is a small town and it won't matter. These guys are ready to clock out and go to the nearest bar. Go right to the back, smile, and get out of there, but don't rush."

"This makes me nervous."

"Want some food?"

She chuckled lightly, driving closer to the pharmaceutical supplier. Sydney let out slow even breaths as she rounded the loading bays and stopped the car.

"Leave the lights on and the key in," he said softly. "But turn it off."

She didn't nod or speak, and did as he instructed. She left the tall vehicle, and strode up the ramp. Her hair was pulled back and she wore glasses that belonged to Peabody. Her heels clicked and she didn't say anything when a worker came toward her.

She thrust out the paper. "I'm here to pick up this order for the college."

He looked it over, took her ID and compared it to her face.

"Doctor, huh?" He looked her up and down, his gaze pausing on her breasts. "I got an ache right here, Doc." He grabbed his crotch.

"If you'd cease playing with that, it just might heal."

He flushed, then grinned. A lurid, nasty smile that didn't meet his eyes. Who raised people like this, she wondered and gave him her best *you're wasting my time* look she reserved for condescending idiots. He went to get the chemicals. They were pharmaceuticals really. Anti-spasmodics, epileptic medications, and two others, along with atropine and a purgative with a charcoal base.

Sydney waited, feeling sweat cling to her skin under her clothes despite the cool temperatures. Below on the asphalt, men loaded supplies onto a truck marked with the name of a nursing home. They didn't pay her much attention, and she smiled tightly, then folded her arms over her middle. Minutes passed. She forced herself not to look at the car, where Jack was on the back floor. She stepped farther into the warehouse and tapped her foot.

The man came back with a small box. "This isn't much."

It was plenty, enough for several doses. "And just how much do you think you need to inject a rat?"

"We usually get orders from the college that are larger."

"Perhaps, but not today." Sydney took the box.

He looked from the box to her face. "This is just not right. Wait right here while I check it out."

"Fine." *Oh, God. Please, just drop off the face of the earth so I can get outta here.* She propped the box on her hip. "Who do you think will be there? Since I'm the department head."

"Now I know you're lying, Ferguson is."

"Ferguson got fired for screwing a co-ed." He snickered. "So if you don't mind, I've got to put these in the lab before security locks up for the night." Sydney turned away, and for a moment, she thought he'd follow her to the car. But the phone rang somewhere in the warehouse. She didn't look back, and when she reached the car, she flipped open the rear hatch window, and deposited the box inside. She gave the workers a smile, waved, then got into the driver's seat and turned over the engine.

"I'm going to puke," she muttered.

"You did fine, honey. Take a breath." Jack closed the phone before anyone answered. "Ease out, watch where you're going. Act normal."

"I've stolen a car and now lethal drugs, nothing about this is normal."

"God will forgive you."

"I hope so. Since I met you, I've been a very bad girl."

"Yeah. You have." His chuckle was dark and sexy. It left a trail over her skin.

She shook her head. "How can you enjoy this sort of stuff?" She turned onto the road leaving the supplier. "Oh, good, he's closing up." The truck the men had loaded rolled in the opposite direction and the bay door slid down.

"Just keep driving. We're fine so far. And I'm used to it. Gets the adrenaline pumping."

"Yeah, all the way up my teeth. I feel like I could run a mile. And I never run except to a good shoe sale."

When she was beyond the line of sight of the warehouse, he rolled into the front seat. "I could think of a couple ways to use up that adrenaline."

She looked over and her heart tripped a little. Head down, he was preoccupied with concealing his weapon. Just how much raw man could a girl take, she wondered, then smiled. *Overdose me, please.* "You're making me feel like a teenager wanting someplace where lying down is the only requirement."

"Who says we need to lie down?" He looked up, winked, his gaze sliding over her like his warm hands. Slow and smooth.

A wash of adrenaline and savage need spilled like hot water, tightening her skin, the muscles between her thighs. "How long till we commit another crime?"

He laughed, then sobered. "You're serious?"

She groaned, wiggling in the seat, not understanding why she was suddenly so keyed up and hot. "When?"

"The witching hour."

She glanced at the car's clock. Hours. "Then we have to do something or I'll go crazy."

He was close, his hand sliding up her thigh and under the skirt. "*I* can do something." He stroked a finger over her center and enjoyed her grab for air.

"Participation is mandatory." She felt giddy when she saw the warehouse and pulled around behind it. "I'm going to attack you, just so you know."

"I'm all yours."

She threw the car into park and cut the engine. Jack grinned as she pulled her skirt up, shimmying out of her panties. Then she rolled to the right and straddled him, the two of them hurriedly unbuttoning her blouse. Jack flicked her bra clasp and cupped her bare breasts. He pushed her nipple into his mouth, sucking heavily, keenly aware of what she wanted. From behind, he found her, toying, thrusting.

She pushed back. "Not good enough. You. Now, Jack." She fumbled with his buttons, his zipper and Jack reclined the seat back as she freed him.

He clutched her. "Syd."

"Oh, God. This is embarrassing."

"Using me for sex?"

"Well, yes, I can't, oh, God, do that again," she muttered when his fingers slid over her sex.

"Condom."

"Unless you can produce one in about ten seconds . . ."

He found his wallet, threw it aside and she opened the packet and rolled it down. He groaned when she stroked him deeply. Then she guided him, his hot length pushing into her; she arched, her hips shoving forward and he filled her.

"Oh that's good. Oh that's *good*."

"It'll get better." He cupped her hips, giving her motion. "Your turn to go to town."

She laughed and pushed. Jack took it all in, her bare breasts, the skirt hiked up—man that was sexy—and the exotic movement of her body. In the setting sun, they were alone, grabbing a moment. He didn't take it as anything more than a release of tension. She wasn't used to living on the edge of life and death knocking constantly. He was. He lifted weights to purge the adrenaline. This was far more satisfying. She cupped his face, kissing him, her tongue thrusting as she rode him unabashed, wildly. The hot slide of her gripped him, her position creating incredible pressure. She quickened and he felt it, the clench and paw that dragged him quickly with her. He latched on to her nipple, sucking hard, and she pounded against him.

"Syd, Jesus, slow down."

"I can't. Oh, Jack."

He gripped her hips, jamming her down onto him, and she arched back, bouncing crazily and he erupted, grinding her to him as she came like a gale, fast and primal. He leaned forward, clutching her, thrusting upward and riding out the tempest. She strained, made a sound that was guttural and passionate. Then she collapsed with him, breathing hard and motionless.

"I can hardly wait till we break into the lab and you make the serum."

"A sex fest, I'm sure."

He laughed and clutched her, burying his face in her throat. "You always surprise me, Einstein."

"You can surprise me by getting us inside without those two knowing what we've done."

He wasn't going to ruin the moment by mentioning they had surveillance cameras all over the place.

"Tell me it's done."

Montoya tucked the phone to his neck. "No, I'm afraid not," he said, snapping off the rubber gloves.

"You couldn't even figure out what was missing?"

"Nothing was. It's the weights and measures. Which would take weeks to test with any increase and decrease she made. She was working in milligrams."

"I knew I should have hired her."

Montoya's lips thinned and he reached for his jacket.

"Keep working at it. We have to duplicate it. We must."

Montoya frowned. Bertrand sounded panicked. The call ended without salutations and Montoya hung up, shrugged into his jacket, then put the folded papers inside his breast pocket.

He needed to publish this paper before Hale did. It would earn him more than he deserved, but he was a man faced with the winning lottery ticket. Freedom and fame were too close to ignore. It didn't matter that she'd created it, developed it. He'd heard enough in the past days to know Hale would be dead soon.

He left the complex, entering the underground lot to his car. He heard noises, a door slam, and ignored it as he climbed in. The car bounced over the speed bumps and onto the street. He drove toward Washington. He'd left a single message. A few choice words that would get him a Nobel Prize nomination.

The moon was missing in the blackened sky.

Jack insisted it was a perfect night. Sydney could barely see past her nose. The elements for Kingsford were in a pack strapped to her back. They both wore street clothes, dark and fitted. Dressing in his commando gear would have been a wide-eyed alert to anyone who saw them, he'd said. Blend in, look normal. Even his two-day growth of beard was enough that he looked sloppy and oh, yeah, sexy. Jack had a small ear pierce with a thread mike that was poised at his cheek. At the other end of the wireless was Peabody, tracking them by bouncing off a Magellan satellite.

Too much techno-babble for her, but the guys seemed to bond over the high-tech gear. Sherman continued to search Chem-Loc files to see if they had reference to Kingsford. Positive proof they were behind the Cradle attack.

Jack ran his fingers lightly as he traced the alarms on the door. With sharp pointed nippers, he inserted them in the jam and clipped something, followed a line she couldn't see and nipped another, whipped out a switchblade and cut something else. It was fascinating to see a crime in action, she thought, wondering just who taught him this skill.

She stood close, scanning the area. Lights in the parking lot shone down on the barren asphalt several yards away. The landscape was thick and overgrown near the building, manicured near the lot. They had about two hours, maybe less. Sherman had hacked the college employee files and they'd had the schedule. But that didn't mean the security couldn't change it at will.

She would have to work in the dark; turning on the lights in the lab was out of the question. Jack had some special lights, they glowed yellow and died after a few hours. Like the type parents hooked to their kids at Halloween, only bigger. It was going to be difficult. That she couldn't test it didn't make her feel as if they'd reach success, and all this unlawful activity would be a waste.

Crouched low, Jack cut the last alarms in the door frame, then used a key card Peabody had created to open the lab. The click was soft and triumphant. He glanced at her, winked, then pulled.

Silence.

"Thank God."

He put his finger to his lips, and opened the door enough for her to slip inside. Jack wiped down the door and alarms for prints, then followed, closing it behind them softly. Sydney let out a breath. Halfway there, she thought, and went right to work, gathering the materials she needed as Jack cracked open the chemical lights and set them around the tall table.

"I don't want to rush you but—"

"I know, I know. I'll try."

"You sure you remember it all?"

She snapped on rubber gloves. "Oh, yeah. I've been reciting it in my mind." She grabbed a rubber apron from a rack and tied it on, then put a chem-lite up her sleeve.

Jack moved to the window, closing the shade nearly completely and peering through the slats to keep the glow of light from the street. In the darkness, it would shine like the sun.

He looked back at her. She had a microscope and was already pushing a slide under the viewer. "Excellent quality," she whispered, then got busy.

It was amazing to see. She had glass beakers and tubes, eye droppers; weighing and measuring each element. Her moves were quick, efficient—skilled. She blended, then went to another part of the lab and she used a long eye dropper to extract a measured amount from the test tube and deposit it in a machine, in another set of smaller tubes. She hit the key pad, and a platform with a hundred or so glass rods underneath moved slowly forward, and dipped into the tubes. She slipped the chem-lite from her sleeve and held it to read the console.

"Yes!"

She removed the tubes holding minuscule droplets of the chemical and brought them back to the table.

Jack checked his watch, then looked out the window. A ghost town. All clear. He went to the next one on the west side. The lateral view was blocked by trees and shrubs. Hell. He went to the doors leading to the center of the building. The halls were empty, the floor glossy with fresh wax. "What are you making now?" he whispered when she repeated a process.

"Solidifier. I had to make it so it wouldn't stop the growth of the enzymes in—" She glanced. "You don't want to know, do you?"

"Just put a fire under it, honey." He moved around the room, checking the exit and the scenery beyond. Jack felt like he had when he was waiting for Decker to load explosives. The kid always took his time. A good reason he had all his fingers. When he died, his mind added. His lips tightened and it reaffirmed him. He was doing this for them, too.

He heard a noise, a whine and snapped a look at her. A centrifuge was spinning.

"Jesus, that's loud."

"I know. It's only a minute, but necessary. The mix will remain permanent."

"That will alert anyone passing, Syd." He made his rounds again, then stopped to watch her lift a thick-bodied syringe filled with gold liquid.

"This is it, Jack."

"Package it and let's get out of here."

"I have to check the solidifier."

"No." He glanced at the time. "Security will be heading this way soon and I don't want to meet up with some rent-a-cop with a gun."

"But I really should, to be sure."

"Trust your brain, Syd, and pack up!"

She deliberately cut her finger and applied a drop to a slide, then pushed it into the microscope viewer. It came up on a large screen in front of the room, and he glanced between it and her. With the syringe, she put a drop onto the slide. His gaze shot to the screen.

His attention flicked to the right, out the hall doors. A narrow beam of light.

"We've got to go, now, God dammit!"

She looked at him, then past him to the doors. The light glanced off the windows of the lab doors. "Oh, no." She packaged the antidote in two vials, stuffed them in her bra, then tossed everything into the supply box and into the pack.

"I'll take it," he said.

"No! I can."

He frowned for a second, then grabbed the chem-lites, putting them inside his jacket to block the radiance. She didn't move from the table. "You're going to get us caught."

"I have to clear the hard drive, and the machines."

He could hear footsteps now, the light growing brighter. The guy was probably on a pension; a night watchman wasn't a cop. Man, he didn't want to tangle with this guy and hurt him. They had to get out without notice. Sydney frantically moved between the machines, taking everything out, tapping keys and erasing files.

"Jesus, Einstein."

"I have to, Jack. The elements to make Sarin gas are in with the formula."

"Oh, hell. Why?"

"I had to make certain my measurements were enough to do the job, and provide the right counteragents."

Suddenly, Jack yanked her to the floor, covering her mouth. The flashlight scanned the room. Sydney reached for the keyboard. The screen was lit up and casting light on the lab, two steps and the guy would see it. Jack caught her hand in a tight grip, glaring at her. They heard the door squeak and shoosh closed.

Jack peered around the edge, at the floor. He's looking for the guy's feet, she thought. She bent with him, her leg wound throbbing, and under the tables, she saw the door swing and shut, then vibrate. She started to rise, and he clamped a hand on her arm.

He shook his head slowly. Then Peabody's voice sounded in his ears. "You were right, they have her formula."

Bingo, Jack thought.

"Some guy named Montoya has been playing with it." Jack started to congratulate them, when he heard, "Oh, shit. They found us, Jack. Someone has an echo on *us*."

"Shut it down," he whispered.

"I can't. They've locked me out of my own system! I can't cut it."

"Cut the power."

"I am, but they have this location, I'm sure of it."

"Get out of there. Now."

Sixteen

A maid let Montoya in immediately and he waited until she closed the door behind him. He looked at the man sitting behind a large desk. Well dressed, slightly gray, he was distinguished-looking in the suit vest and loosened tie.

Then he hit the intercom on the desk. "I won't need you anymore this evening, Mrs. Kartlin. You may go home."

Wise, Montoya thought, no witnesses. "I have something for you." Montoya patted his pocket.

"May I see it?"

"Let's deal first. I want all connection to her erased. All of it. This is mine, I made it work."

"It's her formula, though."

"Not if she can't claim it."

"I see where you're going with this."

"Well?"

"No."

"I have it, you want it."

"You've overstepped, Montoya. Whatever you believe, it's wrong. Leave."

He paled. "What?"

"Leave." He folded his hands on the desk, his gaze dark and narrow.

Montoya flushed with anger, spun and strode out of the

office. Fuming mad, he was in the elevator when he realized he'd just showed his hand in a dangerous situation—to a very powerful man.

He pressed the answering machine, erasing the message. To be certain, he removed the tape, broke it in half and tossed it in the fire. The odor was noxious, but he was the only one here now. He turned back to his desk, lifted the glass of wine, sipped, then settled back in the leather chair. The phone rang, a soft buzz that didn't really disturb the moment.

"He's heading south. What do you want me to do?"

"Get the papers back. The creativity of disposal, I'll leave to you."

He cut the connection and swiveled toward the fire, his gaze on the flames and smoke rolling up the chimney. If Montoya had completed the formula, then they really didn't need Dr. Hale, did they?

"Peabody? Sherm?" Jack whispered as the guard returned. The line was dead.

Syd was oblivious and Jack held her tightly. He felt her heart beat, her expression as if she'd burst with a scream.

"Who's in here?" The light flashed over the lab, flicked high toward the screen. "You kids shouldn't be in here. You wanna make out, go somewhere else."

Jack remained still, his breathing slow and quiet. Sydney's wasn't and he cupped her face, and mouthed *calm down.*

She nodded, and hunched on the floor; she didn't dare move, afraid her shoes would squeak. She still wore the gloves.

Footsteps clicked on the polished linoleum floors as the man neared. He was nearly on them, moving cautiously. Jack glimpsed the man. He was older, though he looked fit, aside from the few extra pounds. He really didn't want to hurt this guy, but he took three more steps, coming around the table. They were under it near the computer hard drive.

He looked again at the screen she hadn't cleared. The hard drive whined. What the hell was making it do that?

"Come on out, I know you're here." The guard walked and still didn't see him, but when Jack realized he was bending and would see Syd, he stood.

The man flinched and drew his gun. Jack put his hands up.

"Easy now. Sorry sir."

"You will be sorry when the cops get here." He reached for his radio, but with the flashlight and the weapon, he couldn't juggle it all. Jack lurched forward and with his forearm, hit the guard in the face. He staggered and Jack rushed to catch him, laying him gently down.

"Oh, my God." Syd stood, staring down at the man. He was old enough to be her father.

"I told you we didn't have time! Let's go."

She spun and went to the computer, tapping keys and he saw the file finish deleting. A disk popped out of the Writer CD and she snatched it, swiping a case from a stack and slipping it in.

Jack grabbed her around the waist and dragged her to the door. "Listen to me when I give orders!" he growled.

"I'm not a Marine! And you can kiss my ass," she hissed back.

"I'd like to paddle it." He pried open the door, pulling her with him into the nearby bushes. He could hear the guard's radio crackle with call letters before the door shut behind him. "They'll come looking soon."

"At least it's dark," she said.

"Yeah, did you remove my prints? I didn't." Though he didn't think he touched anything except the floor.

"Oh, no." She still wore her gloves and took them off, stuffing them in her pocket. "We have to go back in."

He shook his head. "I need to get to Sherman and Peabody."

"Why, what's wrong?"

When he told her, the fear she'd kept bottled exploded. "They've found us, Jack. They know!"

"Yes." And the boys would pay the price if he didn't get to them. He peered through the bushes, then stepped out and turned to her. "Walk at an even pace, no running. We have to make it to the truck before his counterpart gets here."

She slipped her arm around his waist and hung on. "Sherman and Peabody, will they leave?"

"I told them to go, but the line disconnected. Damn, I hope they didn't hang around to get some of their things and just split."

"We have to go to them."

"I will. But not you."

"What?"

"Syd." He kissed her temple and knew she was scared. "I want you to drive off."

"You're leaving me?"

His heart clenched for a second. "Baby, I have to." They reached the car and he helped her into the driver's seat, then hopped in. "Go, come on." When she was too slow, he reached, pushed the key and turned the engine over. The security car rounded the far corner behind them. "Drive, honey."

Hurriedly, she put it in gear and drove. The second guard got out of the car and with a flashlight, walked the area, using his radio. "That poor man."

"He'll be okay. I just stunned him." She made it to the street. "Step on it. I need to get to them."

She focused. "Oh, Jack, I'll never forgive myself if any-thing—"

"Don't think that way, it never helps."

They didn't chat, and he instructed her when to turn, when to speed up. Her fingers kept flexing on the steering wheel and he knew she was scared. He couldn't stop it and as much as he wanted to assure her, the plan had gone to hell too fast.

When they came within a couple blocks of the warehouse,

he told her to pull over and he got out, then grabbed his gear bag, shouldering it. "Drive around, but not in this area. Go north. Stay in the suburbs. Keep making turns to see if anyone follows, then get a hotel room somewhere and stay there; no calls, no contact, keep the cell on walkie-talkie. I'll call you."

She nodded, and Jack suddenly wondered when he'd see her again. He almost couldn't bear the thought and cupped the back of her head, then kissed her ruthlessly. "Don't worry. I'll find you. I swear it." He turned away from her.

Sydney eased into traffic, and her dread turned to tears.

Jack jogged the last block, and when he arrived, the entrance was wide open, the camera destroyed along with the locks. He had his gun out, a penlight following the aim of his weapon.

The corridor black lights were out, and he flashed the light on the floor, sidestepping the broken glass. He flattened to the wall as he moved toward the glow of light at the end of the passageway. The room was in shambles, the computers riddled with bullets and smoking. He checked the perimeter, each partitioned room, the exits, then came back to the computer terminals.

Blood smeared the floor, shoe prints left behind. He followed it, guilt bearing down on him. *This is my fault.* The bloody footprint thinned out, a single drop ending the path. He looked around, above. Rusty catwalks were suspended over his head, a metal staircase leading to them. The blood trail was far from it and Sherman and Peabody weren't all that agile to climb the catwalks without notice. But they had had enough warning, should have. He looked to see if anything was missing. The pile of Writer CD's littered the floor. No way of telling what was on them. They guys had their own method of coding, but the CD's had been riffled. What were they looking for—the formula or the bar code cards? he wondered.

He bent to pick disks off the floor and saw a darkened

spot under the computer desks. He ducked beneath, pushing aside wires and cables. There was a hole in the wall about two feet in diameter. On his hands and knees, he stuck his head in, and his palm touched something wet on the edge. He sniffed and got the metallic odor of blood.

He crawled deeper, hoping he wouldn't find them dead.

Martin watched Wilson enter the building and smiled to himself, then turned away to follow the woman. He could give a bladdie damn if the formula worked or not, but he'd get it for the buyer. Besides, he had the gas and that would give him a few rands for his retirement fund. But first he'd get him a piece of the pretty scientist. After he was done with her, she'd scream that damn formula to the heavens.

Cisco had flown by chopper and was on the road headed toward Chem-Loc when Marcuso radioed.

"We have the location."

He'd found another link to Chem-Loc, outside the corporation. "Let's see it." He tapped the keyboard harnessed to his dash and the GPS came up. "I'm three miles away. Whose is it?"

"A couple of level four systems analy—"

"English," he cut in.

"They debug and make random security checks on some pretty high level classified computer systems, in several government agencies and private companies. One is Lockheed Martin. Another is the U.S. Marshals Witness Protection. The two guys, Kyle Sampinado and Kane Llewellyn, were charged and arrested when they were underage. Hackers. Instead of jail, we hired them."

Pictures downloaded. Kids, great. "Connection?"

"One. NCIS apprehended them. Wilson was on staff at the time."

"Send a team there now. Use the chopper."

"You aren't waiting for it?"

"I'm already here."

* * *

Sydney stopped at a light, swiping the back of her hand across her cheek. *Please be okay,* she thought and glanced in the mirrors, feeling terribly alone without Jack. He was her only anchor and she tried to remember all he'd taught her so far. She checked her rearview mirror again and saw only other cars. It wasn't till she was pulling through the intersection that she noticed the police cruiser beside her, and how the cop was frowning at her and talking into his radio. Then he followed her.

She did what Jack said, and made several turns. The cruiser moved past and she turned back the way she'd come on a side street, then got back on the main road.

I should be behind him now.

She was wrong.

Cisco entered the building alone. He knew it wasn't wise, but he was out of time.

His sidearm tucked to his body, he moved down the black corridor. Glass crunched beneath his shoes and he stopped. He flicked on a flashlight, scanning the ground, then stepped over the crushed purple bulbs. He stepped into the open, his back to the walls as he checked each section. Christ, it was huge, an office and living area was only a small portion of the warehouse. He canvassed the perimeter, and satisfied he was alone, he looked over the destroyed computers. *Now they couldn't access anything,* he thought, and wondered what these two were doing for Wilson. The blood splatters and footprints dragged near the computer. There was blood on a screen and Cisco tried to judge the pattern of splatter to understand the hitter's position.

Then he felt the gun at his back and tensed. Jesus. He didn't hear a thing.

"Give it up, handle out, you know the drill," a voice said.

"Actually, I don't." He gave over his gun.

"Then this will be a new experience for you, Agent Cisco."

He heard the man remove the ammo and throw it somewhere.

It clattered, slid on the floor into his view. The weapon was in pieces.

"Wilson?"

"Your lucky day. Hands on your head."

Reluctantly Cisco obeyed. Wilson searched him thoroughly, taking his extra gun and butterfly blade.

"Where are they?"

"Who?"

"Cut the crap, you see the blood. What did you do to them?"

"My people didn't do this. You know that."

"Your word isn't worth shit, Cisco. Turn around and back up."

Cisco turned slowly and came face to face with Jack Wilson—sighting down his gun. The glare in his eyes told Cisco to tread carefully. Wilson didn't need that gun. He was an expert hand-to-hand fighter, lethal, and he looked pissed enough to kill him right now.

Eye to eye, Cisco found a strange irony in that they worked for the same side, but it was so blurred now, even he had trouble seeing the lines. For a moment, he wondered who and what he was really protecting. National security, or the killers. "You know what you're up against."

"Corporate sons of bitches who killed my men and the Cradle staff to get Kingsford, simple enough?"

"This has the mark of Judas. He got to the hackers first. You know that Chem-Loc traced it. We're linked and traced the echo."

"Tell me something new. Who's behind this mess?"

"We aren't certain."

"Bullshit! You have leads, you have the access, who the fuck did this?"

"Chem-Loc."

Jack shook his head. "It goes further and higher than Raymond Bertrand."

He had more information than he'd suspected, Cisco

thought. "We think—" Wilson aimed the weapon at his forehead. "Lila Handerson perhaps. She's disappeared."

Jack's features tightened. "She's been to see Sydney's mother." That wasn't all, he thought. Treason came from deep inside.

"I have an agent on Mrs. Hale."

The consideration didn't sway Jack. They wanted Syd for her brain, her formula. Jack wanted the woman, alive and free of this.

"You need to bring Hale in, we can protect her."

"Like you did in the Cradle, on my boat? And Kyle and Kane, they're kids and have nothing to do with this."

"Then bringing them into it got them hurt or killed."

"They're smarter than you think." But he didn't feel the truth in his own words. The tunnels were an old air vent leading outside, but there was no trail, no matted grass. As far as he knew they were still inside here somewhere, bleeding. "Who's Judas?"

"Martin Van Meer, South African. He's killed his own team. He's a psychopath."

"Good. I can deal with them."

Suddenly, Cisco shot forward, bringing his arm down on Jack's gun hand. But Jack had been waiting for it, expecting it, and blocked. With short powerful moves, he delivered a fist to his jaw, his elbow into his throat, then swept his foot across and knocked Cisco's legs out from under him. Cisco landed on the concrete so hard his head bounced. It didn't stop him and his leg shot up, a booted toe clipping Wilson in the back and driving him forward. Cisco leapt to his feet, fists primed.

Wilson was already facing him.

"Lila Handerson is nothing, maybe an information leak. But you and I both know this was a top-level breech. National Security Council, R and D committee, Finance?"

Cisco said nothing.

"Just who do you *think* you should be shielding, Agent Cisco?"

"Our country's security," Cisco said, his voice strained.

"Wrong answer." Jack punched and was back in position before Cisco could react.

"You want to waste time with this, fine," Cisco said, turning his head to spit blood. "But you won't last."

"Posse coming, huh?" Jack jabbed, aiming higher, and snapped the other man's head back.

Cisco staggered back, swiped his wrist under his nose. "Good one, Wilson, but we still need Hale. She has to finish Kin—"

Jack didn't give him the chance to finish, to breathe. His rage spilling as he landed a fast, hard hit to Cisco's throat, his temple, then his solar plexus. Cisco folded, and with his hands clasped, Jack delivered a brutal hit to the back of his neck. Cisco went down and didn't move.

Jack stumbled back, then he cocked the gun, and aimed. He fired.

Cisco didn't flinch; the bullet went into the floor. Cisco was out cold. Jack relieved him of his equipment and was putting in the ear mike when he heard Sydney's name.

The police had found her.

With blue lights flashing, over the loudspeaker, they ordered her to stop. Syd couldn't outrun them. She didn't even know where she was. Jack had disengaged the mapping system. She pulled the SUV over near an alley, and waited. The cop was out of his car, and walking toward her all the while talking into a radio mike attached to his shirt collar.

Her stomach pitched. She leaned out to say—she didn't know what—then saw the van speed up behind the police cruiser. "Look out!"

The cop turned, weapon drawn. He wasn't fast enough. A muddy gray van plowed into the back of the cruiser, driving it forward. It clipped the policeman, knocking him off his feet and throwing him backwards against the nearby wall. Syd faced forward and stepped on the gas, but it wasn't enough. The van plowed into the back of the SUV. Metal crunched. Her head snapped forward and the impact pushed her vehicle into the street.

She kept going, trying to outdistance him. "Oh, God, Jack, where are you?" She drove through stoplights, and people honked, tires screeched. A woman screamed. She swerved around a man crossing the street, and laid on the horn.

"Can't you see me?" she shouted; her hands slipped on the steering wheel. The SUV bounced over a curb. The small vials between her breasts clicked.

She was alone. No Jack, no weapon. Just chemicals she couldn't reach, and a maniac riding her like a bull in heat. Sydney knew what she had to do. Ditch this guy, ditch the car. But he was right behind her, knocking aside anything in his path and rolling closer.

He bumped her. She gunned the engine.

The phone beside her bleeped, the walkie-talkie signal. "Where are you?"

She grabbed it, hit the button, trying to hold it and the wheel. "Jack, oh thank God. I'm being hijacked, help me!"

On the other end, Jack heard the crash, her scream, and his insides locked. "Syd! Syd! *Where are you?*" God. The bastard was going to kill her.

"I'm on Weston Road. He's behind me, Jack. In a gray van. He already hit the cop!"

"I'm coming. Get to open space."

"Where? I'm in the middle of the city, oh, shit." She clipped a newspaper kiosk.

"There's a baseball field, go right after the grocery store. Never mind anything else, get to an open area."

The phone slipped from her clammy grip, tumbled to the floor and she cursed, but gave it up, keeping her hands on the wheel. People were stopped on the street to watch as the bastard creamed into the rear of Rick's truck. The bump jerked her neck, and she braced her arms, pushed her body into the seat and made a sharp left, then jammed on the gas and barreled out into the street. Tires squealed.

Then she heard sirens.

Thank God, she thought. Then in the rearview, she saw him open his window and point a gun. Sydney slammed both feet on the brakes. He hit her. The gun went flying. Her air bag deployed.

The siren was close. "Oh, God, we're done. We're done!" She couldn't see.

A black car with a blue light over the driver raced toward them. Cars jerked out of its path, people raced into doorways and flattened to the walls. But the man behind her kept pushing, driving his car into the rear and sending her forward— toward a playground of screaming children. The air bag softened as Sydney pressed on the brakes and managed one honk on the horn before she had to grip the wheel to keep the SUV from heading directly into the playground.

Children scattered in all directions. Parents rushed, sweeping them off their feet and running for cover.

The black sedan with the police siren was there, speeding alongside her.

Sydney couldn't see the officer; she was too high up in the monolith of a truck and couldn't take her eyes off her path. Or the children. *Move please, God, move!* Her legs ached, her body trembled. The van kept pushing, grinding against the SUV. It slid sideways on the gravel and threatened to tip over. She turned the wheel to the left, the back end swerving.

The cop slid back, and she glanced in the rearview in time to see him aim a gun at the other car. He shot at the tires, then into the car. The tires deflated and the man driving flinched and slowed, veering right.

Without the van pushing, the SUV lurched to a sudden stop. Sydney gasped for air, her arms still locked, her body tight like a slat of wood. Pain burned through her wounded thigh. Her gaze shot around to the ball park only a few yards away to the right. Relax, she thought. Let go. She softened like melted ice cream and pressed her forehead to the steering wheel, breathing hard. She prepared herself to be taken away in handcuffs and thrown in the slammer. The driver door flung open.

"Come on."

She jerked upright. "Jack! Oh, Jack." She flicked off the seat belt and fell into his arms.

"Hurry, before the real cops get here."

"What about him?"

They glanced. The van was empty. "Jesus." He glimpsed a figure in jeans and leather running toward the east street corner and knocking people aside.

"Shouldn't we follow him?"

"No." But he wanted to, wanted to wring the life out of Van Meer. It had to be him. Cisco said he'd killed his own team. *Like they killed mine.* He hurried her to the black sedan, helping her in, then got behind the wheel.

"Wait! The drugs."

"No time." He drove off, siren and blue light flashing.

"We don't have enough serum." She touched her breast, feeling the two hard vials.

"They'll have to do."

He drove for a few blocks and he cut the siren, then reached out to remove the light from the roof and tossed it in back. Beside him Sydney rocked, her arms crossed over her middle.

"It was him. It had to be. Oh, God those children, that policeman."

Jack frowned. Her voice fluttered, fading in and out. "Syd, you okay? You did great. Really great."

He reached, rubbed her arm, gripped her hand for a moment. She lifted her gaze. "He would have pushed me right into those children, Jack. He didn't care if I died. They don't need me or the formula. They must have figured it out by now."

It had taken her a year and half to get the measurements right: he doubted it. "If he wanted to kill you, he'd have simply shot."

He tried, and Jack never thought he'd been more afraid when he saw the guy aim.

Syd looked around the car, just noticing all the equipment. "Where did you get this?"

"Cisco."

"He *gave* it to you?"

"Not like he had a choice, and yes, he's alive and about now, really pissed off."

She would have liked to have seen that encounter. "Sherman and Peabody?"

He shook his head.

"Oh, no." He told her what he found; blood, a trail, but no sign of them. "We have to look for them." She said it like there was no choice, decision made, get moving.

"I will when this is done. We can't stop now."

She inhaled sharply as sirens drew close and Jack pulled over to let police and fire engines pass, heading the way they'd come. When they'd passed, he pulled back on the road, drove for another mile, checking the area.

He spotted an old school that looked abandoned. The sign in front said it was scheduled for demolition. It didn't say when. He pulled around the rear and parked.

He looked at Syd. She was hunched over, breathing hard and fast. "Oh, shit." He grabbed her, forcing her head up. "Baby, slow your breathing." She nodded, but her eyes didn't focus. "You're a doctor, you know you'll pass out, get control."

He stroked her throat, trying to get her to swallow. She gasped for breath. "Jack."

"That's it, that's it. Slowly." He got out, rushed to her side and pulled her from the car, holding her tightly. Finally, she softened in his arms. "It's over, he's gone."

"It's *not* over and he'll come back. He won't stop!"

Jack tightened his hold. He'd nothing to say that would assure her. They wouldn't stop. All he and Sydney could do was try to stay ahead of them. He hated this feeling, ineffective, his hands tied. But he was just glad she was in his arms. He didn't give a damn about Van Meer or Cisco right now.

"Hungry?"

Her laugh vibrated against his chest and she looked at him. "I'm so glad you're good at what you do."

He scraped his hands over her hair, her shoulders, then cupped her face. "I've never been that terrified," he admitted, then brushed his mouth over hers. "I thought I was going to lose you."

She whispered his name, clinging to his kiss. It was a gift, this piece of emotion, this confession.

"Oh, Jack, everything we've done seems . . . useless."

"We have an edge now, for a little while." She frowned and he inclined his head to the car. "We've got his computer."

They got back in and Jack opened the computer. It tapped directly into NSA files.

And in moments, they knew what Cisco did.

Agents swarmed in, guns aimed. Cisco was just picking up the pieces of his weapon. Wilson had disassembled it in seconds. He rubbed his middle. Going to be sore for a week, he thought. "Get the tracking up. He's got my car, my computer, my intel!" He'd know everything in minutes.

Wickum was the first in and walked to him, offering a handkerchief.

Cisco blotted his nose. "Van Meer was here."

"He left evidence?"

"I smelled witch hazel." The man must bathe in it.

"Think he killed the hackers?"

"Probably. He killed his own men, what would they be worth? Start a body search. Secure the building, lock it down," he ordered and walked out. Every breath made him hurt. The sound of the chopper blades made his head throb. He put his gun back together and patted down his pockets for a magazine. Wilson had taken it.

Wick produced one.

"Wipe that smug look off your face, Agent Wickum, before I fucking knock it off."

Wick's brows shot up.

Then someone shouted, "Van Meer's been sighted downtown!"

Seventeen

Sometimes you knew it before it happened.

A nagging that didn't let you rest, creeping up your spine, and battering the back of your brain. And when it hits—that moment when you realize your purpose was so jaded you didn't see beyond it—it was shattering.

Occasionally it came in the form of a bare knuckled fist in the face.

Humiliation crawled though Cisco, tightening his features. The least of which was Wilson's efficient beating.

This was his failure.

He was the watchdog and a tight, hot rage flowed with his blood. He hadn't felt like this in years, had learned to control it, but not today. Not today. He'd allowed this to happen. He was willing to believe in the sanctity of national security, the secrets sworn to keep rather than to believe in one woman . . . one Marine.

This wasn't about terrorism. Not in the view 9/11 gave the world. It wasn't even about actually unleashing Sarin gas on the American public.

It was the money. A theft. Stealing the gas was a cover. The formula Hale had created was the real target.

He understood the purpose. It was a perfect weapon against an invisible foe. They would shove the threat down the throats of the Americans that would send them running to doctors for Kingsford—a drug they didn't have. That didn't exist. But that would be only the beginning. Next would come thefts, hijacking the serum, and a stock market battle that would make Chem-Loc huge and give Dr. Hale nothing for her brilliance.

They might as well have launched a terror attack in broad daylight. This one would have casualties. When word hit the street and reached al-Qaeda—they'd use Sarin just to prove Kingsford didn't work. And there wasn't any to be had.

God help us.

Over a dozen lives lost so Bertrand could save his company. Kress was no less guilty of treason. The country was betrayed. The American people's safety net yanked from under them by one of their own.

No one knew, except him—it was sufficient.

He wouldn't let this be swept away. He *fucking* would not.

Cisco touched the black card inside his jacket. He'd make sure that the innocent would never pay for the sacrifice again.

Van Meer strode into the hotel room, throwing off his jacket and holding his shoulder.

Wilson, the bladdie bastard.

"My God, what happened?"

She hurried toward him, her concern touching him in some small way. He didn't like it—it colored his choices. "Just get me some bandages."

She scurried away. He dropped into a chair at the kitchenette. Blood dripped down his shirt, soaking his trousers. He unfastened his holster, laying it on the table, then grabbed his T-shirt and ripped it. He used it to staunch the blood.

She returned, opening the kit and started cleaning the wound.

"It went right through."

Martin said nothing. The bastard aimed for his head and

the only reason he wasn't dead was Hale slamming on the brakes. *The bitch needs to die.* Bertrand couldn't make her stupid experiment work, but he had only half his money and all the gas and bomb. All the cards. He was wasting time here. He could be sunning on a beach somewhere, using up his money.

She dabbed at the wound.

"Oh, for crisssake, woman." He took the bottle of witch hazel, flipped the cap and poured.

"Martin! Good God."

He was immune to the burn.

"It's the meat of your muscle and you need stitches."

"Do it."

"Do I look like a nurse? No way."

He gathered a needle, surgical thread. She lurched back when he jabbed the needle in and pulled. "Hold it closed."

She approached cautiously, pushing on his shoulder. He took large stitches; he just needed to stop the bleeding. He finished, then threaded the needle again, irritated at the quiver of his torn muscle.

"Do the back."

She didn't take it and he glared back over his shoulder, his look telling her there would be consequences.

She took it, and stitched him. "This is disgusting."

"I'm going to pay the fucker back. Bastard tried to take my head off."

"You got cocky. He's better than you thought."

He backhanded her, the crack loud and sending her against the counter. "Shat up."

She clutched her cheek, her eyes watering. "How dare you!"

"You think you matter?"

"I better," she warned.

"You're a fuck, nothing more." There wasn't a shred of hurt in her eyes, only rage, pure and quick-hot. It made him suddenly horny.

"Bleed to death, you pig."

She turned away, grabbed a cloth and soaked it in the sink. She held it to her jaw.

His gaze slid over her body, the thin sundress showing she was naked beneath. His cock hardened, and he moved up behind her, his hands slipping around to cup her tits through the thin dress. She elbowed him back and he kept massaging them, pinching her nipples.

"Get away from me! I hate you!"

"Everyone does."

She wasn't afraid of him unlike the others. Like him, she didn't care about anything except what she wanted and the means to get it. If she could, *he knew*, she'd kill him. His hand slid heavily downward, over her snatch and he pulled up the dress to touch her flesh. He rubbed her, and she kept her hands on the edge of the sink and didn't react. Except her breathing was faster, heavier. He nudged her legs apart and opened his trousers. She bent, pushing back into him.

"Hurry up and fuck me, you bastard."

"I plan to." He flipped the dress up over her back and positioned himself, spreading her. He butted a couple times. She was already wet, and he caught her hips, and thrust deep in one hard jam. She let out a long throaty sigh. He pumped fast and hard, pushing her head down, his mind centered on the tight ass taking him in and nothing more. He didn't want to see her face. Didn't want to be reminded that he had her body, but little else.

Didn't want to be reminded of anything.

Sydney stared at the intelligence on Cisco's computer screen. "That bastard, he knew!"

"Not necessarily. This intel is less than an hour old. Cisco was on the floor then."

"It's right there, Jack. I can see it, can't you? Bertrand has my formula and is trying to figure it out." It was there, the wrong measurements, but it was all there. "And this chemist, Montoya? He was in one of my grad classes. A refresher he said and he'd needed to be there. He was about ten years older than me." She sagged in the seat, covering her face, then plowing her fingers into her hair. "God damn him! He would have taken credit, too, the slimy weasel!" Abruptly, she left the car, storming back and forth.

Jack sighed and got out.

"No, don't touch me," she said when he approached. She put a hand up, in case he didn't get the message.

"Then talk to me."

"What should I say? That I'm damn sick and tired of these people taking what is mine! That I worked my butt off to get where I am and all I see is it going down the river very quickly."

"We're trying to stop that."

"How? They have it. He'll figure it out, he's not a complete moron. Then they'll market it and I'll have nothing."

Jack frowned. There was something more to this than she was saying. "What did you expect to get from it?"

She stopped pacing and looked up. "A research grant, my own lab to do what I really want."

"And that is?"

"To find a way to stop the onset of Alzheimer's."

Her mother.

"Mom's in bad shape and my father died from it at sixty five. I have their genes, Jack. That will be me in twenty years."

She met his gaze and Jack saw fear, almost violent, and hidden from the world. From him.

"I don't want to die like that. Why do you think I have so many degrees? I was learning all I could, so I might be able to find a cure."

"But *we* have the formula, in the right combinations, and they can't recreate it quickly."

"I know. I know. But I feel like it's slipping away from my control. For three years, I had no life to make Kingsford happen; I devoted myself to it."

"For the serum, or the research grant?"

She made a face and knew her answer meant something to him. "The grant was only a slim hope. Some power. I had no research that wasn't already being done, no recommendations, not even a theory. If I got a grant, I could at least try. I just wanted to be involved in the latest studies. But if you think I went through all this just for a grant, you're wrong." She met his gaze, her eyes glossy and she threw her shoulders back and let out a breath. "Believe me or not. It wasn't my motive for joining with you. It was for the dead."

"I knew that. Just wanted to be sure you did."

She touched the spot between her breasts, the vials. Then, as if a light went on in her, she groped her jacket pockets. She walked up to him, and held out a silver CD.

"Take it. Do what you want with it."

She'd saved it to CD, he remembered. "After all the bitching you just did? Hell no."

When he didn't take it, she put it in his hand. "Your friends and mine died for this. You do what you think is right."

"Are you sure?"

She smiled softly, the angry fire gone out of her. "Just give me credit for it."

He looked down at the unlabeled CD, then at her. He was truly moved, a chill running down to his heels. Good God. Her life's work and she was handing it over, trusting him with it. "I don't know what to say. Thank you?"

"Good enough. Though . . . you could kiss me now, you know. Show your apprecia—"

His mouth cut her off and she hummed her pleasure, sweeping her arms around his neck. If anything good came out of this, she thought, it was Jack. She lost herself in his kiss, thinking of things she shouldn't—but secretly wanted—and felt the change in herself. She softened, taking her time, and his fingers dug into her back, pushing her closer. His hand rode her spine, caressed her hair, cradled her head and she knew—he felt it too.

Then suddenly he pulled back and scowled.

"Oo," she said, "not the reaction I want to see."

He looked to the darkened sky, then met her gaze. "Helicopters."

She raced to the car. Jack glanced around, then ran to the double doors of the building, kicking at the rusted padlocks.

"What are you doing!"

"Get behind the wheel." He picked up a fractured piece of wood, and hit the lock repeatedly till it broke. Pulling the chains, he opened the double doors wide, then motioned her to drive in.

Syd gave it gas as Jack waved hurriedly. The car rolled into the building, wood and trash under its wheels. He shut the doors and went to the window, rubbed the bleary glass.

Spotlights lit the dark, zigzagging over the ground. Looking for tracks. They couldn't see them, then Jack remembered the car's GPS. He ran, diving into the front seat and under the dash. The GPS was beeping and he yanked the wires, pulling out his knife to cut through them.

He let out a breath, then looked up at her.

Sydney smiled. "You saved the day again, Wilson."

He straightened. The choppers were headed northwest. "They're not looking for us."

"Then who?" She inhaled. "That guy."

"I winged him. Van Meer." He tapped the computer and pulled up a photo.

Sydney stared at the face. The man who'd murdered so many. She hated the bald, tattooed son of a bitch. He had the raw, dangerous looks that would attract half her girlfriends, but made her stomach coil. "I want you to kill him," she said bluntly.

Jack frowned at her.

"He's a murderer. He deserves to die."

"Yes he does, but I'm not the judge and jury, and neither are you."

"Who was the judge and jury for my friends, your men? They were *slaughtered*, Jack."

"I'm aware of that," he bit out. "What you're asking is murder."

"Eye for an eye. Give me a gun, I'll do it." She took the extra gun from the glove box.

Jack snatched it from her. "You're a shitty shot and we don't know where he is anyway."

"We lure him to us then."

"Hell, no."

When she tried to leave the car, he grabbed her by the arms, giving her a shake. "Listen to me, Sydney. *Doctor Hale*," he pressed. "I want this guy in the worst way, but he'll kill without provocation. He's murdered his own team. Do you want to see the pictures? He has no morals. No conscience. We wouldn't get within feet of him before he killed me. Or you."

Sydney couldn't believe the words were coming out of her mouth, but there was no stopping them. "Then pick him off like a fly. You've done it before, I know you have. You said yourself there was nothing but a cause between you two."

He reared back. "Jesus. What's gotten into you?"

"I'm really pissed off! I haven't even had time to grieve for my friends with people chasing us. You might be used to people wanting to kill you, but I'm not! I want it over. He did it, he needs to die!"

"That won't stop Bertrand or whoever he was working with."

"Then we find out and do it to them."

This bloodthirsty tirade wasn't Sydney, he thought. She was normally logical. Theoretical. Rage and grief she'd suppressed were creeping up on her and when he slid his hand to her thigh, his suspicions were confirmed; it was hot enough that he felt it through the fabric. "Get in the backseat. Now. Take off your jeans."

"You're always saying that," she said not too kindly.

Jack left he car and popped the trunk, riffling through the gear till he found what he needed. A med kit. He brought it to the passenger's side. She wasn't moving.

He opened the door and pulled her out.

"You're mad at me."

He said nothing as he helped her off with her jeans, then with her sitting sideways, he opened a bottle of water and softened the bandage.

"I can do it myself."

He pushed her hands off and pulled slowly. It was red on the edges. He should have remembered. He cleaned the wound, applying more salve to keep it soft, then rebandaged it. He broke open a syringe packet loaded with antibiotics, and without hesitation, injected her.

She flinched. "You enjoyed that."

He didn't meet her gaze and tossed her jeans at her. "Lie down and get some rest."

"Jack, I'm sorry."

"Forget it."

Cisco touched the outside of the van, his hand coming away with gray paint. He rubbed the metal; it was blue beneath. Clever. He stepped to the rear, the doors open. Inside were pools of tacky blood that smelled foul. Flies buzzed. Cisco had already ordered a door-to-door search of the immediate area. Van Meer couldn't have gone far. The blood trail led down the street, and people were more than willing to identify him. Bald with a tattoo on his throat, he wasn't hard to miss. And he was wounded.

Wilson, he thought. The SUV was totaled, but the box of narcotics in the pack told him Hale had tried to recreate Kingsford again. He didn't have to know where, the local college reported a break-in. Kids necking they'd said. Cisco knew better.

With the area cleared for a five-block radius, people were starting to bitch. It was late, they wanted back in their homes.

264 / Amy J. Fetzer

The tow truck pulled away with the two vehicles strapped on a flatbed, and he cleared the area for the public.

"We go after Hale and Wilson?" Wickum asked.

"No."

Wickum blinked with shock. "They have your car, the computer."

"And by now Wilson knows what we do. Maybe he'll get smart and bring Hale to us." But he doubted that.

The radio in the chopper crackled as Cisco approached. "We found where Van Meer's been hiding."

Cisco hopped in and held on. "Any sign of him?"

"No, but he left behind a bag of fingers."

He bit into the sandwich without tasting it, and stared at the crumpled picture of his friends. Sydney had passed out in the backseat, from exhaustion or the adrenaline crash, Jack didn't know. Right now, he didn't care, he told himself, but that was a lie. He was pissed off; he admitted that to himself when he went for food. For a moment there, she'd compared him to a cold-blooded killer. She didn't know that with every shot he took, he knew it would take a life. That sometimes he could be wrong, bad intel, not enough proof, whatever the reason. He wasn't perfect, nor was his aim. Long ago, he stopped dissecting what he did for his government. The lines were thin enough.

But he knew that wasn't Sydney talking, not the same woman he'd come to know. He was used to people hunting him and had grown so accustomed to living with that on his shoulders, he forgot how it affected others, for a newbie who never experienced that kind of in-your-face risk.

She was scared and tired, and hell, when someone aimed a gun and you knew in your soul they wanted you to die horribly, it wasn't easy to handle. It was tough the first time it happened to him. He just shot back. Sydney couldn't do it.

Yet the sting of her words made him recognize how much he cared what she thought of him. He finished off the sandwich, and reached for a bottle of water, washing it down.

"Jack?"

He looked over the backseat, meeting her gaze. "Feel any better?"

Sydney's eyes burned and shame swept her. The last conversation played in her sleep and was fresh and hurtful when she woke. "I'm so sorry."

"I said forget it." He looked away, tucking the picture inside his jacket.

"No, I can't." She sat up and rested her chin on the seat back. He wouldn't look at her. She didn't blame him.

"We finish what we started, Syd, and I'm outta here."

Her heart clenched so tight she had to swallow. "No." Slowly he turned his head to look at her and she saw it. Like an open wound, his pain was there, up front, when he'd hidden it before now. "I don't want that," Sydney said, "no matter what happens, I don't want that."

He started to say something and she put her fingers over his lips.

"I know what I said. I know. It was completely selfish and insensitive. I won't excuse it away, but I wish I could take it all back. I'm glad you do what you do, Jack. I am. I'd be dead if not for you. They chose the best man for it, but I'm not like you. I can't compartmentalize my feelings in a crisis."

He held her gaze for a moment, then said, "What's the real reason?"

"I've never hated anyone like I do that man," she blurted, "and it scares me."

"I understand what you're feeling, I do. Judge and jury comes in a courtroom or on a battlefield. Circumstances make the difference."

"No, Jack." She touched the side of his face and leaned toward him. "People like you do." She kissed him softly, with such an intimate tenderness that Jack felt his entire body bleed with sudden heartache.

Man, he was falling hard for her. "Sydney," he growled and took more, devouring, wanting to bring her inside himself. He tore his mouth from hers and pressed his forehead to hers. "You make me crazy."

"Forgive me?" she said.

"Nothing really to forgive, baby."

He swiped his hand over her hair, kissed her forehead. "Go back to sleep Einstein, rest that big brain."

"But I smell food."

Jack chuckled to himself, then handed her a sandwich. She didn't waste time and bit into it. "When this is over I'm taking you out for a real dinner." She looked over the seat for more and he handed her a soda. "An all-you-can-eat place, I'm thinking."

"Chesapeake Bay's my favorite." She got out and with her sandwich, slid into the passenger seat. The glow of the computer screen lit the inside of the car. "You've been reading this all night."

"It's only been a couple hours." His eyes were bloodshot and he looked beat.

"So what'd you find?"

"Cisco is watching several people, including the Under Secretary of Defense. That's just insane," Jack said, shaking his head. "And Senator Mackleson, a Dr. Daniel Kress and Jabez Nazier very closely."

At the first name, her head snapped up, her eyes going wide. "They're advisors on the council, Jack. I know Kress and Nazier."

"According to this, they own some of Chem-Loc, too."

Sydney laid her head on the back of the seat.

"Einstein?"

"Kress was one of my professors and Nazier was my boss before I went to work at the Cradle. Jabez, Dr. Nazier, recommended the project to the NSC and the Under Secretary based on a theory I'd presented to him. No wonder Chem-Loc got the government contract to test blood."

"And it's probably how the attackers got inside the cradle."

She looked up and shook her head. "Codes were not pre-set. Each person had a four-digit code to get inside at the first level, which is just to the elevators. They wouldn't operate them without a valid palm scan and a second code. It was designed to keep *us* secure."

"Cisco is looking in the wrong direction."

"How is that possible?"

"Kress and Nazier, they're on it, I can smell it. Bertrand is a given. But the palm scan? Not easy to take unless you cut off the hand."

She paused, the sandwich poised at her mouth. "It works with the print and the warmth. Cisco knows that, he came up with the security measure."

"Someone *let* them in."

"They got killed for it, then. Everyone who was inside at the time is dead."

The computer blinged.

"He has a message?" She leaned to look.

"No, we do. It's from Cisco."

"Can't he find us with the wireless connection?"

"Maybe, but his attention is elsewhere."

She waited for the bad news.

"Van Meer is on the loose, they found his hotel."

"He's warning us?"

He slid her a glance. "As much as you dislike the man and his methods, he's just doing his job."

She made a sour face. "How can you say that? He used me as bait. He let my team die down there and didn't vent. He chased us when he should have been—"

"Einstein," he said into her ranting. "He couldn't vent. Everyone was already dead by the time you got back down the elevator. And the fires ate up the oxygen." He'd read the intel, every detail, and wished he'd found something. He rubbed his stinging eyes. "So many dead that the coroner hasn't filed the last reports yet."

"If Cisco's investigating Kress and Nazier then he has a strong lead. See if you can find it."

Jack tapped the keys, pulling up Cisco's private reports and reading again. "He's got next to nothing on them. Financial connection."

"That isn't enough."

"Wiretaps, surveillance. God, he's on everyone's case." Jack shook his head. "But nothing that will stand up in a court. Bertrand can be put away for life. He's got your formula in his computer systems, so that's proof it was stolen."

"So what do we do?"

He glanced to the side and said, "We smoke them out."

In the hotel suite, Cisco nudged the trash can filled with bottles of witch hazel. Forensics were taking prints on every surface, but since the scent of ammonia mixed with witch hazel, Cisco figured Van Meer had wiped the place clean.

The bag of fingers still had him stumped. If Van Meer took them, why leave them? With a pen, he nudged the bag. It was filled with blood. Then he noticed their weren't any wedding rings. The only one who was married was Handerson. Had Van Meer taken them all to cover one? The only reason left was for proof of death. For Lila Handerson.

He didn't have time to deliberate further when Marcuso called.

"Those two hackers, they were deeper inside than us. Near as I can tell, they'd hacked for passwords, remote accessed and got into some files."

"Which ones?" But he knew.

"Some drug formula."

"It's a drug company," he said dryly.

"See, that's the thing, they focused on one, a formula with the saved name of Hale."

None of his people knew about the serum Hale personally dubbed Kingsford. Not even Wickum.

"I need a chemist to understand it, but if I'm reading it

right, there are several versions of the same file with just a minor change. There are several notations of failures. It was saved and copied just an hour or so ago."

"By who?"

"Dr. Ernesto Montoya."

"Find him."

An agent rushed in. "Bertrand made a call, we think it's to Van Meer."

"Get me a location!" Cisco adjusted his holster and grabbed his coat.

"He's ten miles away and moving toward Washington."

Cisco ran, pushing people aside. Jesus.

Van Meer had the gas.

Eighteen

Montoya sat in his house, the shades drawn, and lights off. He fingered the print copy, a disk in the other hand. The house creaked, the emptiness of it bearing down on him. He had nothing left. In one moment, he'd destroyed all he'd worked to get.

His cat purred, moving between his legs. He nudged it aside.

The animal slipped around the legs of a chair, the end table and headed into the kitchen.

He'd fucked up. Showing his hand was stupid. He muttered a curse, wondering what to do next. Bertrand didn't know he hadn't completed the formula. He'd figured what he had was good enough to bluff Kress. The SOB had to be hip deep in this because there was no way he could have gotten anything of Hale's without help. She was government sanctioned, something Montoya had been trying to do since graduate school.

His cat meowed. He ignored it. The noise went on for another couple of minutes and he sighed and turned on the sofa.

"Bathsheba, dammit, shut—"

The hard barrel of a gun pressed to his forehead. He went still, his gaze flicking upward. "Oh, shit."

The man smiled, and pulled the trigger.

The shot blew him backwards over the coffee table with his brain matter. The man walked around, took the disk and printout, then left as quietly as he'd come.

Office of the Under Secretary of Defense

"Daniel, how are you?" The USD came around the side of the desk, smiling.

Daniel Kress shook his hand. "Sorry so late. I've a sensitive matter to discuss."

The USD waved off his aide, and he left the room, closing them in.

"The Cradle, is there any new information?"

The USD folded his arms, resting his rear on the edge of his desk. "The articles stolen are still at large."

Articles, Daniel thought. The room was secure, what was the USD covering?

"You have the same information the rest of the council possesses; what's your interest in this, Daniel?" the Under Secretary asked.

"The council is concerned over Hale's long-time absence."

"NSA is closing in on her, but the gas vials are our chief concern."

"I agree, however, she was my student you know. And not without flaws. A loner, few outside interests, pushed almost fanatically by her father. She could be handing over her formula to the enemy. Not without being forced, I'd like to think."

The USD stared back. "We've considered that." The intercom on his desk sounded and he glanced at it. "Can you excuse me for a moment? Please wait. If you have the time?"

Daniel nodded.

The USD stood and went through a door to the right and behind the desk.

The locks clicked behind him and the corridor went secure. He walked a few steps into a closet-like room, and put on a headset. "Send me anything you've learned on Daniel Kress. Right now."

A system of screens blinked with data. The USD leaned in, slipping on his glasses and reading. "I'm impressed. Did you do a deep penetration search on everyone?"

"Of course, sir. Senator Mackleson, while he owned shares in Chem-Loc, turned control over to a broker, all profits to be in a trust for his grandson; and he hasn't been in contact with the board of Chem-Loc since he took office."

"Good. But not our real problem, is it?"

Kress had accessed the schematics of Mother and the Cradle and had them in his possession. Something he shouldn't have. He was a consultant on the chemical processing, not the Cradle operation in itself.

"Keep me appraised."

"Will do, sir."

The USD cut the connection, and sighed as he removed the headset. He left the room, walking the short corridor to his office. He paused, glanced into a small room filled with video screens, and the men sitting behind the desk watching them. The USD reentered his office. Daniel stood near the windows.

"Forgive me, it's an urgent situation."

Kress only nodded shortly.

"If you have any suggestions on how to handle this, I'm open. We've exhausted a great deal of manpower and money already."

"Perhaps ending it completely is the wisest choice."

"A sweep?"

He nodded, frowning deeply. The stare was so penetrating, the USD felt as if a hawk was circling in his office.

"We've considered that. It's still an option."

Kress's cell phone rang and he glanced at the number, then cut off the call.

"Please keep me in the loop. I have a fondness for Dr. Hale and I truly don't want to see her die for this."

"Neither do I, Daniel."

Kress left and after he closed the door behind himself, the other door opened. Jabez Nazier stepped out and looked at the USD.

"You were right, Jabez."

"I am most grateful for your moment of trust, Mr. Secretary. He will cover his deeds. Quickly."

"He's well beyond that, and I'm praying Agent Cisco is faster."

Bertrand couldn't sleep and scuffed through the house. He was alone in the massive estate, his wife in Boston with her family. A distant cousin's wedding or something. He hadn't been listening, nor did he care.

Montoya hadn't reported his latest attempt in hours and Raymond considered going to the lab. At this hour, it would raise too many eyebrows, even if it was his company. People were already getting suspicious. Montoya was practically living there. Raymond could not. He went to his library, the décor similar to his company office. He liked familiarity.

He poured himself a drink, feeling the burn of the first sip go through his stomach, then bleed out to his chest and shoulders. He took the bottle with him and dropped into a chair behind the desk. He finished off one and poured another, then decided that if he was going to get drunk, he should do it on the sofa and sleep it off there later.

He started to rise, but something pushed him back down.

He turned his head and saw the gloved hand on his shoulder. "Christ, Van Meer, now I know you're insane. You shouldn't be *here*."

The person said nothing.

"This is your fault; if you hadn't left him alive on the mountain we'd be clear. No witnesses and no proof. Now give me the goddamn gas. I can destroy it."

Still, not a word.

"You want the rest of your money. Fine. You can get out of here, out of this country."

When the voice came, it was close to his ear and deadly. "Treason is an ugly thing, isn't it?"

He tensed, and instantly knew it wasn't Van Meer. "Who are you?" The chair spun and Raymond saw first the pistol, then the man behind it.

"We're going to have a little chat," he said.

Bertrand reached for the intercom and hit the button. "Dicky, Dicky!"

"Dicky is incapacitated."

That he let him call out told Bertrand he was alone. Fear slithered over him like a cold November breeze. Then the man grasped the black mask at his throat and pulled it off.

Raymond Bertrand's eyes went wide.

"Surprise."

Bertrand felt his world crash, the empire he'd built toppling in the look in his eyes.

"Van Meer has the gas."

Bertrand nodded.

"Where is he?"

"I don't know, I swear."

"You hired him."

Raymond admitted nothing.

"You had partners, who?" When Bertrand didn't answer, the man pointed the pistol at his forehead. "Start talking, pal, because you don't know how much I *really* want to pull this trigger."

Bertrand didn't swallow when he wanted, didn't gasp for air when he needed it; he just looked into the man's lethal eyes.

"Let me start. I was your last witness."

Good God. "Van Meer hired them."

"Not without your money."

"Why should I tell you anything?"

Jack pressed the gun into his forehead a little harder.

"Because they killed my friends and I'm itching to pay back the favor. You gave the orders."

"But he carried them out!"

"That's not how it works. The commander shoulders the blame!" Jack sucked his teeth, calmed. "Van Meer have the formula?"

Bertrand shook his head.

"Get him on the phone."

Bertrand opened a drawer and took out a cheap cell phone. He speed dialed and held it out, his hand shaking pitifully. Jack took it. Van Meer bitched, thinking he was Bertrand.

"Shut up, and listen. You and me, we deal."

"Who the fuck is this?"

Your worst nightmare, he thought. "You have my bullet in you."

He was quiet as that sunk in. "Go on."

"Twenty-two hundred hours tomorrow."

"Why should I?"

"You can pay me back. Bring the gas and the implosion bombs or no deal."

Van Meer named an out-of-the-way spot off the beltway to D.C. "I haven't set a price. I already have offers for three million."

"That's doable." Jack cut the call, and memorized the number.

"He won't be there," Bertrand said.

Jack said nothing, rage boiling so hard inside him he wanted to destroy the room.

"Van Meer has his own way of doing business and betrayal is a requirement."

When Jack didn't respond, Bertrand understood his choices had vanished. The man's eyes sparkled with rage, and he waited for the strike, the bullet. He didn't dare move, his body sweating under the silk pajamas, but he imagined a reprieve when the man leaned back against the bookcase running the length of the wall.

Jack stared for a long moment, unmoving, then he withdrew something from his vest and held it out. Photos.

"Look. Look at their faces. You don't even know who they are and you had them killed. Slaughtered like sheep, you son of a bitch."

Raymond refused to look, his stomach revolting. This man would never believe that he hadn't known about his men. It didn't matter. He was guilty because he didn't want to know the details, just the results.

Jack came off the bookcase, and slammed the pictures down on the desk, then grabbed Bertrand by the neck and forced him.

"Jason Decker." He pointed. "Staff Sergeant. He served in Iraq, earned two purple hearts and a bronze star. What did you earn when you were twenty-seven? His mother will grieve till her death." He slapped another one down. "Mateo Martinez; we called him Zorro. He liked to fish with his kids and loved his big Spanish family, and adored his wife. Carl Lyons. You widowed his wife at twenty-five! See the child, that beautiful baby girl? He was gone when she was born and he was just getting to know her. You took her father." Jack's rage exploded and he shoved Bertrand's face into the desk.

It gave him little satisfaction.

Bertrand lolled back, clutching his bleeding nose. "There wasn't supposed to be anyone on the mountain!"

"So you set out to kill just the scientists? The people who worked to create that countermeasure . . . to help people like me!"

Bertrand's eyes went wide, and he realized with crystal clarity that he would die tonight.

"You're nothing but a thief, Bertrand, and a murderer." Jack aimed so fast Bertrand flinched. He sighted in; his entire body trembled with rage. He thought of his men who were his friends, how they'd opened up their homes to him, let him know their families and feel like a part of it. His chest tightened along with his throat as his thoughts spun out of control, flashing on Sherman and Peabody, then ending on Sydney. Her pretty face hung in his mind, what she'd think of this, what she'd be saying to him now. He knew. Her exact words, he knew them. But—God—it was eating him inside not to betray all he'd said to her, to believe in himself and to deal his own justice. Right now. His finger flexed on the trigger.

"Wait. Please, I beg you! I—I have a tape!"

Still, he aimed, and Bertrand had no idea of the war going on inside him.

"It's in there, in the safe."

Jack flicked the barrel.

Bertrand rose, sniffling blood, and removed books from a shelf, then slid back a false panel. His hands shook and he tried the combination twice before it sprang open.

"We can make a deal?" He held out the tape.

Jack met his gaze for a moment, took it, went to the answering machine, removed the old one, and replaced it. He hit play. What he heard would destroy Sydney.

He lifted his gaze to Bertrand. "You don't deserve to breathe." Jack took the tape, then went to the safe, checking for more. It was empty except for large bands of cash. Blood money for Van Meer, he thought. He considered taking it. Actually buying the gas from him, then knew that when he met him, Van Meer wouldn't be on this planet that long.

"Get out. Go after him instead."

"You'll be tried for treason, Bertrand. You'll lose your company, all your assets and your family. Only fitting, I'm thinking." As he spoke, Jack inspected the gun, pushing out the chamber, and removing all the bullets except one. He flicked the cylinder back. It was Carl Lyons's personal weapon he kept in his house to protect his family. Jack wiped off his prints.

Raymond's gaze followed his moves. "What are you doing! We had a deal."

Jack laid it on the desk, his gloved hand over the gun as he lifted his gaze to Bertrand's. "The deal is, you do what's right.

If you can figure that out." He scooped up the worn photos, tucked them away, just noticing a line on the phone was blinking with an incoming call. Clutching the tape, he walked out of the house. When he met the front walkway, he ran, hard and fast into the woods.

To the only person who mattered.

Cars surrounded the vehicle, forcing it off the road and into a ditch. From the chopper, Cisco watched as the driver put his hand out the window and waved. Agents surrounded the car as the chopper landed. He was out of it before it touched down, and running toward the vehicle. A CBC team was right behind him.

An agent yanked the man out of the car and slammed him face first against the window. He frisked, but Cisco was already slowing his steps.

It wasn't Van Meer.

The agent turned. "He's got nothing."

"What the fuck do you people want? Who are you? I know my rights."

Cisco stared, a half dozen curses running through his head. Van Meer had chosen a man his size with a bald head. All that was lacking was the tattoos.

He knows we had him.

Agents searched the car, and one straightened and called to him. Over the hood, he tossed something to Cisco. He caught it, and looked at the GPS loaded cell phone—and the number it kept calling over and over again.

Bertrand. His home.

Cisco cut the call and looked around, half expecting to see Wilson. He walked to the man, turning him around and with his forearm, pushed on his throat. The man gasped for air; his hands behind his back, he was helpless. "Tell me about this."

"A guy gave it to me with a grand. He said drive for a few minutes, don't touch the phone."

"Where?"

"Outside a hotel. The *something* suites, way outta my range, ya know."

Cisco pressed harder.

"I'm not messing with you, man, it's the truth. Jesus, he said it was a joke."

Cisco thrust away. "Lock him up."

"Hey. I didn't do anything but drive a car, for Christ sake!"

Cisco turned his head and gave him a stare he reserved for people he wanted to kill. He showed him his ID.

"Oh, man," the guy whined.

She smoothed her shirt, hating that she was wearing wrinkled clothing, but he'd dragged her out of the hotel so fast she didn't have time to be selective.

Her jaw still burned, and from inside the car, she glared at him. He was on a hillside now, lying flat and watching the highway. After a few moments, he eased back and stood, then walked to the car. She liked the way he walked. That hip rolling gait like a cowboy's, though he was anything but.

When he neared, she left the car.

"Get your ass back in."

"No." She winced. "Jesus, my face hurts, you bastard."

He eyeballed her. An ambivalent look she loathed. "There's ice in the back."

It was a small consideration, knowing he didn't really give a damn. She didn't either. She had her money, her nice fat fee and she'd be sunning in the Cayman Islands with a man with a lot more class than this hunk of muscle. She opened the trunk, and pulled off the top of the Styrofoam cooler. She stepped back.

"Oh, my God, Martin, have you completely lost it? Why do you have this *here*?"

He chuckled more to himself than aloud. "None of your damn business."

"Where is the rest of it?"

The cell rang and he glanced up, answering his phone.

"Answer me! You've had it all this time? You were supposed to give it to Bertrand for destruction."

"Shat the fuck up, will you?"

He spoke into the phone, but she wasn't paying attention. Her gaze was on the ice-packed cooler, and the single metal vial of Sarin gas lodged in the center.

Where were the other two?

Jack slipped into the building, moving to the car, the spot he'd left her. She wasn't there and he panicked, looking around. "Syd?"

She popped out from behind a locker that had been torn from the wall. "Jack, oh, Jack." She hurried to him, throwing herself into his arms. "You were gone so long."

He clutched her hard, closing his eyes and burying his face in her throat. "I left him alive, in case you're wondering."

"I know, I know."

She was like a sponge against him, absorbing his anger, all the blunted rage he had left behind. She eased back enough to slide her mouth over his. He groaned, and mashed her to him. He'd felt like a part of him was missing, a slice of his soul, and was almost afraid she'd be gone when he got back. She wasn't all that happy about him going to see Bertrand in the first place. But he knew everything they'd done had brought him here, to her. And when he pulled back to look at her, saw that slow smile, he knew why.

He started to talk and it came rushing out. "I was searching his place when he came downstairs." He relayed every detail. Then he showed her the tape. "He was covering his back, Syd." He handed it over. "You won't like it."

"I haven't liked any of this yet."

He arched a brow. "Any?"

She blushed and nudged him, then slid into the car. "You heard it?"

"Enough."

She didn't like the sound of that. He got behind the wheel and she popped the tape in the player. The voices were low, but she recognized one as they filtered through the car. She looked at Jack, crestfallen.

"I'm sorry, baby."

"I should be used to people wanting me dead by now." She covered her face and rubbed. "But I'm not."

"This make you feel better?" He held up a bag of chips as if it was a shield.

She laughed and took it anyway. "I'm just glad you're okay."

His brow shot up. He looked so wicked when he did that, she thought.

"I expected you to go ape-shit."

She laughed shortly. "I'd like a demonstration of that someday. But I'm feeling numb to anyone who doesn't mean everything to me."

She glanced toward him, almost shyly, and he cupped the back of her head and kissed her deep and slow.

"Wanna get in the back seat and neck?"

He laughed and kissed her again. "I want more than your neck," he murmured, then sat back, shaking his head at how fast she could lighten him up.

From the driver's side, he adjusted the laptop and loaded the CD into Cisco's computer.

She opened the bag of chips. "That's the property of the U.S. government. And classified. I had credit for creating it, but not for anything else. I signed documents to that fact, too."

He copied the file to the hard drive. "And what were their plans for it if you were successful?"

She shrugged, munching. "Manufacture doses, distribute or probably just hold onto stock till it was necessary."

Jack nodded, looking awfully wise for a moment.

"What are you planning?"

"To show some really smart people they have nothing on that wonderful brain of yours."

"Oh." She flushed with embarrassment, then cocked her head. "I'm just a fantastic mind to you, huh?"

"The big brain is a turn-on, and the nice rack, too."

"Well, there is that."

She leaned and saw him type in her name, and the words Kingsford, Sarin gas pre-exposure serum. He saved it. "Now it goes nowhere without your name on it."

"Boy, you really know how to make a girl feel special." She touched his face and kissed him and for a second, he was lost in the feel of her soft mouth beneath his.

He sat back, let out a long breath, muttering something about her mouth driving him to distraction as he attached the file to an E-mail. He typed something in the body, then he made a call. "Hutch, I need a favor."

"If I can. You have an APB out on you with the local cops, you know."

Cisco was desperate to break confidence like that. "I'm sending you a large file now." He hit send, but before it went out, Sydney noticed that in the body of the E-mail was a short list, ending with the line, *Spread it around.*

"This isn't going to get me fired, is it?" Hutch asked. "Wait, it's here."

Jack heard the tap of keys.

"Holy shit, is this for real?" Hutch said.

"Yes, its for real." He winked at Syd. "Send it out now. Do this for me, Hutch, and we're square."

"We could never be, buddy."

Jack cut the call and looked at her. "USD had plans for the serum, but with the gas in the wild, the Center for Disease Control needs to have it right now."

She agreed. "There was more than one name on the list."

"England's CDC, and the military. And military chemical biohazard medical teams. That should cover it."

"But there's a late stage copy in the Chem-Loc computers, and Montoya has it, too, probably."

"That's why we're going to get it back."

"Excuse me?"

"We're taking it from Chem-Loc."

"No, no, no. I've been in there, that's a high-security facility."

"Not so much." He flipped out the bar code card and her features pulled taut. She'd forgotten about that. "All you have to do is erase the files."

"Me?"

"I won't recognize the elements. I need you."

She shoved a handful of chips into her mouth and muttered, "Oh, God. When?"

He glanced at his watch. "Two hours good for you?"

"How do we know you have such a thing, that it exists?"

"You don't." The corners of his mouth lifted. "I could test it on your friend here and then we'll see how it works." They all looked scared to death, gazes searching his person for a bulge. "One vial for sale."

"That's nothing."

"One vial *or* nothing at all. I have three."

He waited while the men talked amongst themselves. Martin arched a brow, catching a few words. Balinese wasn't that difficult.

"We agree. One."

Another man spoke up. "What will you do with the others?"

Van Meer scoffed and stood. "Sell it to your enemy." He walked away, crossing the mall to the store.

As he passed the shop, she slipped out, took his hand and walked with him through the crowd. "Where is the rest, Martin?"

He glanced to the side, his grip suddenly punishing. "Stop asking. You don't need to know."

"You'd better ease up on my hand, or I'll scream."

He patted it, his smile chilling.

"I hope you have the implosion weapon," she said softly. "Without it and her serum, you've got no safety net. You're dead."

He snickered. "Then so are you."

Nineteen

The library represented the distinguished elegance of wealth, the walls permeated with the lingering aroma of cherry tobacco, a sideboard laden with crystal and expensive cognacs. It detracted little from the body slumped over the desk, half his head blow out the back of his skull and splattered on the leather-bound books behind him.

In a glance, Cisco estimated the time of death sometime before midnight. Next to a blood pool and the gun still in Bertrand's hand was a letter. Confession and request for forgiveness in a few lines—and implication of Daniel Kress. Cut and run, point fingers before you go to hell, he thought, and felt cheated by the cowardly act.

The house had video surveillance, this room with only one camera. Cisco left and went to the security room, no more than a closet housing small screens and videotaping of the interior and estate grounds. He watched the feed. His technician was already sitting inside and filtered it, removing Wilson's image and splicing the stream. Cisco watched the clean play.

"It's done, sir."

He nodded and walked out, allowing forensics to enter.

Wilson had found justice.

And Gabe knew he had a little peace with himself.

* * *

Jack looked cool.

Syd looked like a teddy bear on steroids in a Kevlar vest. It weighed a ton and made her posture slump. Squatting beside him on the ground, she shivered. He glanced to the side, concern in his eyes. She forced a smile and he went back to watching the building through night vision goggles.

Breaking in was one thing, but this was the hub of all their troubles. She'd committed so many crimes, she'd lost count. Yet this time he gave her a gun, a slim, heavy nine millimeter that felt like ten pounds on her hip. It meant he'd expected big trouble since she was a lousy shot, as he liked to remind her. And while Jack had an earpiece in his ear, a thread mike poised at his lips like hers, neither was turned on. It was in case they got separated he'd said, but Syd wasn't planning on being more than three feet from him.

"It's getting late, shouldn't we be doing the deed?"

He side glanced a devilish look. "Not now, honey, we have to wait till this guy leaves."

She laughed shortly, then leaned up and looked. A slender man was getting into his car. "Shift change?"

"The guards are two on each level, one at the security desk."

"So we're going to knock them out and tie 'em up, right?"

"Man, you have a barbaric streak, ya know. No, we're going to pass by them. With the help of our little buddies."

As if on cue, the small box beside her jiggled. He'd caught mice in the abandoned school with her last half a sandwich and they were still eating it.

"I hope you enjoyed it," she muttered to the box.

Jack smothered a laugh as the worker drove down the long road to the main avenue. Jack wouldn't have brought Sydney along if he had known what to look for in the computers. Chemistry wasn't his strong suit. She wouldn't have stayed behind anyway.

Chem-Loc was a complex inside a complex—massive, stretching over acres of land; the laboratories, data research, and business offices were each in separate buildings under one colossal roof. A contained area that could be easily secured, and difficult to breach, Jack thought. He'd studied the plans, though some parts were missing. Pure paranoia on the part of the owners. Four entrances, and key cards to get inside. He hoped the card would give him access anywhere, because if they were different on different levels, they were screwed. Explosive charges would do the trick, but he didn't have any or the time to makes some. It was now or never.

Taking back Kingsford would shift the balance. Van Meer had the gas and implosion bombs and he'd use them. Jack didn't doubt it, nor that the man would meet with him—as much as he wanted to come face-to-face with the son of a bitch. Van Meer would play his own hand. Though . . . pounding him into the ground would just tip the edge of satisfaction. At the moment, the rendezvous was a necessary distraction. Wiping out the files was the first step. Van Meer was the next. Just the same, Jack sent an E-mail to Cisco's office, in case something went wrong. He prayed it didn't.

Beyond the fence line, the parking lots were empty, the outside lit with security lights. Guards patrolled the area inside the complex. The outer perimeter was left to sensors.

Jack slipped on infrared glasses, and studied the beams of light crisscrossing the acreage and wide apart. Was this just for looks? The car passed and the gates started to close. Jack shoved the box at her and they moved around it and into the complex. He stopped her, his head bowed as he checked the sensors. They had about fifty yards to go and little cover.

"The sensors are low to the ground. When I tell you, pick up your feet and step as if you're stepping over a fence." Jack slipped off the red glasses, and put them on her for a second.

"Cool. Gotcha."

"Hold tight to those little guys." He took the glasses back and every few steps, he lifted his leg high.

He made a little *hup* sound to signal her. Holding the box of wiggling mice, Sydney stepped in his footprints. They were halfway to the building when she heard a rapid thumping.

They both turned. Jack reacted instantly, picking her up

and racing the rest of the distance to the building. The growl of a dog scratched the silence and Sydney knew they weren't going to make it. Suddenly, he dropped her and turned as the animal leapt. Jack punched. Syd heard something crack, the dog yelped once, then hit the ground. Sydney stared at the motionless Doberman, then up at Jack.

He shrugged, flexing his fingers. "Wasn't expecting that." He helped her up.

They made it to the side, ducking low; lights shone from inside the building, fluorescent and painfully bright. The lower offices were empty.

Jack was at the service door. "Get ready with the mice."

She squatted and held the flaps of the carton. Jack swiped the bar code card. The door clicked open. "Let them go."

She spilled them on the ground. They scattered and when some headed back to her, she lurched into him. He chuckled.

"Disease carrying creatures were Tish's thing. Not mine. Eww." She kicked a cluster.

He held her back, waiting for the mice to do their job, and when the outside sensor went off, he pulled her inside the building with him. The constant blast of the alarm made her flinch, yet Jack was oblivious, flicking on his flashlight. Sydney hung back as he moved forward and tossed something. The camera followed, a light coming on with the movement. "Aren't you going to spray the lens with something?"

"This isn't TV. If I block the feed, they'll come running for sure. We just have to be fast. Get in, get out."

"It's not a landing assault, Jack."

"Who says?" He grabbed a handful of pens off a desk and tossed one. The camera moved in a slow panning motion. He pointed, then moved under the lens. She shadowed him, gripping his belt.

"Stairs."

Jack flattened against the wall, and watched the camera pan, then pulled her with him and flattened again. The camera moved in a smooth motion. It wasn't on a sensor.

They slipped into the stairwell, their breathing echoing up the hollow cavern. Jack scanned with a flashlight, checking for cameras. None. He inclined his head and they traveled upward to the second level to Montoya's lab.

I'm out of shape, she thought, making a face at his back. Jack took two stairs at a time.

Gingerly, he opened the door a fraction and spied the red light on a camera, another on the far side. A second corridor bisected it, leading to the elevators and to lower levels. No other doors except this emergency escape, and the elevator. He waited till the camera panned a couple times. Automated, he decided, then slid around the door, and hurried, this time to spray the lens.

"Jack I thought—"

"I'm betting this lab has a feed to Bertrand's offices." He went still under it, watching the second camera make one cycle revolution, then he darted forward, and shot the lens.

Syd didn't have to talk. Jack had downloaded the architect's plans and he'd traced their path. He had gone over it a half dozen times so she knew what to expect. He flipped a light switch, but with all the information they had, nothing prepared her for the glass-roofed lab. She stepped out into the hall as the overhead lights blinked on and lit up the wide hall. Whoa.

"That," he pointed toward the ceiling, "should be Bertrand's office. Top floor."

"You think maybe he's got it . . .?"

"Possibly. He was a chemist, but Montoya was working on it and he'd have to do it"—he pointed—"so Bert buddy could watch him."

"Nobody would be in here if they didn't have to," she said and he looked at her. Her gaze moved rapidly over the equipment for another moment, then shifted to him. "It's a toxic chem lab," she whispered, pointing to the pewter colored hazardous material suits complete with air tanks. There were four on the outer wall, four inside. "Titanium suits."

She studied the lab, mentally comparing it to hers in the Cradle. Glass, white, it looked unused. The ceiling was high, mazed with silver tubing and funnel-shaped vents dangling over the work areas. They were retracted now, but they'd lower when you were blending. The ceiling was transparent and offered a view of the outer hull of the complex, and the night sky. Bertrand's offices could look down on it. A fish bowl, she thought.

Her gaze moved over the equipment, the computers, and glass cabinets. There were enough chemicals to mix up a decent bomb in there and she leaned to inspect the security panels. He held out the card.

"That won't work."

He scowled and muscled closer.

"It's on an automated system, Jack. Sensors inside there turn on if the levels get too high, but this"—she gestured to the panel—"no hand print. No card, only a password. Now what?"

Jack stepped back, his gaze moving over the glass. There were locking mechanism sensors in the base and top, clear glass in the center that had to be four inches thick, double paned. A gunshot wouldn't break it. Beyond that was a large open floor, then the bulk of the laboratory. None of it looked familiar to him except a microscope. Beside the entrance—a glass pocket door—was another small panel. Three buttons down, three across like a stoplight.

"Auto cleaning," she said. "It keeps the room hydrostatic free. And it has a wash and vent system. If there was a spill, it would vent. If you're not careful, you can suck all the air out of the room. We had it in the Cradle in my lab and in the cold room."

"Those computers familiar enough?" He studied the panel, then checked his watch. The guard would have corralled the mice in a couple of minutes.

"Yes, except that's not the problem, is it?"

Getting inside was.

* * *

The coroner signed the report, releasing two more bodies for burial. He fixed himself more coffee, noticed his hands trembling, then set the cup aside and rubbed his face. He took his clipboard and walked to the next corpse. Two more to go. He flipped back the sheet, and leaned over what was left of the woman's head.

He spoke into the recorder, jotting notes. Cause of death was obvious. Several bullets to the face. He pulled the tray of tools closer and began extracting bullet fragments. His gaze moved down her body. So young, he thought, then frowned and grasped her hand. In decay, the skin had shrunk slightly, the texture papery and peeling. He adjusted the overhead light. Had chemicals done this, he wondered, using forceps to lift the edge of skin.

Then he realized—it wasn't skin.

Cisco was two steps away from Bertrand's body when the phone on the desk rang. The room went quiet. He approached, and realized it wasn't the house phone, but the small cell near his head. He read the number, slipping out a pad to jot it down.

"Find this caller's location." He thrust the paper at Marcuso who was on Bertrand's computer, downloading the hard drive.

Marcuso turned to his own laptop and worked his magic.

Cisco felt his pulse quicken as the green latitude and longitude bars on the screen linked with the satellite and narrowed the cell waves. The phone kept ringing.

Marucso looked up. "From inside Chem-Loc, sir."

"You're certain."

"Yes, sir."

Cisco debated answering the phone, needing to know exactly who was on the other end, but he trusted his instincts. "Let it ring." He hurried out of the house, barking into his radio. "I want full teams, snipers, and hazmat, CBC. At Chem-Loc. Now. Expect Sarin exposure." He climbed into the chopper, and pounded the interior wall. "Get in the air now, now!"

"Open it up, cut wires. Shoot it."

He bent to inspect it. "It's hermetically sealed, I'd need a crow bar to get it open. And we risk locking it permanently with a gun shot."

All this way and then to be stopped now?

Jack patted own his pockets, then found the narrow black spray can. He shot the panel with the powered spray, then blew on the panel. "I'll coat the oil from fingerprints." The most-used keys were visible.

"There're a million combinations."

"You're the brains of this outfit, take a stab at it. But hurry, the guards are going to get wise soon."

She hushed him, studied the board. "I don't know how many numbers." She punched each marred key slowly. An alarm blared and she flinched. "Oh, hell, this isn't going to work, Jack."

"Try again. Think hard, Syd. We're running out of time."

"Oh, yeah, *that* helps." Sydney rubbed her face, took a breath, and flexed her fingers. "Okay, okay. I can do this." She felt time tick by as if the clock were in her stomach. Montoya was a chemist, too. What would he use? What would *she* use? Suddenly her features went taut and she hit the keys. Locks popped up, the glass door slid open.

"Whoa."

"Elements of life. Air and water."

He kissed her temple and pushed her through the entrance. "Get busy, baby. Turn on your throat mike." He stood guard outside the glass doors.

Syd hurried, turning on the computers, powering up the drivers. "This is an awesome machine. But why didn't Montoya use it to synthesize alterations with computer generation hypothesis to get the final result. I did, but the tweaking is what worked. Too much epileptic and the convulsions wouldn't stop, heart failure, and too little, the victim would choke to death."

"Show off."

She searched and found the formula. That Montoya had tried it nearly twenty times with failure made her smile. She'd done it hundreds. But there were zillions of files.

"If he was testing your formula," Jack said, "did he have Sarin?

She called up Montoya's notes. "He had the element of Sari—oh, no." She looked up, then pointed to the glass cubicle to the rear of the lab. "There. He'd put some rats or roaches in there, inject them and release the gas. No wonder he had the titanium suits. This is not a full decon room."

"Meaning."

She deleted banks of files, emptied the trash bin, and kept going. "If the gas was exposed in here, it would vent and wash, but only in there. Every surface would still be contaminated."

"Pleasant." Jack frowned, walking to the glass exit, his weapon out. "You almost done?"

"Close."

"Then hurry."

The alarm stopped suddenly. She glanced up. "Oh, God."

Jack stepped into the doorway, his arms straight as he aimed down the hall.

The elevator lights were on.

"Syd," he warned.

"I'm trying I'm trying. I can't delete the last files. His copy. There's an encrypted password. Damn, that's the closest mix to mine." The most important, she thought.

Jack stayed where he was. "Ghost that computer. Now."

Sydney drew the weapon, stepped back and did as he'd taught her. She fired, emptying the gun into the center of the hard drives, the noise loud in the tall room.

She let out a breath, thinking that was a turn-on as she

rushed to him. Jack pulled her toward the door to the staircase. He reached it just as the locks clicked shut.

"Oh, man, this day is *so* not going well."

"The entire facility is locking down." Jack pulled her back and fired at the door. The lock smoked and he yanked. It wouldn't budge, he pulled harder and Sydney joined him. The door gave and they burst into the stairwell. Jack heard the mechanism snap shut on the level below.

"Move, move. We'll get locked in."

"Oh, hell, no we won't." She ran down the stairs. Jack passed her, grabbed her, taking two at a time. A shot fired inside the stairwell and he covered her as it ricocheted on the railings. He cranked off four rounds without aiming, then wrenched the door, bolted out and headed the way they'd come.

The service doors were locked down, trapping them.

"No, no!" Syd didn't give up and yanked violently on the door till Jack pulled her back.

"This way."

They headed down another corridor lined with doors, their footsteps a brutal pulse to their escape. Jack made two turns, paused at the edge of the hall leading to the lobby, then popped out the magazine. Two bullets. Great.

He checked for the night watchmen.

Sydney felt it before it came, like a wave of despair over him. His shoulders slumped, his expression softened before he took a step.

She inched out behind him, then staggered back, covering her mouth. "Dear God."

Bodies were strewn, one man slumped over the console, another on his back near the main doors. A third was beyond the wall of glass doors on the ground, his head in an awkward position. A lit flashlight was still in his hand. Rats crawled over the poor man. The guard at the console still had his hand on the phone. His blood, spilled over the edge of the desk, dripped on the floor. The gunshots to the chest she could digest, but not the slashing of their throats nearly decapitating them.

"Who could do such a thing?"

Jack was already checking the area, then the guards for a sign of life. "We can't help them." He looked at her suddenly. The doors on this floor were locking in groups. Each snick a dead reckoning to sealing them in with a killer. "Go go go!"

They ran toward the doors. Jack punched the release and nothing happened. She looked at him, panicked. Jack ran back to the desk, moved the body and searched for an override. He found a four-button panel for the doors. It couldn't be that easy, could it?

"Jack, watch out!" she screamed.

He spun, his gun on the man approaching in a casual stroll. Van Meer. His face and clothing were splattered with blood. He held a machine pistol. Jack's gaze flicked to his hands, and instantly, he smacked the button. The doors sprang. A timer beeped off seconds. "Run! Run!"

"For God's sake, come with me!"

"Right behind you." He back-stepped, aiming and knowing he had only two bullets where Van Meer likely had fifty—and the gas. A buzzer sounded and red lights blinked as the doors stopped, then started to close.

On the threshold, Sydney grabbed his arm. "Jack, don't leave me."

"Not gonna happen."

Then Van Meer fired, bullets catching in the glass.

And Jack.

Sydney screamed as he flinched like a snapping whip, the power of it pushing into her and sending her backwards through the narrow passage. When she straightened, the large steel enforced doors sealed in her face, caging Jack in.

Sydney pounded on the doors. "No! Jack! Jack!" She moved to the left to see where he was hit as he fell to the floor. "Please don't die. Oh, God, please don't." The line the bullets took was etched in the glass, veined cracks bleeding outward. The glass didn't break. She struggled to see him, hitting the glass walls. "Jack. Jack." Tears wet her eyes, her worst fears materializing.

The impact to his Kevlar forced the air from his lungs, and Jack grappled to breathe, pain burning through his chest. The Kevlar smoked, the bullet lodged in the fibers. He moved and winced at the spikes of pain. "That's gonna leave a mark." He held tight to his gun, levering to his feet. For a second, residual pain immobilized him down to his heels.

He could barely hear Sydney's screams through the glass, his attention on the silver vial in Van Meer's hand.

This isn't going to end well, Jack thought, resolute. At least she's safe. "Where's the rest?"

"One isn't enough?" Van Meer chuckled and cocked the load on his machine pistol.

If he shoots again, he'll kill Sydney, Jack thought and moved away from the door in slow increments. "I go, you go with me, count on it."

Van Meer reached, his arm disappearing into the doorway to his right, and came back with a woman. He shoved her, and she slipped on the blood pool, but didn't fall.

Jack frowned, out of the corner of his vision got a glimpse. Tish Bingham. The bug bitch.

"Get it," Van Meer ordered.

She sent Van Meer a snide look, the same to Jack before she moved to a bag on the floor behind a visitor's sofa. She unzipped and pulled out a gray sphere the size of a softball and encased in feather-shaped layers of metal. The implosion bomb. Jesus. Did they think they could actually use it and live?

"What did it take, Bingham? How much did he pay you to betray everything they worked for and throw in with a killer?"

She sneered, making her look older, used up. "You know nothing about me, so shut up."

You were her friend. "She grieved for you, trusted you, goddammit!"

The glass thumped and Tish looked to the right at Sydney, who gave her the finger, shouting behind the glass. Tish rolled her eyes.

Van Meer laughed, a dark growl that held little humor. Jack shifted to his right away from Sydney. His chest felt tight, pain billowing out from the bullets trauma and weakening his grip.

"I'll get away, you'll be stuck here, Wilson, dying."

"*I'll*? Aren't you forgetting someone?" Bingham looked so prissy for a moment, her hand on her hip, head cocked.

Van Meer turned his head and looked her dead in the eye. "No." He fired, and the spray of bullets ripped through Bingham's body, nearly tearing her in half. Shock froze on her face as she started to fall. The ball slid from her hand and Jack dove for it.

Van Meer was there, lurching to get it first. He collided with Jack, and the sphere skipped across the floor, out of reach. In a heartbeat, they both had weapons aimed at each other's head.

Van Meer grinned, stretching the tattoo that wrapped his neck. "I'll put enough holes in you they'll bury your bladdie carcass in a boot box."

Rolling to his knees, inches away, Jack stared into the eyes of a mass murderer. "And at this range, I promise, you'll die first."

The vial in his hand, the machine pistol in the other, Van Meer was trapped. In a flash of movement, Jack yanked the magazine from his weapon. Van Meer pulled the trigger and at the empty *click-click* his fury exploded.

He didn't chamber. Jack fired, putting his last two bullets in Van Meer's chest.

Van Meer flew back, falling on his ass and sliding across the floor. He laid flat for a couple seconds, then his head lifted. He grinned. "You don't think I'm that stupid, do ya, kaffir." He spun to his knees, and ripped open his black T-shirt, exposing the vest.

"Yeah, I do. I read your dossier, Van Meer. You're clever, but you're still a fucking lowlife. You always have been. You're as dirty as they come."

With a shrieking growl, the South African lurched and dove. Jack sidestepped and Van Meer's own momentum sent him sliding across the polished floor. Jack went after him. Van Meer didn't expect it, was trying to reload the weapon with the vial in his fist.

Jack threw his weight into him, knocking the weapon from his grasp. The vial went with it, spinning through the air and hitting the wall.

Jack's heart stopped but the vial remained intact.

The moment gave Van Meer the opportunity, and he punched, driving a fist under Jack's chin and snapping his head back. Jack bit his own tongue, swallowed blood, then grabbed Van Meer's shoulder and dug his thumb into the fresh wound. Van Meer grunted, slammed his fist into Jack's stomach and plowed ahead like a tortured bull, knocking them both to the floor.

Without weapons, it was hand to hand and Jack had no intention of dying today.

Beyond the glass, Sydney could do no more than watch. Without a weapon, the bar code, she couldn't help him. The vial lay only a couple feet from them, the implosion device yards away and right in front of her. Inches of glass and steel walls separated her from Jack's only hope.

They were matched, Jack driven by the need to survive and Van Meer the need to kill. She heard every grunt through the throat mike, but Jack had to press it to speak clearly.

He couldn't. Van Meer was wild, throwing desperate punches that missed the mark, while Jack was precise, deadly. His elbow was in Van Meer's kidneys, a fist to the temple. Van Meer staggered, tried to reach the vial, but Jack kept hitting, a leg kick to the face, a sidekick to the solar plexus.

The killer was immune, coming back—savage and mean.

Wind kicked up around her, the sound of a chopper billowing across the open land. Alarms still blared inside, and Sydney could do nothing. Even as men ran up behind her. Even as someone grabbed her arms, forcing her around.

"Cisco! Help him. The vial, the bomb, it's in there."

He pulled her back from the glass. "You can't help, Dr. Hale. He has Sarin."

"But Jack is in there. Jesus, Cisco, shoot the doors!"

Behind him men in Hazmat suits prepared for the worst, and Cisco pulled on a suit. "Complete exposure risk," he said, and gestured for a suit. "Put it on, Dr. Hale. Now."

"The vial is protected."

"Not good enough." He grabbed her arms, and with two men, forced her into a suit.

"No!" Before they got the hood on, Sydney tore from him, pounding on the glass. "Jack!"

Van Meer was on top of Jack, one meaty fist wrapping his neck as Jack clawed at the fingers pressing on the throat mike. She heard Jack choking, each gasp, and could almost feel his windpipe collapsing.

Then his leg shot up, hitting Van Meer in the back and driving him forward. Jack propelled him over his head. Van Meer fell hard and Jack rolled around in his direction primed for attack.

But Van Meer held the vial.

He climbed to his knees. Bleeding from his nose and ears, he smiled at Jack, then looked at the doors, at her, then Cisco.

Then he slammed the vial down onto the floor.

It broke.

Twenty

Jack crawled toward the implosion bomb, his breathing strained, his world narrowing to the next breath, the next thought.

What a way to die, he thought, and wrapped his fingers around the sphere. It took everything he had for him to drive it down into the floor. He turned his face away, felt the blast of cold as it opened. He prayed Sydney was as smart as he thought.

The implosion bomb opened, metal feathers spreading, and spinning the sphere. There was a flash of blue Freon detonation, and she rushed to the CBC officer, grabbing his kit and throwing it open.

"Get a hood on her!" Cisco yelled.

She pushed them off, grabbed a syringe packet and the tubes of Kingsford from inside her bra.

"You had Kingsford?"

"Shoot out the doors!" She jammed the needle into her arm, hit the plunger, then threw it aside to fill the last vial. Her hands shook as she filled it, tears blurred her vision; inside the lobby the implosion bomb did its job, but it wasn't enough. Too much concentrated Sarin. Jack was dying.

Yet Cisco didn't move.

"Cisco, please! Trust me, please! I can save him."

"There is no venting in there. It's the lobby for crissake."

"But there's a fire sprinkler."

Cisco ran to the side of the building, searching and pulled the fire alarm. Nothing happened except the lights blinked and the alarm riddled the air. No water.

Jack was losing consciousness already. She'd only seconds until he was beyond hope. Van Meer was already into convulsions so violent he'd break his own spine.

She pulled on the large yellow hood and glared at him. "Shoot the fucking doors!"

When he didn't move, she lurched, took another man's gun and charged at the doors, emptying the gun in the same area as Van Meer's bullets. The glass started to shatter and she rammed her shoulder into it. It didn't break and then Cisco was there, throwing his weight into the glass, and it shattered in a rainfall of fractures. She fell to the floor and scrambled to Jack, sliding to her knees.

Sprinklers turned on, showering them both. "Jack, I'm here, I'm here."

He was in respiratory failure. He gasped and tried to push her away. She shoved off his hands, ripped open the Kevlar, then jammed the needle into his chest, and pushed the plunger.

"Cisco, help me!"

The team entered, hosing down the area with a wash solution.

Jack rolled into a ball, his nose bleeding, his lungs struggling. He grabbed her arms, his grip losing its strength as men in Hazmat gear rushed in.

"Don't you dare leave me, Jack." She knew it could be her last chance, her last moment. She lifted the hood, and kissed him. "Don't leave me; I love you, I love you."

Cisco was there, yanking the hood over her face and dragging her out as the CBC team quickly stripped off Jack's clothing, hosed him with water, then threw a barrier cloth over him before they took him away on a rubber stretcher.

Outside, Cisco shoved her into the decontamination

closet. Doctors and techs held her under the shower, sprayed and detoxed, then stripped off the suit and her clothing. Sydney didn't feel any of it. Not the hands pulling and cutting her clothes, not the spray of the water, the harsh soap— nor heard the panicked voices. She felt her pulse speed up, her lungs heave to take in more air. Her glands shut down. She slapped the framing bars to hold herself upright.

Cisco was on the other side, his face in the plastic window, and for the first time, she saw emotion in his handsome face.

He shouted, "Do something! Goddammit, do something for her!"

She choked on her saliva, her muscles twitching, and Sydney started to sink to the floor. She was dying. She knew it.

Oh God, it didn't work.

Cisco had seen many people die. Had been the cause of it several times, yet nothing prepared him for Sydney Hale. Men rushed out with the gurney and he could do no more than watch as they put her in the ambulance. Her hand slid from beneath the rubber covering and dangled. Cisco wanted to hold it, assure her everything that could be done was in motion. He ripped off the hazmat hood, pushing his fingers through his damp hair and dislodging the clasp. Biohazard experts spoke to him, pulling him into a decontamination sphere. He obeyed, did as he was ordered.

He was lucky, they all were. Her implosion bomb had worked well enough that the internal gas was nearly non-existent, except for what touched the walls and ceiling, the equipment. And that was being hosed down now. Water and charcoal would take care of the rest.

But Hale had kissed Wilson. The single demonstration of her love could mean her death.

And where, in God's name, were the last two vials?

Eight hours later, Secure Medical Facility, Fort Belvoir, VA

Sydney stirred on the bed, her eyes fluttering open as if they were leaded. Around her was an oxygen tent, beyond that people moved back and forth, talking in whispers. She smiled, glad to be alive, then she laughed.

They turned at once and she sat up. Her bones and muscles ached as she unzipped the partition. The room went silent.

"Hi. Got anything to drink around here?"

Laughter burst and suddenly Cisco was in the doorway, looking rather shocked for his always contained self.

"Good evening, Dr. Hale." He smiled gently at her. Doctors hovered, checking vitals. Her smile fell.

"Jack? Where's Jack?"

He inclined his head and she looked to the right, through the glass walls patterned with wire. Jack lay perfectly still, under a tent, and her gaze shot to his pulse in the monitor, then to Cisco.

"Tell me the truth."

"He's been like that since we brought him in."

She pushed out of the bed, holding the back of the gown and hurried to the room.

"Dr. Hale, please wait. Dr. Hale!"

Someone threw a robe over her shoulders as she stood by the bed, slipping her fingers under the oxygen hood and grasping his hand. His skin was cool and dry, a good sign.

She glanced at the clock above Jack's head. "He hasn't woken? In eight hours?"

"No. No movement either."

Paralysis? "Oh, Jack." Under the hood, she pushed his hair back, glancing over the monitors and drips. "He should be awake."

Cisco waved and people filed out of the room.

Sydney stared at Jack's face for long moments, waiting for

some flicker of life, but he was so still, his chest barely moving, the hood separating him from her. The fluorescent light leeched color from his skin, the hollowness of his eyes were purple, his lips and cheeks bruised from his fight with Van Meer.

She laid her head down on the bedsheets. "I'm sorry, Jack. I'm so sorry. All this and it wasn't good enough." Sydney tried not to cry, but the tears came, followed by the relief it was over, and the new agony. She couldn't think beyond this moment except for him. Don't take him from me, she prayed. *Don't.*

She felt lost and helpless. Cisco moved up behind her, laid a hand on her shoulder. She sobbed harder, angry.

"Dammit, Jack. Wake up, please."

He didn't. He was still as glass.

In the bedcovers, she muttered uselessly, words she couldn't stop, the sound for herself; talking because without him—she wished she hadn't survived.

She didn't know how long she went on before Cisco tapped her. She lifted her head, watched Jack's hand come toward her.

"Einstein," he slurred.

Sydney smiled, tears spilling, and she lifted the hood off. "Oh, Jack." She sniffled, taking his hand, checked his pulse, his eyes, the beds of his nails.

"*Now* you wanna play doctor with me?"

She smiled and laughed, then leaned to hold him. His hand moved sluggishly over her hair, falling to her spine as she cried. "It's okay, baby. It's okay now."

She curled onto the bed. Cisco smiled and turned away. When the doctors scowled and tried to come in, he stood in front of the door, arms folded.

"A classified discussion," was all he said.

Pete Wickum had seen the evidence, but the coroner had called too late. Cisco was already in the air to Chem-Loc and

Tish Bingham was dead. The body in the Cradle had been dead longer than the others, a blond woman kidnapped, murdered and used for the attack. It was likely the reason the odor of witch hazel was all over the packs. The dead didn't keep well. What amazed Pete was that they'd had to drop from the air with a dead body. The young woman, who'd been reported missing a week ago, was an innocent, just riding a bike or walking and was unfortunate enough to be within reach of Van Meer. Her hand had been covered in latex film, which served no purpose except the initial prints for identification. It took two days for the dead woman's skin to shrink and the film to show.

Clever. And deadly. But that's not why he was strolling though Dr. Handerson's house. Lila Handerson was still missing along with the remaining gas, and an implosion bomb. The house had been searched, and nothing had been disturbed since the attack occurred.

But it was Sydney's mother who clued him in. According to Dr. Hale, Lila had visited her mother, yet the elderly woman was a little confused, mistaking the female agent assigned to her as Lila Handerson, then not recognizing her hours later, though the agent had been living next door. It made him think that she probably confused any blond woman and maybe that included Tish Bingham.

Van Meer had more knowledge than Bingham could provide. Dr. Handerson had the knowledge of the codes. Pete was thinking Lila and Tish had helped Van Meer.

Before the attack, Lila Handerson had been questioned like all the others, cleared and released. She never took the trip she'd booked with her husband, and while it seemed viable that she'd want to get away, they were chasing a ghost. He walked through the house, then into the garage and flipped on the light. Her car was missing, the area was packed with household items, sports equipment, and tools. Packed tight, it was more like a storage unit and he moved between the old furniture, frowning when he heard a humming.

Pete moved a set of bikes, a workbench, pushed cardboard boxes aside, digging deeper and following the sound. It was barely there, footsteps would cover it. He wedged himself between an old cabinet and a sofa, stepping on the cushions. Then he backed off and moved enough junk so he could see.

Something rusted and white was tucked under shelving and it took him another five minutes to get to it. A freezer. Small chest, maybe ten cubic feet. It was locked; he broke it, but then had to wiggle it out from under the shelving to get the lid up. The cool rush of air did nothing to cover the stench.

Frozen, and wrapped in plastic—was the beautiful Lila Handerson.

And cradled in her arms were the remaining vials of gas, the implosion bombs, and one man's finger, a wedding ring still attached.

Sydney sat at the foot of the bed, snitching Jack's food. "You owe me dinner."

"I better, I'll never get a decent meal around you."

She smiled, scrunched her face and ate a French fry.

"If you want some of this feast, Cisco, better get it now."

"No thank you, it's all yours."

"You mean *hers*." Jack grinned.

"I even thanked him for bringing it all the way from the Capital Grille."

Cisco stood near the windows, staring out. "It's a beautiful day out there."

"Any day I get to see is gorgeous," Syd said, then whispered to Jack. "He's getting melancholy. Notice that?"

Cisco glanced over his shoulder, a hawkish look that was supposed to be intimidating. He tried hard to be a tough guy, she thought. Then his cell rang.

He let out a long-suffering sigh, then answered it.

"How did you get this number?" Cisco scowled, listened, then held the phone out to Jack. "It's for you."

They frowned collectively as Jack took it.

"Hey, kemosabe."

"Sherman! Jesus, where have you been? Is Peabody okay?"

Sydney shrieked a laugh, and Jack pulled her closer. Jack listened to Sherman tell how they got out, pretending to get inside the tubing, then splitting and hopping a bus and riding it all night. The blood was intentional, Peabody being brave enough to cut himself. They were in Maryland at the university, hiding out in the dorms.

After a moment, Syd had her chance to talk with them. Jack ended the call, and handed the phone back.

Cisco pocketed his phone. "The hackers, right?"

"You charging them?"

Cisco scoffed. "I should hire them." And he'd keep them in mind for the future.

When Jack pushed the tray away, with Hale taking one more bite of food, the pair got cozy on the hospital bed and Cisco felt out of place. And he rarely felt out of place. He said good-bye and quietly stepped out. They didn't even notice.

"Good," she said. "The watchdog is gone, wanna neck?"

Jack chuckled, pulled her down to the bed, and hovered over her. "Did I hear you say something when I was dying?"

Her eyes went soft and glossy as the memory. They'd come so close to death and she didn't want to be near it again. "What did you hear?"

" 'I love you, Jack?' "

That he said it like a question made her see that despite his strength, his valor, he was vulnerable. She was glad it was to her. "Well, I'm glad you're copacetic with your inner being, but it's me that loves you."

He grinned, the smile changing his features, and she pulled him down onto her. "I'd show you, but then, we'd get an audience."

"When has that stopped you?"

She laughed and his smile bloomed, and Sydney absorbed it into her skin, her soul. Then she did what he wanted, hungered for, and laid her mouth over his.

Jack felt something open up inside him, a flow of contented warmth. The wall started cracking the first time he touched her, now it flooded him with emotion: love, hope, a future. All he knew was that the pure crisp feeling left him weak and trembling. He loved her. It wasn't as hard as he thought it would be, and he wrapped his arms around her, wanting to strip her bare and love her all night.

"I'm not up to speed yet, but I can try." His hand roamed her spine and cupped her behind.

"I can wait for the full monty."

Someone cleared his throat, and they looked up. Cisco stood in the doorway, looking serious and too much like his old self.

Sydney flushed, and Jack sat back, pulling her upright and glaring over the intrusion.

He held out the tape. "You left this in my car."

Sydney took it. The tape of Kress.

"The Under Secretary of Defense wants to see you, Dr. Hale. Now."

Another man in Marine uniform entered the room behind him. "Captain Wilson."

"Sir." His commanding officer. Behind him were two men in suits, with badges.

Oh, no, Syd thought, and glanced uneasily between the colonel and Jack.

"I knew it would end like this, Syd. Go on." Not only had he broken laws, the UCMJ, he'd given her serum to agencies and the military.

"No, they can't charge you. My God."

"Dr. Hale, please." Cisco urged Sydney off the bed and she slipped on her jacket. She glanced back at Jack. He mouthed, *I love you.*

She smiled, then looked right at the colonel. "Don't mess with him, Colonel, I have friends in high places, and a couple markers I could call in."

Jack sputtered at her audacity.

The colonel's brows shot up. Cisco pulled her out of the

room and muttered, "Christ, you've gotten a mouth on you, Sydney."

"Yes *Gabe*, I have." She strode ahead of him, the tape in her hand and fire in her step.

Cisco almost pitied the Under Secretary.

Jack stood in full dress uniform at parade rest, staring at the fresh markers. Surrounding his friends was a sea of simple white headstones. Somewhere in here was his own father, he realized. Jack lifted his gaze out over Arlington cemetery, feeling fortunate and somehow cheated.

His friends had been buried with full honors and a twenty-one gun salute. Jack had been in the hospital at the time. They'd forgive him for that, he thought, his lips pulling in a reluctant smile. From Suzanne Lyons he learned that Agent Cisco had seen to it that the families wouldn't suffer any financial hardship. Jack didn't know how he did it, and wisely didn't ask, but he was grateful.

It was over, painfully and justified. But none of it changed anything. Jack thought it would, that he'd feel released from his grief. That would be too easy. To let go of the men who were his family. He didn't feel alone, and looked out over the graves. The brotherhood are here, he thought.

With a white-gloved hand, he placed a copy of the tape on top of the center headstone, then stepped back, snapped to attention and saluted one last time.

"Semper Fi."

Jack spun on his heels and walked, not knowing where to go.

Or if she would be there when he arrived.

Dr. Hale was praised for her creation and would be awarded any grant she desired, but that wasn't her concern. She made demands, forcefully, to one of the highest offices in the government. Cisco enjoyed watching her flex her mental muscles and had to get used to this new woman. She was stronger, almost wild with her determination and the two things she'd requested was Captain Wilson's complete exoneration and to confront Daniel Kress herself. She deserved that right.

Luckily, the USD and his boss agreed.

Captain Wilson had already been debriefed and no charges were lodged. Though continuing his career as a Marine after exposure to Sarin gas would be his decision. He'd survived, but whether it would leave lasting effects only time would determine.

In jeans and leather bomber jacket, Cisco stood back near a column in Dulles Airport, watching as Daniel Kress handed over his passport and ticket, smiling as the woman checked him in.

Everyone involved was dead, and Kress thought he was in the clear. He'd certainly covered his tracks well, except for the phone taps to Bertrand and one to Montoya, who was found this morning in his home, dead for a day. A news release went out three days ago, reporting the death of Dr. Hale and Captain Wilson in Chem-Loc laboratories. The Under Secretary wanted Kress to make a move.

And he had. The bad guys, Cisco thought, are predictable. Especially the ones who aren't used to being bad. Kress had liquidated his portfolio, put his house up for sale and was right now trying to step on a jet bound for the Cayman Islands.

At the increase in chatter, Cisco looked around. Dr. Hale was walking down the wide corridor, maneuvering around people. She had the look of a woman on fire, pure rage rolling off her in waves. Behind her were reporters and TV cameras. Dr. Kress didn't look up, even as the commotion in the airport generated toward the boarding area.

"Dr. Kress," she called and Cisco was glad she didn't have a gun. He didn't think he could cover that up.

Kress grabbed his ticket and tried to board. FBI agents blocked his escape to the plane.

The reporters rushed ahead, cameras flashing.

"Dr. Kress, is it true you betrayed national security and hired a known terrorist to steal Sarin gas?"

"How did you pay him; was it with government funds?"

"What were you thinking when you initiated the sale of chemical weapons to one of Interpol's most wanted?"

Daniel Kress reared back, scowling. "I did no such thing. The sanctity of national security has always been in the forefront of anything I do."

Sydney pushed her way between the reporters. "Really?"

Kress met her gaze and paled, his features going slack. She held up the small tape player and pressed the button.

The sound of Kress's voice was clear and precise. ". . . will make millions on Hale's serum. The terror dynamic only should put us on NASDAQ. She can't be allowed to reproduce it, we must have the only copy." Some conversation, then the distinct, "She's no longer useful, eliminate her."

Reporters shouted questions, cameras rolled. Sydney let the tape play, his own voice revealing the method. She stopped it when it turned classified, and pocketed the recorder. She simply stared at the man who'd taught her to use her brain for good, and betrayed her. Betrayed their country. And nearly killed Jack.

Suddenly, she drew back her arm and punched, her fist impacting with his nose. Kress staggered back into the FBI agent. Sydney shook her hand, rubbing her knuckles.

Cisco muscled his way in, flashed his badge. "Happy?" he said to her.

"Oh, hell yes." She gripped his lapel, yanked him down and planted a kiss on his cheek. "Thanks."

Cisco flushed and turned to Kress, and as agents put him in handcuffs, said, "Dr. Daniel Kress, you're charged with high treason against the United States of America and its citizens." Blood oozed out his nose. "Good shot, Hale."

Sydney looked up at him and he expected a smile.

"You forgot to add twelve counts of murder," she said.

"Trust me, he'll get his due."

She scoffed. "I'll be watching you, geek with a gun."

Cisco chuckled as she turned and left the terminal. Reporters chased her but she ignored them, climbing into the black limousine. The driver looked back at her, waiting for orders.

"Where is he?"

She hadn't seen him in days. They'd been debriefed, hidden away while the news reported their deaths, while the government colored the true story and sanitized it for the public. It was beyond cover-up, they all knew, but some things survived. The Cradle was still secret, and would be operational in a few weeks.

She didn't care. The last place she wanted to be was six hundred feet underground while Jack was on sea level. She felt almost soulless without him near and her heart pounded as she stepped into the Dubliner in D.C., a few blocks from the Senate house, the Capitol building. Sydney blinked, waiting for her eyes to adjust to the sudden low light. The restaurant was elegant but not overly. It evoked an atmosphere of friendly chats and pints of Guinness.

Her gaze slipped over the club, and when she spotted him, everything in her jumped to life again. He was hunched over the polished wood bar, giving his beer bottle intense consideration. He stood out without really trying. His dark jacket was tight across his shoulders, his long legs were hooked on the stool rungs. She liked that no one within five hundred miles knew him like she did. That he was a tender lover when he held her, the perfect weapon when she needed one.

Jack would never let her down, and that he was here, patiently waiting till she was ready said it all. It was so like Jack to leave a simple message on her answering machine. An address and "I'm in love with you, Einstein," and nothing more.

Sydney walked toward him, her pulse quickening. She slipped quietly onto the stool beside him. "I missed you."

His fingers went still on the beer. "Same here. What are we going to do about it?"

"I've got a room at the Crown Plaza."

"Hmmm, good taste. I hear the room service is excellent."

He still hadn't looked at her and the silence pulled between them, tension and awareness rising in breathless increments without their even touching. *Real* chemistry.

"So," he peeled at the label of his beer. "You married or what?"

Sydney blinked and he turned his head and smiled.

"I'm *or what,* Jack. With you."

"Good answer, Einstein." He slid off the stool and pulled her into his arms. "Really good answer."

She smiled brightly. "Well, I do have that big brain and all."

He grinned and, as always, he caught her off-guard. He smoothed his hand over her hair, cupped the back of her head and in the middle of the bar, he kissed her like there was no tomorrow.

But for them, this time, there was.

And wasting a moment . . . was not an option.

Take a look at Lori Foster's novella,
"Playing Doctor" in the upcoming anthology
WHEN GOOD THINGS HAPPEN
TO BAD BOYS,
available next month from Brava . . .

With an indulgent smile, Axel Dean watched the young lady exit the room of suffocating, overbearing people. Damn, she was sweet on the eyes. Tall, nearly as tall as him, with raven black hair and piercing blue eyes and an air of negligence that dared him, calling on his baser instincts, stripping away the façade of civility he tried to don in polite company.

Her straight hair skimmed her shoulders, darker than his own, blue black without a single hint of red. It was so silky it looked fluid, moving when she moved, shimmering with highlights from the glow of candles. The white catering shirt and black slacks didn't do much for her figure, which he guessed to be slim and toned. She didn't have the lush curves he usually favored, but what she lacked in body she made up for in attitude.

And attitude, as he well knew, made a huge difference in bed.

As a waiter passed, Axel plunked his empty glass down onto the tray and headed for the sliding doors. He hated uptight, formal affairs, but being a doctor often obligated him to attend. That didn't mean he had to linger. That didn't mean he had to mingle.

Especially when more enlivening entertainment waited outside.

Making certain no one paid him any mind, he slipped through the doors and onto a wide balcony lit by twinkly lights that mirrored the stars in the evening sky. He waited, saying a silent prayer that no one followed him. Every time he attended a gathering, women hit on him. And that'd be okay, fine and dandy by him, given that he adored women, but not within his professional circle.

He absolutely never, ever, dated anyone in his field. Not even anyone related to someone in his field.

Despite the marital bliss of both his brother and his best friend, he had no intentions of settling down any time soon. That being the case, it wouldn't be wise to get involved with relatives, friends, or associates of the people he worked with. Walking away could cause a scene, and then the entire situation would get sticky and uncomfortable.

There were plenty of women who weren't interested in medicine, like secretaries, lawyers . . . or caterers.

He'd been prepared to be bored spitless tonight. Then he'd seen her hustling around the crowded room with robust energy. At first he'd assumed her to be a mere waitress for the catering company, but given how she performed each and every job, from putting out food to collecting empty dishes to directing the others, she might actually be the one in charge. Given her air of command and confidence, he figured her to be in her late twenties, maybe early thirties. Sexy. Mature. Flirtatious.

His heartbeat sped up just imagining how the night might end.

When no one followed, Axel went down the curving wooden stairs to the garden paths behind Elwood's home. The pompous ass loved to flaunt his money, and why not? He had plenty to flaunt.

Spring had brought a profusion of blooming flowers to fill the air with heady scents. The chilly evening breeze didn't faze Axel as he searched the darkness for her. Then he saw a flare of light, realized it was a match, and made his way silently toward her.

She had her back to him, going on tiptoe to reach the top of an ornate torch anchored to the ground and surrounded by evergreens. Just as the wick caught, Axel said, "Hello."

She went perfectly still, poised on tiptoes, arms reaching up to the top of the torch. Slowly, in an oh-so-aware way, she relaxed and turned to face him.

Here's a peek at "Bottoms Up" from
BAD BOYS IN KILTS
by Donna Kauffman,
available now from Brava . . .

Honestly, she really did need her head examined. One minute she'd been giving Daisy MacDonnell the evil eye, and not ten minutes after her rival had extended the olive branch of friendship, Kat was pouring out her frustrations and desire for Brodie, carrying on about how she wanted him to look at her the way he looked at Daisy. Or any other woman.

To her credit, Daisy thought, she had laughed and taken the news a whole lot better than Kat might have if the opposite had happened. It helped that the only part of Brodie she wanted to get her hands on, or any other man in Glenbuie for that matter, was his publicity business. She'd come to town ostensibly to take over Maude's shop, but in fact, she was hoping to bring her skills and talent as a marketer to the local shopkeepers.

After listening to Kat bemoan her lack of feminine wiles—she still couldn't believe she'd done that and had decided to blame it on the aftereffects of a very long day, far too much of which had been spent brooding over Brodie—Daisy had confessed that back in the States, she'd been known as something of a matchmaker among her friends. And though she didn't claim to know Kat or Brodie all that well, it had appeared clear to her that there was definite chemistry between the two, and that maybe all Kat had to do was get him to open his eyes and notice her in a different way. She said that most men didn't appreciate subtlety and suggested that perhaps it was time to take a more direct, more blatant path to getting his attention. It was all about marketing, really, according to Daisy.

Hence one of the more embarrassing moments of Kat's life. My God, she'd never be able to show her face in Hagg's, or anywhere else in town, for months after her little stunt last night. What the bloody hell had she been thinking? A dress, makeup, her hair hanging all over the place? Could she have looked any more ridiculous? They were probably still laughing it up at her expense.

Sure, sure, there had been that wee moment, when Brodie's look of shock had worn off and he'd actually given her a once-over that at any other time in her life she'd have swooned over. But she'd immediately realized that if the only reason he was noticing her like that was because she'd had to tart herself up, then she didn't want him. Marketing be damned. But it was the truth. She knew right then that the only way she'd have him was if he wanted her for who she was.

And the only thing he wanted from Kat Henderson, she knew, was a hot game of take-no-prisoners darts and a shoulder to lean on occasionally when times were tough. A friend. That's what he wanted. A friend.

She wanted him as a friend, too. She also wanted him naked, sweating, and hot for her.

Here's a sizzling glimpse of
Katherine Garbera's
BODY HEAT,
available now from Brava . . .

Andi straightened and caught him staring. Tuck shrugged. He was attracted to her and wasn't even going to pretend he wasn't. Everything about her turned him on.

Suddenly all the confidence he'd seen seemed to drain away. She held the can out to him and hurried behind her standard issue desk. There was something different in her body language now. This wasn't the same woman who'd joked with her men about strippers.

He hooked his ankle over his knee. Popping the tab on the top of the can, he took a long drag hoping the icy beverage would cool the heat of his body. The heat that was being generated by the woman sitting across from him—eyeing him warily.

He held the Coke can loosely in one hand trying to look as non-threatening as possible. But he wanted her and he knew himself well enough to know that he wasn't going to back away without a fight, or watching her and waiting for everything to click into place.

As an arson investigator he had to be intimately aware of human behavior. The subject had always intrigued him. He'd never met a person whom he hadn't wanted to figure out. Find out why they behaved the way they did. It was the same techniques he used to find arsonists.

He just had to figure out what the turn on was. Why they were drawn to fire. And what they hoped to get out of it.

Shamelessly, he used the same techniques with women. And nine times out of ten it worked. Of course, that one time when it didn't work, had served to keep him humble. He knew on one level that he didn't know everything about women or about human nature. But he'd been willing to turn failure into success.

"Why are you staring at me?" she asked, her voice dropping an octave.

"I like the way your mouth looks," he said, his own voice sounding deeper and huskier than normal. Damn, this woman made him hotter than he'd been in a long time. And, honestly, she wasn't doing anything other than being herself. He didn't understand this attraction to her but he knew himself well enough that he didn't question it.

"You are making me uncomfortable," she said, chewing on her lower lip. "And I don't like it."

"Your mouth is making me uncomfortable." She wasn't helping him get his mind back on business. "And I do like it."

"I can't be responsible for your fantasies," she said, in a way that made him realize that this was a woman at home in the business world but not one-on-one with a man.

"Yes, you can." She was solely responsible for those fantasies. He'd never had this problem on the job before. But if she nibbled on her lower lip one more time, he was coming across the desk and tasting her mouth for himself.

"Why? If I was a guy sitting here you wouldn't be having those fantasies would you?" She sat up straighter in her chair and that fire that he'd seen earlier was back.

It was there in her eyes. She had the kind of passion that most women were afraid of. And he knew she was afraid of it too, but when she felt threatened it came out with her temper.

"No, but neither of us can change the fact that you are a woman. One I can't help but notice."

She opened one of the files on her desk. "Well, stop."